Time
of
Our
Lives

Time of Our Lives

EMILY WIBBERLEY
AUSTIN SIEGEMUND-BROKA

VIKING

VIKING

An imprint of Penguin Random House LLC, New York

First published in the United States of America by Viking,
an imprint of Penguin Random House LLC, 2020.

Visit us online at penguinrandomhouse.com

LIBRARY OF CONGRESS CATALOGING-IN-PUBLICATION DATA

Names: Wibberley, Emily, author. Siegemund-Broka, Austin, author. Title: Time of our lives / Emily Wibberley & Austin Siegemund-Broka. Description: New York : Viking, An imprint of Penguin Random House LLC, 2020. | Summary: When two high school students with different ideas about their futures meet while touring colleges, they come to value each other's point of view, and an unexpected romance unfolds. Identifiers: LCCN 2019014201 | ISBN 9781984835833 (hardcover) Subjects: | CYAC: Universities and colleges—Fiction. | Automobile travel—Fiction. | Family life—Fiction. | Memory—Fiction. | Friendship—Fiction. | Love—Fiction. Classification: LCC PZ7.1.W487 Ti 2020 | DDC [Fic]—dc23 LC record available at https://lccn.loc.gov/2019014201

Printed in the United States of America

1 3 5 7 9 10 8 6 4 2

Text set in Elysium
Book design by Nancy Brennan

✳ ✳ ✳

*To my grandmother, who told me stories of the
Robles and Contreras family —EW*

✳ ✳ ✳

To my brother, who's had my back —ASB

✳ ✳ ✳

FITZ

THIS IS A *terrible idea.*

I watch New Hampshire go by in the bus window. The brittle limbs of the trees on every sidewalk blur together. The bus is close to full, a tall woman holding her service German shepherd's harness in front of me. Despite the crowd and the lurching motion of the drive, the dog looks unperturbed. *Lucky him.*

I wonder what Lewis is doing right now. He's probably drinking with his fraternity brothers. Typical Friday night behavior. Now that he and Prisha have broken up, he's likely looking for his rebound. I'm guessing he won't notice if I don't get in to Boston on time.

The knitting needles of the woman in the back of the bus clack incessantly. I narrow my focus in on the pocket dictionary open on my knees, which brush the seat in front of me. I've had the book since I was a freshman. It's a compendium of obscure, unusual words, and it's become a bit of a pastime to flip through the pages. Words and their definitions are a hobby of mine. I like how they impose temporary control on the world, putting names to the intangible. Not to mention, having a sweet vocabulary makes me effortlessly cool and a hit with the ladies.

The dictionary is open to *So-*, where I find it. *Solicitude.* The state of protective concern or worry. I underline the word in a single pencil stroke.

I put the book in my bag and glance out the window again. If Lewis isn't drinking with his friends, he's probably working on job applications for next year. I know he has other things he could be doing this week. While I'm not in a frat or employable anywhere other than the Froyo place in the mall, I have things I could be doing too.

Going on a college tour down the East Coast wasn't my idea. I've made my decision. My application to Southern New Hampshire University was out the door on December 1. And going with Lewis *definitely* wasn't my idea. It was my mom's. She insisted on Lewis and me having the opportunity for "brotherly bonding." Besides, Lewis is the one with a credit card, which we'll use for meals and hotels. Mom promised she'll pay him back. Having him come with is annoyingly logical.

I don't know what Lewis and I will talk about. The only things I know about him—he's in a frat, and he recently broke up with his girlfriend, Prisha—come from overhearing his infrequent calls home on holidays and the occasional weeknight. The only other things I know about my brother could be summarized on his résumé. He's in his final year at Boston University, he's about to finish his degree in economics, and he's searching for finance jobs in New York. Or Boston. Or Chicago.

Anywhere but home.

I drop my eyes to the folder on the seat next to me. I've only glanced through it once or twice, which makes me feel a little guilty. It contains weeks of my mom's careful research on every school I'm meant to visit from Boston to Baltimore in the next ten days, every program she thinks I could theoretically find interesting, the email confirmations for each hotel she's booked for Lewis and me, an envelope of spending money, even printouts of local restaurants and "places of interest." It's heartbreakingly detailed. Following the first day in Boston, I'm supposed to head to Rhode Island and Connecticut, then New York City and colleges in western Pennsylvania, finally ending in Baltimore and home in time for Christmas.

Tonight, the plan is for me to reach South Station in Boston, take the MBTA bus to BU, and meet Lewis in front of his dorm. I don't know how Mom convinced Lewis to drive me down the coast, but I do know this entire trip was orchestrated to fit *his* schedule. He finished his in-class exams today, and Mom planned our visit to New York to coincide with one of his job interviews. Never mind the timing necessitated I miss a week of school—something my mom found negligible since I don't have finals until after winter break.

I know plenty of my classmates would love the opportunity to ditch for a week. But I like school. I like AP English and debating film noir favorites with my friends. I especially like my perfect attendance record. What I *don't* like is pretending the question of college is worth the weight everyone places on it. It's this blinding prize everyone's rushing toward. Not me. College isn't important enough to disrupt everything else in my life.

The bus rumbles to a halt in front of a post office. On the curb outside the window, a few people huddle in hats and heavy coats, the sunset lighting them in vermillion. It's cold, not yet snowy. In a couple of weeks, plowed piles of dirty snow will line every curb.

The doors open with a hiss and a thud. The first passenger on is a girl who's probably about my age. She's cute, I can't help noticing, with purple lipstick and an Elliott Smith shirt. When she tugs off her beanie, curly black hair spills onto her shoulders. She's the kind of girl who makes me painfully conscious of what a pale redheaded nobody I am.

I could invite her to sit, but I probably won't. I tend to keep to myself in cafeterias and classrooms, content with the close friends I've had for years. Going out of my way to chat with random girls on public transportation isn't quite my style. Even if I occasionally think about doing exactly that.

She catches my eye, and a small smile springs to her aubergine lips. I hesitate.

Fuck me. A cute girl notices me and I *hesitate.* Lewis would say this is why I've never had a girlfriend. Part of me wants to move my folder and offer her the seat. It's just, then she might notice the BU brochure poking out of the folder, and then she might want to talk about college. And then I'd have to explain why I'm not going to any of the colleges on this diligently prepared itinerary. This *punctiliously* prepared itinerary. Or she might want to tell me how great her boyfriend is, and how he plays lead guitar in a band, benches three hundred, and could have his pick of girls but chose her, and then we'd be in *that* conversation.

Whatever. I reach for my folder nevertheless—but she's already walking past my row. I place the folder back on the seat, and in that moment, it feels like I'm destined for a lifetime of putting folders back on empty seats next to mine. The bus doors close, and we veer away from the curb.

In the cool plexiglass of the window, I catch my reflection watching me despondently. I wonder if I'm the kind of guy Beanie Girl would go for. My red hair, pale freckled skin, blue eyes set in a narrow face—I don't think I'm bad looking, but I'm not exactly magazine-cover material.

In my pocket, my phone vibrates. I reach for it with a quickness that's become instinct, but it's only Lewis.

Room 2303 when you get here. It's open.
Will meet you when I'm out of my exam.

Without replying, I shove my phone back into my jacket pocket. The bus pulls up to the next stop, the one I've been waiting for. I grab my things and get off.

The cold bites my nose the moment my feet hit the pavement, the familiarity of this specific street corner enveloping me reassuringly. Tugging my coat tighter, I swiftly walk a block down, then turn the corner. It's a ten-minute trip through the neighborhood I've known my entire life, past the library and the elementary school. Finally, I walk up to my door, fumble for the keys in my pocket, and, with a deep breath, step inside.

I'd know the smell of home no matter what. It's the rosy warmth of hardwood floorboards in the winter, combined with whatever Mom's cooking. Right now, it's eggplant Parmesan. I pause in the doorway.

Off to my right, Mom's seated at the kitchen table, exactly where I left her two hours ago, reading her anthology of American literature. Her head springs up in surprise. Recognition settles on her features, until it's replaced by a disappointment she attempts to smother, not quite succeeding. With gentle bemusement in her voice, she says, "You're home."

"I am," I reply.

"You're supposed to be in South Station," she says.

I take a deep breath, as if extra oxygen is all I need to convince my mom against this plan. "I got off the bus an hour in, and then I . . . I bought a ticket back with my own money. I've thought about this—"

But she talks over me. "Fitzgerald Holton, you're impossible. I've booked your hotels. Your brother is packed and waiting for you. You're not bowing out of this trip. It's happening."

"But what if—"

"Everything is fine," she says, placing undeniable emphasis on *fine* and closing the heavy cover on the anthology she was reading. She gets up from the table and pushes in the worn wooden chair. "Everything will *be* fine. You have nothing to worry about."

I have everything to worry about. "I have a French quiz on Tuesday," I say instead. "And—I'm going to be really behind if I'm out the entire week."

"You'll make up the quiz," she replies, "and we both know you'll mostly be missing movies in class and free study time."

I say nothing. She watches me for a moment.

"It's ten days," she continues, her voice softening. "I'll be okay on my own for ten days."

I want to point out it's not only ten days. It's four years. If Lewis's experience is any indication, it's four years, each increasingly disconnected from home. She might not need me now, but she will soon. I hold the comment in, though. I promised myself I'd never throw her situation in her face.

"I know change is hard," she says, "but give this a chance. You can't make me your excuse not to."

She's not an excuse. She's a reason, a very good one. But pointing that out would only put us on the road to an argument we've had enough times to know neither of us will ever win.

She continues. "You're really going to make your poor mother—who has three dissertation drafts to read—escort you personally to your brother's doorstep? Because I will, you know." The corners of her mouth tug up. "Remember your eighth-grade field trip?"

I can't hide a smile of my own. I'd tried to stay home instead of going on a history class trip to the Paul Revere House. It was my first overnight field trip, and I wasn't interested in sharing a hotel room with three guys I barely knew. But when Mom came home and found me playing video games, she promptly drove me into Boston and deposited me with my teacher with strict orders not to permit me to leave under any circumstances. Even if it was horribly embarrassing, the effort she went to was kind of funny.

She catches my smile, and it's clear she wins this one. I don't enjoy arguing with her, and the trip *will* only be a week and a half. For all her talk of dragging me onto buses, she can't actually force me to choose a college I don't want to. The least I can do is give her trip a chance. "No . . ." I huff. "I won't make my poor *and* very obstinate mother take me into Boston. I'll absquatulate to South Station on my own," I say, hoping she'll enjoy the word choice.

Sure enough, she raises an eyebrow. "Absquatulate?"

"To make off with, humorously."

"I swear, Fitzgerald, I'm a professor of the English language, and I don't know half the words rattling around in that head of yours." She walks to the doorway and straightens my coat.

I can't help it. The nerves set in. I know she notices the change in my expression, because she places her hands on my shoulders and looks into my eyes.

"Everything will be fine," she repeats. From the sharpness in her gaze, I'm almost convinced. "You deserve a chance to know what's out there. If you hate it, I promise, I won't force you to go somewhere you don't want to be. If after everything, you still feel SNHU is the best school for you, I'll proudly send in your enrollment fee. I know it's a great college—I *have* been teaching there for twenty years. I just want to know you're choosing it too."

I place my hand on the door handle behind me. "Remember you said that when I get back and I'm still set on SNHU. I know what I want."

Mom folds her arms. "Just humor me," she says, sounding a little amused.

FITZ

TWO HOURS LATER, I'm in South Station.

JUNIPER

~

"THIS IS A terrible idea."

I hear Tía Sofi in the kitchen as I'm walking toward the stairs. Her voice is brassy, like a trumpet in a parade for which she's the bandleader and every other member. I vent a breath out through my nose, knowing I'm not escaping this conversation. In fact, I might be having this conversation for the rest of my life.

I turn around, preparing to repeat myself for the thirty-fourth time (not exaggerating), and head for Tía.

The kitchen is like every room in the house, dense with inescapable reminders of every Ramírez who's ever lived under its roof. There's turquoise stenciling where the soft yellow walls touch the ceiling, hand-painted by my cousin Isabel, who teaches art at the community college in town. My brothers' homework clutters the desk my abuelo built with wood from his grandparents' home. The wide window over the counter lets sunlight leap in and land on the faded photograph of the first Ramírez who came here from the city of Guadalajara, four generations ago, hanging in its heavy frame beside the window.

Tía, wearing an expression of consternation, cups a ceramic blue mug in her hands at the kitchen table. The scene is unbearably familiar, right down to Tía's posture and the tinny classical guitar coming from the radio I've given up begging my parents to replace.

I cross the room, shutting off the music and then turning to face Tía, who's watching me expectantly. Even though I call her Tía, she's really my *great*-aunt. She's sixty-six and never married or had children of her own, so she's been like a third grandmother to my brothers and sisters and me. Which means one more source of worry about whether I'm eating enough, where I'm going to college, and, of course, how sex is forbidden until I'm forty.

I walk up to her, waiting for the memories to come. Every time Tía's wrung her wrinkled hands while watching me from this very table or compulsively checked whether her charcoal hair is contained in the tight bun on top of her head.

I know exactly what Tía's going to say. Whenever we've had this conversation, she introduces the topic without changing a word. Only when we get into the thick of it and she starts anticipating what I'm going to say do the variations emerge. It's like she's writing a novel or a play, rewriting drafts of this scene until she gets it perfect.

Today, I'm not playing. I preempt her. "Did you take my college binder?" I ask brusquely. Tía blinks, thrown, while I search the counter and the table for signs of my heavy three-ring binder. I know exactly where I left it—next to my suitcase on my bed. When I got home after running the student government ice cream stand to celebrate the official start of winter break, the binder was gone.

"No, chiquita, I haven't seen it." She grimaces, worry lines creasing her forehead. "This trip, I don't think you should go."

I grit my teeth. That only took Tía two seconds. Now it's just a matter of getting away quickly. "I have to visit the schools sometime." I sigh, circling the table and quickly searching the counters. Hoping for signs of my binder, I glance into the living room. "One of them will be my home for the next four years."

I don't need to look at Tía to know her expression has soured. "This is your home, Juniper. *Those* are schools."

"What, then, you'd rather I just not go to college?" I challenge.

Tía's face tightens. "Of course you're going to college. We live close to some of the finest colleges in the country. Amherst, Hampshire, Smith, UMass Amherst, and—"

"—Mount Holyoke. *I know.*" The day Tía found my *Fiske Guide to Colleges* and discovered we lived thirty minutes from the Five College Consortium, my life got way harder. I wander to the couch in the living room and begin rummaging through piles of my siblings' homework, everything from coloring to calculus. I hear Tía get up slowly from her chair, her slippered feet following me into the living room. Right then and there, I take a small, selective vow of silence. I'm done trying to convince her. She'll never understand. All I need to do is find my binder and get out the door.

"Never mind that," Tía says gently behind me. "A road trip like this? What will you even eat?" I blink and round on

Tía, incredulous. This is an argumentative reach, even for her. My vow of silence flies out the window.

"There are a thousand restaurants between Boston and Virginia. We're not going to starve, Tía."

She shakes her head, her frown deepening like I've committed some grave sin. "Take some tamales."

I laugh despite myself. Memories of tamale birthdays and Christmases waft from my subconscious to my nose, the smell of masa, chicken cooking, and steaming chili. "Tía, I can't just bring tamales on a road trip."

Before Tía has the chance to refute me with what will undoubtedly be a well-reasoned defense of bringing tamales on road trips, my mother walks in wearing the harried expression she's never been without since my brothers were born. Coffee in one hand, she's vainly trying to pull her straight blonde hair into a ponytail with the other. I seize my chance. "Mom, have you seen my college binder?"

"It's entirely possible, but I can't even remember if I changed my underwear this morning, so I'm not much help." I watch her eyes run over the room, looking for stuff out of place or things she needs, and I can practically read the to-do lists forming behind her blue eyes.

I didn't get those blue eyes from my mom, whose fair skin looks even paler behind the dusting of freckles I did inherit. I resemble my dad more, with my darker complexion and thick, wavy tresses. It's my younger brothers who ended up with Mom's delicate features and light hair.

Right on cue—like the mere thought of them summoned

their presence—a double-voiced chorus of "Mom!" rings out from the back of the house. I wonder with a twinge of worry what Xan and Walker have gotten into now, remembering the time they had a water-balloon fight in my parents' bedroom, or when they bathed our cat, Malfoy, in the toilet bowl, or both times they tried to cook macaroni in the toaster. With a seven- and ten-year-old brother who incite whatever mischief they can, nothing is out of the question. From the way my mother's head whirls, I know she's imagining similar possibilities.

"Did you talk to Rob about opening early on Monday?" Tía asks, bringing Mom's attention back to the kitchen. I guess no one's safe from her interrogations this morning.

Mom grimaces. "No, I forgot. I can't imagine how," she says, sharing a wry look with me. "I'll do it tomorrow, first thing."

Mom and Tía run a restaurant together. Dad cooks, while Mom does the books and Tía oversees the rest. Rosalita's is the only place to get authentic Mexican food in the city. It's sort of a local sensation, whatever that means in midsized Springfield, Massachusetts. When it was featured on an Eater.com list, my parents were beside themselves. Tía, too, once we explained to her what blogs were. I used to do homework in the restaurant's expansive sunken dining room when I was in elementary and middle school, before I had calc and chemistry and AP US History and real studying. There were days I could hardly concentrate with the clatter of the kitchen and the heavenly smells of homemade tortillas and machaca. Tía and her sister, Rosalita, my grandmother, opened the place nearly forty years ago. Mom and Dad filled in when—

I shut off my thoughts, not wanting to dwell on that.

"Why don't you help your mother remember a couple things around the house?" Tía asks me. "It'd be a better use of that memory of yours."

"Better than my perfect grades?" I snap back. While I do have an exceptional memory—good enough to ace every one of Mrs. Karis's infamous AP European History exams and never forget friends' birthdays—Tía only thinks it's useful when it helps the family. But I catch Tía giving me a stern look and regret my sarcasm. "Of course, Tía," I amend, looking imploringly at my mom, hoping she'll jump in and save me.

She doesn't, her expression distant and distracted. It's a familiar response. I'm decently close with my mom, close enough to have semi-regular Disney movie nights just us two. But my mother divides her time and focus evenly among her six kids. My dad, on the other hand, plays favorites, to my obvious benefit.

"Now, your trip," Tía prompts. She turns her skeptical eyes on Mom. "I don't know why you're letting her go alone with a boy."

I roll my eyes, hoping neither of them notices.

"You know Matt's responsible, Sofi. Gabriel and I trust him. And we trust Juniper," Mom replies, giving me a small smile, but I hear the *don't prove me wrong* behind her confidence. I return the smile reassuringly. "Besides, we've worked it out with Matt's parents to give them money for *separate* hotel rooms."

Even though she's emphasized this every chance she gets,

I hold my tongue and keep from rolling my eyes this time.

"It's not about the hotel rooms," Tía protests. "She's too young to spend so much time with a boyfriend. You know what happened when Luisa took up with what's-his-name."

His name was Chris. And by "took up with," Tía's referring to how Luisa ditched her high school graduation so she could road trip to California with her boyfriend, which, for the record, I thought was badass. But of course, in my family, I'm bound and restricted by whatever has happened to everyone who shares my last name.

"This is our call, Sofi," my mom replies firmly. "We're her parents."

Tía frowns. "Well, this trip could wait until you, *her parents*, could go with her. Instead of some boy—"

"*Some boy?*" I interrupt. "You know his name is Matt. Remember, *Matt*, who helped you rearrange the furniture in your bedroom and drove you to urgent care when you caught pinkeye from Anabel?"

"I did not," Tía says, "catch pinkeye."

Mom cuts me off before I can correct Tía in irrefutable detail. "We postponed this trip once," she reminds Tía, which is true. Matt and I were going to go during Thanksgiving break until Tía convinced my parents not to let me skip school. "Juniper and Matt will be fine."

Before Tía responds, there's a heavy bang down the hall, followed by exuberant shouting. My mom briefly closes her eyes, and I wonder where she goes. Probably a tranquil valley between mountains, or a beautiful waterfall in the heart of a canyon. She opens her eyes again and gives me an apologetic look before darting from the room to stop Xan and Walker from causing any further damage.

Tía eyes me, no doubt eager to continue the argument. It's not the first time she and my parents have clashed in a small-scale parenting power struggle. Tía's opinions and preferences carry weight in this household because she helps my parents, who both work full-time, handle their six children. When conflicts sprout, watered by guilt trips and stubbornness, and branch into towering trees of resentment, my parents are often too busy to chop them down, and their shadows cast darkly over everything.

"I have to go," I tell Tía. "I'm not missing school this time." It's only possible because my school purposefully gives three weeks of winter break to allow seniors time to finish college applications. "This is my only chance before college applications are due on New Year's."

"I don't understand why applications require spending nights unsupervised with your boyfriend," Tía replies with frustrating patience.

I should go scour every corner of the house and under the floorboards for my college binder. Yet there's a part of me that wants to win Tía's approval, even her support. She's the grandmother I have, whether or not she's my actual grandmother, and honestly, we don't have much in common outside of family. Tía speaks Spanish with friends and relatives. I don't. Tía goes to church every weekend. I only go for Christmas and Easter. Tía worries about every member of the family every minute of every day. I really, *really* don't.

Despite our differences, I want her to understand me. To

want what I want, to respect what I choose. It's that part of me that pulls me to reply.

"When I'm in college next year, I could be spending all my time with boys and you wouldn't even know," I say.

She fixes me with a faraway look. When she speaks, her voice is hard and gentle, like sculpted stone. "Next year is next year," she says.

I eye her uncertainly, my brows furrowing. Tía's never been one for riddles. "What's that supposed to mean?" I ask.

"Next year you'll be eighteen."

"I'm practically eighteen now."

"Seventeen is not eighteen, Juniper," she pronounces, like this mathematical declaration carries infinite weight. "When you're eighteen, you get to make these choices for yourself."

I feel the color rise in my cheeks. "I'm old enough to make choices now." We watch each other confrontationally for a long moment.

Finally, she speaks, her voice settling decisively. "Separate hotel rooms . . . and you'll take the tamales."

I scoff, because that's the best I'm ever going to get with Tía. "I won't take the tamales!" I call over my shoulder as I leave the living room and head for the stairs.

"Juniper Ramírez," I hear behind me, "you're not getting out of this one."

JUNIPER

＜

UPSTAIRS, I ESCAPE into my bedroom, the only place where I have an ounce of privacy, despite sharing the room with my sixteen-year-old sister. Marisa is nowhere to be found, probably with her friends or the boyfriend she's doing a terrible job hiding from the family.

I hunt for the binder in desk drawers of student government flyers and physics homework, though I know I won't find it. I would have remembered leaving it in my desk. I don't even venture over to Marisa's half of the room, which is explosively untidy. She could be hiding the bodies of her enemies or a pet Komodo dragon under her laundry piles, and I would have no idea. I do know she didn't take my college binder. She's the only other person in this house eager for me to go to college. She showed me a Pinterest board of her plans for my half of the room. It was . . . overwhelmingly pink.

Right now my side is not pink. It's cluttered but organized, with certificates and photos and watercolors tacked to the bulletin board next to my towering bookcases. I could draw every detail from memory. The collection of Nancy Drew books on my bookshelf, the photos of my friend Carolyn and me ice-skating in sixth grade, the Keira Knightley *Pride & Prejudice* poster over the bed—each a thread tying me to a time and place. The bedroom was my dad's when he was my age, and he's pointed out to me and Marisa the hole where he nailed his high school baseball medal to the wall.

I love home, I do. I love my bedroom and my family. It's just, there's a point where the changelessness of everything becomes enveloping instead of encouraging. There's a claustrophobia in comfort. The threads become a web, confining the person I want to be to the person I was.

I check again around my suitcase for my binder, but it's not there. In case it fell off the bed or something, I drop to my knees on the carpet and begin searching the floor.

Something's out of place. On the floor is my box of old Halloween costume components—Disney tiaras and cat ears and a Ravenclaw robe. It should be sitting on the top shelf of my closet. I spring up from the floor and in two quick paces cross my half of the room to the closet, heart pounding. I check the shelf.

The space behind the costume box is empty.

Without hesitation, I'm bounding into the hall, little bombs of anger bursting behind my eyes. I throw open Callie and Anabel's door and find my younger sisters on the floor next to their bunk beds. They're giggling.

"You went through my things?" I demand from the doorway.

Anabel jumps up. Callie twists to face me, caught red-handed. On the floor in front of them is the shoebox I keep in my closet, behind the costumes, expressly hidden from my eight- and thirteen-year-old sisters.

"That stuff is private," I continue. "You're not even supposed to go in my room without me or Marisa there."

The box holds the items most precious to me, and most private. Because with five younger siblings, my parents, and Tía in the house, I've come to expect prying eyes on everything. But there are things I don't want examined and interrogated. And right now, they're strewn across my sisters' floor—a scarf Abuela never finished knitting, a dried flower from our apartment in Brooklyn, a letter from Carolyn after she moved to Ohio sophomore year.

In Callie's hands is my yearbook from last year, open to Matt's page-long signature. Anabel drops a red marker onto the floor. It's painfully obvious what was happening here— Callie was reading my private messages while Anabel was coloring on the pages. *Coloring.*

Tears well in my eyes. The day Matt returned the signed yearbook to me, I was sitting in the wicker chair on the porch reading *Anna Karenina.* "If you look for perfection, you'll never be content" is the exact line I'd just read when I glanced up to find Matt walking up the driveway, yearbook in hand and a grin forming that perfect dimple on the left side of his face.

He wore his light gray T-shirt and those scuffed Adidas he'd had since freshman year until I finally prevailed on him a few months ago to get a new pair. Even easygoing, confident Matt's cheeks had reddened when he handed me the yearbook, which he'd worked on the whole weekend. I read it right then and there, feeling like I'd never be that happy ever again.

It was the first time he said he loved me.

I snatch the yearbook from Callie's hands. "This isn't okay, you guys. You can't just take people's things and wreck them," I say, hearing the waver in my voice.

Callie crosses her arms, unperturbed. "Did you have *sex* with Matt?" she asks.

I've learned to recognize the attitude she's putting on. This is her "teenager" demeanor. I first noticed it—without realizing how prevalent it would become in my life—just days after her thirteenth birthday, when Mom offered to have Callie's friends over for board games and cupcakes. Callie only rolled her eyes like she was too old for such childish things.

"If you tell on us for going in your room," Callie says, her voice sharp and bossy, "I'll tell Mom about the 'life-changing' night you and Matt had after prom. He wrote *all* about it."

I feel flowers of fury and embarrassment unfurl in my cheeks. Without a word for Callie, I collect the other items my sisters have littered on their floor. Anabel watches with concern and curiosity. It's just like Callie to drop the *S-E-X* word with her eight-year-old sister listening. "Touch my things again," I warn once I've returned everything to the box, "and I won't drive you to the winter carnival." Callie's face falls. "In fact, I won't drive you anywhere. Ever again."

It's an empty threat, not that my little sisters know that. Tía and my parents are always forcing me to drive my siblings places. I'm the only one with a license—Marisa's failed her test twice—and since I'm the oldest, the extra parenting inevitably falls to me. Even with Tía helping out, there's plenty left over. Playdates of Anabel's to supervise and pre-algebra problems to correct on Callie's homework. I'm needed to catch whatever falls through the cracks.

After storming out of their room and into mine, I grab my suitcase from the bed and head for the stairs. I carry the box in my other hand. There's no way I'm trusting my family with it while I'm gone. With incredible fortune, I dodge Tía as I book it to the front door and into the evening cold.

I don't like the cold. I don't like the memories that come with watching those little billows of breath in the air. Or the perpetual gray of the sky, or the way winter turns everyone's yards brown. Fall is my favorite, not only because of school starting, but for the way the tree in front of our porch bursts into flame. The leaves have long fallen now, and only dried husks remain in the hedge from the door to the driveway.

Dad, in his Yankees sweatshirt, is standing next to the car, opening the passenger door. He's holding—my college binder. I'm comforted by the very sight of the turquoise plastic and the perfectly hole-punched pages between the covers. Pages containing the details of the coming week, the seven days I'll spend driving to the University of Virginia, with stops in Boston, Providence, New Haven, New York, and D.C. on the way. I could have easily spent two weeks on this trip if it weren't for the cost of hotels and needing to be home in time for Matt's mom Shanna's birthday. I did my best to maximize schools and cities in the time we have.

Hearing me close the front door, Dad glances up, and his eyes find mine. He holds up the binder. "The girls were eyeing it. I figured it would be safer if I—" No doubt noticing my watering eyes, he places the binder in the back seat and closes the car door. "Go," he says gently, knowing exactly what I need right now. "Before Tía comes out and finds you," he adds with a wink.

I place the box on the roof of the car, then walk into his arms. The fabric of his sweatshirt is soft, and he smells like the mountain-scented deodorant Mom once said she liked and he's worn ever since. I exhale into his chest. "Sometimes I feel like there isn't enough room for me in that house, you know?"

He holds me closer. "For this mind"—he traces his thumb along my forehead—"there isn't room enough in the whole world."

I hug back, hard. I don't know what I'd do if it weren't for him.

Hearing footsteps, I pull away and find Matt coming up the driveway. His house is ten minutes from mine, and he walks over here often for movie nights and family dinners. I feel the familiar flutter in my heart I get whenever I'm with him. He's tall, with broad shoulders from baseball, sandy hair, and a chin Michelangelo would've given his left hand to carve. His smile is wide enough to fit the universe.

He's carrying a duffel bag, and he waves to me and my dad. "I was serious about you getting out of here," Dad says. "Sofi's on the warpath. Don't worry, I'll cover for you." He winks again and walks forward to meet Matt. "Don't do any stupid shit on this trip, got it?" he says, shaking my boyfriend's hand.

Matt swallows. "Of course, sir."

Dad claps him on the shoulder. My dad and Matt have a relationship of their own born of baseball and Die Hard movies, even if Dad likes to pull his "intimidating father" act every now and again. "Tell Mom bye for me," I say, opening the rear door while the guys load the luggage into the trunk.

Instantly, I'm hit with an unmistakable smell, the smell of every Christmas since we moved to Springfield. Memories of Abuela blindside me until I push them away. I notice a foil-covered platter on the back seat.

"Tía," I groan.

I stow the box on the floor behind the driver's seat and close the door, waving to my dad as I get into the front. Matt gets in the passenger seat, and we pull out of the driveway.

"Whoa," Matt says, eager curiosity crossing his perfect features. "What's that smell?"

I nod to the back seat. "Tía's stubbornness. Also known as tamales."

Matt reaches between our seats and pulls out the platter. He opens the glove compartment where—of course—he finds a plastic fork. I roll my eyes. Tía's thought of everything. Matt takes a bite of tamale and groans in ecstasy. "Oh my god," he moans through a mouthful, "I love your family. When can I marry into them again?" he asks casually, giving me a sideways look.

I feel my eyes widen. "Please tell me you're joking."

Matt shrugs. "Seventy percent," he says.

I shake my head, silently scolding. Yet I can't help stealing a glance in his direction. He's wearing his Springfield

High baseball T-shirt. I remember how, when they went to the state playoffs, the whole team threw a huge house party. But even though he was co-captain, Matt told me he wanted to celebrate by going to get ice cream with me.

The best thing about Matt isn't his smile or his shoulders (a close second). It's the way our memories make me feel. They make me feel like *me*.

I nod at the plate of tamales. "I'm relying on you to finish them before we get to Boston."

Matt raises his fork like a conquering hero on a hilltop. "Challenge accepted." I feel his eyes on me from the passenger seat. "Hey, it's pretty cool, isn't it?" he continues, his voice gentler. "This is really happening. We're really going."

I fix my eyes on the road, on the future, on places where I won't be constrained by the expectations of my family. Where I'll have the distance to discover who *I* want to be.

"It is."

FITZ

~

ON THE MBTA bus to Boston University, I text Mom.

Tell me where you and Dad met?

I get the reply I was expecting.

Fitzgerald...

I wait. A couple of moments later, the typing bubble appears, and then her reply.

We were both doing our postdocs. He was
studying French literature, and I was focusing
on American. I was coming up the steps
of the university's administration building,
carrying a cup of coffee, and he was coming
down the steps. I ran right into him, dumping
the entire contents of my coffee down the
front of his shirt. He opened his mouth to yell
and instead asked me to dinner.

It was an epic move on Dad's part, honestly. He could give classes in Advanced Getting-Spilled-On. I've heard the story before, but that wasn't the point. I send her a "thanks" and put my headphones in. With the Shins playing, I watch out the window. Boston's a nice city, even though I have no intention of coming here for college. People bustle on every corner. In the gaps between streets of coffee shops and Chinese restaurants, I catch glimpses of the Charles River, a frozen sheet spanned by stone bridges. Every sidewalk is coated in exhaust, a newspaper bin on each corner.

I thought I understood why Lewis decided to go to Boston, even though he never talked about college with me. He's interested in finance, and Boston is a hub for consulting and banking, and yada yada yada. Once Lewis had started at BU, I was convinced he chose Boston because he remembered the days Dad would bring us into the city for Italian food and cannoli in the North End.

Until Lewis's calls home became less and less frequent. Until Dad asked one Christmas if Lewis ever went to Mike's for cannoli, and Lewis didn't remember the place, or pretended not to. Dad's pretty hard to offend, but I caught the hurt in his eyes then. I decided I must have been wrong—it was dumb to guess Lewis chose a college for family.

I get out when I reach my stop, then walk the blocks between Boston University buildings toward the towers on the riverbank. Lewis lives in a building called StuVi2. While I walk, I watch people on the street, students spilling out of university dorms and lecture halls. I wonder what they're doing, what they're passionate about. What they worry about. I watch a group of guys in coats and ties come out of a brick building and cross the street toward an Indian restaurant. I wonder if one of them will collide with a fellow postdoc holding a cup of coffee.

When I reach the curb in front of what my phone tells me is StuVi2, I double-check the directions. This couldn't *possibly* be right. The building on the riverbank would fit right into downtown Boston or New York or Chicago. It's a modern high-rise, twenty floors or more—a conservative estimate. Walls of brick and window soar into the night sky. It's nothing like the college dorms I've found while halfheartedly paging through pamphlets Mom leaves on my desk. It's definitely a far cry from my two-story home in New Hampshire.

I walk in with a group of students. In the lobby I pause, watching kids in BU sweatshirts studying in the chairs and couches in the common area. For a moment, I imagine myself in one of those chairs, or in one of the groups laughing by the elevators, before the thought is gone.

I ride the elevator to the twenty-third floor, confirming I wasn't far off in my estimate. The doors ping open onto a carpeted and well-lit hallway. I've known that Dad pays for Lewis's dorm and a good portion of his tuition—I didn't know he'd sprung for *this*. I've hardly ever stayed in hotels this nice, not that I'm some experienced traveler. With mom's single-parent salary from the university, we've only gone out of town once or twice in the past few years. In Maine, I liked the scenery but discovered I couldn't keep lobster down. In New York, Lewis was busted for trying to push a penny over the edge of the Empire State Building. I don't love family trips.

I step into the hall, my fingers reflexively finding my phone in my pocket. It's instinct to worry how Mom's doing, even though I only texted her twenty minutes ago. It'd be different if she weren't on her own in the house, if she and my dad hadn't divorced. But he decided to pack up for Canada when Lewis was in high school, before Mom took the test. The test that changed our lives forever.

Forcing my nerves to calm, I knock on the door of room 2303. I'm guessing Lewis is back now. It ended up taking three hours to get from Tilton to Boston and onto the MBTA bus, not counting the delay of returning home after my original departure. I don't think college exams extend this late into the evening, though I guess I'd have no idea if they did.

The door opens. Instead of Lewis or one of his roommates, it's a girl.

Wearing nothing but an oversized T-shirt.

I blink. I know I'm blushing, and for a moment I wonder if I went to the wrong room. Or if I dozed off before my bus careened into the river, and heaven is a Boston University dorm populated with hot girls.

"You're not Becky," she says, betraying no consciousness of the series of complex emotions sending my blood roaring in my ears. "You didn't happen to see a short blonde girl with a physics book, did you? I am seriously screwed for the exam if—" She stops, something like recognition entering her eyes. "Fitz?"

None of the unique words in my vocabulary is helping me form a coherent sentence. Now I feel like the girl definitely notices, because her lips begin to curve upward. Her criminally pouty lips. I might be socially inept, but I'm not blind. And I am a teenage boy. I force my eyes *not* to glance down to her smooth brown thighs peeking out from under the shirt's hem.

Instead, I focus on her face and realize she looks familiar. I know her from Lewis's Instagram. It's the purple-stone nose piercing that helps me make the connection. Hers is the face in the selfie from Lewis's summer trip to Miami and in the photo from a couple months ago Lewis captioned, "Regatta."

"Wait," I hear myself say before I've thought it through, "you're Lewis's ex." For a horrible moment, I wonder if she's gotten with one of his roommates in the weeks since Lewis called home and mentioned the breakup.

The girl only laughs, throwing her long black hair behind her back. It's as stupidly perfect a laugh as everything about her. She's objectively gorgeous, with her black nail polish, her wrist tattoo, the stone in her piercing glittering in the light.

"Did Lewis tell you we broke up?" she asks. She speaks with the hint of an Indian accent, unlike Lewis, who was adopted from Bengaluru before he could talk. When he got to college, he got involved in Indian and South Asian clubs and organizations, or so I gathered from his Facebook. I think he mentioned Prisha running one of them.

I open my mouth, unsure what to say.

"To be fair, we did break up," I hear my brother's voice from inside. The girl opens the door wider, revealing Lewis walking into the room. He's wearing only jeans and pulling a T-shirt over his head. I flush when I realize what I obviously just interrupted, feeling very much like the younger brother.

The girl walks into the room Lewis just came out of and returns with a pair of leggings. I try not to watch her pull them up. "Then we *un*-broke up," she says. "I know it's only for a couple more months, but you could have told your brother we're still together, *Lewis*." She playfully swats him.

"Fine." Lewis sighs. "Fitz, this is Prisha, my girlfriend until spring break. Prisha, this is my brother, Fitzgerald. Happy now?"

Prisha gives Lewis a quick kiss on the cheek on her way to the door. "Very. Have a good trip, you two. Fitz, college is great. What I learned when I visited BU was to hang out with the students. Stay away from anywhere you find guys like Lewis." She winks at him, steps into a pair of boots, and walks—sashays, really—out the door.

Lewis nods in my direction. "Come on in. I have to send a couple of emails before dinner." He waves me in. I'm shocked he waited this late to eat with me. I wonder if he got pressured by Mom, or maybe nine p.m. is a perfectly normal time to have dinner in college. Realistically, he was probably too distracted by Prisha to notice the hour.

I follow and can't help pausing to admire the room. It's like an apartment—a nice, well-furnished apartment, with colorful chairs and a wooden coffee table overlooking the nearly floor-to-ceiling window opposite the door. There's even a kitchen table, and on the TV stand sits the widescreen Dad bought Lewis when he began his freshman year. Lewis and his three roommates, of course, have done their best to worsen their living conditions. Beer bottles line the windowsills. Open on the coffee table is a jar of peanut butter with a knife stuck inside. The room smells like socks and sweat.

But nothing can detract from the view. Right out the window, the frozen river winds through the city, with trees on both banks and a small bridge reaching between them. In the distance, the Boston skyline glitters brightly. The glow reflects dimly on the ice of the Charles.

It takes my breath away.

Lewis sits down at the kitchen table and opens his laptop. I notice stickers for *Khatarnak* and India Club on the case. Since going to college, he's been learning about and embracing his cultural heritage. It's a reminder of how, while we're both adopted, I can never completely understand his experience of being adopted from Indian biological parents into a white American family.

"Good trip down?" he asks after a beat. We both know what happened on my way down—I'm certain Mom texted him the reason for the delay. He doesn't glance up from his computer, and I don't know if he's consciously avoiding my eyes.

I know Lewis considers me not just a younger brother, but a baby brother. When he was going to parties in high school, I was reading and playing computer games. When he was bringing girls home, I was reading and playing computer games. It's not that I don't have a life. I just don't think Lewis thinks I have a life. Admittedly, I'm no future prom king, and I volunteer at the library every Friday and have B horror movie marathons with my friends. But while Lewis is planning spring break with his frat brothers, I'm home with Mom, worrying. Worrying is my primary recreational activity.

I nod, saying nothing more. Uncomfortable, we both wait for the other to speak. Finally, I do. "Why's Prisha only your girlfriend until spring break?"

Lewis shrugs with half a laugh. "She got a job in San Francisco, and I want to be in New York. Neither of us wants to do long-distance since nothing's going to change geographically in probably three years or so. We picked a date to end it, and we're just hanging until then."

I watch Lewis as he works on his emails. He doesn't appear bothered by this in the least. But that's Lewis. He got his even temper—*equanimity*—from our dad's parenting. The day Lewis dumped his high-school girlfriend, the day he brought home a C in chemistry, the parties he threw and the fights he picked with our parents, he couldn't be bothered with guilt or concern.

If we had the kind of relationship where we could talk about things, real, serious things, I might ask him. I might want to know for myself. It's not like I enjoy worrying this much every day. It's that I don't know how not to.

But we don't have that relationship, so I don't ask.

I drop into one of the chairs facing the window. Lewis speaks up again. "How about you? Any girlfriends yet?"

I hate this question coming from Lewis. It doesn't bother me when it comes from Mom—which it does every time I give a girl a ride home from school or work with one on a group project—or even when it's Ben and Cooper ribbing me at lunch.

From Lewis, though, I understand the question for what it is. Judgment. It's the disdain and comedy with which Lewis has long viewed my choices. My whole personality, really.

I do my finest impression of my brother's nonchalance. "No."

"What about girls in general? You got your eye on someone?"

"Not really." I shift uncomfortably in my chair.

I don't mention I pretty nearly did have a girlfriend once, four years ago. Cara Bergen. I talk to her every now and again. It's not awkward. No way, not awkward at all. I asked Cara to the winter dance when we were in eighth grade. I knew her from English, and we'd gotten to be friends once I noticed the Walt Whitman collection she was reading outside of class. She said yes, and we had what was honestly one of the happiest nights of my life. We hung out often after that, and I kept noticing new things about her. How clever she was, how unbelievable her charcoal sketches were, how her nose would wrinkle up at the very *mention* of cilantro.

I was going to ask her out for real, which she knew, in the way everyone just *knows* inevitabilities in love. Then my mom got her diagnosis.

I disappeared. I didn't answer Cara's texts, and then her phone calls. I didn't run into her at school because it was winter break. I *did* feel awful. I just knew I could barely balance my schoolwork with the new fears in my home life. If Mom had worsened, I wouldn't have been able to handle everything, especially a relationship. Cara would have been caught in the middle. It's what I feel with every other girl I've noticed since. I have every reason not to bring new, complicated questions of dating or breaking up into my life.

Lewis doesn't know that, of course. He probably never will.

"Well," Lewis says, closing his computer and jumping up from the table, "this trip could be a game-changer. I bet we could get you a hookup before we hit New York." I shrug. "You're a man of few words," Lewis observes, watching me. "We can work that angle."

"Pauciloquent," I mutter. From the way Lewis tilts his head uncomprehendingly, I wish I hadn't. It was a stupid slip-up, an invitation for exasperating questions. Fifteen minutes in, and I *had* to give my brother something to tease me for.

"Huh?" he says.

"It's a word for that—using few words in conversation," I explain hesitantly, knowing what's coming.

Lewis's expression tightens. "You're still doing the dictionary thing."

I fidget with the buttons on my coat. "Aperiodically."

"Doesn't sound *aperiodic.*"

I scowl.

With a hint of humor in his eyes, Lewis says, "I guess it makes sense. If there'd been a girl, you wouldn't have spent your evenings with Merriam and Webster."

I look up, feeling a flare of anger in my chest. I know there's a gulf between our degrees of experience, but I don't need Lewis belittling me for it. He knows I'm the one who's there for Mom while he's here doing whatever the hell he wants—too busy even to come home and visit. If he'd had more than a fleeting thought for Mom in the past three years, he might not have had the time to notch his bedposts with Prisha and whoever else.

I will Lewis to notice my anger. But one of his roommates walks through the front door, and Lewis glances in his direction. The two exchange wordless nods. When Lewis turns back to me with his insouciant grin, I can tell he's oblivious to how I'm feeling.

"Don't worry, Fitz," he says easily, "college will change everything."

He doesn't know that's exactly what I don't want—for everything to change. I don't want to be two hours from home. I don't want to lose the chance to check in with Mom every day, or to have to wait for a bus or a train or a flight in an emergency. I've worked hard to keep everything unchanging. It's not easy, and it's not something I'm intent on throwing away once I'm out of high school.

"Come on," Lewis says, still oblivious. "I know a pizza place you're going to like."

JUNIPER

TRAFFIC ON I-90 was unbearable. I feel a leg cramp coming on as Matt and I reach the overpasses into the city. We've been on the road for nearly two hours, not counting the hour and a half we stopped for dinner at a highway diner in Allston.

Matt, of course, couldn't look less bothered by the delay, though that might be because the diner had pumpkin-spice pancakes on the dinner menu. His appetite is aspirational, honestly. He's nodding to the classic rock he chose on the radio, drumming his fingers on his thigh.

I watch the city come into view. I've only driven into Boston once or twice, but the route is written into my head regardless.

We drove through here when I was seven, when we left New York for Springfield. Abuela was having heart problems, and Tía needed help running the restaurant. We were only supposed to be in Springfield for a year, until my parents could find permanent help. But things changed. It doesn't matter how much time has passed since I spoke to Abuela or held her hand—the grief never fades.

My phone vibrating pulls me from the memories. "Would you check those?" I ask Matt, nodding to the phone.

He plucks the phone from the cup holder. "It's your family," he says, reading.

I groan. "If it's Tía coming up with some ridiculous excuse for why I need to come home, tell her we have the tamales and this trip is happening."

"It's not just Sofi," Matt replies. "It's pretty much everyone. Marisa wants to know if you'll drive her to some New Year's party when you get back, Callie's wondering where her extra phone charger is, Walker wants to use your computer—I would recommend no—and, yeah, Sofi's just texted, 'Don't forget your family needs you and you need your family.'"

I grit my teeth. I've only been gone a couple of hours and they're wanting a hundred different things from me. It's like I have a job description written on my birth certificate. I get it—with my good grades, my uniquely sharp memory, my oldest-sibling status, I'm easy to depend on. Not like Marisa, who's careless enough to literally lose her backpack for two whole days. Even Tía, while determined, is getting too old to do everything. If only my siblings could handle themselves sometimes, even every now and then.

Instead, it's me. Every time. "Put my phone on silent," I say. He does and returns my phone to the cup holder. My family is going to have to get used to the distance.

We drive into the city center, turning left onto Arlington and circumnavigating Boston Common. Last time I was here, the endless expanse of grass was filled with dogs catching

Frisbees and kids feeding crackers to the ducks. Now, in the nighttime, it's empty except for groups of teenagers sitting on the park benches or wandering the paths.

I pull up in front of the valet for the Liberty Hotel. Matt peers out my window, and his eyebrows furrow in confusion.

"This isn't our hotel," he says.

"Isn't it?" I reply coyly. I get out of the car and give my keys to the valet. Matt follows, pulling our itinerary from his pocket and unfolding the printout.

"Our parents got us rooms at the DoubleTree, Juniper."

Together, we gaze up at the building in front of us. The façade is gray stone, with two wings reaching out from the tower in the center. Vast windows drench us in light. The circular window above us is like a face for this two-armed architectural being.

"This is definitely out of our price range," Matt adds.

I walk toward the front doors. Matt grabs the bags and runs behind me to catch up. "I called three days ago and canceled our parents' reservations. If we combine the money they gave us, two rooms there cost about as much as *one* here." I have a nonnegotiable budget from my parents, and I'll be grounded one week for every fifty dollars I overcharge the credit card. "I'll pay for this hotel, and you pay for the next. Neither of us will go over our parents' limits."

Matt's eyes light up brighter than the windows. "You are a genius," he declares. "A genius who will be grounded if her parents check the hotel name on the credit card statement, but a genius nonetheless."

I hold the door open for him. "I think it's worth a grounding, don't you?"

"Oh, definitely."

We walk into the lobby. With a low whistle, Matt places our suitcases on the floor.

I take in the room. It's dazzling like the exterior, multiplied by a hundred. The floor is a black-and-white checkerboard. White balconies with black railings ring the brick-walled room in tiers. They evoke cellblocks, because that's what they were. The building is a converted jail.

I nudge Matt with my elbow. "Look up."

We both do. From the ceiling hang Christmas trees, upside down, the tops pointed toward us like missiles hung in perpetual motionlessness. Each one is illuminated with strings of tiny lights, just like normal Christmas trees would be. They look like the celebratory ornaments of an inverted world connected to our own by the ceiling of this hotel.

"This is incredible," I hear myself breathe.

Matt just stands there in awe.

We head to the check-in desk. While I'm pulling out my credit card and signing forms, Matt tries repeatedly to hold my hand under the counter. I have to swat him away and restrain myself from giggling. I don't think I do a very convincing job, because the check-in clerk gives me a funny look. Finally, Matt settles for encircling his arm around my waist.

Once we've gotten our room keys, we explore the lobby. With every glimpse of every inch of this hotel, I feel my breath catch. It's a study—no, an exhibition—in contrasts.

In the restaurant on the ground floor, candles flicker under windows with jailhouse bars. On the worn brick walls out-side the bar, huge panels hang depicting flowering trees.

We find the elevator, and Matt punches the button for our floor. "How'd you know about this place?" he asks non-chalantly.

I give him an incredulous eyebrow raise.

He laughs, the noise ringing out wonderfully in the small space. "Right. You've been researching this for weeks. How could I forget you're the girl who prints out item-by-item itineraries when we go to the mall?"

I flush. "That was once," I reply. The truth is, though, I do plan everything. I want to wring every moment for what it has to offer. I want to do everything I can everywhere I go, even the mall. And this trip, this week of nine schools and a hundred million glimpses of my future, is way more impor-tant than shopping.

"Well, it's perfect," Matt says softly.

The elevator doors open, and we walk into the hall. Matt can hardly keep his hands off me as we find our room. I give him a quick kiss and unlock the door. We hurry in, him just a step behind me, and I feel a rush in my cheeks and my chest. Yet when I hit the lights and get a glimpse of our room, I have to pause.

It's not the details that catch my eye, the key-patterned carpet and the hash marks printed on the pillow, like the carvings on the walls of a convict's cell. It's the window on the far end of the room, and everything it overlooks. The lights of the hotel illuminate the street, and behind it, the Charles River. There's a bridge to the side, dotted with head-lights. The river itself is a frozen expanse, gently reflecting the lights of the Boston skyline.

I walk to the window. Matt comes up behind me, one hand finding my waist and the other sweeping my hair over my shoulder. Without a glance at the view, he kisses my neck.

I lift my lips to his and fall into his arms.

FITZ

I HAVE PIZZA with squash blossoms for dinner. Lewis and I hardly talk.

We walk from the restaurant onto the busy sidewalk, Lewis a couple of steps in front, pulling his coat close and glaring warily into the cold. We cross Commonwealth, a wide street with train tracks and overhead cables for the T running down the center. On the opposite curb, I follow Lewis toward the StuVi Commons.

In the lobby, I blurt what's been burning in my thoughts for the past hour. "Do you think Mom's okay with you moving to New York?"

Lewis's step falters, or I might be imagining it, because his voice comes out characteristically easy and level. "Of course," he says, hitting the button for the elevator. "She helped time the trip to coincide with an interview I have in the city."

I bite back my bitterness about skipping school, about Lewis's schedule getting prioritized over mine. This is the way it always is, me making sacrifices—me committing, doing what needs to be done—while Lewis does whatever he wants. "But what will you do when—" I cut myself off. I don't want to say it. I have half a superstition that every time I say it, it comes closer to reality. But I force myself. "When she needs help."

His eyes skirt mine. "I'll cross that bridge when we get there," he says decisively, and I know it's the end of the conversation. The elevator doors open, and I follow him in.

We ride the elevator without speaking. Lewis scrolls sporadically on his phone. He chuckles to himself once or twice. Unbelievable. The second time, he bothers to nudge me with his elbow and move the screen closer to me.

It's a video of a cat on one of those motorized vacuums.

"Wait for it to replay," Lewis mutters. I wait. The video replays. The vacuum, with cat rider, hums toward a couch or coffee table, I can't tell which. The vacuum keeps going, under the object, while the furniture pushes the cat off and onto the ground, where it sits, bored or disaffected.

I muster a smile, and Lewis only chuckles once again and resumes scrolling his newsfeed.

We return to his room. I guess Lewis noticed I'm not in the mood for conversation or cat videos, because I hear impatience in his voice when he informs me he's going to grab his extra blanket and make up the couch for me. He heads to his bedroom, and I wait by the window.

My head is a whirlwind. It's within me to shout at my brother, to force him to take our mother's diagnosis seriously. It's not just some bridge to be crossed. It's the rest of our lives. The rest of *her* life. I don't understand how I'm the *only* one who understands.

Mom has the genetic mutation that guarantees she'll

develop early-onset Alzheimer's disease. We don't know how much time she has before her symptoms set in.

She is the most responsible, resilient, positive person I know. Through college and graduate school, she cared for her own mother, who also had early-onset Alzheimer's. I've heard the stories Mom would tell on the rare evenings when she was in dark moods—the first time her mother ever forgot her name, the nights she called at two a.m. convinced she was being held against her will, the panic in her mother's eyes when confronted with a room full of family she saw as strangers. None of my mom's efforts could rescue her mother from the disease, of course. Her mother died four years following her diagnosis.

She was fifty-five.

That's not unusual—neither her age nor the years she hung on. I know because I'm one of those teenagers whose Google search history includes, "How long do Alzheimer's patients typically live?"

My mother understood the genetics. She knew she had a fifty-fifty chance of carrying the early Alzheimer's mutation. She avoided taking the test for as long as she could, knowing firsthand what the disease would do and that nothing could stop it, and not wanting the diagnosis looming over the rest of her life. However, she understood the game of chance she'd be playing if she had her own children. She knew she could consign them to the wild-eyed nights and empty moments she'd watched her own mother go through.

It's why she and my dad decided to adopt. Lewis came from Bengaluru four years before I was brought home from

Arkansas. We were both infants. I've never met my birth mother, though I've been told she had me when she was sixteen and has since gone to college. We send her Christmas cards, and I know she's not opposed to other contact from me. I just haven't reached out. I might one day, but with everything going on with my mom, it's one question too many.

A year after my mom and dad divorced, she decided she couldn't put off finding out whether she'd inherited her mother's disease. If she was going to be a single parent, she'd have to plan for herself and for Lewis and me. One day, when I was in middle school, without telling either of us, she took the test.

I don't have a great memory for things other than words. I don't remember my first day of high school, or the trip we took to Disney World when I was in elementary school, or the first time Lewis brought a girl over—which, to be fair, might be because he's brought enough of them over that I've lost track. But I remember the day Mom told us her test results. The way the winter sunlight filtered through the window in the front of the house, the smell of apple pie—Lewis's and my favorite, one of the few things we've ever agreed on—from the kitchen when she sat us down in the living room. I remember worrying the threads of the green couch, knowing something was coming even if I didn't know what. Lewis, for his part, stared at his shoes in uncharacteristic stillness while Mom gave us the details on how the results would and wouldn't change our lives.

There isn't a question of *if* she will develop the disease. She will. With a strength I'd never known she had in her, she

never mourned her prognosis. She's only repeated how grateful she is she decided not to have biological children, how
grateful she is to have Lewis and me—how grateful she knew
enough to avoid the weight of worry over whether we're going to share her disease.

She reassured us the coming years wouldn't change and
our lives would remain normal. Lewis took her at her word,
from what I understood from his quick return to texting
during dinners and working on college apps with his friends
instead of coming right home every afternoon. He did become interested in his biological family, writing them letters
in the summer before going off to college. He's close with one
half brother, who gave him the news their mother died years
before.

As for me, I couldn't accept life would "remain normal."
There is no normal, not now.

Normal is a memory. And it's my job to hold on to every
one of my mom's. Every day I watch her for early signs—
whenever she forgets the time of an appointment, or something I mentioned to her, or where she put her keys. What
would be tiny annoyances in the life of a normal high-school
senior fill my head with a parade of red flags.

There's nobody else to watch for her condition developing
or care for her. We don't have extended family. My dad, who
lives in Canada with his girlfriend, was rocked by her test
results. It was never a question that he would continue to
support Lewis and me financially, but nobody expected him
to handle his ex-wife's medical expenses, not to mention the
full-time care she'll one day need. I don't resent him for it,

even if I understand our lives would be easier were our family whole. He and I talk on the phone regularly, and I spend a month with him in Canada every summer—but for practical purposes, I'm on my own.

It's why I'm always asking her where she and Dad met, or what her dissertation was about, or other pieces of her life I want us both to hold on to. It's not only that I want to check on her recall. It's that I want to know she's still the person she was the day before, and the day before that. Because when she can't remember those things, she won't be *her.*

With my mind running over the daily list of worries, I watch Lewis fit the sheets to the futon. Hours later, I'm staring out the window overlooking the river. The lights of the city are undimmed, despite the late hour. Instead of falling asleep, I'm awake and wondering—wondering if Mom's okay, wondering if tomorrow's the day things start to go downhill.

Every day I wait. And one day the waiting will be over, and I don't want to lose the good years she has left because I'm away at college.

Mom said change is hard. Well, yeah. Every change I've ever experienced was for the worse. My parents' divorce, my dad's move to Canada, my mom's diagnosis. Even Lewis leaving for school and effectively removing himself from our lives. Going to college, especially going to college far from home, is a huge, fundamental change, and, honestly, I've had enough of change. I'm not eager for the upheavals and uncertainty it'll bring, not when I know exactly how not okay change can be.

It's why this trip is a waste of time. Everyone puts unnecessary emphasis on the noneducational parts of college—the city, the "feel" of the campus, the perfect "college experience." I only want the degree and the opportunity to learn. The rest is white noise. Instead of drowning in it, I'm focusing on where I'm truly needed.

This tour is nothing but an opportunity to observe everything I'm not interested in—while being forced into a car with the one person who should understand, who should share some of my fears and apprehensions, and who instead appears focused on getting me laid.

I look out the window and wish I were home.

JUNIPER

—≈—

I HEAR MATT'S even breathing beside me. It's eleven p.m. but the lights of Boston haven't gone out. While Matt dozes, I watch the view from the window.

I can't figure out how to be in the moment after sex. Not because of Matt, who is a perfect gentleman. But I envy him for how completely his mind goes clear, how easily restful he becomes. He's utterly relaxed.

Not me. My mind's a tornado. It churns forward, picking up fragments of the future as if they were playgrounds and patio furniture. Hopes, dreams, plans. They rush forward abrupt and unbidden. It's as if the feelings of sex unquiet everything, rushing me into tomorrow's tour and this week's itinerary and the year's exhilarating and enormous decisions.

Matt brushes my temple with his fingers. "Hey, where'd you go?" he asks, no doubt noticing I'm distracted.

"Just thinking about tomorrow," I reply.

He reaches up, pulling me closer, and I notice the sheet slip down his chest. Of course, he notices my noticing. I flush, even as I smile—knowing how moments like this go to his head—and just as I suspected, he grins. *This boy*. I let myself curl up next to him.

"College is going to be just like this," he says in a low voice.

I laugh into the smooth curve of his neck. "I don't think our dorms will be quite this nice."

"Not the room. This," Matt says. He traces his finger down my arm. "Us. No more sneaking around our parents, finding places to park."

His words bring back memories of circling parking lots and playing Ten Fingers until the final car leaves, fumbling on the seats. I pull away a little. "We'll have roommates. And, you know, studying?"

"Oh, is studying something a person does in college?" he asks playfully. "I had no idea."

I shove his shoulder lightly. "Hey, have you thought about that yet? What you might want to study?" I seize on the new subject, not entirely feeling like discussing our college sex plans.

Matt shuffles up onto his elbows. He considers the question for a second. "I'm feeling like something in the arts," he says.

I sit upright, pulling the sheet over my chest. "The *arts*?" Matt's passionate about a lot of things. I've just never seen him pick up a paintbrush or play an instrument or write a haiku. When we play Pictionary, his entries are worse than cave paintings.

"Yeah," he says evenly. "I was thinking . . . the art of seduction."

I wrinkle my nose as Matt smirks, obviously delighted with himself. "I can't believe you just said that." While he props himself up, hands behind his head, I get out of bed and open my suitcase. I rummage for my pajamas and pull them out, my striped bottoms and the UMass Amherst shirt from when I did a college prep day program there my sophomore summer. "For real, Matt," I say, tugging them on. I sit on the edge of the bed and begin to brush my hair. "When you picture yourself in four years, it's leaving college to go do what?"

"Whoa, leaving college?" Matt asks. "We haven't even gotten there yet."

"I know," I say. "It's just exciting. Our futures are out there." I find myself staring from the bed out the open window, onto the lights of the city, unblinking and incessant, each of them a life in motion. I swear I can see every light stretching all the way to Virginia.

Matt's fingers interlacing with mine pull my concentration from the view. On his face when I turn back to him is a rare vulnerability. It's the expression he gets when he's really thought something over—the one I recognize from the day he told his dad he'd decided he wouldn't play college baseball, and the morning he asked if he could meet my family. "My future and my past are the same, Juni, and I'm looking at her."

I feel myself soften at his words. Okay, maybe he *could* major in the art of seduction. It's one of the wonderful contradictions of Matt. Baseball jock though he is, he's melt-your-heart-into-a-little-puddle romantic when he wants to be. In this moment, the city lights become a little less inviting, like they're watching us now, not the other way around.

"The next four years are about you and about enjoying college," Matt continues. "We're going to make memories there. Memories we're going to hold on to the rest of our lives. That won't change depending on a job, or a degree."

I get up and walk to the window. "I'm going to study architecture." I say, scanning my mind for anytime Matt mentioned liking a class or finding an assignment interesting. "What about history?" I suggest. "You were really good at it. Remember?" I face the bed, where Matt's stuffing his legs into his sweatpants. "In April, you got a ninety-five on five US tests in a row."

Climbing under the covers, Matt yawns. "No, I don't remember, Juniper. That class was pretty boring."

I quell a small wave of irritation. I've had to learn not to be surprised when people don't remember things the way I do. Because to me, they're vexingly obvious. Forgetting something like that feels to me like forgetting my class schedule or who my English teacher is. When I was younger, I used to get in fights with my family over what they could and couldn't remember. The times they promised us extra hours of TV or ice cream for dinner, then claimed they hadn't. Disputed recollections of who said what or whose idea was whose. It took years to learn to let those things go.

Matt flips off the light near the bed. He nods toward the window, where the sleepless city still lights our room.

I draw the curtains.

Folding open my half of the covers, I crawl underneath, the hotel linens stiff and unfamiliar. They're comfortable, but not comforting. Within minutes, I hear Matt drift into sleep.

I want to close my eyes and have tonight become tomorrow. But I don't want to ignore my family. Reluctantly, I grab my phone from the bedside table.

Marisa's message is first. I grudgingly agree to be her chauffeur on New Year's Eve. Then Callie, who I tell to look for her phone charger in Mom's car. I throw in a text to let Mom know we got into Boston fine, and I even offer Walker use of my computer *when there's a parent in the room.*

Finally, there's only Tía's text. *Don't forget your family needs you and you need your family.* This is the difference between Tía and my parents. My parents, my practical and even-tempered mother in particular, understand there's tension between how connected they want me to the family, emotionally and logistically, and knowing I need space to grow up. It's why they deflect Tía's guilt trips, when they remember to. But Tía has an uncompromising zeal for the hope I'll never really leave home.

I reply without giving her an inch.

> Glad you're figuring out texting. It'll be great for communicating when I'm in college, xoxo.

Before I even hit the pillow, my phone illuminates with new messages.

I turn the phone over with a long breath through my nose, wishing on every light in the skyline for just one week to myself. One week without obligations, without expectations, with my family's permission to live a future outside the four walls of home.

I know what life would look like if I did what they wanted

and went to college closer to home. First, living in the dorms would be a debate. They'd want me home. Then, every weekend would be a battle. Whether I had to be home for dinner, whether I was obligated to come to this family event or that. Whether I made enough time for Marisa, Callie, Anabel, or Xan and Walker, no matter whether I'm in finals or rushing a sorority or running for student body president. I'd be fighting to write my own answers to things they didn't think were questions.

My family would have me believe there's nothing worthwhile outside the role they've handed me. But when I look toward the window, imagining everything beyond the curtains, I see a different view. Every idea, every world, every possibility is out there waiting for me.

FITZ

~

I WOKE UP in a terrible mood. The blanket Lewis tossed to
me yesterday, monogramed with the name of a consulting
firm, barely covered me through the night on my brother's
creaky black futon. The fabric bore disconcerting stains, and
I tried hard not to speculate on their origin.

By eight in the morning, when my phone chimed on the
coffee table, I'd woken up twice before in the night. Once when
Lewis inexplicably left the room close to midnight, then once
more when he returned hours later with two roommates and
they protractedly discussed *FIFA 19* for PlayStation. I don't
know how Lewis got used to this indeterminable cycle of
emails, random hookups, and nighttime video-game talk. But
if forced nocturnality is a fundamental of dorm living, it's
one more tick in the *not interested* column.

Things did not improve when I went into the bathroom
to shower. They'd left the roll of toilet paper on the floor,
and I'm pretty certain it's because none of the guys know
how to replace it. The cramped cubicle of the shower wasn't
completely covered by the flimsy curtain. One glance and I

knew nobody had cleaned this room in a while. Needless to say, I took a quick and to-the-point shower.

Following a breakfast of dry cereal—the milk in the fridge was profoundly expired—I grab my backpack and head for the elevator. I don't cross paths with my brother, which is fine by me. The folder my mom prepared says I have the BU information session at ten this morning. No way Lewis will wake up before noon. I know Mom will call later wondering how the session went. But I have thirty minutes before I'm due at the admissions building, and I plan to spend it not thinking about college and Lewis and next year.

I rub my eyes in the elevator, my disbelief having not entirely faded over how nice this place is. The doors open, and I wander into the foyer filling with students holding textbooks and thermoses. I'm going to read in a coffee shop. I helped myself to the copy of Henry James's *The Bostonians* on Lewis's bookshelf, the crisp pages evincing it was clearly unread. The choice felt fitting. I walk through the glass double doors into the breath-catching cold of the gray morning.

Halfway to the curb, I hear someone shriek.

I whip my head in the direction of the sound. The source isn't difficult to find. In the middle of the courtyard, I see a girl examining the fresh coffee stain seeping into one corner of her cream-colored cardigan. Her parka is unzipped, and the coffee trickles from her exposed sweater onto her jeans. The person with whom she presumably collided watches sympathetically, holding his Starbucks cup with lid half off.

Coffee. My mom and dad's story flits through my head. I

wonder if this is the beginning of something life-changing for this girl and Starbucks guy. If I've just witnessed a real-life meet-cute. If—

The thought evaporates, because the guy continues on his way, walking hurriedly like he's late. The next instant, a hulking blond guy walks up behind the girl. He's like a fourth Hemsworth brother. While he inspects the stain with a dire expression, he places one hand on the small of her back. *Boyfriend*, I immediately read in the gentle gesture. Definitely not a meet-cute, then. The way the guy is watching her holds an intimacy, a familiarity drawn from considerable time together.

I'm close enough to hear their conversation.

"Asshole," the Hemsworth-boyfriend mutters, eyes fixed on the Starbucks guy's retreating form.

"It was my fault," the girl replies immediately. Despite myself, I notice she's strikingly pretty. Her heart-shaped face frames dark eyes, with freckles dusting her light brown skin. Errant flyaways of her wavy chestnut hair escape from her ponytail. "I was distracted. Too busy looking at the dorms." Even as she's speaking, her eyes return to the campus surrounding us. Her fascination radiates the kind of intensity I thought only existed in fiction. She studies everything with enraptured eagerness—everything except the sidewalk. I now understand how the coffee incident happened.

"Well," Hemsworth says, "we should go back to the hotel so you can change."

"No!" Her eyes dart to him. "We'll be late."

"But your sweater—"

"It's fine," she interrupts. "I'll just take it off when we're inside."

"You sure?" he asks doubtfully. "It'll stain if you leave it too long."

"I'm sure," she says. Excitement comingles with decisiveness in her voice. "I'm not missing this."

He rolls his eyes affectionately. "Yeah, I know, Juniper." They walk down the street in the direction opposite me.

Juniper. I wonder what having her momentum would feel like—literally running into someone because she's intently focused on what interests her, then charging on to whatever she can't stand missing despite the coffee. It's enthralling, her indefatigable energy.

I fight for a moment to imagine having her curiosity, her hunger, for college and the possible futures it represents. I fail, of course. But it's possible I'm briefly better for having put in the effort.

I'm staring, I realize, watching Juniper and her boyfriend. I don't want to become *that* guy. Remembering plans of reading, I divert my eyes from the couple. There's still twenty minutes before the information session begins. Plenty of reading time.

Except I don't want to read. I want to wander. Not the campus, necessarily—I figure I'll just explore in one direction and take in whatever I find until I have to return for the information session. I'm going to have nights in hotels not talking to Lewis to read James if I want.

I follow the road until I reach a tree-lined lane of brownstones. They're grandiose and imposing, fire escapes curling over their curved stone windows. This street's quiet. I hear only the hushed whisper of the wind through the icy branches of the trees, even though I'm just blocks from Commonwealth. For a moment I think I've finally escaped the reach of the campus, until I notice plaques for student living on the doors. Is every dorm here insanely nice?

I check the time, finding I have only five minutes until the information session. Grudgingly, I pull up the campus map on my phone and double back toward the admissions office. Before I'm even near the building, I find I'm slowing my pace. The prospect of sitting through the session, enduring details of the campus life I'll never live dispensed by stock-photo-ridden PowerPoints, taking the tour guided by an overzealous freshman . . . It's too much. Lewis won't know if I ditched. The only way Mom will know is if I tell her.

I have better things to do than this presentation. Find a decent breakfast, for one.

I'm lingering outside the building, searching for the nearest Panera on my phone, when I hear familiar voices.

"In here," Juniper says, walking quickly toward the door next to me.

"I'm coming," her boyfriend replies. He races in front of her and opens the door with a dramatic flourish, earning a laugh from Juniper. She doesn't notice me. As she passes him in the doorway, he pulls her to him, giving her a quick kiss.

My earlier thoughts of breakfast and exploring dissipate. Resolve fading, I follow them in.

JUNIPER

IT DIDN'T FEEL real until now. Well, not *this* real. I can't
deny that every time I've thought about college or the idea of
leaving home, it's felt like a new version of real, like a developing photograph.

But my first on-campus information session definitely is
one of the most real versions. I hold on to every statistic,
every detail, even the ones I know won't figure into my decision. The percentage of students coming in nationally and
internationally, the number of graduates in government and
in science, the well-regarded journalism program. The information flows comfortingly over me. This is exactly where I
want to be right now.

Even if I'm increasingly conscious of the smell of espresso
wafting up from under my seat, where I stored my cardigan. *Marisa's* cardigan, if I'm honest. I'd hoped I could stuff it
into her wardrobe when I got home without her noticing I'd
stolen it. But as soon as she sees the giant coffee stain, she'll
know what happened, and she will retaliate.

I'll deal with her later. Right now, I'm determined to focus
on the presentation.

When the admissions officer opens the room to questions, my hand is the first one up. I'm called, and I project my voice to the front of the room. "What opportunities exist for double majoring?"

I don't need to glance over to know Matt's enjoying this. In AP Bio last year, he bet me I couldn't *not* be the first person to raise my hand in every review session. Of course, I lost. For winning, he requested a complete *Lord of the Rings* marathon, an obligation I grudgingly fulfilled over the summer.

Whatever. He knows I'm eager.

"It depends," the officer replies. "Do you have a prospective major?"

"I'm really interested in architectural studies," I say. "But I'm considering combining the major with physics."

I want to be an architect. I want to pull buildings up from the earth, stretch skylines from the streets. Whatever I do, I want to shape the future. I want to *create*. I considered painting and thought about writing or drama or journalism. Finally, I found myself enthralled with architecture's union of opposites. Art and science, mismatched pieces that decided to defy expectations and fit perfectly.

"Definitely." The officer nods. "The physics program is demanding. If you're interested, though, double majoring is well within reach for the dedicated student."

I thank her. The questions continue, prospective students with inquiries on study abroad programs and sports, dorms and dining halls. When one guy wants to know whether the freshman have intramural baseball, I glance at Matt, knowing it's something he would be interested in.

Except he's not listening. He's looking at his phone. Craning my neck, I find he's exchanging rapid-fire texts with Nathan Fletcher, who I've hung out with enough times to know is probably playing video games with Vincent Zhong and the Klarov brothers in his basement back in Springfield. I frown, nudging Matt's knee, and whisper, "Hey, you might want to listen to this."

He looks up, focusing halfheartedly on the discussion. I wait for the moment curiosity kicks into his eyes, but it doesn't happen. His gaze quickly returns to his phone. Frustrated, I watch a new message from Nathan pop up on the screen.

After a couple more questions, the presentation ends, and everyone shuffles to their feet. Everyone but one boy three rows from the back. He remains in his chair, writing in a paperback book, while the rest of us head for the doors. His red hair stands out in the room, and when I pass him, he glances up for a heartbeat and his eyes meet mine. They're startlingly blue, set in narrow, freckled features. It's a face seemingly sculpted in its precision, with high cheekbones and a serious, contemplative mouth.

I'm the one to break our eye contact, walking on with the crowd.

The admissions officer divides the room in two for the campus tour. Because we're on different sides, the boy and I don't end up in the same group. Finally, in the bustle of everyone finding their tour guide, he closes his book and joins the others.

He obviously hadn't even noticed the information session

ending, and the flush I felt when Matt texted through the presentation returns to my cheeks. This guy is completely checked out, finding whatever is in his book more important than the information he'll use to make the decision on which his future hinges.

I bet I know what he's thinking. Because I bet it's no different from the perception of college I've watched form for countless classmates. There's an interchangeability to the college experience for them, the impression they'll be content with whatever universities check a standard series of boxes. Football, parties, degree. They consider college nothing but doing what they've been doing, being who they've been.

They'd rather read, or text people back home, than look at what's ahead.

I walk out onto the tour, carrying my coffee-scented cardigan, and put the boy from my thoughts.

JUNIPER

~

THE T RUMBLES toward Park Street. The view of the river explodes through the glass of the windows when we emerge from the tunnel, the ice reflecting the oil-paint oranges and pinks of the sunset.

It's nearly five. I'm packed between students with headphones and university sweatshirts and moms corralling children on the crowded train. Matt and I grabbed sandwiches when the BU tour ended around noon. After, I changed my shirt and took the T into Cambridge on my own for the Harvard tour I had scheduled for three. I'd planned to tour both schools today knowing I could cover each in a couple of hours.

The Harvard tour was breathtaking—the wrought-iron gates and brick buildings, the new dusting of snow on the courtyard where poets and presidents walked, the towering library. It felt intimidating, though, even unfriendly, if inspiring. I'd pitched the idea of touring Harvard to Matt weeks ago, but he wasn't interested. Over our sandwiches today, I tried again on the off chance he'd changed his mind. Unsurprisingly, he hadn't. We made plans to meet in the North End when I was done.

While I'm changing trains in the Park Street station, I find myself imagining what Matt's doing now. I know with incontrovertible certainty he napped in the hotel room. Every chance the boy gets, he dozes. *Traverson family trait*, he told me once, which is a bullshit excuse. I'd guess when he woke up, he wandered to the closest coffee shop to grab a matcha because coffee is "gross" to him. It's nice just thinking about it—he's probably befriended half the baristas by now. There's a tender pride to envisioning the person you love when you're not there, being funny with friends, being charming with classmates, having interests and inspirations. It's different from imagining yourself with them, and differently wonderful.

The river of my thoughts reverses course, and I think back to the day he and I began. The hallways of Springfield High were empty, everyone having headed to the cafeteria for lunch. I had doubled back to grab the heavy AP US History textbook from my locker, and I was on my way to rejoin my friends when Matt walked past me.

He was wearing his white Adidas, and his jeans bore grass stains, probably because he'd been sitting in the courtyard with his friends in the mild September weather, no longer summer and not quite fall, instead of in the cafeteria. I remember his confident stride—which hasn't changed—and how he'd recently cut his hair.

Of course, I blushed.

This was *Matt Traverson*. Baseball co-captain, big man on campus—whatever *big* means in our class of one hundred—and the crush of one Juniper Ramírez. Wholly and completely.

One year of sitting next to him in sophomore English, trading eye rolls and glances behind Mr. Ward's back, and I was done for.

He walked past, and I fought down the pink in my face, knowing my friends would call me on my rosy cheeks and discern exactly who'd caused them.

I had nearly succeeded when I heard my name called behind me.

"Hey, Juniper."

I found Matt grinning unevenly and running a hand through that neat blond hair, his bicep the stuff of dreams. I focused on the Celtics logo on his shirt, and this time I failed to keep the blush from my face.

"Hey, Matt," I said with a nonchalance I thanked god I'd practiced in the mirror. "How's it going?"

He jogged up to me, energy in his every movement. Without warning, he ducked down to retie his undone shoelace. When he stood back up, his eyes fixed on mine. "So Tory told me you have a crush on me," he said. His voice betrayed nothing, neither flirtatiousness nor disinterested cruelty.

It was brutal. He knew exactly what he was doing.

In the moment, I figured he'd reduced my crush to hallway chatter because it was trivial to him. Probably just an everyday occurrence. The blood drained from my face, and I vowed to reap revenge on my best friend—*ex*-best friend—for her tactlessness.

It felt like a bad dream, one I wanted to escape. "Don't let it go to your head," I said, hurried and defensive.

I turned to leave, but his hand found my shoulder. Grudg-ingly, I waited.

"I didn't mean it that way," Matt said fumblingly, and I was struck by the oddity of seeing him off guard. "I just—it's true then? You do like me?"

The hesitant inquisitiveness in his voice eroded my defensiveness, and hope fluttered open in my chest. It was funny, I thought then, how a whole year of yearning and imagining could narrow down to a single moment that had come out of nowhere. I leaned on the locker behind me, looking up at him through my lashes. "I do," I replied, feeling bold. "What do you think of me?"

His eyes widened. I could have sworn I saw my flush mir-rored in his cheeks. I took his hand, pulling him closer. He swallowed.

"I think you're the most beautiful girl I've ever seen," he said. "And I have a feeling you're smarter than everyone in this school. Teachers included."

I smiled the kind of smile lit with a thousand smiles saved up for right then. When Matt returned it, I stepped in closer, my chest meeting his. "Let me get this straight," I said softly. "I'm smart, I'm beautiful, you know I like you. Why haven't you kissed me yet?"

He laughed, lowering his mouth near mine, closing the distance between our lips.

The crazy thing isn't how wonderful the kiss felt, the blinding rush of heat racing the highways of my heart. The crazy thing is how that's the way every kiss has felt from then until now. For fleeting instants, they erase complicated choices, and inescapable uncertainties.

The train hurtles into Haymarket Square. I follow the crowd onto the platform, then up the escalator into the fading daylight. Pulling on my scarf in the cold, I take in the street corner. The taxis in front of slush-piled gutters, the pubs with EST. 1826 and A.D. 1795 signs over the doors. I'm walking toward the North End when I feel my phone ringing through my coat.

I pull the phone from my pocket. It's my dad. With gloved fingers, I clumsily pick up and press it to my ear. "Hi, Dad."

"Found your dream college yet?"

It's exactly what my dad would say. Instead of the introductory pleasantries of conversation, he loves just jumping to the point. It's probably—no, *definitely*—where I got my own directness. I hear the clatter of kitchen prep over the phone. He's getting ready to open the restaurant for dinner, chopping vegetables and frying tortilla chips.

"I don't know," I say. "I did BU and Harvard. They were both great, but Boston is a bit close to home."

"Yeah," he says thoughtfully. "Big city, though."

Dad and I both love big cities. He went to college in New York City, and I could fill books with the stories he's told of getting ramen with friends past midnight, living with five roommates in a loft meant for three, his yearlong quest to determine the greatest pizza in the city. The way he describes them, cities exist in perpetual reinvention, sparked by constantly changing populations of constantly changing people.

They're places where the strangers you meet on the street could derail your life in wonderful, unforgettable ways.

"Boston is great," I reply. "I'm going to the North End right now to meet Matt before we drive to Providence."

"The North End," he repeats, excitement jumping into his voice. "Oh man. You can't come home without grabbing cannoli from Mike's Pastry."

"Twist my arm, why don't you?"

He laughs over the clang of pans in the kitchen. "How were the hotel rooms?"

"The *rooms* were good." I emphasize the plural, which I know my dad detects, because he chuckles.

"Uh-huh," he says. "You know, I was Matt's age once." I permit myself a small laugh, understanding this is one of those things we won't be discussing with Mom and Tía. "I trust you to be responsible, Juni," he continues, "and to never, ever tell your sisters about this."

I laugh. "Promise," I say resolutely. I know full well that I, the oldest daughter, provide precedent for my siblings. If Marisa knew I shared a hotel room with my boyfriend, she would be clamoring for the exact same within weeks. It's part of why the idea of leaving home for college is contentious with Tía. If I do, every one of my siblings can, and probably will.

"I have to finish prepping," Dad says. "Enjoy the city."

"I will," I say.

I hang up, wondering if I caught wistfulness in my dad's voice. He'd probably be living in Boston or New York if he could. We both know why he isn't. We moved to Springfield because of Abuela's heart trouble. We stayed because she died. The guilt kept my parents rooted to the restaurant, to Spring-field, to the house of fraught memories and family history.

But I won't spend my college tour ruminating on old wounds. I lift my head and keep walking, fixing my eyes forward.

FITZ

　❦

ENTERING MIKE'S PASTRY, I breathe in the sweet smells of dough and sugar. Everything is exactly the way I remember. The brown tile floors, the glass display cases on three walls of the room, the warm brilliance of the overhead lights. Behind the counters, women in black uniforms, universally gruff and wordless, point to customers for their orders. They pull white string from overhead spindles and deftly wrap cardboard boxes of every kind of cannoli imaginable. The place is packed, the crowd incessantly moving up to the counters and exiting with white-and-blue packages.

I *love* Mike's Pastry. When I was in elementary school and my parents were still together, my dad would drive Lewis and me into Boston for pretty much the greatest day a ten-year-old could imagine. We would catch the Sox in Fenway or visit the New England Aquarium, then head to the North End for Italian and finally, Mike's for dessert.

I text my dad a photo, knowing he probably won't respond for a couple of hours. He went into academia like my mom—archaeology, Grecian art and history in particular—and now he's his university's department chair. He has office hours for undergrads in the evenings. I've dropped in on them once or twice in my life, giving him the chance to recite Euripides and Sophocles to me, eyes bright behind his glasses. While I don't know what I want to study in college, I know it's not Grecian art or history. Despite the ancient pottery shards on my dad's shelves and his trips with students to Athens or Crete—not to mention his irrepressible passion describing some statute or discovery—I never found the enthusiasm for the subject he did.

I don't exactly know what pulled my parents apart. I do know the change was not abrupt or unexpected. I had felt continents shifting under my feet for years, and then one day the marriage was over. I felt them shift again when my mom told us her test results, and again when Lewis left home. I feel them shifting now, shaking the foundations of the life I know. I just want the ground under me to settle.

Lewis doesn't mind the shifting, doesn't reach for familiarity the way I do. Familiarity that today takes the form of cannoli dusted with powdered sugar, ricotta spilling out the ends. When I extended the invitation to Lewis to head uptown with me on the Green Line and revisit Mike's, he declined, his flippancy betraying no cognizance of the childhood trips we would take with Dad. Instead, he suggested I join him for drinks with three friends whose names I obviously didn't know, but who Lewis rattled off like I did. He wanted to hang out with Bruce, Trevor, and Amir before leaving for the week with me. I said no.

I don't care, honestly. I'm content to visit Mike's completely on my own. It's probably better this way, because the week to come will be nearly nonstop time with my brother. For now, cannoli and solitude will be the panacea for the frustration of this trip.

I join one of the lines in front of the counters, although "lines" suggests an orderliness lacking here. While nobody is pushing or shoving, I find myself jostled in the gradually moving pilgrimage to the registers.

Eventually, I notice a girl next to me craning her neck, rising onto her toes to look over the heads of the crowd, checking her place in line a little obnoxiously. Wobbling, she tilts in my direction, her shoulder bumping mine. She glances toward me, and our eyes connect.

Which is when I recognize her.

Juniper, the girl from this morning. She's holding her parka, and I notice she's not wearing the coffee-stained cardigan from earlier. I search the shop for signs of the Hemsworth boyfriend, but he's not here. Maybe they broke up, and she's here to find someone to help nurse her heartbreak. I'm reaching for some small talk when she speaks.

"You were in the BU information session today."

"I—yeah," I stammer, startled she remembers me.

"You weren't interested, though." It's a statement spoken like a question. Her eyes burn into me, holding the intensity I remember from this morning in front of the dorm. It's intimidating when that intensity is directed at me, even if she looks curious, not accusatory.

"What makes you say I wasn't interested?" I ask, puzzled I'm even having a conversation with this girl, and that this is the topic.

"I saw you reading. You didn't even know when the presentation ended," she replies, undaunted. Her hair remains in the uncompromising ponytail it was during the tour, and I'm beginning to learn there's no halfway with this girl.

"You were watching me read?" I say, surprising myself with temerity.

For the first time I catch the force in Juniper's eyes flicker. "I wasn't *watching* you, watching you," she explains. "You just stood out because you weren't listening to the presentation," she continues, recovering quickly.

We've nearly reached the registers, and I wonder if she's going to question me through the entire ordering process. I know the women behind the counter don't have a profusion of patience.

"I was listening," I protest weakly.

Juniper faces me, a hint of playfulness in her eyes. "Well, are you going to apply to BU?"

I sigh. I could lie, but the directness in her gazes makes me rethink it. Besides, in a couple more questions, she'd probably corner me into admitting the truth. "Compunctiously, no, I'm not," I say, and her eyebrows—her perfectly shaped eyebrows—rise. I wince internally. Once again, the pretentious word choice just slipped out. I know from experience that obtuse and antiquated vocabulary generally doesn't go over well with the girls I try to talk to. With anyone, really.

The woman behind the counter gestures in my direction, and I order quickly. Plain ricotta with chocolate chips. She throws together the familiar package of wax paper, cannoli, and enough powdered sugar to leave the dough beneath barely visible. Juniper orders Oreo.

Handing the woman a rumpled twenty over the counter, I'm conscious of Juniper's silence. I probably put her off with the weird word choice. Or—a worse thought hits me. Boston University is probably her dream school, and I've just implicitly insulted her with my indifference. She receives her cannoli. "Look," I say before she can turn to leave, "it's not only BU. I'm on a college tour this week, and I'm not planning on applying to any of the schools I'm visiting."

Juniper's eyes widen. "You're—what?" Gentle understanding settles on her features. "Oh, it's okay if you don't have great grades," she says encouragingly, if a little patronizingly. "Colleges consider lots of other factors in their decisions. I'm certain you could get in if you wanted to."

I blink. "What? No," I rush to clarify, wanting with startling urgency for this girl not to think I'm unintelligent. "It's not that I don't think I could get in. I have fine grades and a practically perfect SAT score."

God, that sounded douchey. But Juniper doesn't look bothered, only curious. The people behind us push forward, breaking our eye contact for a moment. Our shoulders brush, her chestnut curls swinging with the movement. Glancing over the crowd, I see an open table for two in the corner, near the long window.

"Want to sit?" I venture uncharacteristically. Years of lunches and weekends spent with the same three or four friends don't generally lead to spontaneously inviting random gorgeous girls for cozy cannoli dates. Of course, I have absolutely no expectation she won't produce a flimsy excuse for why she needs to return to her hotel because she remembered I'm a complete weirdo who she never wanted to have a conversation with in the first place.

"Okay," she says.

I can't believe what I'm hearing. But incredibly, I keep it together and nod toward the table under the window. We push into the crowd, cannoli boxes held in front of us. We're pulling out chairs when Juniper eyes me again.

"What do you want to do instead of college?" she asks.

"Oh, I'm going to college." I open the white flaps on the box and pull out the cannoli, powdered sugar sprinkling down like snow. "I just don't want to go to any of the colleges on my tour. They're too hard to travel to."

"*Compunctiously*, I have to tell you that's a dumb reason," Juniper replies. There's lighthearted confrontation in her eyes, and I get the feeling she's proving she knew exactly what the word meant when I dropped it earlier. She's probably trying to put me in my place. Instead, I can't help leaning a little closer over our window nook. If this girl intrigued me before, now I'm fascinated. "We're on the East Coast of the United States, not the moon," she continues. "There are buses, trains, flights wherever you want to go."

I don't really want to get into my reasons for wanting to go to college near home. Besides, I want to know about her. "Where do you want to go?" I crunch into my cannoli. It's heaven, exactly the way I remember. "What's your top choice?"

If Juniper notices my deflection, she doesn't comment—but I'm guessing she doesn't notice, because I can tell she's the type who, when she wants to know something, pursues it until she does. "Everywhere," she says easily. I tilt my head, curious. But her eyes have wandered out the window, her expression faraway and hungry. "I mean, if there weren't application fees, I would apply everywhere," she adds. "I'm on a college tour this week too. Already I can tell there are so many great schools out there. It's going to be impossible to decide. Part of me hopes I'll only get into one and I won't have to. I'll probably end up on the East Coast for undergrad because flights cost money I don't have. But maybe I'll get a master's or PhD in California or London or wherever. It's exciting to imagine myself in other parts of the country, even on other continents."

We both realize she's rambling. I think it's awesome. She doesn't. Her embarrassment is evident in the way she turns quickly to face me, tugging that tight ponytail, her cheeks heating.

"What about you?" she asks. "Why go on a college tour if you're not planning to go to any of the colleges on the tour?"

"I'm on this trip because my mom's forcing me," I explain. "But I'm committed to Southern New Hampshire University." Even saying the name gives me a rush of reassurance. Memories flit through my mind of the wide lawns, the brick buildings, the expansive windows, and the elegant columns of the modern library. "I practically grew up on the campus because my mom's a professor there," I continue. "It's close to home. Familiar."

Juniper's finished her cannoli. I'm not even halfway through mine.

"Let me get this straight," she says, pointedly pausing to dust off her fingers. "Your parents are encouraging enough of your college choices to send you on a tour. You have fine grades and a practically perfect SAT score"—she recites my words verbatim—"and I've already explained how travel won't be a problem. Yet you want to return to a campus you grew up on, a campus that's *familiar*?"

"Well, there are things more important than college," I tell her. Frustration stirs in me. I should've known this girl wouldn't understand. Should've expected she'd react the way every one of my classmates has, oblivious to the idea that there are other ways of thinking about the future.

Juniper's nostrils flare, a frown shadowing her lips. She half opens her mouth, like she's fighting what she wants to say.

I suddenly don't want to be talking about this any longer. I want to change the direction of the conversation instead of only being the guy who told this PhD-bound girl he thinks there are more important things than college. But right then, I notice her boyfriend's broad frame push through the door, and I know I won't get the chance.

JUNIPER

I NARROW MY eyes, feeling a hundred retorts about to spring forward. But I hold them in. I don't know this guy, and I know it's wrong to come right out and criticize his whole worldview, even if I think it's ridiculous. Instead, I try to formulate a lighter, reasonable rebuttal. Before I have the chance, a hand drops gently onto my shoulder.

"There you are." Matt smiles down, stepping up to my side.

I glance back to the boy with whom I hadn't anticipated having a full-on discussion of college and the future. I honestly have no clue what compelled me to unload my entire prospective life plan on him. With a family skeptical and even dismissive of my desire to live my own life, I've learned to be a little wary of sharing my highest-flying hopes. Yet here I am. He might not be interested in college, but I'll grudgingly concede he was a welcoming listener.

"This place is great," Matt declares, and I don't know if I love the distraction. He surveys the room, then nudges my shoulder to get my attention, his hundred-watt grin returning to me. "We could come here for date nights if we both go to college in Boston."

"Yeah, when we're not busy," I remind him instinctively.

His green eyes flicker, and I know it's not what he wanted to hear. I feel bad, but I'm not wrong. When Matt envisions college, he pictures the life we have now, the dates and long conversations, except with new freedoms and a new city. I picture problem sets and sorority philanthropic events, having two-hour conversations in the dining hall with people we've never met, and walking each other to class under the fireworks of fall leaves. I just hope our different pictures are two parts of one panorama.

Matt glances at the boy I'm sitting with, whose presence I haven't yet explained. I guess I don't really have a good explanation. "Well," Matt says stiffly, "I checked out of the hotel. Do you want to get dinner before we head to Providence? I know you wanted to explore the North End."

"Yes," I say enthusiastically, standing up and taking his hand. I'm not one for public displays of affection, but I feel bad for torpedoing his date idea.

I turn back to the boy, who's taking his final bite of cannoli. His eyes flit to Matt's and my clasped hands. When he peers back up at me, the frustration I saw earlier after I questioned his decision to go to a familiar college has returned. He blinks, and it disappears, erased so completely that I wonder if I misread him or if he's practiced in letting go of irritation.

"It was . . . interesting meeting you . . ." I pause, realizing he never gave me his name.

"Oh, I'm Fitz," he supplies.

"Fitz?" I repeat. "Like Fitzwilliam?" It's not a name for redheaded teenage boys on college tours eating cannoli in

Boston bakeries. It's a name for snarky Jane Austen heroes.

"Like Fitzgerald. Not that that's much better."

"Damn," Matt says. "Family name? I have a cousin named Eustace, after our grandfather."

Fitz turns to Matt. Even though Matt interrupted us, even though his first words to Fitz were lightly disparaging, Fitz doesn't appear annoyed. I'm convinced Matt is secretly a superhero with powers of uncanny likability.

"No," Fitz replies. "My mom is really into twentieth-century American literature. My brother's name is Lewis, for—"

"Sinclair Lewis," I cut him off. "And F. Scott Fitzgerald." Our eyes lock.

"Exactly," Fitz says, and smiles widely for the first time. It's not a flashy smile, not one used to being on display for large crowds. It's the kind of smile for surprising kindnesses, for doors held open or dropped items picked up in hallways, for book recommendations or discovering you've both had the same favorite band since seventh grade. It's exhilarated in a close-quarters kind of way.

Matt squeezes my hand, and I know he's asking me if we can go.

"Right," I say. "Well, I'm Juniper, and this is Matt. My boyfriend." I don't know why I include the "boyfriend" designation when it's obvious. I continue. "Maybe we'll run into each other again on this trip. You know, if you don't decide other colleges aren't worth a chance."

He nods, and I swear a wry gleam enters his unreadable eyes. "Impossible to say," Fitzgerald—Fitz—says with a shrug.

FITZ

I LIED TO Juniper. It wasn't impossible to say. It is very possible we'll cross paths. I don't do "cool" very well, but in Mike's I miraculously pulled out a noncommittal veneer even though I knew my own itinerary put me in Providence next.

I'm not following this girl to Providence. I'm not. I reminded myself of this important fact on the walk from Mike's to the T, from the train down to my brother's dorm.

It's just serendipity that my tour and Juniper's are putting us in the same city again. Pure coincidence.

It's pretty probable she's visiting Brown like I am—from her unusual preparedness in the BU information session and her use of *compunctiously*, she exuded the overachiever vibe of student council presidents and future valedictorians. But there are plenty of colleges in Providence, I tell myself while packing up my backpack in my brother's room the next morning. Plenty of opportunities for me not to run into Juniper and Matt. It would be impossibly coincidental if we did reconnect.

But even the possibility filled me with nervous excitement, which got me out of bed before six. It's unlike me, wanting to spend time with some stranger. But being a stranger to her lets me be unlike myself.

I took another brief shower and quickly folded the futon back into a couch, then waited while I heard my brother's phone alarm go off three times. I knew he was repeatedly hitting snooze. Lewis never was a morning person. In fairness, I'm usually not either. After the fourth alarm, I banged on his door and heard a groggy, "I'm up."

We were on the road half an hour later, Lewis rubbing his eyes and dressed in a rumpled polo, one of those ones with an animal embroidered on the pocket. It was snowing softly when we headed out. Lewis drove carefully, neither of us speaking while we navigated onto I-93 and through Quincy, passing ponds and white rooftops.

Mom calls when we're nearing the Rhode Island state line. Lewis hits answer on his dashboard display. "Hey, Mom. You're on speaker," he says.

Mom's voice crackles over the car stereo. "Oh, you're driving? I figured I'd be waking you up. I thought Fitz's tour was scheduled for ten." It's a relief hearing how focused and vivacious her voice is, how herself she sounds.

"Yeah," Lewis says, shooting me a lightly disdainful look. "Fitz woke me up early. He was eager to get on the road. Dramatic change from trying to ditch the trip and take the bus back home."

The commentary irks me, and I grit my teeth. It's not

worth calling Lewis out, though. I know he said it to piss me off, and he would only ignore me or continue belittling me if I spoke up. *It's going to be nine more days of this*, I think ruefully. *Nine long days.*

"Well," Mom says, sounding pleased if startled, "it's wonderful you're beginning to take an interest in the trip. Brown would be perfect for you, honey. With your grades and your SAT score, you can really consider the Ivies. I googled the campus, and it's lovely. It looks like SNHU"—she says this in a way I know she imagines is casual—"except, you know, older." She laughs.

"I'm sure it's a nice campus," I reply neutrally. I don't have the heart to explain that my feelings on this college tour haven't changed, except to the extent that the tour puts me in the path of one particular prospective coed.

"I hope you love it. Text me pictures, okay?" Mom charges on. "Love you both."

"I will," I promise. "Love you too."

"Talk to you later, Mom," Lewis says, and hangs up. Of course he doesn't bother to tell our mother he loves her. Lewis is too cool for that kind of thing.

The brick buildings and barren trees of Pawtucket pass by outside. I put my forehead to the cold glass of the window and close my eyes, hoping to check out for the rest of the drive. I wish I could pull out my pocket dictionary, but I don't want to deal with the shit I'd get from Lewis. Instead, I concentrate on cool, nonchalant ways to get a girl's phone number without offending her intimidatingly muscled boyfriend. Hypothetically, of course.

"You don't want to go to Brown," Lewis says speculatively, interrupting my creative process.

I look over, finding him watching the road with thoughtfully narrowed eyes. Sitting stupidly in silence, I realize I'm astonished my brother figured this out. He hardly knows me. Even Mom, who does, was quick to forget I have a plan and I'm not wavering from it.

"I'm just doing what Mom wanted," I reply carefully. "Visiting the schools, going on the tours, you know."

"Yeah . . ." Lewis draws out the word, emphasizing his disbelief. "There's a difference between doing what Mom wants and doing what Mom wants at seven in the morning. Not even you cling that tightly to her every wish." Once again, I ignore the jab. He's only trying to get a rise out of me. "You wouldn't have hauled my ass out of bed bright and early for this itinerary," he continues, pursing his lips, and with dread I watch an idea enter his eyes. "Do you have your own plans in Providence?"

"No," I say quickly—too quickly. The instant the word exits my mouth, I know I've blundered into a conversational bear trap.

Confirming my worries, Lewis grins wolfishly. "Oh, I get it," he goads. "I know what's going on here. You know a girl at Brown? The hot girl from high school who's a couple years older than you who you still have a thing for? Everyone has their upperclassman crush," he pontificates. "Nicole Kepler. Whoo." He bites a knuckle, performing the jock-bro role he's evidently gotten used to. "Went to Berkeley. Your Nicole Kepler goes to Brown, doesn't she?"

"There's no . . . Nicole Kepler," I fumble to contradict him. "It's not that."

"Uh-huh." Lewis glances over. "There's a girl. There's definitely a girl."

"What's it to you?" I ask harshly. Lewis isn't really interested. He's never been interested in my life. He's just playing his favorite game of pressing me about girls, putting on the older brother posture and flaunting his own casualness in romantic conquests. It's Twenty Questions, except with a victim.

"I'm just curious," he answers. "I'm going to figure it out."

"There's nothing *to* figure out."

"Of course there's not."

"Whatever," I reply, fuming.

"Whatever?" Lewis repeats. "Are you feeling all right? Don't you mean *antediluvian vagaracity* or something?"

Here goes the dictionary shit. I didn't even have to pull out the book. "*Vagaracity* isn't a word," I reply flatly.

Lewis ignores the retort, something he's infuriatingly good at, and nods confidently to himself. "There's definitely a girl."

FITZ

~

I GET TO the Brown information session at ten minutes to ten and out of breath. There's a punishing hill between the bed-and-breakfast where Lewis and I checked in this morning and the campus. By the second block of close-to-vertical sidewalks, my legs were burning and I felt sweat stains forming under my parka. They're practically neon lettering over my head proclaiming, *Hey, everyone, Fitz is out of shape.* It's a cool look for possibly running into Juniper and Matt.

The Stephen Robert '62 Campus Center is full of prospective students and hovering parents. Hours-old snow dusts the sculpture in the courtyard and the patio furniture. I walk into the foyer, pretending I'm not checking the hallway for a certain ponytail. In the presentation room, I choose a seat near the back with a view of the rest of the rows.

I watch the door. I don't even reach for the dictionary tucked into my parka pocket. *Sempiternal* and *verisimilitude* will have to wait. Bouncing my knee nervously, I try vainly to remember it's unlikely Juniper and I have booked the same session.

People file in the double doors behind me. I watch kids in

Brown sweatshirts and bright-eyed parents enter the room, quickly picking out seats and, probably, checking out the competition. I couldn't care less who the competition is.

The doors close. Despite telling myself I likely wouldn't see Juniper, I can't help it. I'm disappointed. I guess I was stupid to guess she'd be in today's ten a.m. session just because we'd both been in the ten a.m. BU presentation. It's typical me, hoping nothing ever changes.

The presentation begins. I pull out the dictionary.

While the presenter regales us with the usual routine of facts and figures, photographs and platitudes, I focus on the words. *Quixotic*. Definition: impractically idealistic, foolishly unrealistic, e.g., a quixotic undertaking.

I thumb the pages until finally the presentation ends. We're divided into tour groups, and I halfheartedly follow my guide, who looks impossibly thrilled to be escorting twenty parents and kids like me through his campus in the snow. While David, the sophomore who's concentrating in public health, escorts us into the Ruth J. Simmons Quadrangle, I check out. I catch myself repeatedly watching crowds of visitors and groups of students, looking for familiar brown eyes and wavy hair.

Knock it off, I order myself.

We finish our route, ending up in front of the campus center. David the Sophomore Concentrating in Public Health enthusiastically wishes us good luck with our applications. I decide to keep wandering the campus. The freezing weather reddening my nose and watering my eyes, I stuff my hands into my pockets and walk into the College Green.

This campus is different from BU, contained and classically old. The uniform brick of the buildings, the white columns framing wooden doors, wrought-iron fences around quiet quads. Wandering to the corner, I reach the Italianate tower that caught my curiosity on the tour. The tower's bricks climb higher than every other building nearby. Four clocks the color of old copper face the campus in every direction. THE CARRIE TOWER reads the inscription carved over the door. I circle the structure and find more details carved into the back.

It's a memorial. It commemorates Carrie Mathilde Brown, from her husband.

It feels futile. Sure, everyone who walks this campus will see her monument, and everyone who reads the inscription will know the name Carrie Mathilde Brown. What the tower can't tell them is the color of her hair, the sound of her laugh, what kind of friend she was, what she enjoyed. If we could reduce everybody's essence into enduring physical objects, we would. But we're only pretending the memorials we erect could possibly embody those we've lost. Memory and memorial may share a linguistic root, but they're estranged brothers, not twins.

I think of pulling well-worn novels from bookshelves. I think of folding Thanksgiving tablecloths and eating plates of eggplant parmesan. I think of stacking pages of student dissertations on Hawthorne and Melville and Twain.

Even if you wrote every memory imaginable on to a memorial a million feet high, you would fail to capture infinite others.

I walk from the Carrie Tower onto Prospect Street and gradually explore the rest of the campus. The brick buildings blend together, especially under the ubiquitous blanket of frost. They're undeniably impressive, colonial and imposing in a way I know characterizes the college dreams of countless of my classmates. I barely taste the sandwich I get for lunch in the student center, my eyes drifting to every unfamiliar face that enters.

Heading onto one of the campus's identically tree-lined roads, I wrestle down a growing dejection. I've circumnavigated dorms and paused in front of libraries, passed gleaming genetics buildings and entered empty foyers. No sign of Juniper. I'm left to confront why I'm, okay, obsessed with this girl. I could distract myself from this college tour if I were wondering when or whether I'd run into her. With the chance we'll reconnect pretty much gone, it's only me and the emptiness of this idea of my mom's. I don't want to concentrate in public health. I don't want to read in the Ruth J. Simmons Quadrangle. I don't want to remember Carrie Brown or her husband.

I head downhill for the bed-and-breakfast.

When I reach the room, I find Lewis napping. With the feeling only starting to return to my fingers, I decide I need a shower to warm up. Standing under the scalding water, I systematically remind myself of every reason it's good I didn't find Juniper. Now is definitely not the time to be interested in a girl who could live in Georgia or Ohio or wherever and who has elaborate plans involving possible PhDs in California or London. Oh, and who has a boyfriend.

I step out of the shower and pull on clothes. When I open the door, Lewis is putting on his shoes.

"You have dinner plans?" I ask. It's nearly seven, and it occurs to me I'm going to have to find dinner for myself. I remember walking past a pretty promising burger place near campus.

"*We* have dinner plans." Lewis jumps up. Glancing into the mirror over the desk, he runs his fingers through his hair. "I have a friend here who mentioned a party at one of the coed frats. We'll find a restaurant in town, then head to campus."

"Yeah, no," I reply. I don't even enjoy high school parties. The idea of going to a college one with Lewis doesn't improve the prospect.

My brother ignores me. "It's time to quit moping," he continues. "You have to get out and experience a real taste of college."

"I'm not moping," I say, frustration flaring in me. It's only partly true, but I'm not taking orders from Lewis.

Lewis's expression changes, solemn and searching. "Look, I know you're having a hard time with the Mom thing—"

"The *Mom thing*?" I interrupt.

"It's shitty," Lewis continues, undeterred. "But you have to start living your life. Mom and I are both worried about you."

The casual way he invokes Mom pisses me off. He doesn't know the first thing about what worries her. Knowing would involve visiting or phone calls or even a damn email every now and again. There's no way he's worried about me, either. If he were, he could've visited or called or written me.

But those thoughts are weapons for a battle I'll never fight. "Living my own life wouldn't include going to parties," I say instead.

"How do you know until you try?" Lewis counters. "You might meet a girl there who'll make you forget whoever you were hoping to see in Providence."

I don't bother wondering how he knows I didn't run into Juniper. He's probably guessing. "Forget it," I say. "I'm not going. You don't need me there to get wasted."

"This isn't about me getting wasted," he replies. "Well, it's mostly not about me getting wasted. Just *try* something, Fitz. For once, try something."

I drop down onto the bed. "No," I say resolutely.

Lewis sighs and walks to the door. With his hand on the handle, he pauses. "How about this?" he asks, turning back to me. "Come to this party and I promise, if you want, I'll drive you home tomorrow."

I blink, my thoughts snagging on a dozen discarded rebuttals. "What?" I get out. "What about Mom?"

"I'll explain it to Mom. Let's face it, we both know touring a bunch of schools you've decided not to like won't change your mind about SNHU."

I'm almost afraid to say it. Afraid this is a trap and Lewis is going to ridicule me or leave me behind without another word. "If I just go to this party," I say slowly, "then you promise you'll take me home tomorrow? No tricks?"

Lewis grins. "Get your coat."

JUNIPER

~

I, JUNIPER RAMÍREZ, have officially slept in a college dorm.

There were things I knew I would love on this trip. The grandiose Gothic campuses, the new cities, even the presentations with their wonderfully real projections of the future. The distance from my family. What I didn't know I'd love was every inch of room A314 in Keeney. The Brown flag hanging in the corner, the crooked posters of *The Last Jedi* and Radiohead, the three beanbag chairs, the windows with chipped white paint on the frames.

It's everything I never knew to expect. It's perfect.

We're staying with Carter Wright, Matt's former teammate from the baseball team, who's a freshman. Carter's roommate, Theo, inflated their air mattress, and we slept on the floor in between their twin beds. I didn't care that we were in close quarters. Growing up with five siblings and sharing a room with Marisa my whole life prepared me *very* well for college.

Instead of the usual tour and information session, Carter

gave us his own tour of the campus. We roamed for three hours, which left me plenty of time for every question I'd prepared on the drive down. He took us into places I'm pretty certain they don't include on the official tour. His favorite dining hall for breakfast, the local coffee shop with the shortest lines, the lounge for when you're pretending you want to study and really just want to hang out with friends. I held Matt's hand, and the hours shed from the day effortlessly. It felt possible. It felt real.

Now we're eating dinner out of Chinese takeout cartons as we sit on the beanbag chairs. The door is propped open, and people pass by on their way to the bathroom or to libraries or to parties, popping their heads in every now and then to talk to Carter or Theo. Theo's computer is open on his desk, playing intolerable music from the college radio station. Thankfully, Theo keeps the volume nearly inaudible until the voice of the female host replaces the music. He turns the volume way up to hear Tina Wu's commentary interlude. It's kind of cute.

When I look to Matt, I find him thumbing through the textbook next to his beanbag. I read the cover. *Introduction to Cosmology.*

I nudge him. "What's that?"

"What?" For once, Matt seems like he's elsewhere. His eyes find mine, refocusing. "Oh, this astronomy book is just cool."

"Tell me," I urge him.

"It's about the expansion of the universe." He glances back to the book, and I have to say, his evident interest is kind of a turn-on. "It's just not stuff we've learned in school," he continues. "But the ideas are really, you know, big. Important. It's unbelievable what's out there."

I lean into him. "Yeah."

"I don't know. It could be a cool class." He closes the textbook.

"Definitely," I say. "Could be a cool major, too."

He looks timidly hopeful. I'm thrown forward, a year into the future. We're here—or not here. The place isn't important, because we're together. I'm in an architecture program, and he's in astronomy. I reach my creations toward the stars, while he reaches up and pulls the stars to us.

"What's the senior trip this year?" Carter's question interrupts my reverie.

"Lake Placid!" Matt replies enthusiastically. "White-water rafting, bonfire, the whole thing."

Carter nods. "Okay, dude. Words of wisdom from an experienced college freshman. Don't waste a moment of that trip. Now, college is the bomb," he pronounces, holding up a hand like a Greek orator. "I'm just telling you, once high school is gone, it's gone."

He's not wrong. I haven't contemplated other moments closer in the future—the last time I'll have lunch with Matt and our friends in the courtyard under the warm sun, the feeling of submitting my final papers and finishing final exams, the hug I know I'm going to give Ms. Delores for two years of English classes. They'll be bittersweet moments, tearful congratulations, and half-happy goodbyes.

Matt takes my hand. I have a feeling he's remembering those futures too.

I rest my head on his shoulder. Everything we'll leave behind when we finish high school will hurt in a way I hadn't predicted. But the edge of the pain blunts when I remember everything exhilarating to come. I'm not just leaving things behind. I'm leaving them for lunches in the quad, history lectures in wood-paneled halls, and the look on Matt's face when he comes back from the first class he loves. Maybe it'll be astronomy.

FITZ

ON THE WAY to my first and likely only college party, I observe the contrasts of campus nightlife like I'm watching one of the National Geographic specials I was really into when I got my wisdom teeth out and had hours of daytime to devote to television.

Girls in puffy coats over their short dresses wobble on high heels, and I honestly have no idea how they're handling the ice. It's got to be some secret college-girl skill, because not one of them even stumbles. In the opposite direction walk students probably on their way to the library, wearing sweatpants and huddling books to their chests. Loud music vibrates from dorms near darkened lecture halls.

Lewis leads us to the front patio of one of the dorms where the party has poured outside. People hang out on the porch swing, drinking from nondescript cups, while four guys play cornhole on the lawn. Lewis heads for the open door with what I'm guessing is practiced casual confidence. He probably goes to parties like this every weekend.

Inside, we head directly downstairs. The stairwell is painted with big Greek letters, and the floor is sticky. Bright, discordant murals cover the walls in the basement, which branches into hallways heading in every direction and packed with people. I pass what I assume is the fraternity's crest and pause in front of a figure I recognize from a picture book. *Caps for Sale*. The character, a well-dressed salesman, holds his wares on his head, off of which they're stolen by rowdy monkeys. I don't remember the ending.

In front of one wall decorated with Jigglypuff from Pokémon, Lewis heads left. I follow him into what I gather is the fraternity's taproom. It's chaotically decorated, with white Christmas lights strung haphazardly from the ceiling and trash or people's drinks covering every inch of the wooden countertop. I don't know how people tell which is which.

The room is hopelessly crowded. Girls dance in the center to excruciatingly loud music. The guys hang out in the wooden booths built into the walls, drinks in hand, watching everything and nothing. Lewis heads for the counter of endless cups while I remain near the door.

I feel profoundly out of place.

Lewis returns holding his drink. We head back into the hallway, which is good because with the music and the lights and the jostling bodies and the pungent smell of beer, I'd started to feel a bit dizzy. I breathe deeply in the hall, reminding myself I just have to do this for one night. Then I get to go home, get to put this trip behind me and focus on what's important.

"I'm going to play a round." Lewis nudges me, nodding in the direction of the Ping-Pong table we passed on the way in. It occupies a ridiculous amount of the hallway, and teams of two play beer pong. There's yelling and drinking every time one of the Ping-Pong balls drops into a plastic cup.

I nod wordlessly.

"I could teach you if you want," Lewis offers.

"I'm good," I reply. "I think I'll walk around." I turn in the opposite direction with utterly no idea where I'm going.

"Call me if you go anywhere, okay?" Lewis half asks, half orders.

I nod once and plunge into the crowd, regretting the decision instantly. I'm doubly aimless and overwhelmed without Lewis. I push out of the hall into the front stairwell and head up, passing the door where we entered. Nearby in a narrow foyer, a chandelier draped with toilet paper hangs from the ceiling. I wander in and follow the room to the doorway on the other end, which opens into a larger common area. This room's equally crowded, if fortunately less claustrophobic. Windows line the walls, and the entire room is effectively a dark dance floor.

It feels intensely anonymous. Not in a comfortable way either. In an unpredictable, vaguely frightening way. I acknowledge pulling out my dictionary would render me the weirdest person in the vicinity of this entire college campus, so I focus on putting words to the experience instead.

Discomfiture (n.): the unease, close to embarrassment, I feel walking amid partygoers enjoying the kind of party I'd never go to on my own, on a college campus I'll never call my own.

I force myself farther into the crowd. Suddenly really thirsty, I decide to find the bar—only for a cup of water. I've never had the curiosity for underage drinking I know almost every one of my classmates does. I have a hard enough time holding on to control of my circumstances without the liquid catalyst for risks and abandon. When I've nearly reached the counter, someone barrels into me and I feel something wet slosh onto my sleeve.

Bacchanalian (adj.): characterized by drunkenness and excessive revelry, even on Sunday nights, probably with fall semester finals coming up.

Ataraxia (n.): the peaceful calm I'll feel when I get the hell out of here.

The bar consists only of open bottles from which people mix their own drinks. The girl next to me pours together Sprite and whatever's in the clear plastic bottle she's holding while I reach for the soda water. I dump what's left into one of the plastic cups. It's flat but not terrible.

Turning back to the crowd, I wonder what exactly Lewis imagined I'd do here. Dance with a random girl in this poorly converted common room? Play drinking games with bros I've never met before in my life? Experience a *real taste of college*? The truth is, I don't understand how people do this. What combination of effortless ease and bravado, confidence and poise permits them to walk up to people in dark rooms, play anonymous games, and try things they've never tried before.

I'm not that person.

Theoretically, I could be. Nobody on this campus knows me—it's possible I *could* be whoever I want. Everyone certainly says college provides the opportunity to "reinvent yourself." But I don't know if a dimly lit fraternity and a different zip code can summon from me something that's not already there.

I don't have to find out, not tonight. I promised Lewis I'd come to this party, but that's all. I only have to be *here*, not present.

Pertinacious (adj.): persevering in one's course of action to return home to New Hampshire in the morning, even when what's required is hanging out within the confines of a college party.

I head for the stairs. If I'm going to remain in this building the rest of the night, it's essential I find some peace and quiet. Everyone's streaming down into the basement, but I go up. While I doubt I'll find the upper floors entirely peaceful, they have to be better than down here.

The stairs open onto an empty hallway. Tight doorways run the length with little whiteboards hung on each one of them. I walk idly and read what's written on them. *Janine needs to study. If you hear music (or sex) behind this door, KNOCK AND YELL AT HER.* I find crudely drawn hand turkeys and end-of-year countdowns. On one I read an extensive conversation of song requests for the person who presumably plays guitar in the room.

I figure I'll read my dictionary until Lewis texts me he's ready to leave. Finding nowhere to sit, I settle for the floor near the windows on one end of the hallway, opposite the door to the outside fire escape. While uncomfortable, the patch of hardwood is out of the way and wide enough for me to stretch my legs.

Leaning on the wall to lower myself to the floor, I glance out the window. In the frigid night, packs of partygoers stumble down the front steps. Laughter and shouts echo up from the quad over the vibrating rhythm of the music. My eyes sweep the view of old houses and fresh-faced students until I'm caught up short.

Under a streetlight, I see her.

Juniper hugs her arms over her chest, her hair unleashed from the ponytail I've come to expect and falling onto her shoulders. Her breath makes clouds in the cold. Matt's no-where in sight.

I hit the stairs without hesitating.

JUNIPER

I DON'T DISLIKE parties on principle. I enjoy them, even. I love hanging out with friends, the way the normal routines and rhythms of the day ebb away into the endless expanse of night. It's like entering this universal in-between, a place where pressures relieve and rules change and nobody needs to be exactly who they are.

It's just this party I'm not down with.

I wasn't opposed when Matt suggested we come here with Carter. I was even looking forward to checking out my first college party. But when we got downstairs, it took two drinks and one round of beer pong for me to realize this was no different from every high school party I'd ever been to. Except for the obvious differences—the more extensive alcoholic offerings, the absence of anything resembling a curfew, the venue not being someone's parents' house—this party is identical to the ones I'll go to next week and the next week and the next. I don't know what else I expected. I just didn't think this would be *exactly* what I expected.

Which is why I went outside. Out here, I can watch the campus in the nighttime. It's better than nothing. Facing the cold, I zip up my coat and rub my hands together in front of my face, hoping to generate heat.

I met my abuela on a cold night like this. I remember distinctly our car rolling for the first time into the driveway of the house I now call home. Heavy snowbanks sat on the slanted roofs and the windowsills. The lights were on in every room. When I hopped out onto the driveway, my shoes crunching the snow, the wind stung my cheeks and nose the way it's doing now. I followed my parents up the path to the porch.

The front door opened, revealing a woman framed in the doorway. She greeted my father with a crushing hug and my mother with a hesitant kiss on the cheek, which I know now was because she'd never met her son's wife before. Her eyes caught on three-year-old Callie, held on my mother's hip, and she leaned in to whisper inaudibly to my sister. When she drew back, her eyes had filled with tears. She looked down, and finding me and Marisa clinging behind me, she smiled.

"You don't know me," she said, her voice weathered and warm, "but I'm your abuela."

I blinked. I didn't know the word. Since I didn't meet my dad's family until I was seven, even now I have only a fragmented fluency in Spanish. When we moved to Springfield, I didn't know a word. I knew nothing of my dad's family's culture. Not their food, their traditions, their histories. To this day, I consider those things part of my life but not of me. They're *ours* but not exactly *mine*.

"Your grandmother," my abuela clarified.

I didn't know what to say. Marisa, who hadn't yet exited

her shy phase, stood stock-still in my shadow.

"This is my sister," Abuela continued when a taller, sterner woman entered the doorway. "Your tía Sofi." I had no idea how familiar I'd become with the expression on Tía's face then—reserved and wary, with a kind of proud and loving protectiveness. "We're very sorry we're only meeting you now. We have a lot of missed time to make up for." Her expression turned a touch conspiratorial. "Do you know I make a really special meal for everyone in my family every year on their birthday?"

She looked from me to Marisa, who hid even closer behind my back. "But my birthday is in October," I said.

"Yes," Abuela replied, "and I have seven years to catch up on."

I'll never forget what I felt then, the tentative unfolding of curiosity and surprise and excitement of my own, and the edges of this new indescribable thing I could only begin to understand then. In the span of only minutes, I realized I had a new person in my life who would change everything. It felt like discovering a continent.

"You made me a birthday cake?" I ventured.

"Better." Abuela's eyes gleamed. "Have you ever had a tamale?"

I shook my head. Abuela led me inside, and the smell enveloped me.

My phone vibrates, distracting me from the recollection. I pull the phone out and find a text from my mom. She wants me to check in, and I reply quickly, describing the dorm and my day. I look up, watching the quad from under the streetlight where I'm waiting. Waiting for . . . I don't know what. I feel restless.

I didn't come to Brown to be bored in a fraternity basement, and I didn't come outside to relive old memories. I'm in a new city, on a new campus. I have only this week before I have to return home to everything I know in thorough, inescapable detail. I want to explore. I want to walk through Waterplace Park, over the Venetian-inspired bridges on the river. I want to visit downtown, admire the architecture, people-watch. Instead, I'm spending another night playing beer pong with Matt and Carter like I've done countless nights before.

I've had enough of lingering under this streetlight in the freezing night. I'm going inside to find Matt and ask him if we can venture into the city instead of partying for the rest of the night.

I walk with purpose into the frat, fighting through the throng to reach the stairs to the basement when I'm caught short.

I recognize the head of red hair on the other end of the crowd. I remember cannoli and conversation and the possibility we'd cross paths again.

Fitz.

For F. Scott Fitzgerald. He's pressed to the wall, openly uncomfortable, not holding a drink. He looks incoherent with the revelry surrounding him, in the midst of the party but not part of it, despite the short blonde talking to him. She's wearing a pink tank top with white Greek letters on the front, and I nearly laugh at how she clashes with Fitz's crisp button-down and discomfited demeanor. The blue book I remember from the BU information session protrudes from his front pocket. Of course he brought a book to this party. He read during the presentation. Why wouldn't he read here?

The girl keeps touching him, grabbing his wrist and poking his arm. It's obvious she's flirting with him. Obvious to everyone except Fitz, that is, who appears confused and lightly agitated, his eyes flitting from the girl to the room. I wouldn't have expected him to be the kind of guy who'd attract college-girl attention as a high-schooler. Now that I think about it, though, Fitz *is* kind of cute. His wiry build, his keen, refined features. He has a subtle, soft intensity I understand one could potentially find attractive.

I shake my head, smiling, and head downstairs. Matt's where I left him, playing beer pong with Carter and a couple of other guys in the hallway. When I sidle up next to him, Matt places the ball on the table and hooks an arm around my waist. "Hey, babe," he says. He smells like beer and sweat.

I tug gently on his shirt, pulling him from the table. "Can we talk?"

He nods. "Give me a minute," he calls behind him. I catch annoyance in the expression of the tall, unequivocally handsome Indian guy on the opposing team.

"Do you want to head out?" I ask once Matt's followed me into the stairwell. "I was wondering about visiting Waterplace Park. It looks kind of cool, and I heard it's great to walk around in at night."

Matt checks his watch. "We just got here, Juniper," he says delicately.

"I know," I reply, repressing impatience. "It's just, we're leaving in the morning. I want to explore the city a little more. Don't you?"

Matt looks back to Carter, who's laughing with the other guys. Matt's expression is pained, and the realization settles onto me.

"You're having a good time," I say softly, understanding what I hadn't when I pulled him from his friends. Matt's usually really generous and receptive to what I want to do. He's a good boyfriend that way, and I know he's conflicted. He wants to tour the city with me, but if he's hesitating, it's because he really wants to hang out with his friends too.

"Yeah, I am," he admits. "Could we stay one more hour and then go?"

He's compromising, and I want to feel happy and appreciative, knowing he'd rather hang out here the rest of the night. Instead, I feel the painful pull on my heart of having to compromise in the first place.

I nod. "Sure," I say, chasing disappointment from my voice.

"I could introduce you to the guys. We could play a round together if you want?" Matt offers, obviously excited. "I know you're good. I could use you, Ramírez."

I don't want to deflate his enthusiasm. I don't want to be the girl who puts her foot down, who crushes her boyfriend's plans. I just really don't want to play beer pong, either.

"Maybe later." I try to sound cheerful. "I'm going to walk around a little."

I know Matt can tell I'm withdrawn. He watches me

warily until Carter calls his name behind us. "Traverson, you coming back?" When Matt doesn't reply, I push him lightly toward the table.

"Have fun," I say. "I'll be fine, I promise."

He pauses, reluctance written on his perfect features. I muster a convincing smile, and finally he nods and rejoins the group. From the stairwell, I watch his face light up as he claps Carter on the back and picks up the game.

I'm happy for him. He's toured schools for me, endured presentations he has little to no interest in just because I want to. I'm happy he's enjoying himself tonight, reconnecting with his old friend, recapturing the fun they had in high school.

That's exactly the problem, though. *This* is what's important to Matt. This is what thrills him. Hanging out with Carter Wright the way they did in his basement and their baseball clubhouse, and at parties back home. Matt's found what he wants.

Whereas I'm still searching. Still figuring out which place will thrill me.

I head upstairs, feeling forlorn. Usually I enjoy the rumbling momentum of impending changes. Not tonight. I walk up another flight of stairs to the next level, not because there's anything worth seeing upstairs—just for the peace and quiet.

FITZ

~

I THROW OPEN the front door, and Juniper's nowhere to be found. The path under the streetlight is empty.

It took me ten minutes to get outside. When I made it downstairs, I tried to maneuver through the group of girls holding drinks clustered in the foyer. Unfortunately, one rounded on me and I ended up politely trying to extricate myself from the utterly unilateral conversation. Over the thudding of the music and with the thought of Juniper distracting me, I only caught the girl mentioning some semiformal coming up this week. *Finally*, one of her friends beckoned her into the room with the countertop bar.

I flew to the door. Now I'm searching the quad in the cold. No Juniper.

Not giving up, I decide to check the rest of the house. From the foyer, I take the stairs two by two to the basement. I don't find Juniper, only the wall-to-wall crowds I left when I went upstairs. But I do notice Matt playing beer pong with— Lewis. *Wonderful.* I check the taproom, where Lewis first took me when we got here, then return upstairs. She's not on the dance floor, not by the bar, not near the table with the computer and speakers passing for a DJ booth. She's nowhere.

I move toward the stairs, figuring there's a chance I'll spot her from the second-story window the way I did before. Maybe I'll catch sight of her heading in the direction of one of the other buildings. Careful not to cross paths with loquacious sorority girls this time, I walk to the upper level and pass the whiteboards and closed doors, heading toward my window.

Where I find her.

She's sitting in the exact spot under the window I had marked for my own solitary reading plans. Her head is tipped back against the wall, eyes closed.

"There you are," I say unthinkingly, not meaning to say anything at all.

Her eyes fly open and fix on me. Immediately, I read the sadness in them. The emotion doesn't render her features any softer, only shadowing the usual sharpness of her expression. She blinks, and the despondency vanishes.

"There I am?" she asks. Her tone is edged with accusation, and if I'm lucky, perhaps a little amusement. "Were you looking for me, Fitzgerald?" She gets to her feet, leveling me an imperious eyebrow.

Hardly anyone calls me Fitzgerald, but I don't bother correcting her. My name somehow doesn't sound awkward on her lips. "Um, no," I stammer. She's wearing a light pink sweater tonight, the color of a blush. "How could I be looking for you? I had no idea you were at this party. I wasn't even sure you were at Brown."

It's the wrong thing to say. Her eyebrows flatten over narrowed eyes. "You *followed* me here?"

"Juniper, how could I have guessed you'd be at the random party my brother dragged me to? I only saw you from the window earlier." I'm eager to dispel her suspicion, to ask her why she was sitting up here alone, whether she likes Brown—anything. Everything.

She shakes her head. "No. Not this party. Brown. Yesterday you heard Matt mention we were going to Providence. Did you follow me here?" Her voice is wary, almost nervous.

I understand why. There's a word for following a girl you hardly know across state lines. *Creepy.* She's right to be nervous. I take a step back, wanting to give her space. I will my body language to communicate, *Hey, you could leave at any time, and I will in no way be weird about it.*

"It's purely a coincidence we ended up at the same school again," I assure her evenly. "Just serendipity."

She blinks, her unease fading beneath surprise and something else. Understanding? I'm not sure. It doesn't last long. She juts her chin at me, dissatisfied. "If it's just a coincidence, why didn't you say anything yesterday when Matt mentioned we'd be coming here?"

"I don't even remember Matt saying that," I lie. It's unfortunate, but better than admitting I was too nervous in front of her boyfriend to tell her I'd be in Providence too.

"He did," she says stonily. Her eyes flit to the side. "You and I were talking about college. Then Matt came up and mentioned dates at Mike's, and I said, 'When we're not busy.'" She nods, having found what she was trying to recall. "And then Matt said, 'I checked out of the hotel. Do you want to get dinner before we head to Providence?'" She returns her gaze to me triumphantly. "You definitely knew where we were headed."

"Whoa," I say, blinking. Distantly, I'm aware she's just caught me in a lie, but I'm too impressed by her perfect recall to care.

Her cheeks turn bright pink, and I become suddenly very aware of the smooth skin of her neck. The freckles brushing her jaw. Like she's annoyed by her blush, she doesn't drop her eyes and instead pins me under her scrutiny. "Okay, so I have a pretty good memory," she says. Her voice is determined, but I notice a hint of bashfulness in her tone.

"That sounds like an understatement." I want to ask her more, but not if it's something she's embarrassed about.

"Did you follow me to Providence?" She crosses her arms, obviously refusing to be distracted. I don't think I've ever spoken to someone so wholly single-minded.

"I didn't follow you. I swear my itinerary had me at Brown today too," I say quickly. "I didn't mention it yesterday because, well, frankly—could your boyfriend be any more in-timidating?" Her lips thin into an unamused line. "Besides, I wasn't even sure you'd be at Brown. I just hoped you would be," I continue, not wanting her to cut me off or walk away. "I'll admit, though, just the chance I might get to see you again did increase my interest in the tour."

She frowns and leans against the wall. Clearly, she's skeptical, but she's not leaving, so I'll consider it a victory. I lean on the other side of the hallway, matching her posture. "That's ridiculous," she says. "You don't even know me. You should be excited about your tour because it's your future, not because you might run into some random girl."

"Like I said, there are—"

"—'things more important than college,'" she says, cutting me off. "Ugh, no." I stifle a smile at how easily she reproduced my comment from yesterday. "I am definitely *not* more important than college," she declares.

I shrug. "Maybe not. But you might be." Even I'm aware of how much that sounded like a line when I didn't intend for it to. First inviting her to have our cannoli together, now this? It's not like Ben and Cooper and I spend our spare time practicing pickup lines. I would call myself friendly, not suave. Yet here I am, undeniably in the possession of game.

I expect her to roll her eyes or grimace, but she doesn't.

"Okay, first," she begins, "we just met, and unless you plan to stalk me down the coast, we won't see each other again. Second, you should really prioritize college over girls. Third, we don't even get along." She hardly pauses for breath, each thought proceeding quickly and clearly one after the other. "And fourth, I have a boyfriend."

"None of those points are real impediments," I say, grinning. "Except the boyfriend one. Which it's interesting that you listed last." I don't know what's gotten into me. I don't know who this Fitzgerald Holton is. I kind of wish I did, though.

Juniper ignores the boyfriend comment, which is probably for the best. "Do you really not think college is important?" She's honestly inquisitive, no longer pressing her case.

"It's not that I don't think it's important," I explain. "I just think it's not *as* important as everyone says. Everything we hear this year is, *Focus on college. This is the whole point of high school. This is the rest of your life.* I just . . . think people need to remember other things are important too."

Juniper is grimacing now. I guess I'm not surprised. "Since you don't know me," she says briskly, "let me tell you, college is the dream I've devoted my entire life to for four years. It's really important to me. I don't understand anyone who has the opportunity to go but feels it's not worth their time."

Her judgment sparks something in me. "It's not that," I say harshly, and then the words pour out, fast and free and uncontrollable. "Okay, honestly? When I say people focus too much on college, what I'm really saying is *I don't get* to focus on college. I have to be home in New Hampshire for my mom. She's—she's going to get early-onset Alzheimer's." The admission trips awkwardly over my tongue. I'm not in the habit of telling other people my mom's prognosis. "If I go to Southern New Hampshire University, I could live at home when she needs help. For me? Yeah—that's more important than college."

The instant I finish speaking, it hits me how forcefully the feelings flew out. Which I didn't intend. The emotions just built up, and once I'd begun letting them out, I couldn't stop.

I expect Juniper's face to fall, for her eyes to fill with worry and regret. It's why I don't tell people—the inevitable and inevitably fleeting remorse.

Instead, her features harden. "Come on." She rolls her eyes in exaggerated annoyance. "You're the worst, you know that? Now I can't even be mad at you."

I laugh, the sound echoing in the narrow hallway. Her reaction is surprising and utterly liberating. It emboldens me. "I'm certain I can find other ways to make you mad at me."

"I don't doubt it," she replies, her mouth twisting ever so slightly in what I hope is a smirk. I reach for a witty reply. But whoever this new game-having Fitzgerald Holton is, he's left me hanging. Juniper's studying me, her inquisitiveness ever-present. "How long has your mom known?"

I shove myself off the wall. I don't fault Juniper for her curiosity, not when I'm the one who brought this up. She's being kind, expressing real sympathy instead of burying the topic under pleasantries. But even though the only thing I've wanted to do for days with Lewis is talk about what's happening to Mom, and even though this girl is inviting me to do exactly that, I don't want to. Not right now. Not with Juniper's eyes on me, with the music pulsing under our feet, with the night waiting outside.

For the first time, I'm not worried about what I'm missing at home. I'm only worried about what I might miss tonight.

"Like you said, we might never see each other again. I don't want to waste the night dwelling on a disease that can't be stopped. You're here to see Brown, right?"

She nods.

I cross the hall to the fire escape. Opening the door, I'm suddenly grateful this frat's in such an old building the door isn't alarmed. I turn back to Juniper.

"Then let's see Brown."

JUNIPER

WHILE THE COLD blasts through the open door, I don't move. I don't know if it's really a good idea to follow this boy I hardly know. He seems nice enough, but I'm not dumb. I know what can happen to girls who go off with a guy while college parties unfold downstairs.

But . . . I have my phone. Matt's downstairs with Carter and would come immediately if I called. Which, of course, I'd do if I were uncomfortable in the least.

"I promise this isn't a move," Fitz says, guessing my thoughts. He smiles, and it's not the predatory grin I would recognize on a frat boy. It's authentic, disarming. "I'm not the type of guy who makes moves like this on girls. Definitely not on a girl like you, even if I didn't know you have a boy-friend."

"A girl like me?" I repeat, not sure if I should be offended.

"You're out of my league." He falters a little on the words.

Now I'm even less convinced he's not flirting. I take a step back.

Fitz stands in the doorway. "You don't have to come," he says, his voice softening. "It's just, this party is nothing special, and I'm on this trip against my will, but . . . it could be worthwhile for the memories. I already know what the future holds. It's right now that has the potential to be extraordinary."

His words ring through me. I can practically feel the rush of resonance in my cheeks, my fingertips. I don't generally live for the now. I live for what I can plan for and dream of. But right now is offering me something I didn't know to plan. Something that might be worth experiencing.

I grab my jacket and follow him.

He holds out his hand to help me up. I eye him dubiously, hoping to communicate he's not helping himself with this chivalry crap, and he flushes under his freckles like paint dipped into clear water. His frost-blue eyes dart from mine. But I take his hand. His fingers wrap tightly over mine, and I feel a tingle of warmth despite the temperature.

We walk out onto the fire escape, which looks precarious. But it *is* a fire escape, intended to support people. It can't be that unsafe. I drop his hand once I'm on the metal platform and zip up my parka while the cold wind whips my hair. The noises of the party drift up, shouts and cheers punctuating the echoes of the music. We're both part of the scene and thrillingly isolated, the feeling of being backstage in the middle of a play.

Fitz waits by the stairwell. When I glance over, his eyes hold a question, like he can't believe I'm really doing this. Or maybe he can't believe *he's* really doing this. Suppressing a smile, I concede to myself his trepidation is kind of cute. If I had to guess, I'd say he never would have imagined himself leading a girl to the rooftop of a frat house.

To be fair, I never would have imagined following him.

There's a blanket draped over the railing, dry because the rooftop shielded it from the snow. Fitz throws the blanket over his shoulder and begins climbing the stairs. I test the first step with my shoe and find it feels sturdy. Besides, Fitz hasn't fallen to his death, which is comforting. I climb the single story up, my boots hitting the stairs with metallic reverberations.

When I reach the roof, Fitz isn't waiting. He's walked to the other end of the rooftop, looking out over the edge. I join him, tiptoeing carefully because of the patches of snow.

Coming up next to him, I gaze out over the view, breathless.

The campus spreads out below us, glittering lights in every direction. The warm glow of lamps and windows dot the trees, illuminating the university's fascinating combination of neoclassical and Venetian Gothic. Pathways crisscross the campus. The few students walking them look small from up here. In the distance, the buildings of downtown Providence rise on the skyline.

Fitz lays out the blanket, and it's easy to imagine students in the dorm doing this often on warmer nights. He sits, his knees touching the lip of the rooftop. I join him.

We take in the view in silence. Thoughts of tomorrow and the next day and yesterday and the future press in on my thoughts. But instead of focusing on them, I press back.

Right now does have the potential to be extraordinary. To be breathtaking. This moment, this view, is everything and exactly what I wanted from today.

I turn to Fitz. He's watching the campus, his expression indecipherable.

"By the way, you're wrong," I say, nudging his elbow with mine, coat sleeves swishing. His eyes flit to me. "This is *definitely* a move," I continue.

He tips his head back and laughs, his breath visible in front of the stars.

"Not that it'll work," I remind him. "Nor do I buy that you're not the kind of guy who'd try this on a girl like me. I saw you flirting with that sorority girl downstairs."

Fitz's eyebrows scrunch in what I'm pretty certain is genuine confusion. "What sorority girl?" he asks. "I wasn't flirting with her."

"Well, she was definitely flirting with you," I reply.

"She was not," he protests. "She was just going on about her sorority's semiformal next week."

I roll my eyes. I cannot believe he's this boneheaded. "She thinks you go here. She was hinting that she wanted you to take her to the semiformal," I explain with the patience and clarity I used when Anabel unwrapped my tampons and floated them in the toilet.

"You couldn't possibly know that," he scoffs, leaning back to rest on his elbows. I notice the blue corner of his ever-present book poking out from his front pocket.

"I *could* possibly know that. It's a basic girl tactic, Fitzgerald."

He falls silent. Gazing over the edge of the rooftop, he looks like he's contemplating this unforeseen possibility. "Huh," he finally says. I wonder if he's considering returning downstairs, finding his smitten sorority girl, and escorting her up here to pull his "move" for real, on her instead of me.

Which I wouldn't mind, obviously.

"So you were watching me downstairs," he says suddenly, his voice a little pleased.

I open my mouth, but nothing comes out. I settle for shaking my head and rolling my eyes once again.

I lie down on the blanket, looking up into the endless field of stars. The cold of the night on my face feels wonderful, ice cream in the heat of summer or a cool shower after a run. I'm conscious of Fitz reclining on the blanket beside me.

"First you notice me in Boston," he says. "Then you memorize our entire conversation in Mike's Pastry. Now I hear you were keeping tabs on me at the party. . . . If I didn't know you better, I'd start to think you're into me." He's goading me, and he knows it.

"But you *do* know me better," I say with a lightly warning glance. "Besides, I already told you I only remembered our conversation because I have a good memory."

He turns his head toward me. "How good?"

I turn my head too, meeting his eyes. They're open, bridges half built and reaching toward me. "I don't know," I reply, feeling self-conscious. "I just remember stuff. Grocery lists, the grades I've gotten on every exam this year, conversations I had with friends in September. Facts and dates mentioned in class. Like, here, I remember the number of BU applicants last year, from the information session. It's 62,210." I gesture vaguely in the air. "Google it."

He does. It's quiet for a moment, except for the chorus of drunken guys belting "All the Small Things" coming from below.

"Whoa." He's reading from his phone. "Yeah, 62,210." He returns the phone to his pocket. "That's incredible."

"It's kind of cool, I guess," I reply. "It's definitely useful. Except, of course, when I unintentionally memorize conversations with people I'm definitely not *into*." I elbow him and earn a laugh, low and soft. "But," I go on, "having a great memory won't change the world. It's not like having a talent for inventing things or creating things. If I could exchange my memory for new ideas, for ingenuity, for dreaming new dreams, I would."

"I don't know," Fitz says beside me. "Memory is more than just useful."

The declaration hits me with guilty weight. This is a boy whose mother's memory is going to disappear, and here I am telling him the things I'd trade for mine. I feel insensitive, helplessly ineloquent.

"Because memory is . . . it, right?" he says. "It's who we are. It's everything. Everything we love, everything we fear, everything we think is important or necessary or exciting. It all comes from what we remember. The compilation of experiences that constitute a person. Without them, we're dreaming of nothing, working for nothing. We're unable to love people because we're unable to know people. We're no one."

"You can't think that's true." I remember working on homework in the restaurant, walking home from school with Matt, smelling tamales from the kitchen on winter nights. They're not me. Not the entire me. I want the chance to be more than the person I was yesterday, or the day before, or years before. In my family, memories are nothing but reasons to keep me who I've been. "Memory is part of who we are. It's just not everything. We can't re-create or relive things endlessly. I want my future to be bigger than my past."

We're facing each other, neither of us moving. The curiosity in Fitz's eyes is gone. They're haunted houses now, darkness behind broken windowpanes. He's wrong to think memory is everything, but I understand where he's coming from. While I might resent my family for wanting to tie me to home, I would be terrified to forget them.

I say nothing. I don't know how to express to Fitz I don't *not* understand his fear. I just wouldn't know how to live with his fear either.

Finally, Fitz turns. He faces the night, his features hardened in contemplation. "Logically, I understand your point. I don't know—I don't want to be implacable. I just don't know if I have the kind of future you do."

I want to tell him we both can have whatever futures we fight for. My situation is nothing like his, but I have my own forces pushing me not to leave home, forces I'm fighting so I can pursue what I want. I don't know if he's ready to listen, though, or if it's even my place to say.

"Implacable?" I say instead, wanting to ease the heaviness of the conversation. "What's with the obnoxious vocabulary?

First, you use *compunctious* without flinching. Now *implacable*? You talk like the thesaurus function on Microsoft Word."

Fitz laughs, and I feel his relief that I changed the subject. "I like words," he says simply. He pats his front pocket, where I remember he's put his book. "It's why I travel with this."

"Your book?" Without thinking—because I know what I would and *wouldn't* do if I bothered to think—I reach over him. The gesture is not wholly *un*flirtatious. My chest touches his forearm while I pull the book from his pocket, and I disregard the heat in my cheeks, knowing it's only a reaction to my own boldness. Nothing deeper.

Fitz goes completely motionless. The little clouds of his breath disappear while I reach over him.

I hold the book into the light from the street to read the cover. *"Bishop's Dictionary of Unconventional Usages.* Huh." I open the book, hearing Fitz release his breath beside me. "Unconventional usages," I repeat. "Why didn't they just put *obnoxious words for impressing girls*?"

"I thought you weren't impressed," Fitz replies.

I turn away to hide my grin, but poorly. "I meant *trying to impress girls*. Obviously."

"Obviously. Right."

I shake my head with pretend scorn. "No, really," I press. "You travel with your own dictionary of *unconventional usages* because, what? You just like words?" I'm going for joking, but my voice won't cooperate. It's endearing, the way Fitz feels this passion deeply enough to physically carry it on his person. The idea of putting photographs of fascinating buildings in my purse, or downloading them to my phone, flits through my head.

"Yeah, pretty much," Fitz's voice cuts in. "My mom's an English professor, and she has this policy that whenever we're in a bookstore, whatever I want, she'll buy. It's . . . really generous. I mean, my family's not . . ."

I nod, understanding. "Yeah. Mine's not either."

"It's meaningful, you know? I try not to overextend my bookstore requests. But this one day, I found the *Dictionary of Unconventional Usages* and flipped open to *petrichor*—I remember the exact page—and by the time Mom found me in the reference books, I'd been there for twenty minutes. The words just fascinated me. The world feels comprehensible when you can find the right labels for it."

While he's explaining, I feel my phone vibrate inside my coat pocket. It must be Matt. I texted my parents good night earlier—they're in-bed-by-ten people and it's nearly midnight—and I haven't texted with friends recently. My heart does this unexpected lurchy up and down. I'm enjoying tonight. But obviously I want to find Matt. But I'm enjoying tonight?

I place the dictionary beside Fitz and unzip my pocket. He watches me pull out my phone, then looks away while I reply to Matt, telling him I'll find him later.

"Hey," Fitz says, his voice tentative but even. "Do you think a guy who dreads forgetting the past and a girl who's focused on the future could, you know, be friends?"

I sit up, pulling my knees to my chest, and look out on

the view. Providence glitters brightly, undimmed. *A guy who dreads forgetting the past and a girl who's focused on the future.* We're an improbable coincidence, he's not wrong there. Two perfectly unlikely people to collide in cities like the one before us, buildings and boulevards bustling with people in motion. "I don't know," I say. "But no matter what, I won't forget tonight. Or you."

Fitz props himself on his elbows behind me and lets out an audible sigh. "High praise from the girl who remembers everything."

I blush but throw him a *don't push it* glance. "Okay, well, I won't be *completely* annoyed when I remember the night a boy I barely knew brought me onto a rooftop in the freezing cold. Better?"

Fitz smiles, his gaze traveling off the roof and toward the city.

"Better."

FITZ

IT WAS HER idea. While we sat on the rooftop, Juniper took the dictionary from where she'd put it down between us and flipped the book open. I turned to her, questioning. *"Lissome,"* she read, then let the word sit in the empty night. "I think that's a good one," she commented.

Then she dropped the book on my chest. "Your turn."

We read each other our spontaneous favorites for I don't know how long. *Halcyon.* Referring to times of idyllic happiness and tranquility. *Bucolic.* In a pleasant, often rural place. *Propinquity.* The property of being close to someone. I feel her shoulder edging nearer to mine, and whether it's conscious or unconscious, it's hard not to hope she'll close the distance. Shoulders brushing through three layers of clothing is practically nothing, but it's a nothing I really, *really* want.

I underline one of my early favorites with the pen I keep with me, which I got from the Edgar Allan Poe Museum. Juniper notices. From then on, we exchange the pen with every entry, each underlining our choices.

Hours pass. We only head inside when the temperature inches into the bitterly uncomfortable and we fumble to note our entries with numb fingers. While I follow her down the fire escape, Juniper checks her phone. She's texted a couple times while we've flipped through the dictionary, presumably with Matt.

The party is still going strong when we get inside. The hallway is empty except for one obviously miserable student walking into the bathroom in pajamas. It's whiplash, the contrast of this poorly lit, utterly normal hallway with the intimate vastness of the rooftop. Whatever I had with Juniper up there, it's a firmly closed book now.

Right before we head downstairs—to the party, to Lewis, to Matt, to diverging roads and different colleges—I pause. "Maybe we'll see each other again on this trip," I offer.

"Impossible to say," she replies without a second's pause. She smiles, and I know she knows she's repeating my words from our first conversation, yesterday in Boston.

I watch her walk downstairs—her hips swaying with each step, her brown curls shimmering bronze in the light— committing every detail of her to memory. Memory is likely the only thing she'll ever be to me.

In an explosion of clarity, I realize I *get* girls. I understand Lewis's infatuation with Prisha, with the girls he dated before her, with the girls he's wanted to date but couldn't. I even fucking understand the Nicole Kepler thing. If having a girlfriend means nights like this one, conversations in moonlight, quirks and family histories exchanged—not to mention the *holy hell* rush of her chest brushing my arm and the shampoo-plus-indefinable-girl-ether scent of her body beside me—I *definitely* understand wanting a girlfriend. I'm ready to go downstairs, find my brother, and admit I've been an idiot.

It's strange, this feeling of understanding a piece of Lewis, of maybe even having something in common with him.

I head down to the basement, searching for signs of him. He isn't in the hallway of significantly sweatier and sloppier guys clustered around the Ping-Pong tables where I left him. Even if Lewis isn't exactly the most attentive brother in the universe, I don't figure he would have left without me. Unless he got very drunk.

On second thought, it's entirely possible he left without me.

But when I pass by the taproom, I see him. Immediately, I wish he *had* left me. He's on the dance floor, swaying side to side with a tall girl in a crop top and tight jeans. They're pressed together, facing each other, Lewis's hand resting so low on her back that it's arguably her butt. He whispers something in her ear, and she laughs. I notice her fingers trailing down his chest.

My stomach turns. I don't know how I could have thought he and I had anything in common.

It's classic Lewis. I should've known his feelings on girls and relationships would be the furthest thing from the perfect night I had with Juniper. Instead, he's found one more way to avoid his commitments and forget his life. He *has* a girlfriend. Yet here he is, in this random fraternity, his hands practically in the jeans of a girl he doesn't even know. He couldn't care less about having a connection. For him, it's nothing except drinking and dancing and hooking up. It's the curdled-milk version of what I felt on the rooftop, the unpleasant aftertaste.

I'm suddenly sick of it. I liked Prisha. Despite his carefree manner, I even got the feeling Lewis does too. I won't watch him openly disrespecting her. Disrespecting the entire institution of romance and rooftops and exchanging favorite words in starlight.

I walk right up to them. "Time to leave," I tell Lewis, pulling him by the arm. "You seem nice," I say apologetically to the girl. "He has a girlfriend, though." I haul my incoherently protesting brother from the room, Lewis fumbling over his feet the whole way.

I usher him out the front door. Finally, he pushes me off when we're crossing the quad.

"I'm fine," he spits. "Fuck."

"You're not fine," I reply, reaching for him. He fends me off with both hands.

"I was just drying," he slurs, breathing hard. His brows furrow, like he knows that last word wasn't the one he meant. "With the music . . . and the songs."

"You mean *dancing*."

"Fitz," Lewis declares. "You always have the big words."

Rolling my eyes, I direct us through the campus and toward the hill back to the bed-and-breakfast. It's a miracle I hold Lewis upright the entire trip, but the miracle doesn't extend to him holding on to the contents of his stomach. Three bushes bear the consequences.

By the time we've returned to the room, I'm thoroughly through with this night. In the doorway, Lewis awkwardly shoves me off. "I'm good," he says heatedly, his words heavy. "I can take care of myself."

"Really?" I snap. I don't know why I don't hold in my resentment the way I usually do. I guess Lewis's drunken lack of inhibition is rubbing off on me, or maybe I just know he won't remember this in the morning. "Did you not notice me carrying you here?" I drop my jacket on the bed. "Thanks for a wonderful first taste of college."

"No problem." He waves emptily in my direction and stumbles toward the bathroom. I shake my head, blood pounding in my face. I don't know what I expected him to say. I don't know why I expected him to care. If he'd cared, we wouldn't be in this position in the first place.

Lewis clumsily half closes the bathroom door. "Just one night. I just wanted one night," I hear him mumble under his breath.

One night for what? I kick off my shoes, not caring where they fall. One night to forget his girlfriend? One night to force me to watch his total drunken thoughtlessness? One night to ignore the problems that weigh me down whenever I don't have the wherewithal to distract myself? That's *every* night for Lewis. He does whatever he wants, no matter who it hurts.

I lie on the bed and try to tune out the sound of Lewis retching over the toilet. Willing myself to fall asleep, I close my eyes and wish. If I had Juniper's memory, it wouldn't just be me in this unfamiliar hotel with my inebriated brother. I'd be recalling every word we exchanged on the rooftop over Providence.

But I do my best. *Halcyon. Bucolic. Propinquity.* I hold on to every syllable, hoping they turn into dreams.

FITZ

WHEN I WAKE up, I'm alone in the room. On the pillow next to me, I find a note written on the bed-and-breakfast's stationery. In hasty handwriting Lewis has explained he's gone to grab food. I'm stunned he's awake, what with his penchant for sleeping in late and his extended stay in the bathroom last night.

I lie in bed, squinting in the uncomfortable sunlight. I don't want to heave myself out from under the covers. Really, I don't want to face the fact that last night is over.

It feels like a dream, close enough to impossible, like I really could have just conjured the entire evening with Juniper in my head. In the morning light, the wonder of the night feels nearly unreachable. *Fugacious.* Fleeting, with the tendency to disappear. I know with every passing minute and mile, it'll be harder to imagine it was ever real.

I remember the dictionary—trading the book back and forth, underlining the words we read to each other. I reach over to the nightstand where I left the *Dictionary of Unusual Usages* before I went to bed, feeling a rush of gratitude I have the pages and the ink to tie me tangibly to the night with Juniper. Proof it was real.

I thumb open the book, reading the underlines. *Lissome.* *Desuetude. Embrocate,* which we only underlined because Juniper found it funny that the stately, flowery word means "rubbing on lotion." I'm close to the end of the dictionary when my fingers catch on something. My breath catches with them.

There's a dog-eared page. I never dog-ear pages. I kind of resent the practice, and in other circumstances, the defacement of my dictionary would piss me off. Not this time. With the heady tingle of nervous excitement, I open precisely to the folded page.

I immediately narrow in on the underlined word. It's not one I remember either of us reading out loud, though. *Serendipity.* Fortunate coincidence. Finding what one did not know one needed. The word is underlined in one of Juniper's unmistakably neat strokes.

Next to it, I find ten digits. It's a phone number.

It's *her* phone number.

I do not know how to process this realization. I feel myself blushing goofily, elated yet reminding myself to be cool, to not read into the gesture, to remember she's probably only being friendly. She must have written the number down when I wasn't paying attention, when I was looking the other way, or—I don't know. It doesn't matter. It *deeply* doesn't matter.

I'm staring at the ten perfect little numbers when the door handle rattles and Lewis pushes his way in. He's holding a Dunkin' Donuts bag and a tray with two coffees. In no way does he look like he spent the night hunched over the toilet. He's showered and freshly shaven, his eyes clear.

Oddly, it reminds me how wrecked I feel. Under the elation of finding Juniper's phone number, I'm severely tired. It's only been two full days of this trip, one in Boston and yesterday in Providence. But it feels like weeks since I took the bus—the *buses*—into South Station. Traveling is exhausting.

My stomach growls, like it's hearing my thoughts. Lewis drops the paper bag in my lap. If he thinks this makes up for having to listen to him puke for hours, he's . . . on the right track.

He stands over his open suitcase, sipping his coffee. For a second, he studies me, and I wonder if he's going to say something about last night. About the girl he danced with or how I got his stumbling ass back to the room. About what I said to him.

He doesn't. I don't either. Serious conversations aren't something I know how to have with my brother. Maybe it's because we're not close enough, or maybe it's because Lewis isn't capable of being serious about anything. Probably both.

"So," he says, watching me with keen interest despite his utterly relaxed posture, "are we heading home?"

I glance at the dictionary. At Juniper's phone number. *Impossible to say.*

She wasn't just repeating my words. She knew she'd left her number and was hinting there'd be a way to ensure we saw each other again.

But I won't see her if I go home now.

I return my gaze to Lewis. "No," I say, a grin slipping across my face.

JUNIPER

I'M WAITING FOR an unknown number to light up my phone screen. I waited while we ate croissants out of paper bags in the campus Starbucks this morning. I waited while we drove out of Providence onto US-6, and while we headed in the direction of the University of Connecticut, passing exits for Hartford and Silver Lake, brick buildings and greenery going by in the window.

While we drove, Matt described every detail of the party. I chimed in now and then, listening to him recount his beer pong wins and how he and Carter found this old Nintendo in one downstairs room.

The conversation felt off, though, like we were only carpooling instead of dating. What Matt found hilarious, I found familiar. What I found confusing, Matt found normal. I felt the same unpleasant current I experienced when he wanted to hang with Carter and I wanted to leave the party, an undertow dragging against my feet and the course I'd chosen. One wrong step, and I could slip downstream. I couldn't help continually checking my phone in the cup holder too, which I know Matt noticed. He said nothing, and if he wondered why, he hid his curiosity impeccably.

I think he felt the same weirdness in the conversation I did, because by the time we reach the Middle Turnpike heading toward UConn, we're driving in silence. We pull off the turnpike and head toward campus, passing honest-to-goodness red barns and stone walls like we're in a photo calendar of the idyllic Northeast. The hour we're on the road feels like eternity. I focus on what's coming up on our itinerary to pass the minutes. Rationally, I should feel exhausted from the party and today's early start, but going over the five days of visits we have left invigorates me, from Connecticut to New York to D.C. to Virginia. I guess I like traveling.

It's nearly ten when photogenic provinciality gives way to collegiate Gothic campus buildings. I take in the brick towers, the granite-rimmed windows, trying to distract myself from uncomfortable questions by examining the architecture.

Matt springs out of the car when we park. He gives me a feeble grin, and I truly can't tell if he's sensed the current at our feet or if I'm the only one. He calls his mom while we find our way to the admissions building.

Waiting for the tour to begin, I check my phone once more. Nothing.

Hiding my disappointment, I start to worry. I thought dog-earing the page of Fitz's dictionary would work. None of the other pages was dog-eared—I figured the message I left should be impossible to overlook. But Fitz either didn't notice my number scrawled on the page or he's ignoring me. Both possibilities preoccupy my thoughts for reasons

I don't fully understand. I try to focus on the tour, but I'm distracted, my mind snagging on Fitz like a loose thread while we're led to the student union, the mascot statue, the campus bookstore.

Which is where I'm halfheartedly perusing sweatshirts with Matt when my phone finally vibrates. Unable to control the tiny thrill tugging up the corners of my mouth, I turn from Matt to read the text.

It's from an unknown number: +1 and ten inscrutable digits. Foreign inscriptions. I know the translation without recognizing the content.

Fitz.

Then, the message.

So, Juniper. Where will you be
making memories today?

The typing bubble forms below. I wait.

I won't follow you if you tell me.
We've established I'm not a stalker.

I bite back a laugh. Matt follows a saleswoman into the T-shirt section, and I turn into an empty aisle of license plate frames to reply.

UConn. I definitely don't condone stalking,
but I wouldn't hate it if we ran into each
other again . . . As friends, of course.

As friends. Did I ever suggest otherwise?

Do you really want me to answer that, Fitz?

Hey, you hardly know me, remember?
I could have some amazing girlfriend
in New Hampshire.

I quickly recall our conversations in the North End and on the rooftop. There's no way he has a girlfriend. If he does, that means he deliberately chose not to tell me, which would make him somewhat shady. I may hardly know him, but there isn't a part of me that thinks he's capable of such dishonesty. He's a good guy.

A good guy who I definitely wouldn't begrudge having a girlfriend.

Do you have an amazing girlfriend in
New Hampshire? The way we talked
on the rooftop would suggest otherwise.

What way? (And fine. No, I don't
currently have a girlfriend.)

You know what way. I have
a boyfriend, remember?

It takes him a couple of minutes to reply. I watch the typing bubble appear and disappear, possible conversations erased.

I do remember. Unrelatedly, why did
you give me your number, Juniper?

I hesitate. The truth is . . . I don't know why. I didn't let myself overthink it. There was one moment last night when I looked over at him, the unruly flip of his hair and the straight incline of his nose illuminated in profile under the moonlight. He was staring up at the expanding universe suspended above us, and I realized I could determine whether I went the rest of my life without saying another word to him. I don't know what I expected or wanted, except to ensure our universe continued expanding.

To talk to you.

I'm glad.

It's the perfect response, somehow. It's everything Fitz is, reserved and understated, and yet open and heartfelt. There's another pause, this time without the typing bubble. I wonder what he's doing, what school he's visiting, whether he's in a college bookstore somewhere across the state.

Tell me about UConn. What
do you like about it?

His question makes something in my chest flutter. A girl who looks about my age walks into my aisle, trailed by two younger boys, probably fourth or fifth grade. One of the boys crashes into the rack of key chains, and the other howls in laughter. The girl scowls.

"Go bother Mom," she says, waving them off and turning her attention to the car decals.

I leave the girl and her brothers behind, heading for the stationery aisle.

UConn is actually on Matt's college list.

There isn't a whole lot of overlap in the schools we like, but UConn has a ton of programs and great resources.

"Hey," Matt says, suddenly behind me. I startle, whipping around to face him. He's holding a UConn polo shirt. "You talking to your dad?" he asks.

"Oh, no, actually," I tell him, my stomach sinking guiltily. I don't hide things from Matt. Whenever Tía is being impossible or I get a grade I'm unhappy with, Matt is the person I go to. "This is, um, Fitz."

"Fitzgerald?" I hear puzzlement in Matt's voice, not resentment. "I still think it's crazy you ran into him again last night."

"Yeah. I know." While we walked home from the party last night, I told Matt I ended up talking with Fitz for a couple of hours. I didn't mention how we went up to the rooftop, and Matt didn't ask. "He's smart. I'm determined to get him to diversify his college list."

Matt rolls his eyes with a smirk. I know exactly what he's thinking. For the past year, I've played unofficial college counselor to pretty much our entire grade. From telling Colleen O'Connell about Kenyon's creative writing program to encouraging Tory to reach for Berkeley, I've become the go-to source for everything college-related. I'm College Confidential in human form.

"Tell him to apply here," Matt says. His friendliness is touching and completely charming. He's that kind of guy, inclusive and welcoming. "Then the three of us could hang out," he continues.

My expression falters, and I hope Matt doesn't notice. He's been unusually engaged today—admiring the campus, asking questions during the tour, picking out this UConn polo. It's honestly been wonderful to watch. I don't know how I'll muster the heart to tell him that after last night, I might be falling in love with Brown.

"I will," I say weakly.

Matt nods and wanders off toward the sweatshirt rack, either not noticing or choosing not to remark on my hesitancy. When he's gone, my phone vibrates in my hand.

This is coming from a place of complete friendship and has nothing to do with any potentially non-platonic hopes I may have, but I feel like you're not the type to pick a college for a guy.

I read the text once, then twice, each time with a twist in my gut. Fitz has known me for two days, and he recognizes this fundamental truth of who I am. My boyfriend of over a year . . . doesn't. I don't want to contemplate the questions that realization brings.

I glance up from the phone, finding Matt chatting easily with a guy in a UConn soccer sweatshirt who's holding a pile of new notebooks. Matt says something, and the student laughs. I'm not surprised. Matt's the life of the party. Not only the "party"—the life of the campus bookstore, the lunch table. It's why I fell in love with him.

It's why I *still* love him.

I watch him, adoration warring with whatever hint of

reluctance I felt when he brought up going to UConn together. I don't blame him for wanting college to feel the way high school does. I've loved high school. I've loved high school with *him*. Finding notes he's written me stashed in my locker, sitting in the bleachers at his games, having him help me poster for pep rallies.

It's not that I don't cherish those memories. They might even be the best I've ever had. But I don't know yet. I need to explore, try new things—with him and on my own—and uncover memories I can't begin to imagine now. Matt might not understand I crave those opportunities, the wide-open world college could represent. Every day, I wonder if he'll only ever want the Juniper he knows. The Juniper of the past.

And that frightens me. I feel the fear in little perforations when we're kissing or he's waving to me on those bleachers or we're walking out of house parties hand in hand. They're would-be perfect moments, punctured until I force myself to forget the dread it's not exactly *me* he loves. Only *this* me. *Now* me.

I unlock my phone and begin replying to Fitz.

But I don't finish the message. I won't write this relationship off. Not that texting Fitz would be doing that—I just can't deny that somehow this new friendship feels like a tentative move in that direction. I won't close my eyes while the current knocks me off my feet and pulls me toward the unknown.

Matt's a good guy. He deserves my trust, and my efforts to *try* to make it work. No matter where he and I end up, I can give him that.

I put my phone away, leaving Fitz's text unanswered.

FITZ

LEWIS DIDN'T QUESTION what changed my mind. We devoured the doughnuts and got on the road to Wesleyan by eleven, following Mom's itinerary. With the radio on and the heater cranked, we left Rhode Island in the rearview.

It took every iota of my self-control not to text Juniper immediately. I could acutely feel my phone in my pocket the entire drive, its weight pressing into my thigh. It was an onerous test of willpower to resist texting her when I took my phone out upon entering Connecticut to tell my mom we'd nearly reached our next destination.

I respect Juniper has a boyfriend. Besides, I would be deluding myself to imagine one night under the stars, trading my dictionary back and forth, is the foundation for an epic romance involving two people who don't live in the same state or plan to go to the same college and who couldn't be more fundamentally different.

But her number is a promise. Of what, I don't know. Something I don't know how to define yet.

We're in a diner outside Middletown when I finally decide I've waited a respectable amount of time before texting her. Though it's a little past noon, the Monday lunch crowd is thin. In the booth opposite me, Lewis is scrolling on his phone, looking bored. I pull mine out and open a message to the number I've had programmed in since early this morning. Keeping the message brief, I ask Juniper where she's visiting.

The waitress brings plates of burgers and fries for Lewis and me, but I hardly taste the food because I'm distracted by Juniper's incoming texts. The conversation continues, and like last night, it's easy. She says she's visiting UConn, and that she wouldn't mind if we ran into each other again. I fight the thrill those words spark in me.

"You texting a girl?" Lewis asks. I don't reply. "Yeah, you are," he crows, apparently finding whatever confirmation he needed in my silence. What's infuriating isn't his confidence. It's him being right.

"A friend," I clarify coolly. I reply to Juniper, wanting to know why she's excited to visit UConn.

"The best girlfriends are often friends first," Lewis points out.

He's obviously trying to project older-brother wisdom and experience with girls, which ordinarily I would permit without interrupting or bothering to reply.

Not today. Not with Juniper's reply staring up from my phone screen. Instead of chasing dreams and following futures the way she described yesterday, she's visiting UConn because she wants to follow her boyfriend. Meanwhile, I'm here with my brother, who I had to watch grind up on the random girl he found at Brown last night.

The twin frustrations put fire into me. "Is that what Prisha was?" I ask, terser than I intended.

Lewis glances up from his phone, his eyes narrowed but not exactly surprised. I get the sense he does remember our conversation from last night. It was the first time I've come close to losing my temper with him. Now I'm near losing it again. When he was home, we'd fight over stupid stuff, but I've hardly ever stood up to my brother on real things. I don't know what's different, but something is.

"Yeah," he says evenly, following a moment's pause. "She was. She lived down the hall from me freshman year. I think we collectively hooked up with the entire *rest* of the hallway before figuring out how we felt about each other." He dips a fry into his ketchup. "But we did," he continues, "and I had to put an end to random hookups. For a little longer, anyway." He winks, and once again, I'm irritated.

I put down my burger. "Why do you do that?" I ask calmly. The anger hones my questions into needle points.

Lewis studies me. "Do what?"

"You ask me about girls, or tease me or whatever, or tell me about your gorgeous conquests." I give him a look that I hope comes off pitying or dismissive. "Is getting laid the only thing you care about?"

"When you get laid, you won't ask me that question," he replies.

I've had enough. I'm tired of Lewis treating me like I'm nobody because my life doesn't resemble his. I'm *really* tired of him playing everything off like it's easy or a joke or insignificant. The only people who never get frustrated are people who don't care.

I get up from the booth and throw my napkin onto the table. I don't even know where I'm going. It doesn't matter. Just not here. But when I start for the door, Lewis's hand grips my wrist, holding me back.

"Hey, hold on," he says, his voice softening. I reluctantly face him. "I didn't mean—" He shakes his head. "It was a joke. I'm sorry," he continues, sounding surprisingly genuine.

I wait by the booth, unmoving, reluctant to stay. But I have no choice, really. Unless I want to spring for a four-hundred-dollar Uber to New Hampshire, I have nowhere to go except Lewis's car.

I sit back down, scowling. Lewis says nothing. "Just because I haven't dated a dozen girls doesn't mean I'm a loser," I say eventually. I've known for years what my brother thinks of me, and I've chosen to ignore it or, at the very least, hide my resentment of it, convincing myself he couldn't possibly view me that way. It's liberating and dangerous to finally put words to the feeling instead.

Lewis's face falls. His bravado disappears, and for once I'm seeing my brother as himself, not the debonair role he plays for his friends and job interviewers and probably even his girlfriends. He's serious, even somber. "I don't think you're a loser," he says.

The lack of prevarication in his reply startles me. It's not like Lewis to speak so straightforwardly instead of playing it cool and letting me read whatever I want into his detached dismissiveness.

I don't believe him. He probably only wants the easy way out of this conversation. He doesn't know how to deal with me talking back, and he doesn't like it.

"I don't," he insists. "I think you take everything really seriously."

It's the understatement of the century. "Some things *are* serious," I say, knowing it's futile to try to convince Lewis to care, and feeling irrationally compelled to regardless. "Like Mom."

Lewis looks away, his eyes flitting to the parking lot outside, gravelly pavement under the slate-gray sky. "Some things are," he says. "Not everything. I just want to make sure you're cutting yourself some slack."

I notice how once again he's dodged discussing Mom and once again completely misunderstood what it's like inside my head. *Cut myself some slack?* I wrestle for the right words to explain this fundamental fact to him. "I'm not like you, okay?" I say quietly, staring at my plate. It's hard to admit—hard to confirm what Lewis has said and felt and implied about me for years. We *are* different. He's effortlessly cool, and I *am* a loser.

Lewis snorts. I look up, surprised to find him close to laughing.

"Well, duh," he says. He picks up his burger and takes a huge final bite. I watch him uncomprehendingly while he chews. "I know we're different," he continues. "Sometimes I can't believe we were raised under the same roof."

I start to smile, unable to stop myself. His constant carelessness does hurt—I haven't forgotten the feeling—but right now, the humor of the moment eases the sting. "Well, we were adopted," I reply.

Lewis waves his hand. "That doesn't mean anything."

He glances at the bill and puts cash down on the receipt. We slide out of the booth, and I feel a sudden warmth in my chest from his words, a gratefulness for this unique instance of my brother's universal easygoing acceptance. It's me he's accepting this time, and it's foreign and friendly and kind of fun.

We walk toward the door of the diner. In the corner of the restaurant I notice a family of four red-haired children and their parents, who look beleaguered.

Lewis pauses in front of the door, and I nearly ram into him. "I didn't hook up with that girl last night," he says. I don't know why he's telling me, or why now. I stay quiet. It's a stiff, strange moment. "I just got her number," he continues.

"Okay." I nod.

"I wanted you to know." He runs a hand through his hair, looking troubled. "I was only trying to have some fun," he says with resignation, and I detect unusual weight in his words. "I'm still with Prisha. We'll stay together until the day we've decided to break up."

"And then?" I ask, wondering how I can reconcile his purported commitment with his hands on the other girl's jeans, their faces close to touching.

Lewis shrugs and opens the door, letting in the cold. "Then I guess I'll use the number."

FITZ

WHILE WE DRIVE to Wesleyan, Lewis tells me about the trip to Florida he and his fraternity brothers have planned for spring. After reaching the campus, we walk toward the admissions building, where I have a tour booked today. I have to admit, the admissions office is charming, a custard-yellow bungalow with gray roofs and white-edged windows. Lewis walks me in and says he'll find me here when the tour's over. I nod. We're not exactly friends now, but it's coming a little easier, the uncomfortable disconnect replaced by an unfamiliar détente.

When the tour begins, it's not long before I find myself distracted. The possibility of seeing Juniper might be keeping me on the road this week, but it's doing nothing to increase my enthusiasm for any of these colleges. I pull out my phone while the tour group passes the impressive white-columned façade of what the guide explains is the library. I'm hoping for a text from Juniper, who didn't reply to my previous message.

I click on the screen. Nothing.

It feels weird, knowing we're both in Connecticut, an hour apart, and yet ignoring each other. I consider whether to text her again. *Pro*: the possibility she'll reply. It's unlikely, though, since she didn't reply when I texted that I didn't think she'd be the type to follow a guy to college. *Con*: she'll think I'm an obsessive creep, delete my number, and forget I ever existed. I'll end up celibate, living with fourteen cats and my extensive collection of detailed model trains, rueing this exact moment when my life went wrong.

I put my phone back into my pocket.

Eventually, we return to the admissions building where the tour began. Lewis is waiting out front, carrying two Starbucks cups, steam seeping from the lids. He holds one out when I reach him.

"I don't know your drink," he says. "I went with cappuccino."

"Cappuccino's great," I say instead of explaining I'm nowhere near enough of a habitual coffee drinker to have "a drink."

"How was it?" Lewis asks. It's the middle of the afternoon, and the sun is peeking through one sliver in the frigid sheet of clouds. We cross the street, returning to the parking lot. Lewis's car is in the back row, overlooking a giant field in the middle of the campus. The snow hasn't stuck here, and the grass isn't completely brown yet. I briefly wonder what the field looks like in summer. *Verdant.* Green with plants or grass.

"Same as the others," I say with a shrug.

He nods. Instead of getting in the car, he walks to the edge of the lot, surveying the lawn and the brick buildings on the other side. "I bet Mom spent every afternoon reading on this field."

It takes me a moment to process his words. "Wait, what?" I ask, following his eyeline. He's so focused, like he's actually envisioning Mom here right now. But all I see is dry grass under barren trees.

Lewis gestures at the campus buildings around us. "She went here for two years before she had to transfer to take care of Grandma."

I blink. I knew Mom transferred schools when she had to move back in with her parents. Grandpa couldn't leave his job, not when his insurance was paying for Grandma's medications. But it meant Mom had to be home to help with the caretaking. It took her two extra years to finish school while she drove her mother to doctor's appointments, cooked for her parents, managed medication schedules—all while she fought the disease she'd one day inherit.

I guess I never thought about where Mom had gone to school before Grandma's diagnosis. Never considered what kind of life she was embarking on before her entire world was upended. I'm surprised Lewis has, though. It makes me wonder if he's closer to our mom than I'd assumed. He's paid attention to her in ways I wouldn't have guessed given his careless demeanor. This new information has me questioning if there are other pieces of him I've overlooked.

"I never knew that," I say, gazing out at the campus across the field. They're no longer brick buildings and libraries and dorms and labs I don't remember the names of. No longer a blurry addition to a string of nearly identical schools.

This is part of my mom's history. She was here. She made memories here, began her studies here.

"She loved this place," Lewis says softly. It's a tone I hardly recognize from him. Fragile, almost. "I think she was always sad she couldn't come back, but—you know . . ." He trails off, not needing to finish the sentence. Of course I know.

We stand together a moment longer. I don't know why this campus has Lewis pensive. We still haven't talked about her, about what our family is facing—not quite. But this shared meditation, this quiet stillness is the closest we've come.

"Ready to head to the hotel?" Lewis asks abruptly.

"Actually, could we walk around some more?" I surprise myself with the question. But I'm not ready to leave yet. Not when I feel like I've just uncovered something to treasure.

Lewis's face lights up. "Of course."

We retrace the route I walked with the tour group. This time, though, I study everything.

This school isn't part of my future. It's better. It's part of her past.

While we walk, I don't just immerse myself in the scenery, the buildings, the trees, the endless gray of the clouds over campus. I imagine myself describing them. The words I'll pull when painting the portraits my mom no longer remembers. *Arboreal. Caesious. Austere.* The details, from the incongruous architectural cross-section to the gentle curvature of the palatial library's outer wall. I imagine myself in my house, the fireplace warming the front room while my mom listens. I'll say every word I collect on this campus, but really I'll only say one.

Remember.

Remember.

Remember.

JUNIPER

~

I WAKE UP to my phone vibrating on the nightstand in our cramped Connecticut hotel room. It's not the half-conscious waking of confused dreams or sunlight through bedroom windows, either. The rattling noise throws my eyes open, my nerves rushing with instantaneous ugly energy. I'm a light sleeper, which Matt jokes is the least surprising thing about me. Honestly, I know what he means. Even unconsciously, I never want to miss a moment. It's why I leave my phone on vibrate even though just one text could pull me from sleep, not to mention a call like I'm getting now.

Grabbing my phone off the bedside table, I check the name displayed. *Marisa.*

I quickly take in the numbers over her name. It's 2:34 a.m. My oldest younger sister is not in the habit of calling me past midnight, which means this must be important. Careful not to disturb Matt, who's predictably sound asleep, I tiptoe to the bathroom, ease the door silently shut behind me, and pick up.

"Marisa?" I say, squinting in the bright light. "Are you okay?"

Music crackles through my phone's speakers, distant and thudding. I hear my sister shouting something incoherent through the noise, trying to get the attention of someone named Michelle. Michelle, presumably, hollers something back. They sound far from the phone, their voices a thin accent above the melody.

She butt-dialed me. I would hang up, except *what the hell is my sister doing out at 2:34 in the morning?* There's no way Mom and Dad know about this.

"Marisa," I try again, louder this time. "What's going on? Can you hear me?"

The rustling of fabric scratches the speakers. "Yeah," she says. "I need you to pick me up." Her voice is slurred, her consonants lost under extended vowels. Okay—so it's not a butt-dial. "Steve's . . . house's driveway." Words run together, caught in her heavy breathing.

"What?" I turn the volume up on my phone, hoping it'll make her easier to understand. I've never heard my sister so drunk before, and it spills worry through me.

Marisa sighs into the phone. Except it's not a sigh. Her breath heaves, and I realize she's sobbing. Panic rushes through my chest. I clutch the phone to my ear, feeling electrified through my exhaustion.

"*Steve's party,*" Marisa gets out. "Pick me up from *Steve's party.*"

With horrible rising dread, I understand what's happening. My sister wants to come home from a house party, where she's drunk and overwhelmed and in tears. Not good. Really not good. I hurriedly comb my thoughts for memories of whoever this *Steve* is. Marisa and I go to the same school, but I hardly know everyone in the junior class. I dredge up the recollection of driving the two of them home from school last year. They were sophomores and partners on a *Macbeth* project for English. I wonder if he's the mysterious boyfriend she's been keeping a secret. Under the harsh light, I feel queasy.

"I'm not home, remember?" I explain patiently. "I'm in Connecticut. I can't come pick you up right now."

Marisa's sobs come harder. "Jessie said boys only like me because I dress trashy," she says breathily, and this time it's less like she's talking to me than like she's talking to everybody and nobody and I'm there to hear her.

"Jessie isn't a good friend," I tell her calmly, or as calmly as I can. "I'm sorry she said that." Jessie and Marisa have been friends since third grade, but really frenemies. Jessie throws birthday parties without inviting Marisa. Marisa routinely ditches Jessie to have lunch with other friends. Their social-media relationship is fraught with "accidental" unfollows and passive-aggressive comments.

"So you'll pick me up?" She's heartbreakingly hopeful. "I can't ride home with Jessie. Everyone else here is drunk."

I restrain my frustration. She's not listening to me. "I can't," I repeat, slower this time. "I'm in Connecticut. You have to call Mom."

"I can't call Mom!" Her voice explodes into my ear. Her sobs have stopped, and I can practically hear her fuming over the line. To be fair, I wouldn't want to call Mom if I were in Marisa's position. It's not even that Mom will be that mad.

Dad, yes. But Mom's anger is a firework. A bright bang, then smoke drifting to the clouds. She has too much to do to stay angry.

The problem with calling Mom is she'll tell Tía and Tía will tell the whole family. Second cousins in different states will hear a Ramírez daughter snuck out and got drunk at a party. Great-uncles will offer lectures and advice next time they're in town. Family gossip is an epidemic with the only cure the next scandal.

"I need *you*," Marisa pleads.

"Marisa, you're not understanding. I can't—"

She cuts me off. "God, Juniper. You're so *selfish*." The line beeps, the call disconnecting.

She hung up on me.

Selfish? It's not like I've never heard it before from my family. Studying instead of working in the restaurant, hanging out with friends instead of distant family in town, considering colleges out of state. I'm the most selfish Ramírez there is.

Still, it stings. I remember other requests, other drop-everythings, other obligatory kindnesses. Searching countless cardboard boxes in the garage to find old photos for Tía. Planning Marisa's thirteenth birthday party. Driving her home with Steve instead of doing homework or having Froyo with Matt or whatever *I* wanted that afternoon. I don't remember my family calling me selfish then.

But I don't remember them thanking me either. I'd reached up to what I imagined was generosity, only to find I'd done nothing but reached the normal, unremarkable, expected standard for family contribution. Every time, I would hide my pride and my futile frustration, my fear that the love I thought would be unconditional was becoming . . . kind of conditional.

By now it's turned into a truth not worth fighting, like things that hurt tend to do. As long as I am doing *one* thing for myself, I won't be the daughter or sister my family wants. Eventually, I learned not to think about it, to keep my eyes on the road ahead.

I'd like to ignore my sister right now, but I can't. Even if I can't drive her, I need to make sure she gets home safely. If she weren't a drunk teenage girl on her own, I'd call her a Lyft, but I don't want her in some stranger's car.

Without hesitating, I call my home phone. I know the ringing will wake up the whole house, and I don't care. When I explain, neither will they.

My mom picks up, her voice hushed but hyper-focused, the way mine was when I took Marisa's call. "Juniper?" There's rustling over the line. She's sitting up in bed. "Is everything okay?"

"It's Marisa," I explain urgently. "She snuck out. She went to a party and she needs a ride home."

I hear my dad in the background. He wants to know what's going on. My mom's voice becomes distant while she explains, then returns to normal volume. "Has Marisa been drinking?" She sounds casual, like she's trying to lull the truth from me by pretending the question is inconsequential.

It's a thoughtful effort, though it doesn't fool for me for

an instant. I breathe in, preparing myself. "Yes, but—"

Mom interrupts me. "Gabriel, call Marisa right now," she instructs Dad. "Keep her on the phone until I get there." Her voice comes closer, addressing me again. "Where is she?"

"Steve's house," I say, quietly thankful Mom knows what to do. I knew she would.

"Who the hell is Steve?"

I don't bother to recount the one project Marisa did with Steve over a year ago. Remembering the hedges in front of Steve's house, the sequence of turns I took from the school, the trampoline in the yard on the corner, I fumble to pull the memories together into understandable directions. "It's—on Pelham, off Peer. The white house with red trim."

I hear doors opening and Mom's footsteps moving from the carpet in their bedroom to the tile of the living room, her keys jingling in her hand. "If she calls you again—" Mom starts to say.

"I'll tell her to wait for you there," I finish.

I hear Tía's voice over the phone, fuzzy and faint. "What's going on?" She's talking to my mom. "Where are you going?"

Hearing Tía, I remember I haven't talked to her in days. The realization hits me with, not quite homesickness, but one of homesickness's cousins. The consciousness of finding myself far from familiar things, from the routines and routine details of my life up until now. While I've talked to my parents on the phone every day, I haven't eaten breakfast with my brothers, haven't bumped my head on the cabinet in the bathroom, haven't picked Malfoy's hair from my clothes. I haven't spoken to Tía except for one text—haven't heard her voice.

"I have to pick up Marisa," I hear Mom tell Tía. "From a party."

There's rustling over the phone. Tía's voice comes through closer and harder. "How could this happen? Marisa going to a party at two in the morning?" Mom's evidently handed the phone over to Tía, who's now questioning me.

I grope for words. Tía is ruthless in an interrogation, and I don't understand why I'm the subject. Nor do I have the emotional energy to muster either patience or resistance. I'm exhausted. "I don't know, Tía," I say honestly. "I wasn't there."

"Exactly," Tía replies. I understand a moment late I've given her what she wanted. "Do you think this would've happened if you'd been home, Juni? Do you think your sister could've snuck out if you were here?" They're questions, but really they're points driven in with practiced precision.

Defensiveness gets the better of me. "You're being ridiculous," I reply sharply. It's true, though. Had I been home, Marisa wouldn't have been able to sneak out. Everyone knows I'm a light sleeper. But that's not the point. "You can't make this my fault. *Marisa* chose to sneak out. *Marisa* chose to get drunk. *She's* the one you should be lecturing."

"She'll have her turn, don't you worry," Tía says. "Right now is your turn." I roll my eyes, grateful she can't see me. "We have to look after each other." Her tone is softer now, heavier.

It pulls me to the cold tile of the bathroom floor. I put my back up to the door, tucking my knees to my chest.

"Marisa needed you to look after her tonight," she continues. "Who will look after you when you are far away? Who will you call? You need your family, Juniper." The bite is gone from her words, replaced entirely by the gentle persuasiveness of a person who believes wholly in what she is saying.

"I have to find myself," I plead, feeling the enormous inertia of this conversation, the weight of having fought this exact fight with Tía tens, even hundreds of times before. Tears well in my eyes, partly because it's nearly three in the morning and I'm curled on the floor of a hotel bathroom, and partly because I know how this conversation will end. For all Tía preaches about family, she never even tries to be the great-aunt I need. To encourage and respect my choices and the life I want. The futility and the loneliness overwhelm me.

"I know who you are," Tía tells me. "You're Marisa's older sister. You're the girl who did her homework in the restaurant while her father cooked enchiladas, the girl who taught her brothers long division when they needed help in school. The girl who cut out paper angels to decorate her abuela's room after she was gone. You're a Ramírez. You don't need to find yourself because you're not lost, niña. You can never be lost if you have your home and your family."

The tears in my eyes burn, fury flushing into my cheeks. "You know, I used to wonder why my dad moved to New York. Why he married a woman none of you had ever met. Why he didn't come home for eight years," I say, fuming. "Now I understand. The only way to have even the smallest stretch of freedom from this family is to leave completely. Don't make me do it too."

Icy stillness settles over the line. I know I've said outright what I've only hinted and half expressed for months. "Do you need to be reminded of what happened the second time your father tried to leave his family?"

The question knocks the wind out of me. It's cruel of Tía to use those memories like weapons, to turn them on me. It's unnecessary—my parents and I never need reminding of this guilt.

My parents had moved our family to Springfield to help run the restaurant while Abuela had heart problems. We'd been living there for six months when my dad found permanent help to take over, lightening the load for Tía and Abuela and giving my parents the chance to move back to New York. When they brought Tía and Abuela together to tell them, they weren't expecting their stunned indignation. They'd thought we'd moved to Springfield for good. It turned into a huge fight, and the stress pushed Abuela's heart too far. It was the night she died.

Tía blames us for it. Not that my father doesn't blame himself enough on his own. As long as my parents run Abuela's restaurant and live in her house, they will be reminded of the costs of trying to move on. Of being *selfish*.

I hang up the phone.

I don't need to hear Tía's guilt trip. I refuse to buy into it like the rest of my family. Fights happen in families, and it's no one's fault. Abuela died because she had a bad heart.

Not because my father helped her and then tried to leave. Tía may try to convince me otherwise. She may even believe that my going away to college could set us on a course to another family tragedy.

I refuse to give ground to her accusations, to allow my abuela's death be used against me. I won't have something in the past dictate my future.

I put my phone on silent and return to bed, pretending it doesn't matter to me if I have Tía's support.

Maybe one day, that'll be true.

FITZ

OUR CONVERSATION ON the Wesleyan campus continued to thaw the weirdness between Lewis and me. On the
drive to New York City the next morning, I mention the Red
Sox, and we pretty quickly delve into preseason hopes and
predictions. In a way, it's brotherly, this banal banter. But I
remind myself we're not discussing the real, fundamental
things I don't know—what jobs he's interviewing for, where
he'll probably live next year. Mom.

We take the scenic route toward Manhattan, where I'm
touring NYU this afternoon. The interstate winds down the
coast, the view breathtaking. The water glitters in the midday
sun, flashes of light flickering from the waves.

I end up taking ten or fifteen photos on my phone, compil-
ing my favorites into a text to Mom, who's thrilled, of course.
Any indication I might be enjoying the trip is undoubtedly
cause for celebration. She recognizes the entrance to South-
port Beach from a trip she took with her college roommates
during her freshman year. They rented a tiny house with a
white picket fence, went for ice cream in town, and one of her
friends had a weekend-long fling with a local lifeguard—that

part I didn't need to know. But I'm quietly reassured she re-members the trip in detail.

We pass the sign for Sherwood Island State Park. Lewis slows down and glances over to me. There's a familiar gleam in his eyes. "How much do you care about making your NYU tour?" he asks.

I imagine the desultory hour I'll spend listening to the NYU presenter spinning off facts and figures irrelevant to me. Then I imagine watching the horizon over the water, passing the hour in the winter sun instead. "Not at all," I say.

"Okay," he says, looking decidedly pleased. "If we're doing this, we're going to need food."

We continue on the turnpike to the sandwich shop and market I found on Google Maps. It's perfectly Connecticut, with pale blue clapboard and bright red benches. While Lewis waits in the car, I pick up two BLTs, and then we head back in the direction of the beach.

We follow the grassy drive past trees and into the park-ing lot. When we get out, wind buffeting our faces, the water is right in front of us. The grass gives way to sand in a gentle slope down to the shore.

I watch the waves roll in. It's different from the other times I've visited the beach, which were in the wrong con-texts for reflection or concentration. Outings with friends, full of plans and preparations and constant conversation. Field trips for state geography units in school. Chaperoning a kindergarten camp for my community service requirement in health class freshman year. They weren't exactly restful ex-periences. The beach in winter is nothing like it is in warmer temperatures, either. For one thing, I don't have to apply SPF 60 every half hour—a necessity for gingers in summer. With the weather frigid and the sand wet, there's no onslaught of tourists to break the quiet with rattling beach chairs and the commotion of water games.

The empty landscape calls to mind hundreds of words. *Cinereous.* The whitened gray of the clouds over the water. *Clement.* The mild temperature on the pristine sand. *Susurrus.* The whisper of the wind and waves.

Yet none of them quite do this place justice. Words in isolation often don't. It's part of why I want to know every one of them I possibly can. It's in their combinations that words find their worth. If I'm going to use them to capture the world the way I want, I have to know how to reach for every possible permutation.

Lewis walks up next to me. "Wow," he says. "Right?"

Simple words work too sometimes.

"Yeah," I reply.

We head onto the sand and unwrap our sandwiches, eating in silence near the waterline. Watching the waves, I feel unexpectedly free. It takes me a few minutes to recognize the feeling, or really, the *not*-feeling. The not-worrying, the jarring release of being far from home and yet not feeling Mom's health hanging over me. Not that the worry is distant. I just know it'll be there when I return home in a few days, and I'm okay with permitting myself this hour on the beach. This respite.

The clouds shift. There's a moment where the sun streams

through over the water, shedding gold streaks onto the shore.

I pull out my phone. I haven't texted Juniper since we discussed UConn yesterday. Of course, she hasn't texted me, either, which is a detail I decide to ignore. I've tried hard today to be cool, to not pester her. But it wouldn't be overeager if I texted her now, I rationalize. I send her a picture of the glittering waves, then return my phone to my pocket, pretending I'm not hoping she'll reply.

It's a now-recognizable thrill when my phone vibrates in minutes. I read the message immediately.

That wouldn't happen to be on
the way to New York, would it?

While I reply, I notice Lewis eyeing me. I ignore him.

This IS on the way to New York. (Does
this mean you're coming to New York?)

Indeed it does.

Okay, so after taking in that view,
you still want to spend the next four
years right where you grew up?

I don't know why she dropped the conversation yesterday. She's evidently willing to have this one. Whatever is different in her day or her outlook on me, I definitely won't question it.

Yeah. I do.

If circumstances were different, though.
Would you want to leave home?

I face the water, weighing her question. It's a question I've told myself time and time again wasn't important, one I've avoided while assuring myself college isn't everything. Talking to Juniper, I'm forced to wonder if that wasn't just a lie I told myself to make my decision easier.

It's close to impossible to imagine my life without my mom's impending Alzheimer's. Nevertheless, I try. I try to remove every trace from the image in my head of the next four years, every visit to her doctor, every question of her care. It's not my life. It's foreign, unrecognizable.

I'm not sure.

What about you? What's so horrible about home that you're desperate to leave?

Nothing's horrible. I just want the freedom to be my own person, to try new things and figure out what I want. You know?

I don't.

Yeah.

Definitely.

Well, assuming you don't live in New Hampshire, I'm wondering if you've

considered the venerable institution
of Dartmouth College. It's only an
hour from my hometown. . . .

Juniper's typing bubble appears before I have the opportunity to doubt the forwardness of the question.

HA.

It's a possibility. . . . I'll
apply if you will.

It's honestly the closest I've come to entirely reconsidering my college plans. I reply embarrassingly quickly.

DONE.

I rolled my eyes so hard, I think
I strained something. You're
kind of impossible.

I grin reading her text. Lewis claps me on the back. "You ready to go?" he asks. I nod and stand up, swiping the sand from my jeans. While we walk to the car, I reply to Juniper.

You're not the first
person to tell me that.

JUNIPER

FITZ AND I are friends. *Just* friends. When he texted me today, I decided in a rush of wonderful clarity I wouldn't be giving up on Matt if I were to text a *friend*. I would be lying to myself if I said the decision had nothing to do with my conversation with Tía in the middle of the night. Her implication I would have no one to call, no one who would be there if I needed someone when I'm in the world on my own, might have kindled my desire to have one more friend.

We drove into New Haven that morning, Matt leaving me to my Yale tour while he explored the city. Wanting a break from the constant college touring, he convinced me to spend the rest of the day in Westport, which was only forty minutes away. He'd read it was one of the wealthiest towns in the country and decided he had to see for himself. We wandered the pristine sidewalks and around the perfectly trimmed hedges, imagining ourselves living together in each of the palatial houses, me a Pritzker Prize winner and him the owner of the Red Sox.

While we stopped for coffee and sweet potato scones, my

dad called to fill me in on the state of affairs at home. Tía is livid I hung up her, obviously. Mom found Marisa at Steve's house, and she's been grounded for the rest of winter break. Dad recommended I enjoy my trip and then "put together a respectful, even if fake, apology to Tía" when I get home. I told him I'd think about it.

I did text Marisa, hoping she would understand why I had to violate the sacred sibling code and tell on her, but she ignored me. Usually when Marisa and I fight, I can expect angry emoji responses to my olive branches—flames, puking faces, skulls, or the dreaded frowning cat. But today, nothing.

I'm trying not to think about it. I know I did the right thing. For now, I'm allowed to focus on this trip. But no matter how much I tell myself to ignore the conflicts waiting for me at home, I can't. Not completely. It's a layer of frost on my window, making the world look cracked and gray.

Texting Fitz is the best distraction I've found.

We leave Westport in the evening. With night falling, in the gridlocked expanse of highway leading into New York City, we continue messaging. He tries to convince me to apply to Dartmouth, and then the conversation threads through everything, like the Hudson River out the window on its way to the sea.

> I used to live in NYC, you
> know. Well, Brooklyn.

Why did you move? (Where
did you move btw?)

My grandmother was sick. We moved
to Springfield, Massachusetts, to
help her run the family restaurant.

How about you? Have you lived
in New Hampshire your whole life?

Yeah. Tilton to be exact. I've stayed
with my dad in Canada a couple
times, though. He lives in Toronto.

✳ ✳ ✳

I couldn't get a pic fast enough,
but I swear I just passed a billboard
for the eyes of T. J. Eckleburg.

. . . the eyes of who?

From The Great Gatsby!!
The optometrist's billboard!

I wouldn't know. I haven't read it.

I'm sorry, FITZGERALD. You're named
after the author and you haven't
read The Great Gatsby?

✳ ✳ ✳

You're into architecture, right?
Are you applying to the schools
with the best architecture programs?

Why do you know I'm interested
in architecture?

You mentioned it in the BU
information session, remember?

Of course I remember. But I'm
the one with the good memory.

What's your excuse, Fitzgerald?

✳ ✳ ✳

If you love words, are you a writer?
I bet you'd be great at poetry.
You have poet face.

Poet face?

. . . Is that an insult?

✳ ✳ ✳

I hope New York's worth it.
If I weren't a homebody already,
this traffic would do the trick.

It's worth it, I promise.

And I think you'd leave New
Hampshire for the right girl.

Is she asking?

IMPOSSIBLE, I say.

Fitz texts me a photo of himself looking disgusted by the guy in the driver's seat, who has one hand on the wheel while gnawing determinedly on a piece of jerky. I recognize the tall, angular-featured Indian boy. Matt played beer pong with him in the basement of the Brown fraternity.

Lewis is currently eating python
jerky. Please send help.

Wait, that's your brother?

I know, I hardly believe it myself.
He also bought alligator.

Well, yeah, and ... you know,
you look nothing alike.

Oh, did I not mention
we're adopted?

＊ ＊ ＊

Here's my favorite. Hiraeth.

What's it mean?

Homesickness for a home to which
you can never return or that never was.

JUNIPER

I'M THOROUGHLY EXHAUSTED when we reach New York City. It's nearly eight, the daylight long gone. We check into the hotel our parents put into our itinerary, one of the nondescript kinds that host new rotations of out-of-town businessmen and convention-goers every weekend. Of course, we only check in for one room. I canceled the other a couple of days ago when I restructured all our hotel plans.

I text my mom we got into the city okay, and she replies immediately with the thumbs-up emoji. As we pass used room service trays on the beige carpet, I trudge behind Matt to the elevator and into the hallway. He's quiet, and I wonder what he's thinking or if he's only tired.

When he unlocks the door, I hardly look at the room. In this moment, the only thing I care about is the bed. I collapse onto the comforter, the over-washed threads scratching my face. The miles we walked in Westport, the two hours of traffic, and the uneven night of sleep are catching up to me.

"I think I've figured out how to take the subway to Justin's place so we don't have to deal with New York traffic or pay for a cab," Matt says, letting the door swing shut behind him.

I crack open an eye. Matt drops his duffel bag and checks something on his phone without removing his jacket or scarf. Justin is another former teammate of Matt's who's now at NYU. He invited us over to a party tonight. When Matt mentioned it a week ago, I said it sounded like fun. But that was before the party at Brown, before I decided I didn't want to waste time on this trip doing what we could do at home in a week.

"I'm beat," I say, dragging myself up to sit on the edge of the bed. "How about we walk somewhere for pizza, take in a bit of the city, and then call it a night?"

Matt frowns. "We promised Justin we'd go."

"Yeah, but I'm sure he'd understand if you told him we're exhausted."

"You're too exhausted to go to our friend's party but you want to walk around the city?" Matt's eyes flash. He's never been quick to anger. In the history of our relationship, I've only seen him upset a handful of times, and it was never with me. Not even when I overslept and was an hour late to the pancake breakfast he made me, or the time I drank too much and threw up on his favorite shoes. Matt is imperturbable. I don't quite know how to contend with the sudden resentment in his gaze.

"I guess I'd rather spend the energy I do have out in the city," I say.

"Fine. Go ahead. I'll go to Justin's on my own." Matt's tone is utterly unlike him. Cold. Spiteful.

He turns for the door, and my temper ignites. "Seriously? You're mad at me because I don't want to go to a dumb party right now?"

"No. Why would I be mad about that?" he returns.

I know he's being sarcastic, but I ignore him. First Marisa and Tía, and now this? I'm done holding my tongue. "We can hang out with Justin tomorrow after the Columbia tour. If we have time," I add. "I want to make sure we see the city, too."

Matt throws his arms up. "Sure. Whatever fits into your schedule, Juniper."

The hardness of his voice wakes me up completely. This is bigger than Justin's party, and I don't know why.

"What's that supposed to mean?" I ask.

Matt sighs, and the sound is a gust of cold wind on my neck, sending chills tingling down my arms. "It means everything is about *your* dreams, *your* schedules. These are all your colleges we're visiting."

I stand, indignant. "That's not true," I protest.

"Fine. The majority are," he fires back. "You think *I* have a shot of getting in to Brown or Columbia or Georgetown?"

"You could try—"

"You don't understand," he says, a new desperation awakening in his voice under the anger. He tears off his scarf and flings his coat on the dresser. "I don't *want* to try. I don't want to go to those schools. I want to go to a school with good parties and good sports. I want to tailgate with my friends before football games. I want to meet people in my classes who care about the things I care about. I want to have enough free time to visit you. But you don't respect what other people want unless it lines up with your priorities."

"I never said you couldn't go to a school like that," I argue, my face heating. It's unbelievable. I tried countless times to get him to open up about what kind of future he wants, to describe to me his hopes and his horizons. "I asked you if you wanted to come on this trip, and you told me you did. If you had a problem with the itinerary, if you wanted to add schools, you should've said something. You should've told me what you wanted out of college. But you didn't. You didn't give me the chance to *respect your priorities*."

Matt's eyes narrow. "Right," he says, clipping the word. "It's all my fault."

"Fault?" I repeat. I can feel the argument spinning out of control, car wheels skidding on black ice. "I don't even understand what the problem is. You've known since the day we started dating that my dream was one of these schools. Remember? We talked about it on our second date when we walked to the bookstore after dinner and I found that college guide—"

"Don't do that," he cuts me off. "Don't use your memory against me like ammunition. I can't compete."

"It's not ammunition. It's who I am," I reply, stung. I take a breath, hoping to slow my racing heart. Matt's chest is heaving too, and I want nothing more than to find our way back to an hour ago. "Look," I say finally. "I just meant I've never made my aspirations a secret. I would hope that you, my *boyfriend*, would know how important college is to me." My vision blurs, and a tear slips down my cheek. I wipe my eyes hurriedly, not entirely knowing why I'm crying. I drop my gaze to the floor.

It's a long moment before Matt replies. When he does, his voice is different.

"You're right," he says softly. "You didn't mislead me about anything. I've known all along what you wanted. I just—" His voice breaks, and I look up to find he's crying. He thumbs away his tears, but they keep coming.

It's heartbreaking, jarring and wrong, watching Matt cry. Tall, broad-shouldered Matt. Compassionate Matt. Life-of-the-party Matt. His shoulders quake, and the thought crashes through me, consuming everything, *there is nothing that hurts worse than this.* Than the person you love falling to pieces in front of you.

"I didn't know what it would feel like," he continues. "Seeing you tour these schools, knowing you're looking forward to a future that could be far from me. You have one foot out the door. It's like what we have . . ." He pauses, as if he's fighting the pain of what he's going to say next. "What we *had* doesn't even matter."

I cross the room. Taking his hands, I look up into his red-rimmed eyes. "It matters," I say with the force of a year of weekend coffees and study dates, good-morning texts and kisses good night. "It's always mattered."

I hiccup on the final word, and with a twisting breath I realize how hard I'm crying. There's finality in my sobs now, the unstoppable momentum of this horrible conversation collapsing into its inescapable end.

Matt wraps me in his arms, and I cry onto his shoulder— his achingly familiar shoulder. It makes everything worse and yet is the only comfort I could want right now.

"We don't want the same things, do we?" he asks finally.

I don't answer. I don't know how to answer. I don't know

how to do this. I'm holding the map and unable to find the destination. The helplessness overwhelms me, the impossible reality of this moment.

For the first time, I want to put off the future. I want to stay in the present. I want Matt's arms around me, his heart beating against mine. If I don't think about tomorrow, then right now, with him, is enough. But his question hangs in the air perilously, waiting to crash down on us.

"We don't," I say when I can't hold on to the moment any longer.

He hugs me tighter, and I bunch my hands in his shirt, knowing this is it. We both know. There are no dramatic declarations. No *I'm breaking up with you* or *we're over* or *I don't love you anymore*. We hold each other, and it's the end of us.

"We could stay together until graduation," I suggest weakly. We had plans for the rest of this year, plans I've daydreamed of and yearned for. Right now, they're blurring out of focus, fading fast enough to frighten me. There was Valentine's Day, prom, the senior trip to Lake Placid. I even have his Christmas gift wrapped and hidden in my closet—a *Lord of the Rings* DVD box set.

Then there are the bigger plans. The trip we talked about taking to Ireland when we had enough money, the first apartment we'd rent together, what type of dog we'd adopt.

We'll never have those plans, but we could have this year.

He steps out of my arms. "You don't want that," he says. I begin to protest, but he continues. "You're not the kind of girl who holds on to things that are already over. You'll want to face tomorrow with a fresh start, ready for something new."

I close my mouth. He's right. It hurts how right he is, how well he knows me.

I don't deny it. "I want you to have your perfect college experience," I say instead. He was right. I could have tried harder to understand what he wanted. It's too painful to admit, the thought tightening my throat. Between him and Fitz, I guess understanding other people's priorities is something I'm working on. "I know you'll find the girlfriend who wants to go to parties with you," I go on, "who will stand at your side for everything that's exciting to you." I meet his eyes, finding his expression slightly disbelieving. I know the feeling. A year together, and it ends in a handful of minutes in a New York hotel room. "I'm just not her."

"And I'm not the guy who's going to take on the world with you," he says. His tears have subsided, leaving his face wrecked.

"If it's worth anything, I really wanted you to be."

He smiles genuinely, sweet and sad. "Yeah, it's worth something," he says. "You know, I still think you're the most beautiful girl I've ever seen, and smarter than everyone I know."

Then why haven't you kissed me yet? It's my line. It's what I replied the day we started dating. Except the scene's over. The memory of Matt, confident and cheeky, walking up to me in the school hallway, draws new tears into my eyes. I divert my gaze, not wanting this to feel even worse.

Matt grabs his bag and jacket from beside the bed, then returns to the doorway. "I'll stay with Justin tonight," he says gently, and I catch myself loving him for not dragging out the breakup. Which is such a wrong, confusing thing to love him for that I nearly break down right then. "In the morning I'll take the bus home," he continues.

I look up. "You don't have to," I say. "I'll drive you. Really."

But Matt shakes his head. "No," he replies with intensity I didn't expect. His eyes meet mine. While they're watery, they've regained the clarity of purpose I remember from batting practices and the moments before kisses and endless— except, I guess, not endless—conversations.

I'll probably remember those moments, his eyes, forever.

"Have your trip," he tells me. "Have everything, Juniper."

I open my mouth, but nothing comes out. I'm not used to not knowing what to say, to fumbling for the right words. In student government speeches or confrontations with Tía, they come easily. But what could I possibly say right now? "Thank you"? "Okay"? "What if this is the happiest thing I ever have"?

With one final smile, tears drying on his face, Matt walks out. He closes the door softly behind him.

FITZ

I DON'T KNOW how to read this girl. Or possibly girls in general. But right now, Juniper's the riddle. Yesterday she texts me for hours while we're on the road, exchanging favorite words and cities, swapping family stories and photos of the highway. Today, nothing. Well, not nothing—she replies to my texts. But I notice long pauses in between her replies, no punctuation, and none of the ebullience or humor of our conversation yesterday.

I know I'm reading into it, and I kick myself for playing into introspective-hipster-boy tropes. Teenage ginger Joseph Gordon-Levitt decoding the texts of Zooey Deschanel or Zoey Deutch or other Zoeys while wandering New York City. Find me a Joy Division T-shirt and fancy coffee, and I'm ready for my close-up.

I really could go for a good coffee, though.

I'm on my own while Lewis interviews for one of the finance jobs he hopes will keep him from Tilton, New Hampshire. Five hours of interviews for Bright Partners, one of the top VCs in the country, he told me in the hotel this morning, though really it was more like a monologue to himself in the mirror. I thought I caught uncharacteristic nervousness in the waver of his voice. He told me he'd text me for dinner, and emptily I wished him luck. Despite the friendlier moments we've had on this trip, I still don't love the idea of him taking a job in New York.

I have no college tours today while Lewis interviews. Though I could have made up yesterday's NYU visit, I found myself interested in the city instead. I decided to walk downtown on Broadway, which is when I began texting Juniper.

It's not worth speculating why her replies have changed, I remind myself. Crossing from street corner to corner in packs of pedestrians, it dawns on me that I'm halfway through this trip. In just five days, I'm returning to New Hampshire, to home-cooked meals and familiar friends and the unchanging prospect of SNHU. Those things are your future, I find myself repeating. They're important.

Because, I guess, part of me *does* want more. More new cities. More time with a hypothetical girl who could potentially be interested in architecture and possibly, theoretically want to live "everywhere."

It's better I don't turn this funny light-speed friendship with Juniper into something more. We're inchoate. Yet unformed and undefined due to newness. It would only hurt worse when I have to return to my life of waiting for the inevitable. Because I *do* have to return.

It's why I could muster only a hollow "good luck" to Lewis. It won't be him home with Mom. It'll be me.

I know I could have years until Mom declines. I *could* commit to other schools in other cities. Except I won't do what

Mom did. I won't go to some other school and then withdraw when her condition worsens. I won't fall in love with a college or city and have to leave. It's the same with Juniper. It's better in the long run if things don't progress.

Whatever's out there, I'm certain of one thing. I would rather never know than force myself to forget.

It's within my rights to be frustrated that I'm living like this, always focused on my mom's health, every decision hinging on her. This isn't the first time it's pissed me off, of course. But I guess at some point over the years, I realized if I bothered to resent this reality every single day, I'd burn out. It would be equivalent to resenting the sun for rising and setting. This—the inevitability of me losing some years to responsibilities I'm too young for—won't change.

I don't think Mom fully understands how entirely I've structured my life around her well-being. That's fine with me. It's not her fault, and it's the one thing I have the power to keep her from worrying about.

Resolute, I walk down Broadway, immersing myself in the details. They're keepsakes. The rare winter sun remediates the chilly weather, lighting the cloud cover blindingly white. I enjoy the crisp warmth on my face. Trash overflows from curbside cans and dumpsters in front of buildings. It's not gross, though. It's this bold, in-your-face reminder of the towering number of human lives on top of each other in this endless city.

It's nothing like home. It's the exact *opposite*, in fact. I cross Fourteenth Street in front of Union Square Park, somewhat uncomprehending of the momentum, the sheer concentration of people heading purposefully in every direction. The hectic cacophony of car horns, cyclists whizzing past me, and people in suits talking into headsets. I can't help imagining future Lewis among them. It's dizzying, in a good way. The propulsive energy pulls me in.

I recognize the feeling. Not from this city. From conversations. From debating college over cannoli. From discussing if a boy who dreads the future could become friends with a girl racing for it.

Juniper told me she lived in New York City when she was younger. It figures. She has the restlessness of this place, the inertia. I walk the brick pathway into Union Square, picturing her here, on the lawns hemmed in by wrought-iron fences and perusing the crowded farmers' market on the perimeter.

There's nothing wrong with thinking about her in New York, I tell myself. It's not the same as hoping I'll start something with her I could never finish. It's just meaningless wonderings.

I walk without purpose or destination for I don't know how long. When I pause for a second to text my mom, I notice I'm in front of a row of red-and-white carts lining the sidewalk, filled with books. Their quantity is like everything in this city—enormous. The edges of the carts, and the red awning of the building behind them, read STRAND BOOKSTORE in white lettering. 18 MILES OF BOOKS.

Curious, I head inside. I have an enduring love of bookstores from when Mom would take Lewis and me when we were kids. I could honestly devote hours to browsing the collection, crashing in the comfy chairs with the first chapters of whatever intrigues me, and of course, breathing in the heady scent of new pages.

I bet Juniper likes bookstores, I think, then immediately try to un-think. I can't go through my day comparing everything to what Juniper I-don't-even-know-her-last-name likes or dislikes.

For a bookstore fetishist, the Strand doesn't disappoint. The stairway in the center faces tables of new releases and bookshelf upon bookshelf. There are notebooks and literary socks, bookish tote bags and T-shirts. Everything is identified in bold red-and-white signs, with "staff pick" cards on the shelves and clever thematic displays. The smell is *exactly* right.

I send my mom a picture and head for the fiction and literature section, noticing familiar editions from my mom's own bookshelves. The Modern Library edition of *Ethan Frome*, the Norton Critical Edition of *The Adventures of Huckleberry Finn*, the Oxford World's Classics edition of *The Jungle*. I'm really glad Mom didn't name me Upton. I pause in the *F* names, finding *The Great Gatsby* under the marginally better name she did choose for me. My mom's shelves hold multiple editions, one recent and two from her PhD program because her notes in each got too numerous and crowded to decipher.

I don't know this edition, though. A Penguin Modern Classic. It's beautiful, with gold designs and lettering on the hardcover's pristine white jacket.

I decide I'll buy it. It'll thrill her even when she no longer remembers the words. Opening the cover, I find the first line, the one I've heard her repeat countless times under her breath and in the SNHU lectures I'd visit every now and then—even to me or Lewis without context or provocation like she just loved the sound out loud. *In my younger and more vulnerable years my father gave me some advice that I've been turning over in my mind ever since.*

Juniper incredulously asked me how I'd never read the book that inspired my name, and I dodged the question. The truth is, I've thought about reading it often. My mother wrote her dissertation on *The Great Gatsby*. She references it constantly. Besides, it's not like I don't enjoy classic literature. I do. I've read nearly all of her recommendations.

Except this one. The biggest one.

I guess part of me was holding on to it like it could be some safeguard from her disease. How could my mother really get sick, how could she forget her years spent ruminating on F. Scott Fitzgerald's words before I'd had the chance to discuss *Gatsby* with her?

It's stupid. Nothing is going to stop my mom's illness—not this week pretending I could have a different life, not enrolling in a distant school, and definitely not *not* reading *The Great Gatsby*. She will get Alzheimer's, and I will be home for it. The end.

I resume reading the first page. Then the next and the next. Before I know it, I'm at the register, then walking out of the store, my finger holding my page.

I return to Union Square Park. The first free bench I find, I sit and open the book.

After years of waiting and avoiding, I read without intention of stopping, the constant motion of the city continuing around me.

JUNIPER

I LET THREE alarms go by before I decide to wake up.

When the first went off at seven this morning, I rolled over to jostle Matt awake—he's never been good at getting up to an alarm. But when my arm hit his empty pillow, I remembered last night and the reality that I'd never wake up next to Matt again. He was gone, and I was supposed to return to my tour without skipping a step. There were a couple of hours before my Columbia information session, enough time to shower, find breakfast, and navigate the subway to campus.

I got up to draw the curtains and returned to bed.

The thought of continuing the trip without Matt, driving in my empty car to D.C. and then Charlottesville, was too huge an undertaking. Climbing Everest in a snowstorm.

It's not that I won't do it. I just need time. I need to let my heart finish breaking.

Around ten, I admit I'm too hungry to stay in bed. There's no way to make the Columbia tour. Part of me is pissed at myself for sleeping through it, for missing the chance to see a school because of a boy. But the other part of me, the bruised part that can still smell Matt on my shirt, is glad. Ending our relationship deserves a moment of pause. A moment to recognize there will be no more of Matt's easy smiles at my locker, no more daydreams of our future together, no more hurried kisses in his car five minutes before curfew.

It hurts, and I let it. It hurts every time I think of what Matt and I used to have. The past versions of ourselves who worked perfectly together in ways we don't now. It's the undeniable truth, and it's awful, and it recedes into healing with every passing hour.

I haul myself into the shower, hardly feeling the warm water against my skin.

Pulling on my parka, I head downstairs, ferociously blocking out the thought that the last time I walked down this hallway, I was following Matt. It's funny how places can feel completely different depending on who you're with, or who you're not.

Downstairs, I quickly find a hole-in-the-wall bagel shop, the line spilling onto the sidewalk. It moves quickly enough I'm not convinced there isn't magic involved, and in ten head-spinning minutes I'm standing on the street corner again holding my everything bagel with cream cheese.

I gaze up.

The Chrysler Building soars into the sky in front of me. I study the iconic spire, the way the curves cascade unconventionally into the needle point. Facts explode in my head. The building was the tallest in the world for eleven months in 1931, until the Empire State Building was finished. The thirty-first floor displays replicas of the 1929 Chrysler hood ornament. With the details comes the realization *I'm in New York City.*

I'm in one of the greatest cities in the country for the thing I love. The thing I want to devote my entire academic and professional life to. I grew up here, but I was too young to understand or appreciate the architecture of New York the way I do now. I resolve right here, with the curb under my feet and the titanic towers over my head, to throw myself into an architectural tour of the city. Even though I skipped Columbia, I won't waste today. I'll let my dreams of the future heal the wounds of the past.

It takes me twenty minutes to compile my itinerary for the day. I pick five buildings spread across Manhattan along Fifth Avenue. The architectural greatest hits of the city, from historic to modern, Gothic to art deco.

I begin with the Flatiron Building. I know the history of the wedge-shaped structure. I can summon a perfect image of it in my mind's eye. The limestone changing to terra-cotta as the building rises. The rounded corner at the peak of the triangle. It's a perfect medley of styles from antiquity to the Renaissance Revival.

In person, it's more than that.

The point of the building rises between the streets like the prow of a ship cutting through the sea, the entire city expanding behind its hull. Taxis glide along its smooth sides like waves. In a city of colossal skyscrapers and more than eight million people, the Flatiron still manages to command attention.

I stand on the sidewalk for several minutes, admiring the shadows cast by the skyline against its windowed walls. No wonder the surrounding neighborhood took the building's name. The Flatiron District—a place of people and businesses defined by a single structure. Not everyone understands the influence of architecture. But here, under this twenty-two-story sentinel, it's undeniable.

I soak up the view until the alarm I programmed into my phone to keep me on my itinerary rings in my hand. It's not a long walk to my next stop—the Empire State Building.

I'm reaching the skyscraper when my phone vibrates once more. It's not my alarm this time, though. It's Fitz.

Is New York everything you remembered?

I stare at his name on the phone, at the trail of our previous messages leading down the screen. Talking with him was effortless yesterday. I have a feeling I could fall back into those conversations today without thinking. I could let Fitz into my heartache. He'd probably have the perfect word to describe it. He'd hand me some centuries-old adjective that wraps up the cyclone of emotions in my heart in a way that makes them understandable and easier to bear.

It's unusual, his thing with words, but not in a bad way. Knowing the repertoire he has at his disposal gives everything he says to me a deliberateness it's difficult to find in casual conversation. He speaks to me like he's reading dialogue from a novel, each word chosen with care and precision. The effect is . . . disarming.

We're in the same city today. I could find him, laugh at

his jokes—be disarmed. He'd make me feel better. Less alone.

But I want to feel alone right now. To stand with nothing but my dreams at my side, in the shadows of buildings that have towered over people just like me and people completely unlike me. The Empire State Building reaches higher than everything around it, but it doesn't appear lonely.

I reply, knowing he'll pick up on my terseness and not minding.

> Yeah. It is. Full schedule today.

Being alone and without Matt—or Fitz—I feel more keenly the non-interruption of my family. Normally, they'd be bombarding my phone with texts. I know Tía's resentful I hung up on her. My dad's working today. My mom's probably still dealing with the fallout from Marisa's night out. The quiet is weird, and I have to admit, a little unpleasant. Not that I don't appreciate the peace. I'm just unexpectedly aware of it.

I'm particularly aware I haven't talked to Marisa in days. Impulsively, I take a picture of the Empire State Building, even though I can't fit the entire structure in the frame, and pull a moment from my head into a message.

> Remember when Mom took us here when you were three? You were NOT into it.

I don't get a response.

I continue on from the Empire State Building, covering this city properly explored on foot. Every crossing, every hot-dog cart, every flock of pigeons pecking crumbs from sidewalk corners resonates with what I remember from when I was younger. The energy of the city is unforgettable, not only in my recollections, but in the instinctual rhythm I feel walking the curbs and corners among inescapable crowds.

Rockefeller Center is next on my itinerary. Couples and children crowd the ice rink in front of the iconic Prometheus sculpture. The enormous Christmas tree points toward the sky, looming over the pedestrians like an emperor over his subjects, bedecked in fineries of multicolored lights and a massive shining star.

On the road, it's easy to forget Christmas is only a week and a half away. In my house, the days before Christmas come with constant competing family obligations and traditions. While I'm sad not to be home for Callie's cookie-decorating party, I don't regret skipping some of the chaos of the holiday. I'll have nearly a week once I return to host cousins and aunts and uncles, to help Tía dig out Christmas dinner recipes, to be a Ramírez for a holiday synonymous in our house with family.

Right now, I'm on my own, exploring my old city with new eyes. It's been ten years since we moved to Springfield, and I'll be back there before long. I circumvent the rink and head to the foot of the Rockefeller, where I gaze upward, examining the façade's perfect intricacy.

I snap a selfie with Prometheus in the background and send it to Marisa.

Your first crush.

He really was. It was honestly adorable when she announced he was her husband. She was six.

I'm undeterred when there's no reply. I decide I'll text her with every new building until I wear her down.

I pause in front of the ice rink. I swear I fall in love with art deco every time I see design like this. It's the very idea of the style, the philosophy—art deco is devoted to *progress*, to relentlessly emulating every future its creators could envision. To imagining tomorrow into today.

Fitz continues texting me. The boy is sensitive, I'll give him that. He gives me time in between replies, he jokes gently and not often, and he asks me what I'm doing without pressing me for details on the rest of my itinerary this week. He doesn't ask what's wrong, which I appreciate indescribably. He's definitely intelligent enough to know I'm not acting totally normal, yet he apparently understands that getting me to divulge the details will do more harm than good. I feel myself opening up during these off-and-on conversations, describing my day and hearing what he's doing with his.

I visit St. Patrick's Cathedral, its skeletal stone in imposing defiance of the silver and steel surrounding it, where I send Marisa a reminder of the day she threw a tantrum because Dad wouldn't let her bring ice cream into the church. When my stomach growls, I grab a quick lunch from a nearby deli. Finally, I head to the Guggenheim.

It's a long walk, and I've unzipped my parka and taken off my scarf by the time I reach the museum. At first, I can't tell if I like Frank Lloyd Wright's pairing of unconventional spirals and sharp angles, but the more I walk around the building, the more I appreciate it. Wright was a master of architecture emerging organically and harmoniously from its surroundings. The Guggenheim is a perfect example. The concrete walls flow up from the sidewalk into shapes reminiscent of the modern art the museum was designed to house.

In front, I find a sign advertising a special Kandinsky exhibit. I take a photo for Marisa, who famously detests art museums. She says they're just excuses for people to pretend they're cultured.

I pay the eighteen-dollar student rate and enter the museum. While I'm wandering up the curved walkways, my phone buzzes with a text. I assume it's Fitz, who hasn't replied to me in an hour. Admittedly, I'm curious about whatever is distracting him. But when I unlock my phone, I find a text from Marisa.

Do you know how much of a
dork you are?

I smile, stopping to lean against the railing overlooking the interior.

I've never claimed otherwise.

I'm still mad at you for
getting me grounded.

She follows up the message with a string of emojis—the frowning cat—and I know her anger is fading.

Be mad at yourself. You
know I didn't have a choice.

She replies immediately with a new row of emojis. Flames and the purple devil face.

I wait. I have a pretty good feeling the conversation's not over, and I'm not surprised when the typing bubble pops up. It disappears, and I gaze over the railing into the museum while tourists examine the artwork opposite me. The typing bubble reappears, and finally my phone vibrates.

How's your trip?

The question is whiplash. I'm immediately grateful to my sister for her effortless reconciliation. The very next instant comes the nasty yank of remembering she doesn't know Matt and I broke up. I can't tell her, either. I know what would happen if I did. The news would reach my parents, who would definitely try to convince me to come home, and then Tía.

Tía, who would turn my heartache into a tactic. Who would feed my loneliness to the arguments never far from her reach. Who would hint and imply and eventually remind me outright I wouldn't be hurting on my own if I were home in the comfort of my family. To her, my breakup would just be proof that I'm not mature, that I still need my family.

I won't give her the chance.

Really amazing. You'd love the campuses.

Don't worry, I'll invite you to visit me next year.

I hate the forced cheeriness of my replies. This is the one

time I don't want to talk about college. I want to talk about my boyfriend—*ex*-boyfriend. Instead, I have to pretend everything is wonderful and I'm enjoying my trip exactly the way I'd planned.

I could really use sisterly commiseration right now, which is unlike me. We've never been the type of siblings who braid each other's hair, who share every secret and every detail of our lives. But this is one time it'd be nice to open up to her. The fact that I can't doesn't just frustrate me. It frightens me.

Because I'm beginning to recognize this feeling. I don't want this to be the rest of my relationship with my family, this dynamic of their constricting tendencies forcing me to push and push until I no longer remember wanting to be close to them. I don't want to not reach out to my sister when I need her. Or dread coming home from school on holidays because of the lectures and judgment I know will be waiting. And I don't want to move far from home and never return, not even when I get married, not even when I have kids, not until it's one of my own parents who is ill or dying.

I explore the museum for half an hour, but my heart's not in it. As I walk out the front I check my phone, hoping for a text from Fitz. I can't confide in my sister, but there are eight million people in this city. It's nice to know I could confide in one of them.

FITZ

OKAY, I UNDERSTAND why my mom loves this book.

I lift my head from the final page, gazing out the window of the café where I holed up when the temperature dropped in the park. I spent the remainder of the day reading, and the sun is lower in the sky. The streets glow with golden light breaking through the buildings. Walking out into the park, I rub my hands in front of my face while I watch the passersby, *The Great Gatsby*'s final words echoing in my head.

So we beat on, boats against the current, borne back ceaselessly into the past. My chest loosened when I read them. I sat up straighter, feeling lightened.

I don't fully understand the effect the ending has on me. Hoping to figure the question out, I walk through the park, holding my trusted companion *Gatsby* to my side. I pass couples hand in hand and evening dog walks, circling the park three times before I've organized my thoughts.

Gatsby spent his entire life trying to recapture the past. He failed. Time worked against him like it does everyone. Everything he accomplished, every piece of his meticulous planning, was in the pursuit of something already behind him, something receding in a rearview mirror he mistook for a windshield. And for what? Gatsby lived a half-life, the warped reflection of human existence.

I won't repeat his mistake.

I lift my head to the road ahead and pull out my phone.

JUNIPER

FOR A MOMENT, I wonder if I've wandered into a fairy tale. Except not one of the fairy tales Mom would read to me and Marisa and Callie from her hardcover anthology with the pastel-painted cover, with stories of princesses and witches and occasionally dragons. No, this is the kind of fairy tale Juniper Ramírez would live, if magic whisked her from the college tour she was enjoying in the present day and transported her to this incredible, impossible wonderland between buildings.

I've just come up the grimy bolted-metal stairs from street level. What spreads out in front of me is a walkway—or park—or both. Sheets of rough concrete stretch in either direction, with smaller pavement pathways and wooden decks interspersed. Plants entwine the paths, the trees brittle and the bushes brushed with snow. The walkway hangs high over the streets, cutting through the skyscrapers rising up on both sides.

The High Line, Fitz called this place. When he texted with nothing but an invitation—no dictionary words, no college questions—I didn't recognize the name. I promptly found the place on my phone and hopped on the subway.

I stare over the edge, watching the churn of cars below and the colors of the sunset. Turning back, I imagine the High Line in spring and summer, the foliage green, the trees waving in the breeze like guests enjoying a party to which they have no idea they weren't invited.

I'm envisioning the vivid vein this place would cut through the city when Fitz walks up the stairs. His eyes meet mine, and he smiles.

The effect is instantaneous. I notice he's different, somehow. There's an easiness to his motion, or even his momentum, like he's headed in a new direction. I haven't known Fitz for long, but he's definitely never had *momentum*. He walks over while I take in the unusual freedom to him.

"Thanks for meeting me," he says.

It strikes me as a funny expression. Thanks for meeting me on the High Line tonight? Or, thanks for meeting me for the first time days ago? For unconsciously organizing your life to bump into mine?

I smile back softly, wanting to thank him for meeting me too, though I know it's not the meaning he intends. He confuses me. Or, rather, the feeling I get when I'm with him confuses me, especially now. The undeniable tug of my heart toward him is wrapped up in the pain of breaking up with Matt. I don't know what's genuine connection and what's simply the shock of being without the person I expected to be with. I do know his invitation lit up my phone right when

I needed someone to talk to and someplace to go besides my empty hotel room.

"This place is unbelievable," I say finally, the one non-confusing thing I can get out. "I didn't even know it existed."

"I thought you'd like it." He nods in the direction of the path, and we walk. We enter a stretch of thin-limbed trees, branches dusted with snow, the city on one side and the river on the other. It's perfect, dreamlike, this out-of-context winter wonderland. "I sort of had an epiphany today."

I watch his profile out of the corner of my eye. With the wind blowing in our faces, his hair is swept back on his forehead. His gaze bounces around like he's taking in everything around him, continually caught on something new—the couple kissing on one of the modern lounge chairs, the lit-up interior of an apartment's opulent dining room overlooking our path, the violin player busking under the bridge.

"I know that in the dictionary sense of the word, we are hardly more than strangers . . ." Fitz begins.

"Matt and I broke up," I say abruptly, cutting him off. Fitz skips a step, then stops and blinks at me with those piercing blue eyes. I don't know why I blurted out my romantic status in the middle of his speech, but I realize it's the first time I've said it out loud. Maybe part of me just had to tell someone. Or maybe part of me had to tell *Fitz*.

Fitz's stunned expression drifts into a grin, which he immediately flattens. But he fails, and I can't help rolling my eyes.

"I know what you're thinking," I tell him.

"No, you don't," he replies hastily. "I know you think I'm into you—"

"I know what you're thinking," I repeat, "because I'd be lying if I said I hadn't thought it myself."

This shuts him up.

"Now, did you want to finish that denial, or do you want me to continue?" I ask.

"I'm good," he says.

"There's something between us," I start. "Which I do *not* get, because you're honestly kind of annoying and you're not really my type and I don't even know you, which I keep forgetting."

Fitz's face glows, like he didn't hear anything after "something between us." In hindsight, I probably should have predicted he wouldn't.

"I feel it too," he says.

"What?"

"Pulled to you," he replies, his eyes full of emotions written on top of each other until they've become indecipherable. Hope and hesitation and dread and doubt and certainty. I swallow, fearful of how quickly this conversation is careening toward an edge, and of what waits below.

"But Matt and I broke up because we didn't see our lives going in the same direction," I say decisively. "I want to explore, learn what's out there, and find out who I am in the process. Matt didn't want anything to change. Do you see what I'm saying? I can't just pick up with someone who's exactly the same. Go through that again only for it to end when one of us is brave enough to admit it can't work."

Fitz nods. "I read *The Great Gatsby* today," he says simply, like this is a logical reply to what I said.

I'm thrown. "Okay . . ."

"I don't want to always be looking back," Fitz goes on. "I don't know how much time my mom has, but I don't know how much time I have either. I can't live my life wishing things were as they'd been, missing a home that's no longer there."

Hiraeth. I remember the word from the conversation we had while driving into New York City yesterday. Yesterday, which feels like a lifetime ago.

He steps closer to me. "Because if I spend every minute wishing everything would stay the same, I'll lose so much more than the past."

His declaration strikes a harmony with the noise in my head and my heart, the dull roar I've found impossible to drown out this entire day. The pain of Matt leaving is awful, but right now, it begins to fade. I study Fitz, the gentle narrowness of his face, the unreadable line of his thin lips, the features it's hard to believe I've only known for five days. There's a look in his eyes, a characteristic exactness to his words, an undeniable spark between us. They quiet the whole world.

"I'm not asking anything of you, Juniper," Fitz starts again.

I pull myself together enough to glance pointedly at how close together our feet are. "No?" I raise an eyebrow.

"It's not that I don't want to ask," he clarifies. "I definitely do. It's only, you just got out of a relationship, and we don't exactly make any sense. The only thing I want is to tell you I'm not going to waste the rest of this trip. I have four days of this college tour left. I'm going to see more schools, and if I fall in love with some of them, I'll apply. All I'm asking is if you'll see them with me."

The harmony narrows to a single note, pure and perfect. In the echo, I'm left recognizing I didn't expect this from Fitz. He's stepped enormously far from his comfort zone, into territory he wouldn't have dared even last week. He's facing huge, frightening things, and he's staring them down the way not everybody would. "I think that's really brave," I tell him truthfully. His expression softens.

"So?" he asks. "Will you come with me? I'm traveling with my brother, and we could go wherever. Or if you don't want to, you could send me a list—"

"I'll come with you."

He looks surprised. "You will?"

I ask myself the same question, half shocked that the answer has already flown from my lips. *I will?* The more my impulsive response rings in my ears, the more right it sounds. I run through the logistics in my head. I'd planned our trip in order to be home in time for Matt's mom's birthday dinner on Sunday, which I obviously won't be going to now. If I'm smart with my money and careful with my parents, I could extend my trip a couple days.

I nod. "As your friend," I clarify.

Fitz beams. "Okay then. Where do we start?"

JUNIPER

⌐

WE START CONSTRUCTING our itinerary right there. Walking the High Line, I describe schools in New York while Fitz questions me on dorms, departments, dining halls, everything. It's nice, having someone want to know everything I know, every item of college minutia I've collected over the past couple of years. I remember the way Matt would either furrow his brow or fake interest every time I would exclaim over a new program or campus location I'd found online.

I banish the thought. I am *not* comparing Matt and Fitz.

After finding benches looking out on the skyscrapers, we pull out our phones, exchanging information on distances and campus tours while plans begin to form. Eventually, we reconcile our diverging itineraries, selecting the schools we want to see from each and combining them into a logical order for the drive. Fitz defers to me on a couple of choices, canceling schools his mom suggested in western Pennsylvania so we can make it to D.C. and UVA. He says his mom won't mind if we extend his trip a couple of days, and he'll just have to check with his brother.

We decide to tour NYU and Columbia tomorrow, which

will be one more day than either of us had planned in the city, but when we learned we both missed those tours for different reasons, it felt like fate. Tonight, we'll have to rebook hotel reservations to fit the new schedule. I'll probably have to pay my parents back for a couple of nonrefundable cancelations, but I'll work it out. Fitz and I coordinate new hotels together too. Separate rooms, of course.

The minutes pass, dusk darkening into night.

We begin walking again, passing frosted trees and bushes, gleaming high-rises and office towers. When we're nearing the end of the High Line, our hands touch. It's innocuous, and yet I feel it throughout my whole body. The cold on my cheeks disappears. The realness of the world feels a hundred times richer. We become the heart of the city, the center of countless buildings and crisscrossing streets. I don't know how it even happened. I guess we drifted nearer to each other while we walked, pulled by whatever imperceptible gravity drew us together in Boston and again in Providence.

Between one breath and the next, my hand slips into his. Our palms press together, his fingers closing over mine with a soft certainty. It brings us closer, in the way holding hands does. Our forearms entwine, our shoulders touch, our strides match.

I tell myself to drop his hand. It'll give him the wrong impression.

But it doesn't feel wrong. When we're touching, I don't feel lonely. I don't hear the terrible echo of Tía's question, the broken record repeating in my head since Matt left our hotel room. Who *will* I call when I'm in college on my own? With

Fitz, who I didn't even know a week ago, I'm reminded con-
nections can come from the unlikeliest of places. With Fitz,
the questions go quiet.

Even so, I vow I'm going to release his hand. While we
walk, I pick the place. I'll let go when we reach the girl eating
gelato on the bench.

We pass the girl eating gelato on the bench.

I pick my new landmark. The barking dog by the bushes.
Then the couple watching the river from the deck. Then the
curvature of the train tracks embedded in the concrete, which
Fitz explains is from when the High Line was an overhead
railroad. Each one passes, and my hand remains firmly in his.

We reach the end of the High Line, where the Hudson
River opens up in front of us. Together, we lean on the railing, watching the glittering New Jersey waterfront.

Fitz nods to our intertwined fingers. "So . . ." he says.

I grimace. "I know. I'm working on it."

He grins. "Don't work too hard." I roll my eyes. "I could
let go if you want," he continues, his voice gentler.

"Do you want to?"

His eyes travel unmistakably to my lips. "No," he says.
The syllable is a relief I don't know how to reconcile with the
platonic requirement I gave him. "It's just—" He stops suddenly. "Wow, I understand limerence now."

"Limerence?" I repeat.

"The state of infatuation with someone, characterized by
frequent thoughts of—"

I drop his hand. "Nope. None of that," I interrupt. "No
word-defining. It's not making this easier."

Fitz rounds on me, curiosity illuminating his freckled features. With his newly free hand he reaches up, and before I know it he's tucking one loose strand of my hair behind my ear. "Why?" he asks. "You don't happen to find my vocabulary charming, do you, Juniper?"

Ignoring the tingle his touch leaves on my skin, I huff, turning to walk down the stairs from the raised platform of the High Line. From this overly romantic place where I've ended up with a boy who's beguiling me with his dictionary definitions.

He follows. "A turn-on, perhaps?"

"No!" I reply, walking in front of him to hide my flushed cheeks.

"Right. Out of curiosity, do you know what *pulchritudinous* means?"

I hit street level and spin, facing him. He pauses one step up from me. "We're going to pretend none of this happened. The hand-holding and whatever this"—I gesture to the two of us—"is. We have a couple more days together, and I'd like to enjoy them as friends. Nothing more. So let's just forget the whole thing."

His mouth flickers halfway to a smirk. "I will if you will," he replies.

I frown. "Not fair," I say. "You know I don't have a choice."

"Oh, and I do?" He drops off the step in front of me, crossing his arms. "The rest of us can't just choose what to forget. It doesn't work that way."

"Forgive me for not knowing," I reply sarcastically. I start walking without caring where I'm going. The destination isn't important, not when I know he'll follow me until we finish the conversation. Not when I want him to. "I'm used to people not remembering things I think are obvious."

"I couldn't possibly forget," he says. "Trust me."

"I—have to get back to my hotel." I crash into the subject change like a train careening off the rails. "The next time we see each other will be the NYU information session at ten a.m. tomorrow. Where there will be no hand-holding."

"Or we could grab dinner," he replies.

I shoot him an incredulous glare. "Fitz!" We cross the street in a crowd of tourists who part to circumvent us. "Dinner sounds suspiciously like a date, which is something I definitely would *not* agree to. We need to separate, or do something strictly platonic."

We reach the corner, where Fitz stops.

I turn and find him nodding, an idea in his eyes. "I think I know what we could do," he says.

He pulls out his phone, glancing up from the screen to orient himself with the map, and I wait. I wait while I could be dismissing the invitation. While I could be returning to my empty hotel room. While I could be telling myself I definitely, unquestionably hated holding his hand.

"It means 'breathtakingly beautiful,' " he says out of nowhere.

"What?"

"*Pulchritudinous.*" He looks up, his eyes finding mine. "It means 'beautiful.' "

FITZ

JUNIPER WAS RIGHT. We do only have a couple of days. It's why I had to invite her to dinner when she was considering heading back to her hotel.

We walk side by side through Koreatown, passing cars rushing up to every curb, kids shouting to each other from neighboring stoops. It's nothing like New Hampshire, where everything closes by nine and nighttime entertainment is the local theater's two-for-one movie screenings.

In ten minutes we've reached the restaurant, which can in no way be confused for date territory, I note with satisfaction in one half of my brain and deep disappointment in the other. The place is corporate clean, with white fiberglass tables and booths. Behind them, people wait for to-go orders in front of the brightly illuminated counter. It would be cold and minimalist if not for the smell, which is the exact opposite. Rich and vibrantly flavorful, it's practically a tangible presence. It's so spicy, the temperature in the room prickles with heat.

I turn to Juniper, who looks grudgingly curious. "Korean fried chicken," I answer her unasked question.

She nods, and I can see intrigue winning out over skep-ticism on her stony features. I walk into the restaurant and fist-pump internally when she follows me.

Near the front of the restaurant, we find Lewis reading the menu at a table. He's in his interview suit, his tie loos-ened around his neck. I sit down opposite him. "Okay," he says, head down, studying the menu, "they say spicy means insanely spicy, but I'm feeling daring—" He glances up, stop-ping midsentence when he sees Juniper. She's standing next to me, her mouth folded into a confused frown.

"Dinner with your brother?" She sounds doubtful, if a little amused. "That's your idea?"

I grin winningly. "Perfect, right?" It *is* perfect, I note, congratulating myself in my head. *Excellent job killing the mood with the girl you like.* I can imagine nothing more platonic than Lewis jumping in every time conversation with Juniper veers in the direction of . . . not-platonic. I'm guessing Juniper will understand the plan's inexorable logic. "This is Juniper," I tell Lewis.

My brother stands, recovering his composure immedi-ately, and extends his hand. The gesture's precision makes me remember how frequently he's probably repeated it to-day in his five hours of interviews. "Lewis Holton," he says with confidence, and for a moment I'm pricked with familiar jealousy for his instantaneous, easy warmth with people. Ex-cept this time, there's something else alongside the jealousy, something possibly born of this week together. Something like pride.

Juniper doesn't introduce herself. She blinks. "Holton?"

It takes me a minute to understand the question. She's never heard my last name. The realization shakes me. I can't quite wrap my head around the idea that this girl I feel remarkably close to doesn't even know enough of my name to find me online. She knows exactly as much of my name as Starbucks baristas do. It seems dumb, idealistic, the way I've presumed with very little foundation that I have this incredible, genuine connection with her. I don't even know her.

Juniper's eyes jump to mine. "My last name is Ramírez," she says, like she's reading my mind.

It's weirdly reassuring to know. Learning her name doesn't change who she is to me, doesn't change why I like her, or how much I enjoy her ever-present wit, or how utterly unpredictable I find her. It just gives whatever our relationship is a longevity it previously lacked. We're more than baristas to each other.

Juniper takes the seat next to me. I turn to Lewis, who's openly gaping at the two of us. It's like I can hear the questions formulating in his mind, and I quickly head them off. "Juniper's going to be leading our college trip now," I inform him. "She's an expert," I say like it's a real justification.

"Um—what?" Lewis asks, evidently trying to process this development.

"Only if it's okay with you," Juniper interjects, addressing Lewis. "I don't want to derail any of your plans."

Lewis ignores the comment. "I remember you," he says, studying her. "You were in the basement at Brown. The Alpha Delt party." He faces me, and I recognize his expression instantly. "I *knew* it." My stomach knots with dread. "You tried to deny why you were in a hurry to drive to Brown," he continues. "You were texting all day yesterday, and you pretended you were talking to *a friend*. But *I* knew." He's irritatingly impressed with himself. "I knew there was a girl."

Juniper rounds on me, because the world is cold and unfeeling.

I deflect desperately. "What, um"—I pick up Lewis's menu—"what were you saying was spicy?"

"Are you two a thing?" Lewis asks, predictably unwilling to let it go.

"No," Juniper and I say simultaneously, and with too much conviction.

Lewis watches us, obviously interested. "I see."

I notice Juniper blush, which is unusual. She's not the kind of girl who's often embarrassed or self-conscious. Not when crashing into students in the Boston University quad or when striking up conversation with people she's never met in the middle of Mike's Pastry. The fact that her cheeks have colored now gives me hope that Lewis thinking we're together thrills her in some way. It's hope I'm hesitant to hold on to, but that's the only kind of hope I know.

"I'm game for the spiciest thing on the menu," Juniper says, reading the folded laminate over my shoulder. I glance down, surveying the color-saturated photos of crispy, sauce-drenched chicken and remembering how hungry I am.

"I like her," Lewis declares, looking impressed with Juniper's choice. He pulls his tie off in one quick motion. "I don't know if ultra-spicy is the choice I would've gone with in your position," he continues with a meaningful look at the two of us, "but, respect. Let me know if you want me to leave, by the way. To give you some privacy for your date."

"It's not—" Juniper and I start to say simultaneously before we catch ourselves.

"It's not a date," I finish.

Juniper buries her nose in the menu, looking like she doesn't believe me.

I don't blame her. I don't believe me either.

JUNIPER

IT DOESN'T TAKE long for me to learn Fitz and his brother are nothing alike. Lewis is relaxed in the way only truly confident people are, and he clearly loves an audience. I understand why. He recounts his hours of interviews with humor and charisma, and I even catch the waitress eyeing him appreciatively once or twice. In fairness, I understand that, too. From the fit of his suit, he definitely works out. His face is highlighted by his strong jaw, brown eyes in deep brown skin, black hair, and an irrepressible smile. I know he and Fitz are adopted. Nevertheless, it's striking just how different they look.

I'm surprised how instantly included I feel, how comfortable with the rhythms of the conversation. I find myself describing my college picks and plans when Lewis asks, and then I'm asking him more about his interview. I notice Fitz's discomfort when his brother elaborates on the company, on his prospects in New York, on his plans to split a "sick" place in Queens with friends if he lands the job.

Lewis seems to notice too. He changes the subject, questioning Fitz on what he did today. Fitz describes walking in

Union Square Park and visiting the Strand. He doesn't mention *The Great Gatsby* or the High Line, which leaves me wondering if he routinely dodges the important stuff with his brother.

We finish dinner in forty-five minutes. The chicken really was insanely spicy. We all agree the menu didn't exaggerate with labels like "inferno" and "killing blow," which is saying something coming from a Mexican girl and an Indian boy. Fitz was worse off, visibly suffering, sweating profusely and gulping down water. We walk out of the restaurant with our mouths on fire, grateful for the cold air numbing our lips.

We ride the subway to my hotel, the train empty enough for Fitz and me to sit next to each other while Lewis crooks his elbow around a pole. When we reach my stop and climb the stairs to the street, Fitz's phone rings. He pulls it out and checks the screen.

"I'm sorry," he says, giving me an apologetic glance. "I have to get this."

Without explaining, he walks ahead, holding the phone up to his ear.

I fall into step with Lewis. We say nothing for a few moments, realizing in unison we're without the only person we have in common. We're like kids holding two tin cans with the string connecting them cut.

"It's probably our mom," Lewis says finally, nodding to Fitz.

"Oh." I remember everything Fitz told me. "Right." I watch Fitz walking in front of us, noticing things I probably wouldn't have if Lewis hadn't brought up their mother. His posture, hunched and tense, the quickness of his footsteps, like he's running from something.

"I'm glad you're joining us, Juniper," Lewis says, his voice nothing like when he was telling stories in the restaurant. It's softer, more vulnerable. "You're going to be good for him. I can tell," he continues. He smiles cautiously. "He's . . . always worrying."

His eyes drift to his brother. They're clouded with concern.

"You worry too," I observe.

It's funny. In Fitz's descriptions of Lewis, I didn't get the impression he was the protective older-brother type. Fitz's offhand comments instead conjured the image of a stereotypical frat dude, content to play drinking games with his friends and get whatever finance job he wants. It's not who I recognize walking next to me. This Lewis is watchful, insightful.

He laughs a little. "I guess I do."

Fitz finishes his call. He waits while we catch up. "Mom wants you to call her," he says when we reach him. "She wants you to tell her about the interview."

"Yeah, sure," Lewis replies. "Later."

Fitz frowns. He opens his mouth like he's about to reply, but then closes it, his expression flattening. Whatever he wanted to say, it's gone, hidden where I have the feeling he's hidden his words for a while. I don't have to know Fitz and Lewis well to see everything they're not saying to each other. It's a weight pressing down on them both.

I want to encourage them to speak up. Fitz should know

Lewis worries about him. Lewis should hear how his hopes and dreams in New York make his brother nervous.

Except then I remember how I didn't tell Marisa what happened with Matt. Why I've hidden the end of my relationship and the start of this new friendship with Fitz from my own family. Sometimes honesty in families is worse. Sometimes it doesn't end with everyone coming together, commiserating or celebrating or understanding each other. Sometimes it ends on the floor of a hotel room in the dead of night, with tears and fighting and finally not talking for days. The way it worked with Tía, or didn't. Honesty can bring you together, or it can drive you apart.

"What's going on tomorrow?" Lewis asks while we walk.

"NYU," Fitz replies.

Lewis nods and doesn't follow up.

I could fill in the details. I don't, deciding I trust the quiet.

FITZ

I'M DISAPPOINTED WHEN Juniper walks into the revolving door to her hotel. I knew I would be. Even though we've hung out for the past four hours, it doesn't feel like enough. I could walk the High Line and discover new restaurants with her for the rest of the night. *Limerence.* It's the strangest feeling, one I don't remember ever having before and one I'll never forget.

I chew my lip, watching the cabs cycle in and out of the hotel driveway. Lewis stands next to me.

"Should I have offered to walk her up to her room?" I finally ask.

"It is generally date protocol." Lewis grinds the heel of his Kenneth Cole oxford on the curb like he's looking for something to do.

I cut him a look. "We just gorged ourselves on fried chicken *with my brother*," I remind him. "For the hundredth time, it wasn't a date."

He shrugs. "Felt like a date."

I don't realize I'm smiling until a second later. I'm not used to being the subject of Lewis's easy optimism, and it's welcome in the present context. "It did, didn't it?"

Lewis laughs. "You know," he says, getting a very *Lewis* gleam in his eye, "I'd head back to BU and leave you both to it if I didn't know Mom would kill me."

I nod. He's right, she would, and without Lewis's credit card, I couldn't pay for hotels and food. What's more, in a way I don't exactly understand, Lewis's presence keeps the idea of this trip with Juniper grounded. Juniper and I are *teenagers*, crossing paths in cities not our own. If we were to embark on this with only the two of us, it would be inconceivably impulsive. With Lewis, we're just fitting her into a shape that already exists instead of drawing the outline of some new romantic odyssey.

"By the way," I say, "Juniper and I want to extend this trip a couple days of days. I don't know what your schedule is. . . ." I trail off, not knowing how to ask for this.

"It's fine." He shrugs. "I don't mind traveling with you guys. But if it were up to me," he continues, "I wouldn't be here cockblocking you."

The warmth of my brother's earlier friendliness frosts over. I register the joke for what it is. He's decided what I'm supposed to want, to find important, and he's implicitly judging me if I don't.

"It's not like that," I say. "Just—just, chill," I finish fumblingly. The word feels weird and uncharacteristic.

Lewis raises an eyebrow but doesn't comment on it. "I'm chill, dude, I promise. In fact . . ." He nods in the direction of the hotel, the illuminated logo reflecting red on the nearby buildings. It's similar to our hotel, just twists on the same template of business-casual rooms and unused rooftop bars. "I'm so chill, I won't wait up if you want to follow her. You don't have to," he adds. "I'm just saying *if*."

If. The word is wonderfully open-ended.

It has me looking up, weighing Lewis's suggestion and wondering which one of those rooms is Juniper's. It's not like I'm considering the hookup he's obviously insinuating— it's very possible my brother literally does not understand the existence of other things you could do in a girl's hotel room—but I won't deny I'm contemplating other ways the night could go.

The possibilities play out in a montage in my head. I'd text Juniper, asking if I could come up. She'd tell me her room number and invite me in. We'd watch something dumb on TV and share the overpriced candy on top of the fridge. When we tired of TV, we'd talk, describing our friends, our home-towns, our high schools, our favorite movies no one else likes, our favorite childhood board games. I have a hunch she's a Trivial Pursuit fiend.

Except what if she's not?

I don't know why Trivial Pursuit is the detail that does me in, but it does. In a horrible lurch I recognize I've con-structed this entire fantasy in my head founded on nothing. While I feel like I know Juniper, I don't. I'm enjoying embark-ing on this indefinable thing with her, but I don't do well with unknowns. Juniper is enchanting and fearsome, and a huge freaking unknown.

I decide not to follow her up to her room. It's a fear-driven decision, just like not confronting my brother when I feel the tension between us pushing us further and further apart. *Pusillanimous. Timorous.*

In a blink, I hate the dictionary-definition thing I do. The point of memorizing words is feeling a degree of control over the unstable, unforeseeable world. It hits me now—cataloging and describing every feeling in the world isn't control. Having the word for *cowardly* doesn't change me. It changes nothing.

I turn and follow Lewis, feeling things I no longer want to name.

FITZ

THE NEXT MORNING, I shower early to meet Juniper for the NYU tour. When I step from the shower into the steamy bathroom, I overhear Lewis on the phone. "They said I'd hear from them this weekend. No idea when," he says. There's a pause. He's recapping his job interview.

For a moment I wonder if he called Mom like I mentioned. The possibility vanishes instantly. It's probably Prisha.

I ignore him. Wiping the mirror, I focus on my reflection.

God, I'm pale. And skinny. I usually only glance into the mirror in the morning. Today I linger, viewing my appearance from Juniper's potential perspective—in the unlikely event she ever sees me shirtless.

I need to cut the red hair flopping onto my forehead. I have freckles *everywhere*. Not cute freckles like Juniper's, either. I look like my entire body got splashed when someone dropped the world's largest pot of marinara sauce. Instead of the six-pack and V-formation upper body everyone expects from TV, I have a flat stretch of stomach and shoulders devoid of definition except my collarbone poking out halfheartedly.

Juniper is way out of my league.

I wish I'd devoted even minimal effort to exercise of any kind in my entire existence. Even though I just showered, I drop to the floor and begin doing what could be considered push-ups.

I do twenty and feel like my arms have been forcibly detached from my body. I only have stumps now. Excruciating stumps. I don't understand why people do this frequently. Except I do. The Junipers of the world are why. I mean, I know other people exercise for personal pride and enjoyment. But *my* reason is five foot three, unfairly curvy, and infatuated with college.

I hear Lewis through the door. "Babe," he says chuckling. Definitely Prisha. "You know I'd hate San Francisco. The start-up culture and everything? Come on."

I scowl, nearly frustrated enough to do five more push-ups. It's obvious Prisha wants him to consider a job close to hers next year, and Lewis couldn't be more careless with his disinterest. He's probably looking forward to being single, free to follow through with girls like the one he danced with in the basement at Brown.

I dress quickly and collect my jacket from the bedroom. Lewis is still on the phone, typing on the computer and giving only half his attention to whatever Prisha is saying. I wave quickly on the way out.

Juniper is waiting when I reach the lobby. Her hair is in her characteristic ponytail, and when I walk up, she holds out the brown paper bag in her hand.

"I didn't know what bagel you like. I got you plain with cream cheese. Sorry if you hate it," she says.

I smile. She's direct even when it comes to breakfast. "That's my order, actually," I tell her, digging the bagel from the bag. I unwrap the tinfoil while we walk out of the hotel's revolving door.

"Why does that not surprise me?" She takes a bite of her everything bagel. "Let me guess. You've never tried any other flavor."

"Don't psychoanalyze my bagel preferences, Juniper."

We walk in the direction of NYU, following the map on her phone. It's colder today, the sun smothered in gray. The hotel Mom picked for Lewis and me is a couple of blocks from the NYU admissions building. As we head along West Third, Juniper hits me with a barrage of information about the university. I find it intensely attractive. She details the number of dorms and dining halls, facts about financial aid, and the early decision process. I retain about half the information because while she's talking, she unzips her jacket halfway, revealing a triangle of skin at her collar.

We reach the admissions building five minutes early. A couple of teenagers and their parents are waiting under the purple NYU flags adorning every building, demarcating the university's territory in the indistinguishable expanse of buildings. I notice one boy sitting on the ground, his back against the building's stone. He's reading a worn science-fiction paperback, its cover the rocky surface of some faraway planet. His dad stands over him, wearing an NYU sweatshirt and darting frustrated glances at his son's novel. I recognize the expression on the boy's face. He doesn't want to be here.

"NYU has over two hundred programs," Juniper says,

pulling my attention from the reading boy and continuing her college trivia.

"I don't know why we're even going to the information session." I tug Juniper's ponytail playfully. It happens too fast for me to overthink the gesture. Days of admiring that ponytail, and I release it almost as soon as I touch it. "You know everything already."

She swats me away, but her lips curve upward. "I don't know *everything*. Besides, haven't you ever finished a book only to flip back to the first page and start over again? Knowing everything doesn't take away the fun."

"Only you would compare a lecture about college statistics to reading an amazing book." Her passion is irresistible, though. She's kind of right. I've been listening to her rattle off facts all morning about a college that yesterday I wasn't even planning to apply to, and now I'm genuinely looking forward to this information session. It's an unfamiliar excitement. If I'd come here without her, I'd have my nose in my dictionary, counting down the minutes until I could resume my day—resume my life. "Do they have an architecture program?" I ask.

Her eyes light up. I make a mental note to prompt her about architecture more often just to see that soft warmth settling her features. "Yeah," she answers immediately. "It's called the Urban Design and Architecture Studies program, and it looks amazing. Wait—" She stops suddenly and blinks, her focus returning. "What about you? I never asked what *you* want to study."

"Oh." I don't know why the question surprises me. Even when I was set on SNHU, I would have needed to pick a major eventually. I guess I never peered that far into the future. "I haven't really thought about it. Undeclared, I guess."

Juniper looks scandalized. She grabs my arm, and I feel the contact everywhere. My toes, my stomach, the tips of my ears. She drops her hand almost immediately, but it doesn't matter. Her touch reverberates through me. "After the tour let's go to the campus bookstore. You can browse the course books for different classes. Maybe something will stand out to you. Literature, like your mom?" she suggests.

It's a great idea. A perfectly Juniper idea. But the thought of literature and my mom stokes the worry never far from my mind. I decided to tour these schools, to entertain a future I never envisioned, but making that choice didn't erase my every concern. Everything I've worried about is still there, behind every thought, making me feel guilty for even thinking about leaving my mom.

"I don't know. I might," I say.

I'm spared having to continue the conversation when the door opens in front of us. We're ushered inside by a woman wearing a crisp blue blazer, who looks unreasonably cheery for eight thirty in the morning. She directs us into the kind of large conference room with which I've become familiar over the past week. While we file in, I notice the boy with his sci-fi novel following his dad, who's already deep in conversation with the admissions officer. Overhearing the guy's father obnoxiously questioning the woman on Greek life—

despite the fact that his son looks like he'd never in a million years pledge a fraternity—I catch the kid's eye. I offer him a weak smile, which he doesn't return.

I sit down next to Juniper, recalling how just days ago I was envying Matt for being by her side in the BU presentation.

I'm happy. I really am. Happier than I remember being in a while, in fact.

It's just not what I'd define as pure, untainted joy. What interrupts the feeling is the sneaking suspicion I'm deserting what's really important with every step I take into a future that's distinctly mine.

I wonder if I'm right to imagine more, or if I should bury my nose in a book of my own.

JUNIPER

IF THERE'S ONE thing you have to do in New York City, it's find yourself some pizza.

When we finished touring NYU late in the morning, Fitz and I grabbed unfulfilling café sandwiches, then took the subway uptown to Columbia. We'd scheduled two schools for one day, not wanting to miss either even though we knew it'd be exhausting. Finally, finished with Columbia and desperately hungry for dinner, we ducked into the hole-in-the-wall pizzeria we found near the campus. It didn't disappoint, the way New York pizza never does. Dripping with delicious grease, scald-the-roof-of-your-mouth hot, with crunchy crust—the two, or it might've been three, slices Fitz and I each devoured were perfection.

Lewis didn't have dinner with us. He volunteered to drive ahead to Philadelphia and "make sure everything's okay with the hotel." It was a flimsy excuse if I ever heard one to leave Fitz and me alone and force us to carpool, considering we'd chosen the new hotel and called them this morning. While we finished off the pizza, Fitz explained he's overheard Lewis have increasingly frequent phone calls with his girlfriend,

Prisha, and Fitz suspects relationship stress combined with worries over his job interview have put his brother on edge. Lewis could probably use the time on his own, Fitz says.

We check out of my hotel and hit the road. I can't help the awkward disjointedness I feel every time I notice Fitz in the passenger seat, where Matt would sit. It's like I've tumbled into a parallel universe. I keep glancing in Fitz's direction because I feel like if I don't, I'll forget and say something to Matt. Which would be a level of uncomfortable with which I completely could not deal.

"Do you want to listen to music?" I blurt while we head toward the interstate. I'm conscious of how direct and desperate the question comes out. It's just, Matt would have reached for the radio while we were pulling out of the hotel. The newness of having Fitz in the passenger seat draws the differences from driving with my ex into unbearably crisp focus.

"Up to you," Fitz replies. "What do you usually listen to?"

Matt would've started pressing for his eighties playlist he knows I can't stand. *This is too weird.* "Podcasts?" I suggest.

"Cool. Let's do that." He's holding his dictionary in his lap, lightly tapping his thumb on the spine in a steady pulse. The sound is booming, my brothers jumping in the upstairs hallway while I try to study. He picks up the tempo, the beat audibly anxious in the silence.

I don't know why things are suddenly so stilted between us. We've never struggled in conversation before. Words normally flow *too* easily. I remember texting him nonstop on the drive to New York, earning irritated glances from Matt every time my phone buzzed with one of Fitz's replies. We weren't even talking about anything and yet we had everything to say.

Now something is different, and I don't know what. It might have to do with this car ride being the first time Fitz and I don't have distraction. There are no colleges to tour, no stars to watch, no definitions to trade. Just us. Fitz and me— and a two-hour drive. Cold sweat prickles my hands.

"Which podcasts do you like?" I ask desperately. I'd put anything on at this point, even the show Anabel is obsessed with devoted entirely to American Girl dolls.

"Oh, any of them." Fitz doesn't look pleased with his reply. He turns his gaze to his shoes. I fix my eyes on the highway.

"Pick one."

"I, um, don't know any," Fitz answers. "I don't actually listen to them. But put on whatever you like. I'm sure it'll be interesting."

I almost take him up on the offer, but it feels like giving up. Like stalling the silence instead of breaking it.

"We could talk?" I'm pretty much pleading.

"Yeah," Fitz replies. "Okay."

We proceed to *not* talk. The car fills up with quiet, like water rushing in following our plunge off the bridge of this conversation. It's not long before the hushed hum of the road under my tires becomes unbearable.

I give up and reach for the radio knob—right as Fitz does too. Our hands collide before we both instantly pull back.

It's one of those romance-movie moments, where the hero and heroine both blush, the heady current of contact rushing between them. Except it is *not* romantic. It's cringe-worthy. The mutuality of our defeat makes the whole thing way worse.

"Um, sorry," Fitz fumbles to say.

I reach for chagrinned politeness like his and find only exasperation. "Hold up," I say loudly enough to startle. "Why is this suddenly the most awkward car ride of my entire life?"

I steal a glance at him. He looks physically pained. "Surely you've had worse," he suggests weakly.

"Nope. This wins."

"Well, it's definitely your fault," he replies.

I round on him, tearing my eyes from the highway for a brief moment. "*My* fault?" I repeat incredulously. "It's definitely not my fault. I think it's because we don't have enough in common. We probably exhausted everything we have to say to each other, and we're not compatible enough for, you know, daily conversation." The whole idea of this drive, this trip, is beginning to feel ridiculous.

I expect my theory to worry Fitz, because honestly it worries me. It's the fear I've been pressing to the corner of my thoughts for this entire car ride.

But it doesn't appear to bother him at all. Bizarrely, it seems to relax him. He leans back, pushing up the sleeves of his sweater and revealing—nice forearms. I don't know why my brain has decided to zero in on his forearms, the light lines of muscle running to his wrist, while I'm questioning the entire premise of our compatibility. Probably because it's not my brain doing the noticing.

"That's not it at all," he says easily. His confidence relaxes me, and I focus on the road, somewhat relieved. "It's because you began this trip with Matt, you imagined this trip with Matt. Instead you have me, but you're thinking about him."

Wincing, I open my mouth and I find I can't deny what he's saying. "I'm not anymore." It's the truth. I haven't thought about Matt since we broke this conversation open and began examining what was wrong with it.

Fitz grins. "Good."

Heat races from my cheeks into my fingers on the wheel, and that's when I realize I'm not, in fact, thinking about Matt. Not at all. In the start-and-stop traffic I find myself stealing looks in Fitz's direction. His recently exposed forearms, his hands resting delicately on his dictionary. I didn't know I had a thing for hands, but I definitely have one for Fitz's. Kind of the way I have a thing for the winter-sky blue of his eyes, the untidy curtain of red hair covering his forehead, the precise angle of his nose, the restless twist of his lips.

I blink. *Focus, Juniper.* I'm going to crash the car if I keep this up.

Fitz's phone vibrates. He pulls it from his pocket. "Lewis got to the hotel," Fitz tells me, reading the screen. "He's checking in now." He frowns, reading his phone.

"What?" I prompt.

"Oh. Just Lewis," Fitz grumbles.

His tone has me curious. From my conversation with Lewis last night, I've started to get one brother's side of their relationship. I don't know Fitz's, but I wonder if it's something he might not want to keep to himself. "What do you mean?"

"He's . . . He made a dumb joke about whose room I'll stay in tonight." Fitz puts the phone down and looks up. "He's constantly saying stupid stuff like that. I apologize in advance for how obnoxious it is." He forces a smile, one I know is hiding his frustration. "I did explain Lewis and I aren't biologically related, right?"

I laugh, because I can tell he means it as a joke. "I think you guys are pretty similar actually." Out of the corner of my eye, I notice Fitz's eyebrows quirk in surprise. It's not disdainful surprise. It's interested, even flattered. "No apology necessary," I add. "But you'll definitely be staying in his room." My eyes dart to him, and the next comment on the tip of my tongue leaps off before I have the chance to tell it not to. "I don't blame Lewis for wanting us to be together, though."

Fitz's whole posture shifts. He leans forward, and I feel his eyes on me, focused and penetratingly blue. "No," he says. "One couldn't blame him for that."

I don't know if it's me, or if by an unexplained, undiscovered meteorological phenomenon the temperature in the car jumps up fifteen degrees, or thirty, or fifty. Fitz chews his lip. The sight is intolerably cruel to inflict on me in the middle of the New Jersey Turnpike. I have the impossible urge to pull over the car, lean across the gearshift—and kiss him, bunching the collar of his sweater in my fingers, pulling him closer and not letting go. I try to banish the thought immediately, which is when I notice the corners of those lips curving upward.

"Juniper," Fitz says calmly, "you're staring at my lips."

I whip my eyes forward. There's a long stretch of empty road where the car in front of me moved forward. Someone behind me honks, and I guiltily step on the gas. I'm certain everyone on the Turnpike knows I spaced while fantasizing about a boy.

"No, I wasn't," I say vehemently, the fire in my voice matching the fire in my face.

"Wow, you're blushing. Were you thinking about kissing me?" His voice is teasing on the surface, but rough underneath, jagged edges and disbelief. It's a terrible question. It has me considering forgetting architecture and going into public service in order to draft legislation illegalizing direct questions about kissing fantasies.

"Of course not," I get out.

Fitz's grin dances irresistibly—*no*, infuriatingly. "You are not a competent liar," he remarks. I scowl, and he continues. "Do I need to remind you that kissing me wouldn't exactly fit into your platonic plans for us?"

"Please," I shoot back, "you've been staring at my lips since we met. It doesn't mean anything."

"Yes, it does," he replies instantly. "It means I think about kissing you often."

I have no response to the confession, which sounded nothing like a confession given his impossible straightforwardness. I'm stunned. Not only by his nonchalance, which is honestly in violation of the laws of nature—but by the irrepressible, boundless excitement I feel when I replay his statement over in my mind.

Which I do. Three times.

I reach for words, knowing I'm leaving his comment to expand in the emptiness between us. But I don't find them. I don't think I remember what words are. So I don't use words. When the traffic ahead grinds to a halt, I stop behind the car in front of me.

I glance at Fitz. But his eyes catch mine, and then it's not a glance. It's eye contact. It's instantaneous, irreversible. It's our gazes locked together like lips and arms and bodies. This time, I let the fantasy play out. I imagine kissing him. I have a feeling he would be a very deliberate kisser. His mouth pressing precisely to mine, every brush of lips the exact right word in sentences upon sentences of touch. *Limerence.* The word leaps into my head, which is the moment I know I'm done for.

I don't know what I'll do in the next second. Whether I'll kiss him for real or turn back to the road, leaving the fantasy in my rearview mirror.

My phone rings over the car stereo, deciding for me. It's connected via Bluetooth, and the ringtone is deafening in the quiet of the car. I tear my eyes from Fitz, a tremor prickling down my shoulders. And in that moment, with the opportunity flown out the window, I know what I would have done.

I totally would have kissed him.

JUNIPER

I HIT ANSWER on the stereo display. It's my dad, and I'm immediately happy to hear his voice. We text every morning, but we haven't talked on the phone in two days. The wry tenor of his voice fills the car.

"How's the trip? What did you see today?" he asks quickly. I have a feeling he wants to vicariously tour New York.

I hold a finger to my lips, motioning to Fitz to stay quiet. None of my family knows this random boy has joined my road trip. "It's great," I reply. "We did NYU and Columbia, and New York was incredible. I went to all my favorite buildings in the city."

"Rockefeller Center, right? You say hi to Marisa's ex-fiancé?"

I laugh. Fitz's eyebrows wrinkle in confusion. I make a mental note to explain the Prometheus story to him later. "Of course," I say.

He pauses for a moment. "And how's Matt?"

I falter, knowing I should have anticipated the question. Fitz watches me warily, undoubtedly putting together I haven't told my dad about the breakup. I haven't even told my parents I'm changing my itinerary or extending my trip. I know I have to eventually. I'm just used to hearing no so often, I usually ask them for forgiveness, not permission.

"Matt's, um, good," I say, hearing the high strain in my voice. Fitz might not have been completely off when he told me I'm not a competent liar.

"Can I talk to him?"

I'm really glad this isn't FaceTime and he can't see every ounce of color drain from my face. "You . . . want to talk to him?" I repeat. My dad and Matt aren't exactly chatting-on-the-phone friends.

"Yeah," he says. "I watched a movie last night I think he'd like. Can you put him on?"

"Um." I'm a deer in the headlights unable to avoid the speeding car that is this interrogation.

"Um?" Dad's tone revs, and I brace for the collision. "*Um*, like he's in the bathroom and can't come to the phone right now?"

"Uh." I don't have it in me to lie to my father. Not even now, when I really, *really* want to.

"Or *um*, like you can't because I saw him today in Spring-field, Massachusetts?"

I swear under my breath. I should've known this would happen. I live within six blocks of Matt. We go to the same grocery store, he orders Chinese takeout from the same place Marisa does, and he walks his dog in the park where Callie has soccer. The chance of him encountering one member or other of my enormous gossipy family before I came home verged on the upper end of 99 percent. I guess I should be grateful my dad was the one who saw him.

"What happened?" he asks.

"We broke up, Dad," I say, nearly whispering. It's hard to admit to my dad in a way it wasn't to Fitz. I'm in a new world with Fitz, and telling my dad brings the breakup into my old world, into the life I was living and the life to which I'll return. The family movie nights Matt won't come to, the birthday dinners in the restaurant where we won't share a fried ice cream.

"I'm sorry, honey," he says softly. All the anger is gone from his voice. "I know how much he meant to you."

Fitz shifts uncomfortably in his seat, and I suddenly wish he weren't overhearing this. "Yeah," I say, choking the word out awkwardly.

"Maybe you should come home," Dad suggests. "We could go ice-skating in the park. Remember how we used to do that when you were little?"

I do remember. We would go every Friday when we first moved to Springfield. I remember thinking the park rink was so small compared to the one in Rockefeller Center. "How about next week? I want to finish my trip."

"On your own?" He sounds skeptical. "That wasn't the agreement. I don't want you driving hundreds of miles by yourself."

"But I can't come home," I protest. I flip my turn signal sharply and merge into the left lane, the traffic finally clearing up. "I'm not done yet. And—" I ready myself for the plunge, knowing I can't put it off any longer. "I want to extend my trip a few days. I don't have to be home for Shanna's birthday now, and there's more I want to do. I'll use my own money for the extra nights—"

"I don't know, Juniper," he cuts me off. "We can find a weekend to visit the schools you're interested in as a family." I hear his argument hardening, encasing me within his decision. I have to break through before I'm stuck.

"No," I say too forcefully. "I mean, it's a nice offer, but I want to do this by myself. I just . . . want to see the schools on my own, without anyone telling me what to think or how to feel." I don't elaborate. I don't say that once my family is involved, what's best for me won't be important. It'll turn into what's best for them. "I know you understand, Dad," I continue. "You remember how domineering family can be at my age."

"What do you mean?" he asks. I can tell he's genuinely confused.

"How you moved to New York and never came home," I remind him.

"I'm not proud of that decision, Juniper. I regret not having your abuela at my wedding. I wish she had been there when you were born. Yes, the family was domineering. But I was stubborn. I refused to give them the chance to accept I couldn't call every night and visit every weekend. Instead, I cut them off," he finishes evenly.

I don't say anything. I didn't know he regretted his time in New York, the distance from his family he created while exploring ramen restaurants and living with his best friends. I thought he regretting leaving.

Only the rhythmic hum of rubber on the road fills the emptiness in the car, waiting for me to say something. I glance at Fitz. He's looking out the window, and I know he's making an effort not to intrude. Days, schools, conversations, moments I can't yet imagine wait ahead of us. I don't want to give them up. If I drive home now, they're gone. With the possibilities unwinding in front of us, I don't want to cut the threads and ruin whatever fleeting future we're weaving.

"Are you forcing me to come home?" I ask my dad.

He'll recognize the challenge in my voice from conversations with the rest of my family. He just won't expect it coming to him. "No," he says after a pause. "You're seventeen, you're nearly an adult. This is your choice. Use your own money for the extra nights, and send me your *exact* itinerary every day. If you're not home by Christmas Eve, I'll sic Tía on you. Just . . . don't forget we're here when you need us."

"Thank you." I exhale with relief. The thought of returning to Tía right now, to endless lectures about what I *should* do next year, to the constant demands of my siblings, to facing school without Matt—it's overwhelming. I need this trip in more ways than one.

"And, Juniper," he adds, "it's okay to need your family sometimes."

FITZ

~

IT'S DIFFICULT TO decipher everything I'm feeling after overhearing Juniper's phone call. I'm relieved her father didn't force her to go home, returning us to our separate lives. It's impossible to deny I'm a little jealous of the way her face broke when he mentioned Matt. Her feelings for him aren't gone, which I guess I knew but didn't want to dwell on. And I'm kind of confused by her adamancy to keep her distance from her family despite her dad saying he regretted doing the same.

"Sorry for the interruption," Juniper says, her voice jarringly bright. "What were we talking about?"

I don't understand her readiness to jump back into conversation like nothing happened. I'm unable to match her instantaneous avidity. "Your dad just wants to be there for you," I say, knowing I'm probably overstepping.

Her smile fades. "I know."

"It's reasonable for him to worry about you being on the road by yourself," I continue. I don't quite know why her reaction bothers me.

"Yeah, but I'm not by myself. You're with me," she points out, effortlessly logical.

"He doesn't know that."

She huffs a laugh. "Believe me, he would not be cool if he knew I was traveling with a guy I just met."

"Well, yeah," I reply with force I fail to restrain. "It's his parental right to be concerned. It's what family does. Worry about each other." Juniper is watching me, but I'm elsewhere. I'm thinking of Lewis, who's chronically unwilling to give a shit about my worries. Juniper owes her dad respect for his fears, his uncertainties. Unexpectedly, I realize the final emotion that was rising in me during Juniper's phone call—anger. "I know it's easy for you to move off to college without even a backward glance," I continue. "But for everyone else, for your family, it's a huge change. It's hard."

Juniper scoffs. "This has nothing to do with my family. I don't care whether going to college is hard. It's necessary. It's part of growing up, whether you like it or not. But you want everything to stay the same, forever." She shakes her head, reproach in her eyes while she scrutinizes the road. "You're just like Matt," she finishes.

It's the worst possible way to be compared to Matt. I turn from her, focusing on the trees passing on the right while I push down indignation. "You know it's different for me. I *can't*—"

Juniper cuts me off. "Just because you use your mother's Alzheimer's to justify your fears doesn't mean the rest of us need to find something to hold us back."

I glance over and see immediate regret in Juniper's expression. She doesn't take the words back, though. She can't, because she meant them. They're a wall between us, solid and infrangible. It occurs to me distantly, only moments ago she looked like she wanted to kiss me. I can't wrap my head around how hard this conversation hit the ground, and how ugly the wreck.

I face the window and say nothing for the rest of the drive.

FITZ

⌇

WE REACH OUR hotel in Swarthmore, outside Philadelphia, a little past ten. Unspeaking, we pull our luggage from the trunk of Juniper's car. The *thunk* of the hard canvas hitting the pavement, the metallic clicks of the extendable handles—everything is painfully, precisely loud while we're deliberately quiet.

I'm trying to forget our fight. The tension is taking up more of the fleeting moments we have, and I want to enjoy this time with Juniper. It's not working, though. There's a new resentment in me, pushing back every time I think about bringing up our coming college visits or joking about whatever. I want to let go, but I don't.

It's confusing.

We walk together up the path to the hotel lobby, our breath visible in the night. If tonight had gone differently, I would be trying to wring this night for every minute together. I would wait with her, walk her to her room, even stay up late with her watching TV or talking until I can't keep my eyes open. But I turn for the elevators, leaving her at the front desk to check into her room.

"So we'll meet down here at ten tomorrow and head to the Swarthmore campus?" Juniper asks behind me. She sounds tentative, even nervous.

"Yeah. See you then." My reply is terse and tepid, and I hate it. I wish I could forget the last hour of my life. Not just the distance widening between Juniper and me, but how I now know she views me. It's a huge thing to put behind me, to erase from my thoughts.

I continue to the elevators and punch in the floor Lewis texted me. Walking down the hotel hallway, I let myself hope that a night's sleep will fix us. Tomorrow morning will be a new day. It has to be, because I'm not ready for Juniper and me, for this trip, to be over. I'm not ready to return to the life I had planned.

Lewis opens the door in his sweats when I knock. He gives me a bro nod that I don't bother to figure out the right response to. I ignore him and walk in, planning to pass out on the bed immediately. Except somehow Lewis has managed to take over both of the queen beds with what I can only guess is every item from his suitcase. I pick the less cluttered one and remove Lewis's shirt and jeans.

"Sorry about the mess," Lewis says. I'm distantly grateful when he begins grabbing loose items and tossing them back in his bag. "I thought you might be staying with Juniper."

"We're not even dating," I mutter. I pull my sweats from my suitcase, hoping to escape this conversation quickly.

"Yeah . . ." Lewis draws the word out. "That's not really the way things work in college. Come on, dude. This is one of the perks of traveling with your chill older brother."

"I wasn't aware there were *any* perks," I snap.

In the corner of my peripheral vision I catch his expression falter. It's not a frown, not a flinch—only a nearly imperceptible fading. It's enough to make me feel guilty, not enough for me to be conciliatory. Especially not when he's prodded and joked and insinuated every chance he gets.

He continues to consolidate his unpacked clothes, saying nothing. I change quickly, and it's not long before we hit the lights. Even with the room dark and quiet, I feel the tension pressing out on the walls, unwelcome and impossible to ignore. We've had moments, flickers of levity and something like friendship, over the past week. But the pressure beneath them is growing. I don't know how much longer I can pretend it's not.

Tomorrow is a new day, I remind myself, the starchy hotel pillow crunching under my head. I roll over once, twice, becoming gradually aware how far I am from sleep. It takes me longer to figure out why, to realize it's not only the disconnect with my brother or the unpleasant tension with Juniper.

It's the possibility she's right. I know I'm not wrong to worry what'll happen when my mom's prognosis turns into a diagnosis. What's wiring my thoughts right now is the question of where real worry ends and where excuses begin. I've convinced myself for years I don't care where I go to college, convinced myself I couldn't try things because of my mom's situation. But furthermore, I've convinced myself she's the *only* reason I wouldn't have tried those things. I didn't consider the possibility I would've found other excuses if circumstances were different.

It's disorienting because I honestly don't know if I've been lying to myself this whole time.

JUNIPER

I WALKED INTO the lobby fifteen minutes early to wait for Fitz and Lewis to emerge from the elevator. Swarthmore's only tour today was full, so I prepared my own in the hours before I went to sleep last night, hunting up destinations and history on my phone while under the covers in my empty room. But today, I'm hardly thinking of touring Swarthmore, too wrapped up in the regret that preoccupied me while I showered in the tight hotel bathroom and robotically threw on my clothes, my scarf and jacket.

I want to correct the things I said to Fitz. I went too far, criticizing him for using his mom as an excuse. It's not that I don't believe what I said—I do—only, in the context of the fight, it sounded like it's the only thing I think of him. Which trivialized how difficult I understand his situation is, how brave I know he's being in the face of hard problems. There aren't many people who would challenge themselves the way he has. He needs to hear those things too.

Five minutes past the hour, the elevator dings open and Fitz steps out. Lewis is right behind, rubbing his eyes. Fitz looks everywhere but at me.

"Good morning, Juniper," Lewis says wearily when they reach me.

I give him a tight smile, but I'm focused on Fitz. His expression is muted, his eyes distant. It's not the cold expressionlessness of a statue. It's closer to the apprehensiveness of a statue that's just come to life and has no idea who he is.

Lewis seems to notice the off-kilter dynamic between us. "Well," he says, clearly trying to sound cheerful, "I'm off to find a café. I have a take-home final due by midnight, and I have *not* studied. Have fun."

"Good luck." I tug nervously on my scarf.

Lewis glances at his brother, and I read the concern in his eyes. Instead of saying something, though, he walks toward the door, leaving me alone with Fitz.

The unspoken words between us hum unpleasantly in the hubbub of the hotel lobby. I can't take it anymore. "Look," I start, "I was out of line last night, and I'm sorry." I inhale, preparing to continue when he preempts me.

"It's fine," he says.

I study him, unconvinced. "Is it? Because—"

"Fitz?" A voice echoes from across the lobby. I turn to find a girl standing a few feet behind me wearing a Swarthmore sweatshirt. She looks our age. Her hair is wispy and white-blond, light and fine like spun silver. She's nerdy, if in a cute way.

I've hardly processed her saying Fitz's name when he turns to her, a range of expressions I can't decipher crossing his face.

"Cara," he says, closing the gap between them. "Hi. How are you? What are you doing here?"

"I'm good," Cara says enthusiastically. I wonder how much of that enthusiasm comes from seeing Fitz. "I'm here with my parents to talk to the Swarthmore coach. What about you?"

"Wow, really? For soccer, right?" I can't help comparing Fitz's genuine interest in Cara with his remove toward me.

Cara nods. "I applied early and got in." She sounds proud if a bit embarrassed to share the news.

"Then you're definitely going?" Fitz asks.

She grins. "Yeah. It's been my dream school forever." She self-consciously tucks a strand of her blond hair behind her ear.

"That's amazing. Congratulations." Fitz beams. His unrestrained happiness for her hits me hard. It's funny how when you're fighting with someone, they split into two people. One is friendly and generous with everyone else, and the other is angry and resentful exclusively for you. "We're here to tour the campus," Fitz tells her.

Cara finally shifts her eyes toward me like she's only now noticed I'm here.

"Oh, sorry," Fitz hurries to say. "This is Juniper. She's looking at Swarthmore too."

Her posture stiffens, and I immediately pick up on a jealous vibe. "Hey, I'm Cara." She watches me with something short of suspicion, if nothing close to friendliness. "How do you guys know each other?"

"We just happened to meet while on our own college

tours. We kind of hit it off right away," I tell Cara, sending a small smile at Fitz. His expression softens, and I'm swept off my feet by a wave of relief. "What about you guys? I'm guessing you go to school together?"

"Yeah. Since elementary school," Cara says emphatically. *I get the message.* "Fitz was my date to the eighth grade dance," she continues, eyeing him and blushing.

Fitz blushes too, and suddenly it becomes apparent I'm the third wheel in this conversation.

"Cara very graciously put up with my first and final public display of dancing," he comments, and I get the feeling he's enjoying the recollection.

Cara laughs. "It wasn't *that* bad," she replies. She elbows him gently. "I remember having a good time."

"Me too," Fitz says, and his humor is gone. He looks sad, but I can't quite interpret why. If he's still carrying a torch for Cara, he wouldn't have a reason to be upset, because she's right here in front of him, unmistakably delighted to see him. It's something else.

"Well, I should go," Cara says. "I have to drop my bag in the dorm I'm staying in tonight. One of the freshmen on the team is hosting me. But hey," she continues, her eyes lighting up, "the girl I'm staying with mentioned there's this big midnight breakfast tonight to kick off finals. In Sharples Hall. You should come. Both of you," she clarifies reluctantly. "It sounds totally weird and great."

I have to admit, I'm intrigued. It's exactly the kind of real college experience I went on this trip wanting. I doubt Fitz will go for it, though, remembering how much he didn't want to be at the Brown party.

"That sounds cool," Fitz says. "I think I will." I turn to him, not bothering to hide my disbelief. I don't know if it's because he's frustrated with me or because Cara's there or what. Whatever it is, it's thoroughly unfamiliar.

"Great," Cara says. "I'll see you there." She gives Fitz a quick hug, then runs over to meet her parents, who are holding her bag near the revolving door.

"You don't have to come, of course," Fitz says to me. He sounds generous, but I can't help wondering if he's hinting he doesn't want me there.

"No, I'll come," I say, trying not to be hurt. "Hey," I venture. "Are we okay?"

"Totally."

It's exactly the response I wanted, and he says it with enough conviction that I should believe him. But I don't. We walk toward the revolving door, then into the cold day, and I can't help feeling unbalanced. Fitz has become an unlikely handhold while the other pieces of my life tilt and tumble. With my grip slipping, I don't know how much longer I can hold on until I tumble too.

FITZ

~

ALL DAY, I make the effort to be normal with Juniper. I *want* to be. Otherwise, our limited time together will be wasted. But while I don't resent what she said, I'm desperate to con-vince her I'm not the person she thinks I am. How to do it is the problem.

We're completely cordial to each other while we tour Swarthmore. I follow her on the route she's compiled through the campus, complete with facts on important buildings and campus lore. Our fight doesn't come up, nor her apology. But our connection is off, interrupted, altered in a way I don't know how to fix.

While we tour the campus, I try to concentrate on the beautiful stony buildings and the wide cropping of trees. American elms, Juniper informs me. Forcing myself to com-pare this campus to others I've visited in the full week now I've been on the road, I struggle to think the way I did in New York. To imagine a possible future here.

I can't. I keep circling back to Juniper's words, and to the weird excitement of seeing Cara in our hotel. Cara, who I'd danced with, whose drawings I'd admired, who I could've fallen for had I not fallen into the habit of hiding from things in deference to my mom's health. It's not like I'm interested in Cara now. But she's a reminder of everything I've given up, one of the formerly open doors in my life that I closed because I had to.

The thought preoccupies me while we perambulate Swarthmore. We have lunch off campus, kabobs and pita. Juniper invites me to tour UPenn with her after we eat, and I hear lingering uncertainty in her voice. I do no better, declining with the excuse I want to rest in the hotel before the midnight breakfast. I nap in the room for a couple of hours and then find dinner with Lewis. He brings his laptop with him to the restaurant and works on his exam the whole time.

I don't head back to the Swarthmore campus until close to eleven thirty. I'm expecting the every-which-way energy I remember from Brown, the chaos of partygoers and red cups littering porches and drunken choruses ringing from the windows. Instead, the campus is subdued. It's quiet. Not the tranquil quiet of normal weeknights, either. There's a nervous tension everywhere, like Lewis's unreachable intensity when I left him working in the hotel room.

I text Juniper to tell her I'm close to Sharples Hall. She doesn't reply, which I try to keep from bothering me.

Sharples Hall is wide and low, the walls of gray stone with steep sloping rooftops covered in snow. I walk inside, entering one of the Hogwarts-style dining halls I've come to recognize from the week's campus tours, with rows of long wooden tables and huge circular chandeliers in the reddish-wood room. Everyone filing in with me looks exhausted, trudging in with bleary eyes, untidy hair, and three-day beards. But despite their obvious weariness, they seem upbeat, even lively. Students flit from table to table, laughing, consoling their friends in the occasional pre-finals panic. It's the very definition of camaraderie.

I watch from the entryway, regretting the decision to come. I don't know anyone here. When I get to college, wherever I go, it'll be no different. A college acceptance doesn't come with a cool, close-knit group of friends. I'll be on my own, lingering uncomfortably on the edges of every event, waiting for the one friend I've made to spare me from spending the night shifting on my feet and saying nothing.

I think of texting Cara but ultimately decide not to, knowing I'll only end up ruminating on everything I've given up.

Juniper emerges from a crowd of people on the other end of the room.

Or everything I will *give up.* I shove the thought from my head, focusing instead on the Juniper in front of me now. She looks beautiful. Her ponytail bounces as she walks, her cheeks pink with the cold, her eyes brilliant with their ever-present curiosity.

She searches the room, not yet finding me. I watch her say something to a girl texting by the window. The girl glances up, and then just like that they're having a conversation. It's that easy for her. She approaches people, and they're instantly friends.

It's the final push I needed. The last unwelcome indication I'm not part of this world—not part of Juniper's world. Watching everyone enjoying themselves, close and convivial, I realize I have no reason to be here. I turn to leave and collide with a tall, harried-looking guy.

"Hey, how much time is left?" he asks me. "I forgot my phone in McCabe."

"Uh." I falter, looking behind me to see if he's talking to someone else. There's no one. The guy watches me expectantly. "How much time until what?"

"Midnight. The scream?" he clarifies, except it's no clarification to me.

I pull out my phone, though, and check the time. "It's 11:58. What's the scream?"

"Freshman?" For some reason, the guy sounds delighted.

"Prospective student, actually," I reply.

"Dude, awesome." He drops a heavy hand onto my shoulder and shakes me congenially. "The Primal Scream is when everyone literally screams, letting out the stress and pain of studying for finals. Then we have breakfast. We'll be up all night studying anyway. Might as well have pancakes, right?" I nod, unable to refute his logic. "Hey, what's your name?" he asks.

"Fitz," I tell him.

"Fitz?" he repeats. "Cool name. I'm Dave."

Behind Dave, a girl clambers up onto one of the dining tables. People quiet, eyes turning to her. *"Ten!"* she shouts. Voices join her as she counts down. *"Nine. Eight. Seven."*

"When she reaches the end, scream as loud as you can

about whatever you want. Whatever you have to let out," Dave says.

"I—" I want to tell Dave I'm not interested in screaming or traditions or breakfasts. Except the words don't come. Dave waits with me in the entryway, counting down.

"Two. One."

The room explodes. Everyone raises their heads and screams, shouting shared frustration and fury and maybe even elation into the packed room. It's the loudest sound I've ever heard. It rings deafeningly, and I swear the roof beams shudder. It stuns me for a second, until Dave jostles me with his shoulder, and like the strange energy in the room compels me, I follow everyone.

I scream.

I send everything weighing me down into the din. The fear I've held on to about my mom, the huge questions I'm facing in my future, the doubt I can be what Juniper wants. I shred my vocal cords, hearing my voice disappear into the chorus of release.

Next to me, a guy I don't know steps between Dave and me and throws his arms around our shoulders. The three of us, me and Dave and this complete fucking stranger wail together until we're out of breath.

When finally the scream dies down, I'm grinning. The entire room feels calmer. A line for food starts to form, and I spot Cara in the midst of a group of girls wearing Swarthmore soccer sweatpants. She's flushed the way I undoubtedly am. The girl next to her in line has her arm hooked through Cara's, the two looking like longtime friends.

Cara sees me and waves. I wave back.

"What'd you think?" Dave nudges me, wild-eyed and visibly hyped.

I don't think before I reply. "Obstreperous." It's the first word that jumps into my head, and I regret it immediately. It sounds obnoxious, pretentious.

Dave looks momentarily thrown. "Does that mean loud?" he asks.

"Loud and unruly," I supply hesitantly.

"Yes. Exactly." He nods fervently. He walks past me, heading for the food line. "Come on, Fitz. I need bacon."

I follow through the dining hall, threading between tables and chairs draped with coats. While we pile our plates, Dave introduces me to a few of his friends, guys in the political science program, one of whom is writing his thesis on the political plausibility of *The Handmaid's Tale*. They're friendly, full of questions on my hometown and what I want to study. I notice my nerves from the beginning of the night are gone.

It makes me wonder whether Juniper was right. If my fear of change is something I have to face and fight, and my mom is only my excuse not to. Because tonight had nothing to do with my mom, and yet I was ready to give up on it before I'd even given it a chance. I was going to write this experience off like I did with Cara, like I'd planned with college, like I was preparing to do with Juniper. But I didn't give up on tonight. I let it sweep over me, and the only consequence was that I had a memorable, wonderful night. If I let other things in, it might be fine. It might even be wonderful.

Maybe I've made Mom my excuse every time. For Cara, college, my future.

But if my fear comes from me, I can fight it for myself.

Sitting with Dave and his friends, a plate full of half-finished pancakes before me, my thoughts return to the one thing I need to do. I stand up from the table, searching the room for a particular ponytail.

JUNIPER

I LOVED THE Primal Scream at first. The frenetic buzz was exactly how I'd imagined it when I read up on the tradition over my solitary dinner in Philly. When I entered Sharples Hall, I went up to the first girl I found and asked if she comes every semester. She told me she did, and I wanted to keep talking to her, but she got a text and walked off to join her friends.

Enveloped in the crowd, I wove through tables, looking for Fitz. But the countdown began before I found him. The seconds wound down to midnight, and the room erupted. I prepared to join the hundreds of voices screaming themselves hoarse, pouring out their every emotion in one cathartic rush.

I couldn't. My lungs, my heart, wouldn't. I have things I want to scream. The day with Fitz, everything with Matt, the pressures of my family. I just couldn't.

I hated the feeling. Everywhere around me, students were clinging to each other, laughing, coming together, and all I felt was alone.

I walked out of Sharples Hall into the night, where I heard the echoed screams of students who couldn't come to the dining hall joining in from their dorm rooms. I've been wandering the campus for the past ten minutes, my thoughts a blizzard colder than the wind on my face. I can approach someone and ask her about her school, her major, whatever, but that won't make me her friend. I could be in exactly this position next year, in a crowd of friendly faces and yet entirely alone. Except next year, I won't be returning to high school with my friends, with my sister, at the end of winter break.

When I'm in college, I'll be finding my place and finding my people anew. And with every day I'm connected to my family only through FaceTime and phone calls instead of breakfasts and carpools, I'll be deciding what parts of home to hold onto. How I'll put myself together from the pieces of my past and my present, of old friends and new, of my family, of the two cultures I grew up in.

The pressure won't just be about fitting in with everyone else—it'll be about figuring out where I *want* to fit in. The newness of college will force me to reconsider who I was and refigure who I want to be. Whether I want to keep doing student government. Whether I'll have every meal in the dining hall or will want to cook for myself. Whether I'll find friends who speak more Spanish than I do or less. It's inevitable in transitions, and it's daunting. There's a loneliness in feeling like you no longer know yourself, one that looms large when facing the enormity of the future.

I want peace and quiet to pull myself together, far from the students streaming from Sharples, returning to libraries and dorms. From touring the campus with Fitz, I remember exactly the place I need. I walk in the direction of the woods.

It's not snowing. The night is cloudless, stars spilled on the seemingly endless black of the sky. I huddle in my parka, resenting the cold. It's skin-searing, intense enough to reach through the fabric of my jeans. While I wish I could stay out here longer, I'm no stranger to New England winters. I know I have to get inside soon.

I find my destination on the edge of campus. The Scott Outdoor Amphitheater sits in the midst of the forest behind the college, the semicircular stone steps smothered in snow. I read online they hold commencement here. For a second, I picture this place full of people, proud parents and jittery younger siblings. The image couldn't be in sharper contrast to right now. It's empty, completely quiet.

I wipe snow from the edge of one of the steps and sit. Alone, I let the tears sting my eyes.

In all my college research and anticipation, I never considered the day-to-day details. Having friends, fitting in, finding my place. I never wondered whether I would ever feel lonely, because when I'm home, with nine people in the house, loneliness feels impossible. I never imagined I could feel lost.

For the first time, I wonder if college won't be everything I've envisioned. The thought is harrowing. Worse, if I go to college far from home, far from my family, and I feel this way, I'll *really* be alone. Tía will be right.

It's infuriating. I bitterly wipe the tears from my eyes, hoping if I rub hard enough I'll force this feeling out of me.

It doesn't work. The tears don't stop, and the feeling remains, stuck deep in my chest.

FITZ

SHE COULDN'T HAVE gone far.

I search Sharples Hall for Juniper, scouting every table, every conglomeration of Swarthmore students enjoying the post-Scream solidarity. I don't find her, which is weird. The Primal Scream and midnight breakfast are exactly Juniper's thing. Figuring she might've gotten a call from her family or wanted a minute outside the slightly claustrophobic dining hall, I go out in front of Sharples.

No Juniper. Eventually, I start walking into campus, no sense of where I'm going.

As I wander aimlessly down a path, my boots crunching the salted pavement, my phone buzzes.

I'm at the amphitheater.

I spin and jog toward the outdoor amphitheater Juniper pointed out on our tour. I can't think of a single reason she would be there now, in the middle of the freezing night, except the possibility of some other campus tradition I don't know about. I've heard some schools partake in winter streaking, which admittedly is not something I'm eager to witness. But if Juniper's there, I'll willingly risk naked butts.

When I near the stone steps, I see her immediately. It's not hard. She's the only person here. Sitting in one of the rows, she's illuminated by starlight, her huddled posture strangely small and forlorn in the empty theater.

I walk up to her slowly, not wanting to startle her. She says nothing when I sit next to her. "What are you doing out here on your own?" I ask.

"I wanted to watch the stars," she says. Her voice is off, tight and overly nonchalant. "It's a really nice night." She doesn't look at me, her face turned to the sky. I study her. Shadows and moonlight mingle along her neck, her cheeks. The clouds drift, revealing the moon, and the light touches Juniper's features. Her eyes are puffy. Only slightly, with the barest hint of red rimming the edges. She's been crying.

"Yeah, it's beautiful tonight," I reply. I don't know how to comfort her, or if it's even my place to comfort her. Would it be prying to ask why she's upset? I get the sense she doesn't want me to know she's emotional.

She shifts, angling her legs toward me. "Did you have fun tonight?"

I don't want to talk about my night. But this is Juniper. She directs the conversation exactly where she wants it. "I think I sort of did," I answer, trying to come up with a way to turn the questions on her without being demanding or insensitive.

She smiles faintly without a trace of pleasure. "That's great. Did you find Cara?" Her tone is . . . jealous? I know some guys find jealousy flattering. Immediately, I learn I do not enjoy it on Juniper. The idea she is hurting over something I have done—it's the furthest thing from flattering.

"Juniper, what's wrong?" The question escapes me before I can think of a way to bring it up lightly.

Sure enough, her expression hardens. "Nothing. I'm fine," she says quickly. A tear trickles down her cheek, and she turns away, hurriedly wiping her face with the back of her hand.

"Hey." I reach for her, wanting to take her in my arms, but she leans away.

Her shoulders start to shake, her breaths turning clipped and wet. "God, I hate this," she says between sobs. "I shouldn't even be crying. It's so dumb."

I touch her arm. Just a brush of fingertips on the hem of her sleeve. It's nothing—the suggestion of comfort, a reminder I'm here and I care. It's so much less than I want to give her. "Whatever it is, it's not dumb," I tell her.

Her sobs subside a little. "You shouldn't be nice to me. I was awful to you last night." She meets my eyes, tears clinging to her cheeks. "I'm sorry I said you use your mom as an excuse."

All day, I waited for her to take her words back. To acknowledge she'd gotten me wrong. But it doesn't matter to me now. "I'll admit you were direct," I say with a hint of humor, "but you were right. I do hold myself back." Her tears have stopped, and it's possible her shoulders have drifted toward mine. "Like with Cara," I go on. "I liked her in eighth grade and was planning to ask her out." I make the past tense explicit, hoping she understands. "Then I found out about my mom, and I gave up. I thought I did it to spare her from having to deal with my problems, but now I think it's because I was scared of risking something else that might hurt me."

Her expression hardens. She rubs her nose with a punctuating sniffle. "Oh, well, great," she says shortly. "I'm happy for you, Fitz. Cara's here now. I guess you can make up for lost time."

I open my mouth to reply, and instead I laugh. It's wildly, outlandishly ridiculous.

My laughter only incenses Juniper further, which I probably could have anticipated. She rounds on me, glaring, her dazzling eyes full of indignant combativeness. "What?" she challenges.

"You're not serious, right?"

"Oh, I'm not?" I hear her chiseling her voice into the logical confidence I've heard in every conversation with her. I guess it's her natural instinct. "You can apply to Swarthmore, go to college together, and be happy."

I can't help it. I keep laughing, and now the noise is fuller, ringing out in the empty woods.

Juniper's stained cheeks have colored furiously pink. "What is so funny?" she demands, her voice pitchy.

"Juniper," I get out, "I liked Cara in *eighth grade*. Not now."

She's quiet for a beat, guarded and uncertain. "Not now?" she finally repeats.

"No," I say. "Now the only thing I want is to finish this college tour. With you." It's the truth. For the past few days, I've welcomed uncertainty I never would have before, exploring colleges with real eyes and forsaking my conviction I was bound for SNHU. Instead of deciding my future was written in stone, I've embraced not knowing what it holds. The only thing I *do* know for certain is how much I want Juniper in my life every minute of our remaining days together.

Her expression evens with what I sense is relief. Her eyes remain distant, though, fixed on some hurt I can't see.

"Cara wasn't the reason you were crying," I say gently. It's not a question.

I don't fully expect her to reply. But she hugs one knee to her chest, perching her foot on the step, before she explains. "I guess partly," she says. "But no, I just . . ." She inhales deeply. When she speaks, her words come in a clear, unqualified rush. "I'm not used to feeling alone," she says. "I never have the chance. Three sisters, two brothers, an overbearing aunt. Tonight, I felt lonely for the first time, maybe ever, and I just kept thinking this is what college will be like. Except worse because I'll have moved away from my family, and I'll be feeling alone in the place I've chosen as my home."

The thought that Juniper Ramírez could share my own insecurities momentarily stuns me. She's beautiful and outgoing and smart and fearless. It makes sense for someone like me to anticipate loneliness in college, but her? It's comforting, in a way. "I know what you mean," I say.

Her eyes lift to mine, searching and hopeful. "You do?"

"Of course," I answer. "I'm beginning to suspect everyone feels lonely some of the time. But, Juniper"—I take her hand—"you have to know you're the last person who needs to worry about this. You're charming and outgoing and fearless. You didn't even know me a week ago. Now look at us." The corner of her mouth curls, and I squeeze her fingers. "You're not alone. Not now. Not by any definition. And I know you'll find amazing friends wherever you end up."

She leans in to me, pressing herself to my side. I wrap my arm around her and try very hard not to let the closeness of her body affect me.

Her head rests on my shoulder, the incline of my neck. I turn my head, lowering my cheek and nose to her hair, the curls pulled tight into her ponytail. I remember the way she smells from the rooftop overlooking Brown. There's the floral ether probably from shampoo, and then something infinitely more complex, entirely her. Her body is tucked warmly to mine, her figure nestled into me exactly.

It's perfect. Except for one thing.

"Juniper?" I say.

"Yeah?" I feel her speak on my shoulder.

"It's freezing."

She laughs dryly, pulling herself upright. I kick myself for precipitating this unfortunate turn of events, but I did notice my fingertips starting to purple.

Juniper releases my hand and stands up, shivering once. "Walk with me to the hotel?"

Obviously, I nod. I try not to betray how freaking ecstatic I am we were just holding hands, again, and I had my arm around her.

We walk together from the amphitheater back toward campus. My ears have recalibrated from the din of the Primal

Scream, and I pick up the noises of the outdoors while we walk. The rustling of animals that've found homes in the bushes, the hum of the occasional car, the hooting of a far-away owl. We walk in silence. It's not uncomfortable this time, not like the disastrous echoing emptiness of the drive down here. I'm mentally replaying the conversation we had in the amphitheater, finding myself unable to stop reexamining every detail.

"So you *were* jealous of Cara." I don't say it to pry into or delight in her frustration, but because there's something I have to make clear.

"No, I wasn't!" she protests, righteously indignant. It's one of her top three moods.

"I'm getting pretty good at reading you, Juniper Ramírez," I reply, knowing it's a bit of a bold thing to say. I'm becoming increasingly comfortable being bold with her, and I'm definitely enjoying it. She huffs, and I continue before she hits me with some perfect retort. "But let me tell you, you have no reason for jealousy." I pause. Admitting how I feel is unquestionably scary. It's a huge risk—possibly the biggest risk—but after tonight, I'm ready. It could go horribly. Or it could turn into something wonderful. I'm ready to find out. "I like you." I say it quickly but not without confidence.

Juniper's lips twitch with either a pleased smile or contained laughter at the ridiculousness of my affections. "Tell me," she says abruptly, "what's your favorite word for sorrow?"

I'm thrown by the question, still trying to decipher her reaction. "Dolor," I answer after a moment, hoping my confession hasn't flung her into hopeless dolor and that's why she's asking.

"Thank you for curing my dolor, Fitz." She takes my hand.

It's not horrible. Far from it. It feels like the start of something incredible. In the time since the High Line, we've joked and fought and fallen out, and even though it's been only days, I'm boundlessly grateful we're reconnecting.

I walk with her through the campus, now hardly feeling the cold.

FITZ

~

EARLY THE NEXT morning, I'd only just finished pulling on
my sweater when I heard knocking on the hotel room door. I
swung the door open and found Juniper. We smiled stupidly
and said our hellos with a breathlessness I didn't know hellos
could have. I think we both felt like last night never really
ended, only continued into today.

She looked past me and said hi to Lewis, and then de-
clared she'd changed our plans. Instead of driving to Baltimore and Johns Hopkins, which was on my original itinerary,
she'd decided we would instead visit Pittsburgh. She wouldn't
say why, only commenting cryptically she had something she
wanted to show me.

I'd nodded like this was completely normal and expected and didn't ask any questions. I probably kept smiling my
same stupid smile. Honestly, she could drive us to the world's
biggest ball of twine or the horology museum. As long as I
was with her, I'd be thrilled. This trip has been nothing if not
a testament to how wholly and completely places can change
because of the people in them.

When she left, Lewis asked me if he needed to come up

with an excuse to put me in Juniper's car for the drive. I shook my head, thinking of her hand in mine and a snowy walk lit by starlight. I think Juniper and I both know we're driving together.

✳ ✳ ✳

We've been on the road now for nearly four hours, though it's felt like less. I'm hardly paying attention to the outside world—trees, off-ramps, more trees, I'm guessing. I don't even register the difference between the brilliant day and the illuminated darkness of the numerous tunnels we drive through under mountains in the Pennsylvania wilderness. We've talked about everything, the conversation flowing easily from our families to our friends back home, extracurriculars and irritating classmates. While the highway passes in the windows, it feels like the rest of the world is on pause.

Finally, we pull over for gas. I noticed the meter on Juniper's dashboard drop into the red an hour ago. Despite my repeated efforts to convince her to fill the tank, only now have I prevailed. She's one of those people who claims she "knows her car." I suspect she really just doesn't want to stop when she's on her way somewhere.

We park, and I reach into the back seat for my parka. It's fallen onto the floor and is covered in detritus I don't recognize. Scraps of paper, bent photographs, and what looks like an unfinished knit scarf have tumbled from a large shoebox tipped over from the back seat.

"What is this stuff?" I ask Juniper. I hold up the half-finished scarf.

Juniper glances back, and her eyes darken with protectiveness and possibly melancholy when she sees what's in my hands. "It's nothing," she says. She reaches in the open car door and starts returning the items to the shoebox with a care I don't expect. I hand her the scarf, which she doesn't exactly look happy to see, but she places the fabric into the shoebox like it's precious. "They're just, I don't know, important keepsakes," she explains. "Private stuff I didn't want to leave home with my sisters."

She stows the box under the driver's seat and shuts the door. We walk toward the convenience store. "So sentimental," I say, teasing. "Juniper Ramírez holding on to pieces of the past?"

Juniper rolls her eyes. "Caring about the past and wanting to live in it forever are completely different." She shoves me playfully.

"Ow," I say.

"Ow?" she repeats incredulously. "I hardly even touched you."

"I'm, uh . . ." I start, regretting the direction of this conversation. "I'm sore."

"We've been sitting in a car for four hours. How could your arms possibly be sore? Have you been sneaking to the gym in the middle of the night?"

I feel myself flush. It's not the nice kind of flush, either, the kind you get from compliments or a girl's head resting on your shoulder. "No, I've just been doing push-ups in the morning," I say, letting my voice get quieter with each word and hoping the subject vanishes into nothing.

It doesn't work. Juniper narrows her eyes. *"Why?"*

"I don't need a reason." I walk quicker, entering the store ahead of Juniper, desperately fleeing this conversation.

She cuts in front of me and spins to face me. Walking backward, she says, "I think you have nice arms." She winks and darts into the snack aisle. "I'll get chips. You get candy. Nothing without chocolate," she calls over her shoulder.

Not even trying to wipe the grin from my face, I pick up a handful of candy bars and head to the front. While Juniper fills up the tank, I notice the postcards on the rack next to the register. They read *Frank Lloyd Wright's Fallingwater,* with pictures of a house like none I've ever seen, stone columns and concrete ledges stacked in the midst of trees and small streams. Under the name, the postcard heralds the house as *the greatest example of American architecture.*

I pull one out and show the clerk, who's reading a magazine. "Hey," I say. "Is this nearby?"

"Thirty minutes," the clerk says without looking up. "Take exit ninety-one."

I buy the postcard and candy and walk to the car, where Juniper is returning the nozzle to the pump. When we're both settled in the car, I drop the postcard in her lap. "Think we have time for a detour?"

JUNIPER

FITZ IS TRYING to talk his way into a Fallingwater tour. Apparently, it's a reservation system, and the next tour group is fully booked. Fitz refused to be deterred. He's watching the woman behind the ticket counter while she types his name into the computer.

"I'm afraid I'm not finding you," she says with a put-on frown. "Do you have the credit card you used to purchase the tickets?"

Fitz hands over his card, which I know is actually his brother's card. After we decided to take this detour, we called Lewis, who was only minutes behind us. He met us at the gas station, and we explained to him our new plan. With a knowing glint in his eyes, he gave Fitz the card and told us he would just head straight for Pittsburgh, giving us the afternoon to ourselves.

Fitz steals a glance at me, and I hold in a laugh. It's kind of impressive, though. Put a minor logistical hurdle between this boy and his early-twentieth century Prairie School house of choice and he becomes James Bond.

"I'm not finding any purchases on this card," the woman says. "Are you sure this is the one you used?"

"Definitely." Fitz nods. "It was months ago. Right, Juniper?"

I plaster on a profoundly concerned expression. "Yeah. For my birthday in October."

While the woman continues typing, Fitz turns to me. *October?* he mouths.

I hold up eight fingers. *The eighth,* I mouth back.

He grins, and our eyes lock, and we're held in this moment of heartbeats, improbabilities, and undeniable chemistry.

"I don't know what happened," the woman says, her voice interrupting our connection. Fitz's eyes flit to her. "I don't have your name or your card. I'm so sorry. We have openings tonight if you'd like to purchase tickets for this evening?"

"But I did purchase them," Fitz insists. "For right now. We planned our whole day around this. I promised her."

I sigh in fake frustration. "It's fine," I say, enjoying the theatrics. "Let's just go." I step away from the counter.

Fitz leans in toward the woman. "Please. My girlfriend is going to be pissed if I screw this up. It's her favorite work of architecture." I'm thrown by how natural the label sounds. The word *girlfriend* feels right, the expected destination of the road we've been traveling from perfect strangers to whatever we are now. Fitz continues, lowering his voice. I'm only able to make out what he's saying thanks to years of Marisa and me eavesdropping on our parents. "Between you and me, it's been a rough few months. We're facing a long-distance relationship in college. This"—he gestures in the direction of the house—"could make the difference for me. For us."

He looks genuinely forlorn. I'm impressed with his performance—or perhaps he's not acting. I wonder if he's heard echoes of his words for the past few days. *College. Distance.*

"All right," the woman says, sighing. She hands over two tickets, and Fitz looks enormously pleased with himself.

When he hurries back to me, he takes my hand without warning. I look down. "Nice cover story," I say dryly.

"It felt appropriate."

I shake my head, pretending I'm scornful instead of delighted. "She definitely wasn't convinced. We're way too platonic to pull it off."

"Right," he says. "Feel free to drop my hand anytime now."

"I promise you, I will. When she's not looking," I fire back. "Wouldn't want to give you the wrong idea."

I expect Fitz to reply with a joke. Instead, something complex comes over his face, and his lips part like he's considering a question, but he doesn't get the chance to ask it. The tour guide greets the group and ushers us in the direction of Fallingwater.

I want to know what he's thinking, how the electric humor of before shifted inexplicably into whatever just entered his expression. But we're silent while the tour guide introduces the house and Wright's work. Before I have the chance to make good on my promise, Fitz drops my hand.

JUNIPER

THE TOUR IS breathtaking. I walk up to Frank Lloyd Wright's iconic house with Fitz and the tour group, which is almost entirely middle-aged people wearing bulky cameras around their necks. The home emerges from the trees like it was meant to be here. Snow-covered branches embrace the wide windows overlooking the trees and boulders, where the cream-colored walls fit in like pieces of the scenery. The structure sits on top of an icy stream, the levels of the house mirroring the waterfalls beneath them.

It's not just beautiful. It's the unique beauty of being in exactly the right place. This house could have been built in hundreds of forests, over hundreds of streams in the country, but Wright decided to design a masterwork on this one. This piece of Pennsylvania where it belongs. It reminds me of the schools we've passed through and what I'm hoping to find in them.

We tour the interior, stories of stone pillars and minimalist staircases. Every room feels sculpted, perfectly planned. We walk outside to view a staircase suspended over the icy water, and it's one of those moments where the passion I have for architecture shifts from something I know about myself to something I feel with imperative. This is what I love.

I catch Fitz studying the shelves and wooden furniture, and I'm hit with enormous gratitude. Everything about this detour is better because he thought of it. He knew me. He did this for me. While we wander the second story, I notice myself admiring him as much as the architecture. His inquisitively pursed lips, his blue eyes and their unreadable intensity.

His hands. I'm done for.

He glances my way, his expression questioning, hopeful. I know he wants to know if I'm happy, if this place captivates me the way he intended. I give him a smile I hope says, *It's perfect.* He returns the smile, and I recognize the gift he's really giving me, even if he doesn't know it himself. He understands the person I'm becoming. He understands not only who I am now, but who I want to be.

By the time the tour ends, his arm has wandered around my waist—a development to which I don't object, letting my hip press to his. We grab lunch from the café and return to the car. We're headed for Cucumber Falls, which the guide mentioned was a "romantic" destination ten minutes from Fallingwater. I jokingly suggested we go and then hid my delight when Fitz nodded decisively.

We park in the small lot in front of the trailhead and stroll down the path into the forest. Finding our way through the trees, we climb over rocks my boots don't handle well, clambering down to the base of the waterfall. Because it's winter and it's snowing lightly, there isn't anybody else on the trail.

The forest is quiet except for the crunch of brush and ice under our feet.

Reaching the bottom, I come up beside Fitz in front of the frozen lake. It's not large, the surface dark and glassy in the frigid day. The waterfall drops from the rocky ledge overhead into the water—or would drop if it weren't frozen. Instead, it's a wall of ice, suspended in perpetual descent. Icy rivulets ripple on its edges. Everything is coated in white powder.

"It's beautiful," I breathe.

"Yeah," Fitz agrees. I feel his shoulder brush mine.

I elbow him lightly. "Surely you have a better word to describe it."

He grins. "Several, actually."

"Tell me."

He walks to the edge of the ice, eyes roaming the clearing. From how he's intently studying the waterfall, the snow, everything, I know he's taking the request seriously. I don't ignore the genuine excitement I feel welling in me. This boy and his words. They're irresistible.

"*Riparian,*" he finally says. "Being on the banks of a river. *Quiescent.* In a period of dormancy. *Gelid.* Extremely cold," he continues.

His eyes shift to mine.

"*Sublime,*" he says.

I feel my breath hitch, the cold captured in my chest.

"*Intimate,*" he says, softer.

My heart thuds, deafening in the empty forest.

"*Resplendent. Bewitching. Breathtaking,*" Fitz concludes.

He watches me for a moment more.

"Juniper," he says. "You're looking at my lips again."

"So?" My voice is breathy. I know without a hint of doubt it's not the temperature or the *resplendent* natural beauty holding the air from my lungs. I'm guessing Fitz knows too. His eyes fix on my lips, and I wait. I wait. I wait.

"It's giving me the wrong idea," he says.

The pull is undeniable. It's a new definition for what I've felt between us during the past few days. It's no longer a hint. It's now a demand. Not from him, but from the universe, calling on us to decide here and now what we're going to be. What we could be.

I step forward. Our boots nearly touch. I could put a hand on his chest or reach up to his sculpted cheekbones and the stretch of his neck exposed to the cold. *"Wrong* isn't the right word," I say.

"What is, then?" he asks, his face suddenly serious.

"This." I pull him close, lifting myself on my toes. For a moment, when I lean forward, I feel the warmth of his breath in the air.

I kiss him.

FITZ

~

I KNOW HUNDREDS of words to describe kissing. In this moment, I forget every one of them.

Part of my mind wants to find the right words to define Juniper's lips on mine, a way to categorize and recall right now for years to come. The rest of me, though, isn't thinking in words. Only feeling. The feeling of everything in my entire being rushing into the precise point where we connect. The softness of her skin, warm and electrifying and undeniably her. The cumulative charge of a week's worth of unlikely crossings and surprising closeness. Instinctively, my hand finds the bend in her back, pressing her closer. Our lips part. The kiss deepens, and the world disappears.

Eventually, we pull away. It was only seconds, but they're seconds that could have been eternity for their irreversible impact on me.

From the dizzied echoes of my brain comes one thought. I say it without thinking. "*Kissing me* isn't a word."

Juniper frowns with flushed cheeks. "What?"

"You said *wrong* wasn't the right word," I explain. "I asked you what the right word was, and you kissed me. *Kissing me* isn't a word," I repeat, aware of how dumb this sounds.

Coyly, Juniper hooks her fingers in my belt loops and tugs me to her. "No," she says. "It's better, right?"

"Considerably." With her chin tilted up toward mine, I feel my mental faculties beginning to leave me once more. This time, it's me who bridges the inches between us, brushing my lips to hers. It's just like the first time, right down to the awe I even get to kiss this incredible girl. In this place frozen in time, the river poised on the edge of falling forever, I genuinely believe we could remain here forever too.

Between kisses, my mind finally figures it out. The word to describe this moment.

Perfect.

FITZ

⌐

WHILE I WOULD have welcomed the idea of spending the rest of the day making out by the waterfall, when we part, Juniper checks the time on her phone and immediately declares we have to go. I don't press her to explain, knowing the interruption has to do with her itinerary, and nothing gets in the way of Juniper's itinerary. We eat our cold, somewhat-squashed sandwiches in the car while Juniper drives the final hour to Pittsburgh.

The city is thick with trees, ice hanging from their bleak branches in front of low concrete-and-stone buildings. The streets have the nonsensical, uneven directionality of colonial roads retrofitted for cars. We pull into the visitor parking lot for Carnegie Mellon University, a school Juniper must have chosen without telling me. It wasn't listed on either of our original itineraries or the one we created together.

I close the car door and then pull out my phone. "Should I look up how to get to the admissions building?"

"Nope," she says quickly. She starts walking, and I follow her. "We're not going to the admissions building."

"Then where are—"

She silences me with a kiss. "Just follow me," she says.

I don't object. She leads me through the wide-open fields cutting through the campus while she consults her phone for directions. We end up in front of a low beige building with arches over the green-trimmed windows. Wordlessly, Juniper opens the door for me. We file in, bumping shoulders with college students holding heavy textbooks and looking exhausted. Juniper turns corners in the hallways of white-and-burgundy brick until we reach the entrance to a large lecture hall. Students trickle in, taking seats spread out across the auditorium.

Juniper stops by the door and faces me with nervous excitement. "I thought we might sit in on this class."

"Is that allowed?" I ask, stepping aside to let a short woman wearing a long dress and boots pass us. She walks right up to the podium and pulls a laptop from her bag.

"I emailed with the department head, and he said we were free to audit whatever class we wanted," Juniper says. "Since it's the middle of finals here, the only classes are review sessions."

I lean past her to peer into the filling auditorium. The sight of students flipping through notebooks, halfheartedly typing in their computers, sipping coffee from Starbucks cups is striking in a way I can't quite describe. There's something distinctly quotidian about the scene. A day-to-day ordinariness I hadn't anticipated. With every tour I've been on, I've built this perception of college as this huge event. Something we work toward and then achieve. The object of countless discussions and brochures meant to exaggerate and entice.

But this review session, these somewhat sleepy students, this half-full hall—they're nothing grand. It's quiet and common and real. It's one moment in thousands of nearly identical moments these students will have. *I* will have. If not here, then somewhere.

It makes next year real in a way nothing has before. This everyday, unremarkable view of college life is somehow bigger and more significant than a thousand tours or information sessions, parties or Primal Screams.

It's scary, but kind of thrilling.

"What class is it?" I search the room for indications, titles on textbooks or handwriting on the whiteboard. I figure it's probably related to architecture, given Juniper's evident anticipation.

"It's called the Nature of Language," Juniper tells me. "Carnegie Mellon has an excellent linguistics program. This is the introductory course."

It takes me a moment to understand. "Linguistics?" I repeat. It's not a topic either one of us has expressed interest in.

"You have a gift for words, Fitz. I thought . . ." She takes my hand. "Let's just go in and listen."

I nod numbly, touched and overwhelmed by her thoughtfulness and her effort in talking to the department head, finding the class, rerouting her trip. I guess I should have expected Juniper would bring the same care and intensity to others that she brings to her own life.

We walk in and find seats in the back of the lecture hall. While we wait, the gentle clatter of laptops being placed on desks and jackets dropping onto empty chairs gradually dies down. I feel like an interloper, but in a good way. Like I'm meant to be here. I'm only early.

The professor launches into a review of what I'm guessing is the entire semester's coursework. I listen, swept up, following the thread she's tracing of how words work and evolve, how language relates to psychology and philosophy and literature. It's captivating.

Sitting beside Juniper, our shoulders pressed together, I feel a thought steal slowly over me. The interest I have in words could be more than a marked-up dictionary, more than a vocabulary my brother finds odd. It could be an entire future.

JUNIPER

FITZ IS FLIPPING through a linguistics book while we wait in the student center. He loved the class, which I knew he would. He even went up to the professor at the end of the lecture. I watched from the door, unable to hear the conversation and entirely adoring the obvious interest illuminating Fitz's expression, the animated way he nodded and hung on to the professor's every word.

She recommended a few books for him to read, and we went directly from her class to the campus bookstore. The bookstore clerk, a junior named Daniela, helped us find the books, and we ended up talking while Fitz decided which one he wanted. She told me about nearly missing a final because she'd driven to New York City to see her favorite band the night before, and her easy, confident rebelliousness reminded me of my cousin Luisa. I found myself wondering how Luisa's liking UC Santa Cruz and if she ever gets lonely so far from home. I don't know if talking to someone with the subtlest accent like my aunts and uncles was unexpectedly nice, or if I just miss my cousin, but I decided I would call Luisa when I get home.

Now Fitz and I are waiting for Lewis, who's meeting us for dinner after doing who-knows-what today in Pittsburgh. The guy is a master of giving us space. I steal a glance at Fitz, wondering if he's going to call his mom. He normally does whenever we have extra time. He hasn't today, though, and I can't help thinking he's uncharacteristically comfortable taking time for himself, getting distance from home.

While Fitz reads, I look up directions to Washington, D.C., for our drive tomorrow. Pittsburgh was considerably out of our way, but thinking of the lecture and Fallingwater and what happened at the waterfall—the detour was completely worth it.

I hadn't planned on kissing Fitz. At least, not consciously. I realized it was inevitable when he was right there in front of me, finding the perfect words for the waterfall and for us, being exactly the person I needed. Truthfully, I've been replaying the kiss in my head the entire day. The way his surprise melted into wanting, the way he kissed me slowly, like we were skirting the edge of something desperately wonderful. I was right—he was a deliberate kisser. But before long he shed the deliberateness, and neither one of us was in control. We collapsed into the rush of being together. It felt like we weren't below a waterfall but on top of one, and we'd just embraced each other and thrown ourselves off.

Bickering from the adjacent table yanks me from the reverie. I glance over, irritated. It's a couple fighting, I think. The girl is a gorgeous blonde with a perfect tan and effortlessly cool clothes. The boy has unruly brown curls, and he's wearing a T-shirt that reads NAUGHTY DOG.

The girl throws her fork down and shoves her plate away. "The food here is terrible," she declares. "I don't know how you stand it."

"It's not terrible," the boy replies. "It's just not LA."

LA. It explains the girl's Urban Outfitters style and the magazine-cover bronze of her skin.

"Exactly," she shoots back.

The boy sighs. "Then go home, Cameron. I don't know why you're even here."

"Fine. You want to do this now?" She leans back, and from where I'm sitting, it looks like the girl—Cameron—very much wants to do this now.

"I don't know what *this* means," the boy says, exasperated. "We already broke up. A month ago. It's over."

I glance at Fitz, not wanting to hear this, yet I can't help but listen. I don't want to think about breakups. Not now. Not yet. Fitz looks focused on his book, and I consider getting up and joining him on his side of the table, immersing myself in philology instead of dwelling on fights and distance and endings.

"You broke up with me in the middle of a fight," Cameron says, crossing her arms. "I had more to say."

The boy lets out a harsh laugh. "You flew across the country to get the last word in an argument?"

"Yes," Cameron says simply, like it's reasonable.

The response nearly cracks the boy's anger, but he finds it again quickly. "What did you want to say, then, Cameron? We tried long-distance. It didn't work. You said yourself you weren't happy." There's heartbreak in the way the boy admits it. I can tell he's still hurting over it, over losing her.

Cameron furiously wipes tears from her eye. "Stupid," she says under her breath, like she's frustrated by the show of emotion. "I'm not even sad," she tells the boy. "I'm mad. I should've been the one to end this." She looks upward, no longer meeting his eyes. "I still can't believe Brendan Rosenfeld dumped *me*."

"I can't believe I dumped you either," Brendan Rosenfeld replies. "Everyone from Beaumont must be reeling." They share a look, and this time it's not bitter or despondent. It's halfway to humorous.

Then Cameron's face falls. "Paige told me you weren't coming home for winter break. She said you're doing some winter program and staying with your roommate's family for the holidays." She self-consciously runs her hand through her sun-bleached hair. "That's why I flew across the country."

"You didn't wonder if you were the reason I didn't come home?" Brendan asks. "I knew seeing you would be hard, and I was right."

I glance up, hoping Lewis will walk in and deliver me from having to overhear the rest of this disastrous conversation. He doesn't. The student center remains nearly empty, and there's nothing I can do to block out Cameron and Brendan.

Cameron frowns. "Yeah? Well, too bad," she replies harshly. "Because sometimes being with the person you love *is* hard. Sometimes it sucks. Sometimes you're unhappy. Sometimes you need time to adjust to your formerly reclusive boyfriend now having fifty million friends who are stupidly smart and, in certain cases, frustratingly attractive."

"You think it was easy for me when you started college?" Brendan's voice is low, his eyes fixed on hers. "You think I enjoyed hearing about the fraternity parties you would go to with your sorority? No."

"You could've spoken up," Cameron says, her face flushed. "You always shove everything down and then you use it against me. Speak your mind, Brendan," she orders. "Like this. I'm pissed at you for breaking up with me when we were having a real conversation. It was immature, stupid, and selfish of you."

Cameron is close to combusting, but I notice Brendan's lips twitch. "Don't tell me you're trying to apologize," he says, sounding like he finds this funny.

"Of course I'm not apologizing, Brendan," she replies with a withering glare. "If anything *you* owe *me* an—"

She doesn't finish the sentence because Brendan reaches forward and takes her hand.

"Cameron," he says. "I'm sorry. Take a walk with me?"

I watch Cameron's anger evaporate. It's uncanny, how her expression, her whole person changes. It's like there are two of her, one fiery and one forgiving, and they coexist in imperfect harmony. "Okay," she says.

They get up from the table and head for the door. I try to forget their conversation, to focus on my phone and not on the tightness in my chest. It doesn't work. The thoughts tumble one over the next like rocks falling from a crumbling mountaintop. Cameron and Brendan clearly broke up because of the strains of going to college in different cities.

I don't know why I'm taking their breakup personally. It's

not like I'm contemplating a long-term relationship with Fitz. But being faced with this reality takes hold of the memory of our kiss and gives it a painful twist. Whatever happens in the rest of our time together, I don't want to think of Fitz and me being over. When we part, I'll have nothing tying him to my present. My family doesn't even know he exists. Tía won't question me about him, my sisters won't pry and tease. He'll exist only in my memory. I don't want to imagine our connection consigned to the past, which I've disregarded for years while putting my hopes in the future. I don't want him to become a piece of everything I'm leaving behind.

It's bound to happen, but I'm not looking forward to it.

I glance at Fitz. He's no longer reading his book, his eyes fixed on the retreating couple. His expression reflects mine.

Neither of us says anything.

FITZ

I OVERHEARD THE entire fight. It's a harsh reminder of exactly how unlikely this thing with Juniper is to outlive the week. *Thing.* Ironically enough, I don't even know the proper word for whatever we are. It's that new and uncertain. Fling? Relationship? Pattern of kissing I hope continues? Whatever we are, I need to prepare myself to say goodbye in a couple of days. I don't know if I can.

"I got the job." I hear my brother's voice behind me.

I turn, finding Lewis standing by the table. He's holding his phone, looking stunned.

"The recruitment officer just called me. . . . I got it," he says, repeating the news like it hasn't set in.

I jump up without thinking. In a corner of my mind, I know what I'm expecting to feel. I should be upset, should be frustrated that he'll be going to New York when he graduates, leaving me with the obligations of home and the entire emotional weight of our mom's situation on my shoulders.

Improbably, I'm not. I'm happy for my brother. Elated,

actually. Even though there's an unspoken well of resentment lingering between us, I want this for him.

It takes me a second to comprehend why. Lewis living in New York will make things harder for me eventually, but I understand wanting something the way Lewis wants this future. I get having hopes and dreams big enough to push the fears from your periphery.

"That's great, Lewis," I say, meaning it. "We should celebrate."

Lewis nods, looking distracted. "Yeah. Yeah, we should." He sounds distant.

I study him, wondering if he's finally feeling guilty for leaving home. I quickly extinguish the thought. It has to be something else. Maybe the offer is shitty. Maybe he didn't like the boss. I can't imagine Lewis would mope about details like those when it comes to this opportunity.

"This is what you wanted, right?" I ask tentatively. Juniper watches wordlessly from her seat.

"It is," he replies, staring past me. "I've been working toward this moment for years. It's my dream job. I should be thrilled." He speaks slowly, unevenly, like he's reciting the details of someone else's life.

"But . . . ?"

His eyes find mine, his expression broken. "Prisha will be in San Francisco."

I pause, not quite understanding what I'm hearing. "I thought—weren't you planning to break up?" Whenever Lewis talks about his and Prisha's future, he's cavalier to the point of careless. I never predicted she would figure into his career considerations.

"We were. We *are*," he corrects himself morosely. "I guess it's just hitting me now."

I don't know what to say. I've never seen my brother like this. Not when he got rejected from Columbia, not when he broke up with his high school girlfriend, not even when we heard our mom's test results. Juniper and I exchange a look.

"You're right," Lewis says, straightening. "We should celebrate." He sounds like he's convincing himself. In the next second, the old unflappable Lewis returns, and in the interim, I feel like I've seen behind a curtain. I've stolen a glimpse into how efficiently Lewis stows whatever is bothering him into someplace unseen. "Sushi?" he says cheerfully.

"Are you sure?" Juniper asks, still looking concerned.

"I want to focus on the win tonight," Lewis replies, his voice taking on a hint of the sincerity it held moments ago, before his collected persona returned. "The rest will be waiting for me tomorrow."

Juniper nods. With that, we collect our jackets and head from the student center into the snow and wind. Juniper searches for sushi restaurants on her phone while I walk with Lewis, neither of us speaking. It's a tentatively comfortable silence. We settle on Sushi Fuku and head for the city.

We're stepping off campus when I see the couple from earlier. Cameron and Brendan. They're wrapped in each

other, kissing like they have forever to do it. Warmth flut-
ters in my chest. I reach for Juniper's hand. When I inter-
lace my fingers with hers, she smiles.

Lewis was right. Focus on the good tonight. The rest is
waiting.

JUNIPER

⌁

"I CAN'T BELIEVE you told Dad you and Matt broke up before you told me."

I'm on the phone with Marisa in the hotel room. It's nearly ten, and I'm uncomfortably full of sushi and sashimi and soy sauce. The evening was fun, despite Lewis's momentary melancholy. He ordered saké, though not enough that Fitz had to carry him home. I was getting out of the shower when Marisa called, having just heard about Matt from Dad.

"I didn't want to tell him," I protest. "He trapped me."

"I'm just glad he didn't force you to come home," she replies. "Having the room to myself is kind of the best. Hey, could you not come home very much when you're in college? Or ever?"

"You butt." I laugh. "I know you miss me."

She scoffs loudly over the line. "Miss you? More like I miss your car."

"Yeah, well, I don't miss you talking in your sleep. Or your morning breath." I put the phone on speaker and pull on sweatpants and a T-shirt.

"You're such a liar."

I start distractedly packing in preparation for leaving for D.C. in the morning. Picking up the Carnegie Mellon pamphlet I grabbed from the admissions office, I remember Fitz's enthusiasm in the linguistics lecture. I wonder if he's mentioned to his brother why we're here, why I rerouted the trip to Pittsburgh. Lewis admitting his feelings about Prisha today was a rare confidence between the brothers, and I can't help hoping it begins a pattern of letting each other in. Fitz could use a brother to confide in. Lewis could too, even if he doesn't show it.

"Hey, Marisa?" I say. I take the phone off speaker and return it to my ear like bringing her voice closer to me can close the geographical gap between us. I don't want to keep everything from my sister. I don't want us to fall into Fitz and Lewis's uneasy relationship of unspoken words and silent resentments.

"What?" She sounds somewhat distracted. I figure she's painting her nails. Her favorite shade, Indignantly Indigo. I like that I know that.

"I kind of met someone on this trip," I say. It's funny— just mentioning Fitz gives me a giddy, weightless feeling. I find I'm smiling into my phone.

Marisa gasps exaggeratedly. *"Juniper Ramírez.* Is this someone why you and Matt broke up?"

"No," I insist. "Matt and I wouldn't have lasted regardless." I cross the room carrying the clothes I wore today. When I fold and place them in my suitcase, my hand brushes Marisa's sweater with its impossible-to-ignore coffee stain. "Oh, and I have to come clean about something. I, um, stole your sweater and sort of got coffee on it." I wince in anticipation of the explosion I know is coming.

"You *what*?"

"I'm sorry. I'll buy you a new one," I rush to say.

I can hear her fuming over the line, probably plotting how to inconspicuously murder me in my sleep. I remember when I dropped her phone two years ago, cracking the edge, and she retaliated by writing *Juniper is a loser* on the back of mine in permanent marker. I followed a YouTube tutorial in-volving dry-erase markers to rub the ink off.

"Wait," Marisa says suddenly. "Does Dad know?"

"About the sweater?" I ask, not following.

"No, dummy," Marisa replies exasperatedly. "This guy you met. Does Dad know?"

"No one knows but you," I say, grateful to move on from the subject of her stained cardigan. "Please don't tell anyone," I continue hurriedly. I have no idea how she'll feel being my confidant. This is uncharted territory for us.

"You mean like how you didn't tell anyone when I went to Steve's party?"

I kind of deserve the jab, but I'm not going to concede that to my sister. There's a knock on the door. "Marisa, please," I say, getting up.

"Fortunately for *you*," she singsongs, "I'm a better sister than you deserve. What's his name? What's he like?"

"I'll tell you everything later," I promise, walking to the door. "I have to go now."

"You're a tease," she replies. "I expect details tomorrow." I hear in her voice how obviously happy she is. It's clear how much she wanted this kind of sisterly relationship—this kind of friendship—which makes me realize how much *I* wanted the same. I've shared a bedroom with Marisa for years. I don't really have a reason why we're not closer, why we're not encyclopedic, citable, peer-reviewed authorities on every detail of each other's lives. I'm starting to suspect being that to each other might be easier than I expected.

"Say hi to everyone for me," I tell her.

"Have fun," she says suggestively. "I'll be expecting my new sweater for Christmas."

I roll my eyes. "I know, I know." I hang up and throw my phone on the bed behind me, then open the door, the handle clicking heavily. Fitz waits in the hallway.

I beam, because it's become instinct with Fitz. He turns my insides into a collection of clichés, butterflies on roller coasters with wings of melting ice.

"Hey," I say casually and with Herculean effort. "What's up?"

"Oh, nothing," he replies, matching my nonchalance. "Just stretching my legs. Nothing to do with how we kissed today and I can't stop thinking about you."

I raise an eyebrow. "*Nothing* to do with that?"

"Nope." He runs his hand through his hair, and I'm suddenly a little self-conscious with my shower-slick hair dangling in a rope down my shirt. He looks profoundly kissable. "Lewis is on the phone with Prisha," he explains. "I wondered if I could hang out with you." His bravado fades, replaced by a hint of trepidation.

"Of course," I say, opening the door wider. I don't know why he's nervous until he walks in and I close the door. I'm instantly aware we're alone in a hotel room together.

My recently showered state of dress promptly becomes the least pressing thing on my mind. I'm not nervous, exactly. I'm just a mixture of excited and uncertain and incredibly conscious of our present circumstances. I have no idea if the combination is combustible.

Fitz sits on the bed. Then he immediately jumps back up.

"It's fine," I say, trying to sound casual and hearing my own jumping nerves come through. "You can sit there."

Slowly, he does. "I want you to know, I'm not— I don't mean— This isn't a move," he says haltingly. "I really did need to give Lewis privacy."

"Would it be bad if it were a move?" I sit next to him on the bed. Our shoulders come close to touching.

"Not bad, no," he says. His voice is hushed and even, like he's trying very hard to control something struggling to escape.

The ground shifts under me. I don't fight the feeling. I'm ready to fall.

"I agree," I say.

When he says nothing, I recline onto the pillows and reach for the remote. "Should we see if they have movies here?"

His eyes find mine, and they hold on for a few moments before he replies. "No, I don't think we should."

The words wake up every cell in my body, and not a second too soon, because then he's leaning down, his lips rushing to mine. My thoughts a whirlwind, I hear only one distinctly. *I have never been kissed this way before.*

There's urgency to the way he deepens the kiss. I under-stand why. Our time is limited. He's racing the days, hours, minutes we have together with every brush of his lips on mine.

It won't be enough. Feeling something I don't have the words to name come over me, I reach up with clumsy, hur-ried hands and pull his shirt over his chest. He has a nice chest. Limber, lithe. It's like good poetry, perfectly crafted to hold everything it needs and nothing else. I run my hands down the contours, to the ridges where his skin meets his waistline. Freckles cover his neck and shoulders, uncount-able. I could study them endlessly. For now, I settle for kissing one I choose randomly on his shoulder, then one on his neck, then one on his jawline. My thoughts fall away, and it's only me and him, here and now.

I remove my own shirt. I don't feel bare, because his gaze covers every inch of me. *Pulchritudinous*, I hear in my head, and it's in his voice.

He kisses me gently. Then he pulls back.

"I really like you, Juniper," he says breathlessly.

"I like you too," I say.

"It scares me sometimes, how much I like you," he contin-ues. "How much you can change my world. How much you already have." There's a tremor in his tone, one I know is not entirely from us being nearly naked. Because it's the same tremor running through me.

"It scares me too," I say.

He looks up. "Yeah?" He shifts so we're lying opposite each other on our sides, our forearms gently touching.

I nod. "It scares me how much I want this, despite everything with Matt. I don't want to repeat heartache like that. I don't want to be looking back on what you and I had, unable to move forward." If this were to continue, how could I not factor this boy into my college decisions? I don't want him to influence my wide-open future, even unconsciously, but I can't ignore what lying next to him is doing to me. I'm trapped between a really exciting rock and a really, really attractive hard place. "But this feels special," I go on. "I don't want to miss it."

"Me neither," he says.

"Why couldn't we have met earlier? Or later?" I ask. "Why did it have to be now, when we're on the brink of everything?" The question comes out choked. We both know the end date of this new itinerary we've built together. In two days, we're going to turn around and start driving home. It's unavoidable. We can't just wander the country, traipsing from hotel to hotel with our lives on hold forever.

"How about this?" His hand finds the curve of my forearm. I glance up. The beautiful blue of his eyes catches mine and holds on, unwavering. "We only have a few days together," he says. "Let's live in the present."

His words relax the tension in my chest, calming the tremors. He knows exactly what to say even when he's not using his elaborate vocabulary. "Fitzgerald Holton wanting to live in the present?" I chide gently. "I really am changing you."

He smiles. "You really are."

FITZ

~

WE DIDN'T HAVE sex. I wanted to, and I'm pretty sure Juniper did too. It would have been my first time, which I understand objectively is a big deal, yet with Juniper somehow it feels natural, fated—and completely awesome, of course. Part of me is still hoping for my first time to be with her. But last night, we wordlessly decided we didn't want sleeping together to complicate the upcoming couple of days.

We did literally sleep together, though. We talked for hours before nodding off, facing each other under the pillowed comforter of her hotel bed. I never imagined it could be this easy connecting with someone—never imagined *I* could feel this comfortable and confident, could know the right way to reply to everything Juniper says. I wonder if this is what people mean when they talk about reinventing yourself. It doesn't feel like I've reinvented anything, though. It just feels like me.

It's morning now. The early sunlight peeks through the crack in the heavy hotel curtains. While she sleeps, I grab my dictionary from the nightstand. I had an idea in the middle of the night. After finding the word I want, I scribble a message in the margin. I rip the page cleanly from the dictionary, though it occurs to me the behavior borders on sacrilegious to the book I've brought with me everywhere for years.

I tuck the folded page into the box of Juniper's cherished items, which I find next to her suitcase, and close the lid over the unfinished scarf.

We're on the road by seven for the long drive to Washington, D.C., four hours of Juniper's favorite podcast. Every episode centers on the one of the weirdest buildings in the country, and I find myself engrossed in the one about the Winchester Mystery House. We reach the city just in time for our Georgetown information session. I enjoy the tour, but undeniably my favorite part is watching Juniper's eyes rove over the intricate Gothic details of the buildings. After, we meet up with Lewis at the National Mall.

We walk from the Lincoln Memorial to the Washington Monument, up the frozen expanse of the Reflecting Pool, where a few intrepid couples have walked onto the ice. In front of the obelisk, Lewis tells us he's getting lunch with former teammates from the entrepreneurship competition I didn't know he did his sophomore year. Juniper and I grab burgers nearby and bring them to a bench in the Constitution Gardens.

It's one of those winter days with an unusually blue sky, warm but not warm enough to melt the snow into brown slush piles along the sidewalk. With the sun on my face, I sip from the double-chocolate milkshake Juniper insisted we get to share. The order didn't surprise me. Juniper has a serious thing for chocolate in any form. It's odd, how quickly a person can begin to predict the patterns and preferences of another. A couple of days together, and I know Juniper likes to eat dinner no later than seven, never blow-dries her hair—not even if she's showered in the morning and her hair will literally freeze when she leaves the hotel—and will always opt to eat outside if given the choice.

Sometimes, in moments like these, when we're not touring a school or planning an itinerary, it's deceptively easy to convince myself we're already freshmen in college together. That I've known her for years, and this is only one day of many. It's a beguiling fiction.

"So tomorrow we head to the University of Virginia," Juniper announces beside me, pulling me from thoughts of endless afternoons. She's looking at the Notes app on her phone, where I know she tracks our itineraries. Her hair isn't in a ponytail today. It hangs down her shoulders in loose curls that change color in the sun. Dark brown with golden blond at the edges. "Then I have us driving back to Boston, but the drive is nine hours, so we'll stop somewhere for the night and see one more school," she goes on. But my eyes are lost in the kaleidoscope of colors in the hair tucked behind her ear. "Fitz, are you listening to me?"

I meet her eyes. "No, sorry. You're just very distracting when your hair is down."

She rolls her eyes, but her cheeks color. I don't think I could ever be used to the wonder of being able to make this girl blush. She slips the hair band from her wrist and puts her hair back into a high ponytail. "There," she says. "Less distracting?"

I let my gaze wander to her newly exposed neck. "Not at all," I reply.

Laughing delightedly, she shoves me. I lean forward to kiss the skin beneath her jaw, which I know from last night is warm and soft.

My phone rings.

I brush my lips against her neck. She shivers, giving me half a mind to toss my phone onto the icy lake. Glancing at the screen, I see it's my mom. Usually, I'd feel slightly guilty to be reminded of her in a moment like this. Guilty that I'm kissing a beautiful girl in a city hours from home, contemplating a future far away. But the only thing I feel guilty for is not calling her yesterday.

In one distant corner of my mind, I've noticed how aside from telling her about extending the trip, I haven't kept in touch with my mom in the past couple of days quite as often as I normally do. I'm well aware why. Juniper and the genuine interest I'm taking in this tour have distracted me from things back home, for better or worse. It's liberating, but somewhat unnerving, how easy I'm finding it to put behind me the problems that usually preoccupy me.

"Be right back," I promise Juniper, then stand and walk a couple feet away. "Hey, Mom," I say when I pick up.

"Hi, Fitz. You . . . didn't call yesterday." She doesn't sound upset, just curious. Maybe slightly concerned. "Everything okay?" she asks.

"Everything is great," I reassure her, my eyes fixed on Juniper. She doesn't notice me as I watch her steal into my bag of fries.

"I'm so glad," my mom says. I know she means it. Her tone matches the pleased expression I can't see but know she's wearing. "Are there any schools you're considering applying to?" The question comes out delicate and hesitant. I can't say I don't know why. I remember my words to her when I left for this trip. My certainty that I would only be applying to SNHU.

"Yeah, actually," I reply. The declaration feels foreign, in a good way. "I think I want to look into linguistics programs. Possibly Carnegie Mellon." Just thinking of the day in Pittsburgh with Juniper, the lecture, the books I've perused, makes me look forward to next year in a new way. Not to mention, the day we went to Pittsburgh was the day I first kissed Juniper, which gives the whole recollection an irreplaceable luster.

"Linguistics?" she repeats. She sounds startled for a second. "Of course," she says like she's just realized how obvious it is. "I'm happy for you, Fitz. Tell me about Carnegie Mellon."

I describe everything to her. The campus, the class, the city. It's extraordinarily freeing. This is the kind of conversation I've known my friends have had with their parents and college counselors, the kind I overheard when Lewis got home from touring BU with Dad. I just never thought it was one I would care about having. My mom was the main reason I resented this trip, but every day, the resentment has faded a little.

While I'm watching Juniper, she turns in my direction. Our eyes meet for a brief, boundless moment.

Then she gets up to throw out our trash. I know she's

anxious to move on to the next item on our D.C. itinerary. A museum, if I had to guess. I make my way over to her.

"It sounds perfect," my mom says. It's nice, how obviously proud she is. "I think you'll do really great in sociology."

I pause, halfway to Juniper. "Linguistics," I say.

"Hm?"

"I said linguistics," I repeat, ignoring the roaring in my ears.

"When?" Mom sounds confused, if cheerful. "You were just saying how you were interested in sociology. The Carnegie Mellon program."

The bottom drops out. "I was saying I was interested in the *linguistics* program, Mom. Remember?" *Remember. Remember. Remember.*

"Uh. Of course. I misspoke. Linguistics. You were saying you're interested in Carnegie Mellon's linguistics program," she repeats, an automatic stiffness to her voice.

I want to believe her. I want to un-know the things I know. To have never read that one of the earliest symptoms of Alzheimer's is forgetting recently learned information. Information like appointments, or names. Or what college major your son says he's interested in.

But I do know those things. They douse my veins in icy worry.

"Mom," I say casually, hiding my dread. "How has your memory been?"

"I'm okay, Fitz," she replies quickly. "Don't worry about me. I want you to enjoy your trip."

The worry flashes into anger. I know she's evading me.

"Can you honestly tell me that you're really okay? That you're not having early symptoms?"

"Fitz—"

"Mom," I cut her off. "Tell me the truth."

The silence on the other end of the line says everything. "I wanted to wait until you were home." Her voice is different now, unrecognizably shaky. I sink onto the nearest empty bench, my legs unsteady. Out of the corner of my eye, I catch Juniper noticing. She starts to walk in my direction. "This was expected, okay?" Mom continues. "You don't have to worry. I've just been presenting early symptoms for a little while. Sometimes I forget the newer students, miss the occasional deadline, that kind of thing."

"Have you gone to your doctor?" I ask. It's the first question I can think of, and I grasp onto it, my only lifeline.

Juniper sits down next to me without speaking. Her expression is wrought with concern.

"Yes. We have a plan. I'll share it with you when you come home," she reassures me, except it's anything but reassuring. It's worse, in a way. It means her symptoms have gotten severe enough that she went to her doctor without telling me.

Furiously, my mind recites the prognoses I've read a hundred times over online. She could have ten years, or she could have as few as three.

"How could I not have known?" It's half rhetorical.

"I knew you would worry," she says. "I didn't want my health to influence your college decisions."

It's infuriating, how wrongheaded she is. Of course her health was going to influence my college decisions. It was only a matter of when and how. How much opportunity I would have—how much freedom she would mislead me into feeling—to fall in love with schools far from home. How horrible it would be when I discovered that freedom was founded on a lie.

I laugh harshly. "You sent me on a college tour *knowing* you were presenting symptoms." She tries to cut in, but I continue, harder. "How could you? How could you show me these places knowing I might never have the chance to go to them?" I let the bitter truth fly. "I was *happy* going to SNHU before this."

She sniffles over the line.

It tears me in two. The resentment splits off, and suddenly I'm left with only overwhelming remorse.

"I'm sorry," she struggles to say through tears. "I'm sorry, Fitz. I should've told you. I just . . . I didn't want it to be real. I guess I wanted to pretend I was still a normal mother who could send her son away to his dream college." Her voice chokes. "I wanted more time."

I understand everything she's telling me. I understand the profound difficulty of her position, why she would put off revealing this the way she did. A few forms of grief unfold in me. Grief for her, for the unraveling she knows is coming. Grief for myself, for the watching and the waiting. Grief for the visions of the future I've entertained the past few days, which have vanished in an instant.

But there's one more thing I understand with cutting clarity. This isn't about me.

"It's okay, Mom," I say over the ragged breathing I know

she's trying to stifle. "It's going to be okay. I promise. We're going to figure it out."

Juniper's hand finds my knee, reminding me she's here and she's definitely heard enough to know what's happened. I turn from her, from her worried frown, her caring eyes. From every way I've let her change me. I want to continue being the emboldened new person she thinks I've become. The person I know she's expecting, even with her comforting hand on my knee.

I just don't think I know how. Not anymore. Not when every fear I've quieted during the past few days has come raging back.

FITZ

~

WE SKIP THE rest of the day's itinerary. While I explained the conversation with my mom to Juniper, she said nothing, which was the only thing she could've said. I didn't need to ask her to set aside our plans of museums and monuments and return directly to the hotel instead.

On the way back, I text Lewis that I have something I need to tell him. He agrees to meet me in the room.

Juniper leaves me with one final reassuring squeeze of my hand in the hotel. When I reach our room, I start pacing the narrow stretch of floor spanning from the beds to the dresser. I'm really not looking forward to breaking the news to Lewis. He's irritatingly cavalier when it comes to Mom, but I have a feeling, even for him, this will be a blow.

I walk the length of the room for five interminable minutes before there's the clatter of a keycard in the lock and the door beeps. Lewis enters looking confused and disheveled, like he hurried here.

"Have you talked to Mom?" I ask. I don't bother flattening the waver from my voice. I don't care if Lewis thinks I'm overwrought or anxious. Because I was right.

"I talked to her yesterday. Why?" He unzips his parka and throws his hat on his bed.

My heart drops. I'd held out hope Mom had called him after she got off the phone with me. The fact she didn't is its own painful punch. She was evidently too overcome by our conversation to handle having one with her older son. "Okay, there's no easy way to say this," I begin. "Mom is sicker than we knew." Lewis frowns, his expression puzzled. I continue. "She's been showing symptoms for . . . a while now."

Lewis pauses. In the interim, my mind cycles through the hundred ways he could react. I wonder whether this time, he'll finally be upset.

"I'm sorry, Fitz," he says.

I don't understand. "Why are you sorry for me? This affects both of us."

"I know," Lewis replies. "I'm just sorry you had to find out this way. During your trip."

It takes me a moment to put his words together, to unwind the implications. When I do, I hardly have the presence of mind to put forth the never-ending questions exploding into my head. "How long have you known?" I struggle to ask.

"Since she made an appointment with her doctor." Lewis swallows. "Three months ago."

"And you didn't tell me?" My voice is shocked and hurt and uncomprehending and pissed off *and and and*. I don't understand how my mom could share this with *Lewis* and not me. What could Lewis possibly do to help? Why didn't she trust me?

I feel fear and frustration, fury and hopelessness coursing through me. I've hidden the abandonment I've felt from my brother for years, and right now, I can't. Not for a moment longer.

"You and Mom—what? Had a conversation and decided you'd keep this from me?" I clench my hand, feeling my fingernails bite into my palm. I don't recognize this Fitz, whose anger writes in capital letters.

"It wasn't my place to," Lewis replies. I detect a defensive hint in his voice. "She didn't want you to know yet."

"You didn't think that was fucked up?" I fire back. "You've been with me this entire trip. You've watched me . . . have fun, think about college, try things." I don't say the really important one. *Very possibly fall in love.*

"That's exactly why we didn't tell you," Lewis argues. "Fitz, your whole world was just waiting for Mom to need you, and you could have more than that. I—we—wanted you to see how much more."

"You know why I worry about Mom so much?" I drop my voice, my anger narrowing into raw honesty. "It's because I'm all she has. You're certainly not going to change your plans for her. You're not going to skip a single fraternity event or job interview or date with whichever girl you've moved onto."

"That's not fair," Lewis says.

"How? How is it not fair, Lewis?" We're facing each other from opposite ends of the room, and the distance is like an endless expanse separating us. "Because from where I'm standing, you've already moved on from this family."

"I'm here, aren't I?" He flings a hand toward the window, toward the city outside.

"Only because Mom forced you." I almost have to laugh. "You drive me down the coast for a week and a half, and you think that undoes years of silence? Of being on my own with Mom? Waiting for things to get worse? Do you know how many nights I've spent researching her disease?" I grind out the next words. "Don't you think I could have used a brother to check in on me? To care?"

Lewis's eyes darken. My mind overloads with words. *Choler, wroth, irascible, ire.* I've never seen this side of my brother before, and then it hits me how often over the past few days I've seen new sides of Lewis. In an instant, I figure out why. I don't know the other sides of him because I don't know *him.*

"Like you check in on me?" His voice is bitter. "You show zero interest in anything related to my life."

"Because your life is incomprehensible to me!" My hands start to shake, and I clench them, trying to iron out the nerves. "Like I want to hear about your killer ragers, getting blackout drunk, hooking up with your freshmen floor. None of those things are real."

"Real?" Lewis repeats. He shakes his head. "Did you ever fucking stop to think that I might have needed a break? The smallest shred of a *life* to distract me from what's going on with Mom?"

Whatever I was going to say next vanishes from my head. I'm stunned for a moment, speechless.

Lewis continues, his chest rising and falling heavily, like he's dragging each sentence out of somewhere deep and lonely. "You know nothing about me. You have no idea what it's like to not have the same skin color as your family. What it's like to go through college and face the real world while dealing with Mom's disease. You have no comprehension of anything outside of yourself. You pretend you carry this burden on your own. You *enjoy* it, the idea you're this poor, put-upon, long-suffering martyr. But the truth is you're too selfish to see what others—what *I*—do for you."

This snaps me back into indignation. "What *exactly* do you do for me? Drag me to parties? Pressure me about girls? You just want me to be more like you."

"Oh, and that would be terrible, right? Being like me? Because I'm worthless to you." He sounds genuinely offended, which gives me pause. "Never mind that I *volunteered* to take you on this trip, that I've been busting my ass to get a job to help support Mom, to help pay for full-time care for her."

I blink, honestly not certain if I've heard him right. It never occurred to me that Lewis had considered the care Mom's going to need or how it's going to be paid for. The idea he's not only considered it, but planned on paying for it himself, hits me like a wave. The guilt is frigid, paralyzing.

"You think I *enjoy* hours of interviews?" His words come faster now, breathless, like he's opened something and his feelings have become unstoppable. I understand he's furious, but his fury no longer provokes the same in me. I feel unsteady, overwhelmed. "You think consulting and finance were my first choice?" he continues. "They weren't. But this job will help Mom, will help the family. It'll help you go wherever you want for college."

I say nothing. I knew there were things I held back from telling my brother. It makes me feel small and very stupid to recognize there were things he held back from telling me, too.

"Screw this," he says, grabbing his jacket and turning to the door. *There's* the Lewis I know. The one who leaves the second things get hard, forcing me to pick up the pieces on my own. "You have no idea what you're talking about," he continues. "You don't know what I've done or why. You don't know me at all." He throws open the door, and he's gone without a parting glance.

I have no argument to that. Every moment of half friendship on this trip, every tentative truce, has been engulfed by the insurmountable resentment between us, by the reality of Lewis's and my relationship. We're brothers in name only. The connection is hollow.

I drop onto the bed, broken by the weight of everything this means. I was right from the very beginning. No matter what Lewis says about supporting our mom, he only means financial support. I won't leave her, not when I'm the only one who can remind her who she is.

I have no choice in my future. I never have. The past few days have been a fairy tale, a fantasy not meant for me. Lewis will move to New York, and I'll return to where I've always been. Where I'll always be.

Home.

JUNIPER

~

I WALKED DOWN the hallway to my room and then found I couldn't go in. I couldn't plan college visits, couldn't text my parents or mindlessly scroll through my phone when I knew what Fitz was wrestling with. When I could imagine the conversation he and his brother were having. The thought drove me back into the elevator, into the hallway to Fitz's room, and to his door, where I've waited for the past few minutes, pacing.

I feel useless. I know I can't help.

Not that I won't try. While I wait, I furiously Google information on Alzheimer's and compile my findings into three different speeches in my head, one of which I'll deliver when I feel I've given him time to deal on his own. I'll decide which depending on the mood I find him in. I find positive data on recovery trends, new treatments, experimental programs.

I'm telling myself it'll help. In the unpleasant depths of my heart, though, I'm not convinced. This isn't *a* problem, *a* tragedy. It's *his* tragedy. Unfortunately, not much comes out when you google "how to help Fitzgerald Holton, of Tilton,

New Hampshire, when his worst fear comes crashing down upon him."

When I think it's time, I take a breath and lift my hand to knock.

Before I have the chance, the door bursts inward and Lewis barrels into the hallway. He's blinking furiously—I glimpse tears in his eyes.

It freezes me. The door falls shut, and Lewis continues down the hall, not even registering my presence. He's not heading in the direction of the elevators, and I can't tell whether he knows this or just doesn't have a destination in mind at all.

I glance at the door. Fitz is in there. All I have to do is knock.

I turn and follow Lewis.

I have no speeches prepared for Fitz's brother. I hardly even know him, and he definitely hasn't asked for my help. But I've seen enough of Lewis to suspect he's the type who won't wave for help when he's drowning. He'll wait for the water to cover him, hoping nobody onshore will notice the spray of the whitecaps pummeling him.

Fitz can wait. Lewis . . . I don't know.

"Are you okay?" I ask when I reach him. I hate the inadequacy of the question. Of course he's not okay. He pauses when he hears my voice, facing me and looking like he doesn't entirely know where he is or doesn't care.

"I'm not sure I remember what okay feels like." His voice, like his expression, is stripped bare. I want to help. I want to put a comforting hand on his shoulder, to give him a hug, even. But everything feels insufficient. I stay silent, and he continues. "I try so hard to keep it together. To be the role model Fitz needs."

Role model? I genuinely like Lewis, but I never exactly thought of him as trying to be some shining exemplar to his brother. Fitz told me how he had to carry Lewis home from the Brown party. I must frown involuntarily, because Lewis lets a self-conscious smile crack through his distress.

"Not a role model for school or responsibility," he says. "But, like—an example on living."

"How?" I want him to keep talking, to keep bringing the emotions wearing him down into the open where I can shoulder them with him.

Some of the sadness fades from his eyes, replaced with something like conviction. "Living despite whatever else may be going on. If I didn't have my fraternity, if I didn't have Prisha—" He stops suddenly, like her name is a lump in his throat threatening a sea of tears. "I just mean," he continues, his face paler, "if I were constantly thinking about Mom the way Fitz is, I'd be a wreck. I wanted to show him how to search for fun, for happiness, because he deserves those things. Sometimes I can't sleep because I'm worrying what his life will look like when everything with Mom is . . . done."

I register the pause, the euphemism. *When everything is done.* I'm seven years old for a moment, in my family's apartment in New York, overhearing my parents discussing my abuela's health and why we needed to return to Massachusetts.

Lewis goes on. "I guess I take it too far sometimes," he says ruefully. "Go out too often, flirt too much, get too drunk. But it's . . . an escape." His chest heaves.

I run through the things I could say. I could offer blanket sympathies, empty encouragements to keep talking. Or I could push him to face this head-on, even if it's harder. "I think Fitz feels you don't care about him because of all the fun you're having," I say. "Because you have this other life. This perfect job."

Lewis looks up, raw with wounded incredulity. "I *know* he thinks that," he says. "He just told me."

I open and then close my mouth. I thought Lewis stormed from Fitz's room because he was overwhelmed with the news of their mom's symptoms. It never occurred to me it was because they'd fought.

"I fucked up," Lewis chokes out. "I thought he'd imitate me, not resent me. I didn't want to put my stress on top of his. So I hid it. I hid how desperate I've been to get the kind of job that can support our whole family—regardless of whether it's something I care about or not. I hid where I *really* want to be next year. Because if it were up to me, I wouldn't be moving to New York, not when I could be in San Francisco with my girlfriend. I'm only staying on the East Coast for my mom." His voice is gathering volume now. "I hid my sacrifices because I hoped I could help Fitz have a normal life. Now he hates me. My mom's sick, my brother despises me, and the girl who made everything bearable is moving to the other side of the country. I'm going to be alone."

Tears tumble from his eyes. He raises his hand to his face,

his grief garishly out of place in the hotel hallway.

His words touch bruises in me I've tried to ignore for too long. I've fought loneliness on this trip. I've wrestled with the lurking suspicion nobody in my family really supports the future I want. I've come out of those fights more hurt than I knew.

I reach for Lewis, putting my hand on his shoulder. "Lewis, you're not alone." I'm not expecting my own conviction. "Not even close."

He doesn't contradict me.

I gesture toward his and Fitz's room. "Fitz is in there," I say. "I think you have to tell him what you told me. Tell him everything. He needs you, and you need him."

I wonder if it's the kind of thing only a close friend could say, or only a complete stranger. While I don't have faith in predetermined paths or destiny or mystic workings of the universe, I wonder if, in some improbable way, I'm exactly where I'm supposed to be. Maybe the fact of our joining up into this instantaneous, unlikely group will be important for Lewis and his brother. Maybe it will for me too.

Lewis looks up, and he's worked whatever magic he uses to hide his wounds. His expression is stony, and determination is starting to flicker into his reddened eyes. He nods.

"Go," I say.

He hesitates. I wonder if he'll try to put this off, if he's too proud to bring this emotion to his brother.

"I'm really glad Fitz met you, Juniper," he finally says.

"Yeah," I say, holding Lewis's gaze. "I'm really glad I met him too."

I walk with Lewis to his hotel room. He takes a breath, and then he opens the door. Inside, I glimpse Fitz gazing out the window from the foot of the bed. Lewis enters, and while the door inches closed, I watch him walk up to his brother.

Without words, Lewis sits next to Fitz and wraps him in a hug. I don't know what it is, but something in Fitz seems to loosen. It's the slightest shift in his shoulders, the gentlest release of exhaled breath. It's ice thawing in the first rays of daylight. The relief of having his brother is nearly imperceptible on Fitz, and yet impossible not to see.

I let the door close, wanting to give them time on their own, and head for the elevator.

In the empty hallway, I hear my dad's voice, the echo of our phone call returning in pitch-perfect detail. *It's okay to need your family sometimes.* I weigh the idea against one fundamental of my life for years now, the feeling I need freedom from my family. I'll never *not* want room to become my own person, to lead my own life. But watching Fitz and Lewis, I know my dad isn't wrong.

I hardly even notice the elevator descending. I won't give up my dreams for my family, I decide. I just won't cut them out, either. Because there might come a day when, like Fitz, like Lewis, I need someone to hold me when the rest of my world has imploded.

My whole life, I thought needing them carried a cost. That I couldn't find myself unless I forced distance between me and the people in my past. I decided I needed college to remove myself from the old Juniper in hopes of finding the new one.

But maybe that's not how finding yourself works. In college and in everything after, I won't be discovering new pieces of myself. I'll be uncovering what's already there. And if that's true, I don't need to fear growing into myself while remaining connected to my home. I don't need to force college and family into harsh opposition.

Everything in my past will become pieces of the new Juniper. My family, my home, my heritage. My friends. Fitz. Even when we've parted and he's out of my life, Fitz will have left an imprint on me. Like Matt did. They'll both be part of me forever.

I head from the hotel lobby to the street, where I wander aimlessly. The city feels new, or perhaps it's only me. I follow the sidewalk past Metro entrances and parks with shoveled paths in the snow. While I walk from corner to corner, images come to life in my eyes.

I'm in D.C. for college, and I'm showing my family around. I'm walking them to my favorite restaurants, my go-to coffee shops. I'm touring the campus with them, pointing out my lecture hall, bringing them into my dorm, rolling my eyes when my mom frets over the close quarters, and chasing Callie and Anabel from my desk drawer. I'm growing up, on my own. Except I'm not. I'm with the people who got me here.

I smile, the wobbly kind I couldn't resist if I tried. I keep walking, envisioning everything I never thought to want. Turning onto residential streets, I pass brick towers with pillars of narrow windows. In front of one of the buildings, I smell something unmistakable.

It's tamales. The smell wafts from the open window of

one of the apartments, spicy and strong and full of familiar flavors. It's the smell of home.

It fills me with memories. Memories of Abuela folding closed cornhusks with weathered hands, of raiding the freezer with her for leftovers months later.

This time, though, they're not only memories of Abuela. Tía is there too, in the vista opening wider in my head. Tía, cooking tamales for dinner the first Christmas we celebrated without Abuela. Tía, bringing pans of them to the student government fund-raiser I helped organize when I was a freshman. Even the recollection of finding Tía's Tupperware in my car holds bittersweet joy.

They bring tears to my eyes. It takes me a moment to comprehend the feeling.

I'm homesick.

It hurts. I'm grateful, though, because the hurt feels *right*, like discovering pain in places I thought were numb. I pull out my phone, knowing what I have to do. What I need right now. I find *home* in my contacts and hit call.

I hold the phone up, gloved fingertips brushing my face, while the dial tone rings once, then twice. Tía's voice comes through on the other end. "Juniper?" She sound stiff, urgent. "Is everything okay?"

"Yeah," I say, my voice breaking on the word. "I'm fine. I just wanted to say hi."

There's a long pause. The longest in the history of tele-phone conversations, and I feel every agonizing second. I'm holding my heart out over the canyon dividing us and wait-ing for her to reach forward or refuse.

"I'm helping your brother with his winter break home-work," she finally says, "but Walker is telling me I don't do the math right."

I laugh. It's gunky and overjoyed, and it's the exact right laugh for the day I've had. "Put me on speaker," I tell Tía. "We'll help him together."

Tía pauses once more. I know she understands the sig-nificance of my offer to help the family while I'm away, while I'm in the middle of my college tour. It's not an offer I would have made a week ago, or even yesterday. But though she understands the gesture I'm making, my aunt is nothing if not stubborn. She's incomparable at holding a grudge. Only a niece who's refused to speak to her since they fought on the phone could rival her.

"Thank you," she says. "First, though, I want to hear about your trip. Will you tell me about the school you like best?"

I wipe tears from my eyes. I want to tell her everything this means to me, except I know she knows. In one sentence, she's strung a bridge over the canyon separating us. It's easy to walk across.

"Yeah," I say. "I'd really like that."

FITZ

I WAKE UP the next morning feeling completely exhausted, yet somehow lighter. Sitting up, I exhale slowly. The room is dark, the drawn curtains letting in only a hint of daylight. It feels annoyingly like a metaphor.

The news of my mom's health still weighs on me. It's better since Lewis and I talked, though. I sit, listening to the water running while Lewis showers, and memories of the night rush over me. We spent hours saying everything we'd been holding in. I told him his ever-present cool and easygoing demeanor made him feel unreachable and uninterested. He told me how much he worried for me, and how much pressure he felt to provide for our family. Eventually, we got into how I resented him for disappearing into his partying and job-hunting, vanishing from my mom's and my life, and he explained he needed room to deal with Mom's disease on his own.

It was the longest conversation we've ever had, and oddly heartfelt. Not because it felt wrong, but because it felt like, *why haven't we done this before?* We fought and laughed through years of hidden fears and resentments in one night, and while it was wrenching and totally draining, it felt like a bond. Right now, we're shattered in the same way. It's something we have in common, something connecting us as strong as the name we share.

I went to bed around three in the morning. Lewis called Prisha from the bathroom, a conversation I overheard with uncomfortable clarity through the thin door. Prisha couldn't talk long because she's visiting a friend at another college and they were at a party. His feelings for her, stripped of the casual veneer he usually puts on, are something I can understand too.

While I wait for Lewis the next morning, I run through our itinerary in my head. We're driving to UVA today and then beginning the drive back to Boston tomorrow.

I hadn't considered the rest of the trip in light of everything yesterday. Typing the destination into Google Maps, I realize I *really* don't want to visit another school. Over the coming weeks, I'm going to have to package up whatever newly formed dreams I had of college outside New Hampshire. It won't be easy. Going on one more tour of a campus I'll never call my own definitely won't help.

There's only one reason to go. Juniper. It's reason enough a thousand times over. I'm not ready to part from her, not yet. If UVA's where she's going next, I'm going with her.

Like magic, there's a knock on the door. I roll out of bed, conscious I'm wearing a rumpled T-shirt and sweats, and open the door. Juniper's in the hallway, looking perfect. Her hair is still wet, her nose pink from the cold. She's holding a paper bag I know without a doubt contains bagels—plain for me and chocolate chip for Lewis.

"Hey." Her voice is gently questioning. "Sorry, I should've texted. I hope I didn't wake you."

"I was up," I say defensively, my self-consciousness over my shirt-and-sweats combo and bed head skyrocketing.

She doesn't seem convinced. "I brought you breakfast." She holds out the bag. "How are you guys?" she continues delicately.

Her eyes have filled with sympathy, the respectful kind where it's clear she's not pressing me to confide or be okay. It makes me want to kiss her and cry in equal measure.

"We're good," I say, taking the bagels. "We talked and . . . it's nice to have him understand me. To understand him." The sentences come out clumsily. I guess I have to get used to them being true.

Juniper nods. "Is he awake?" She glances past me into the room.

"He's showering. We'll be ready to hit the road in thirty minutes."

"Actually," she says, chewing her lip. "I was thinking, maybe we should skip UVA."

I frown. "Skip it? What about your itinerary?"

"Forget the itinerary," she replies. "I think we're all about ready to head home."

I'm half relieved, half heartbroken. True, I don't want to see any more schools, but canceling the tour means bringing Juniper and me closer to goodbye. I imagine how hard it's going to be, hugging her for the last time, backing away before driving out of each other's lives. "Yeah," I say. "That's probably a good idea."

She smiles, but I notice the sadness in her expression. "Great. It's a seven-hour drive. We could do it in one day, if you're up for it."

"Sure." I'm forcing every word, every gesture. I feel like I'm following commands to break my fingers or something. "Do you want to head out now, before we're ready, or . . . ?"

The sadness flees from her smile, and she crosses her arms authoritatively. "We have seven more hours together, Fitzgerald. You're riding with me."

Relief races over me. "Good. Maybe we'll hit traffic," I say hopefully.

She tugs my shirt, pulling us together. "I wouldn't complain." She kisses me fiercely, like she does everything.

I try to lose myself in the kiss. My hands find her hips under her jacket, and I take in the unforgettable smell of her skin, the brush of tongues. With her lips on mine, I try to forget the voice reminding me this is one of the last kisses we have left.

FITZ

IN HALF AN hour, we're on the road returning to Boston. I'm in Juniper's car, while Lewis follows in his.

There are thousands of things I want to say. I want to thank Juniper for understanding I needed to skip UVA. To hear her thoughts on each of the colleges we've visited, to listen to her mind working through variables and contingencies, possibilities and plans. To tell her I think she's beautiful with her hair down, bronze waves cascading onto her shoulders.

Except I can't. Everything I could say carries the unsupportable weight of being one of our final conversations.

The silence in the car is suffocating, the way it was in our first drive together. We've come heartbreakingly full circle. I know without having to confirm it out loud Juniper isn't speaking for the same reason, the inescapable knowledge our relationship ends in Boston.

"Want to listen to a podcast?" I finally ask jokingly. Anything to split the silence.

"No, I think we should get the goodbyes out of our system." Her voice is confident, upbeat.

I don't see how she can be cheerful. "Explain," I say.

"It's hanging over us, isn't it?" She glances from the road to meet my eyes briefly. "We're not talking the way we usually do because we know tonight will be goodbye."

It's one thing to understand we're probably dreading the same parting moments, the imminent end of us. It's something else entirely to hear her put the feeling into words, not to mention with such effortless, immediate efficiency. I know I've presumed our relationship will end with this trip, but truthfully, we haven't had the conversation.

"Will it?" I ask. "Be goodbye, I mean?"

Juniper's confidence softens into something delicate. "A long-distance relationship in the final semester of our senior year doesn't really . . ."

"I know," I say.

I do know. I know this probably isn't *literally* one of our final conversations. I know there's texting. There's social media. We could stay friends, stay in each other's lives. It wouldn't be the same, though, and honestly, it probably won't happen. I know Juniper well enough to know she could never be content clinging to our one week together, memories drifting unreachably into her past.

I muster a smile, hoping to trick myself into being okay with this. "You were saying something about getting goodbyes out of our systems?"

Juniper nods, and I can practically feel her trying to recapture her cheerful momentum. "Whatever we're planning on saying in Boston," she explains, "let's say it now. That way we'll have the goodbye behind us. We won't have to dwell on it during this entire drive."

I'm not convinced the idea will work. That *anything* could banish our impending goodbye from my thoughts. But I'm willing to try. "Okay," I tell her. "You go first."

Her expression goes stony. "Fitzgerald Holton," she says. "I did not expect to like you when we first met."

I laugh, improbably. "Oh yeah. This is working. I'm feeling better already."

Juniper swats my shoulder, permitting a laugh past her lips. Her dark-pink lips, which she chews when she's making one of the million decisions her mind processes every day.

No. I won't do this right now. I focus on her goodbye.

"But what I feel for you has gone past 'like' into . . . I don't know," she continues, earnest again. She watches the road intently, like she's searching for something. The right description, maybe. "It's something bigger," she says. "I feel like I'll carry your fingerprints on who I am for the rest of my life. I'm excited for the future. But this week with you has taught me I can still run toward what's to come while holding on to the past. The boy I traveled down the coast with, the fights I'm glad I had with my family, the feeling of a kiss by a frozen waterfall. Everything."

I say nothing, and not because of the conversation's weight. I've told Juniper she changed me, and I will never forget the ways she opened my world. I had no idea I changed hers.

"I guess it's a part of growing up I didn't understand," she says. "Who I am, the home I come from, they'll never be gone even though they'll never be the same. *Hiraeth*, right?"

She throws me a small smile. I try to return it, but *hiraeth* has pulled open torn edges I'm trying hard to mend. "The home you're talking about only lives in memories," I say. I hear the hurt in my voice. It's impossible to hide. I didn't want this conversation to veer into my mom's health, and yet, I have a feeling it's inescapable.

I have no doubt Juniper understands what I mean. She doesn't reply for a moment.

When she does, her voice isn't fragile or sympathetic. "You know," she says, "I remember more about nearly everyone than they remember about themselves."

I blink, thrown. I don't understand why she's changing the subject.

"Do you remember the first thing you said after we kissed?" She glances over, and in a half second of eye contact I catch the endless intensity I know well.

"What?"

"Do you," she repeats, slower, "remember the first thing you said after we kissed?".

Not getting the game, I play along anyway, re-creating the picture in my mind, immersing myself in the image. The waterfall pillared into the frozen lake. The powder covering everything. Juniper's lips meeting mine, melting the cold of outside. The two of us parting, and—

I can't quite remember my words exactly. "Something about being glad you kissed me instead of answering my question?" I venture.

Juniper shakes her head, looking pleased.

"'*Kissing me* isn't a word,'" she says in what I recognize is an impression of me. It's . . . not terrible.

The funny thing is, I don't know if she's right. The sentence sounds familiar, but I can't recall with certainty whether I said it. I'm only convinced because I have other evidence of Juniper's incredible memory. The college-related facts and figures she would rattle off, the driving directions she wouldn't need repeated.

"I could probably tell you what you ordered in every restaurant we went to, and what questions you asked on every tour," Juniper continues. The pride in her voice turns gentle. "I remember more about you than you do. But does that mean you're not the person I know?"

The question breaks me. I understand her point now, and tears well up in my eyes. I clench my teeth to fight the tremor in my jaw.

"Just because one person doesn't remember something doesn't mean the memory is gone," she says. "It doesn't mean the person isn't who they've always been. You'll be there to remember who your mom is even when she can't. You can carry those memories for her. Just like we'll carry the memories of this week together. Even if memory is the only place we'll exist for each other, we won't be less real for it."

My throat feels thick. I put my hand on her leg because it's the only way I have right now to tell her how desperately I needed this. While we pass highway exits in the cloud-white daylight, she gives me time to find my voice.

"Here's what I wanted to say to you tonight," I get out. "I'm glad I met you, Juniper Ramírez, for more reasons than I can say. And my feelings for you have gone way past 'like' too. Admiration. Respect. Gratitude. Love, or the beginning of it." I continue hastily, not wanting to linger on the word.

"Knowing you has inspired me. *You* inspire me."

While I speak, something unfinished in me races ahead of my words. I realize I've made a decision, one I need to voice.

"I have no idea how much time I'll have before my mom needs me," I say. "But I'm going to go to whatever college I *want* to for as long as I can." I don't feel a triumphant rush when I finish the declaration. The fear isn't gone. It probably never will be. But I think I have what I need now, truths I've found on this trip, to keep the fear quiet.

I might have one year at my dream college, or two, or four. It doesn't matter. If I've learned anything from this week with Juniper, it's that change can be wonderful, and wonderful doesn't need to last to be worthwhile. Would it have been easier to have never known her so I wouldn't have to face this goodbye? Maybe.

But I wouldn't trade this time, however fleeting, for a thousand painless returns home. Even if things have to end, they're worth having, no matter how difficult the goodbye.

The thought gives me an idea. I sit up straighter and check the rearview mirror. Lewis's car follows behind us. Pulling out my phone, I call my brother.

Juniper glances over, looking understandably confused.

Lewis picks up on the first ring. "Fitz? What's wrong?"

"Nothing," I say. "I overheard you on the phone with Prisha last night. Where is she right now? What school?"

Lewis pauses. "Princeton."

I turn to Juniper with a grin. "What do you say we add one more school to our tour?"

JUNIPER

PRINCETON IS AN hour away when we pull off the highway into a gas station, a square of pavement cut from the grass in front of the roadside woods. When Fitz explained his idea to give Lewis and Prisha time together today, I was immediately on board. It's not like Prisha is moving to San Francisco tomorrow. They'll have the rest of the school year together. But I know, and Fitz knows, no time is worth wasting.

We've driven for two hours on I-95, and it's nearly noon. The gas station is crowded, three of the pumps occupied. I pull into the only open pump. Lewis, behind us, parks in one of the parking spaces. He gets out of the car and walks briskly toward the convenience store. I've never seen him move so fast, with this uncontainable energy, like he's reaching for something with every step and gesture. He passes me on his way.

Pivoting, he walks backward toward the gas station while facing me. "What do you want to eat?" he asks without stopping.

"It's fine." I unscrew my gas tank and reach for the nozzle. "I'll get it myself when I finish."

"Nope," Lewis replies. "It's on me. A thank-you for last night." He winks. It's a total frat move, except I know Lewis well enough to no longer see the distant, disaffected bro in him. He's being genuine.

I shrug. "Whatever looks freshest."

He throws me a thumbs-up. "Solid."

I watch him walk up to the store, where he catches up with Fitz. Lewis claps his brother hard on the shoulder. Startled, Fitz rounds on him—then looks glad to find Lewis. He shoves him off, laughing, and they walk in together.

Grinning, I return the nozzle to the pump. I recognize that laugh. It's the laugh of Callie and Anabel pelting each other with snowballs in the front yard, the laugh of Marisa and me busting up while fighting when one of us drops a spectacular insult. I look toward Boston, and it hits me how I'm looking forward to those insults, those snowball fights.

Wanting to text my parents, I reach into the back seat for my phone, which is in my purse. The sleeve of my parka brushes the shoebox on the floor, knocking the lid off. I know the contents of the box like I know my memories, and instantly I identify what's different.

I pull out a folded piece of paper. Its edge is jagged, like it's been torn from a book.

Unfolding the page, I realize it's from a dictionary. Fitz's dictionary. My eyes jump from word to word, from *impecunious* to *inchoate*, before they light on an underlined entry. *Indelible (adj.): impossible to erase or forget.*

I refold the paper carefully, understanding Fitz completely. Our time together is the definition of unforgettable. If this were one of those dictionaries with illustrations for certain words, I know what picture would come with this entry. A bitterly cold night, a rooftop, a boy and a girl, and a reach of endless stars.

I look up as Fitz and Lewis walk out of the convenience store, and I make a vow. I'm going to enjoy every moment of our final night together.

JUNIPER

~

WE PARK IN a narrow treed alley that runs along one of Princeton's Eating Clubs. Remembering the clubs from my online research, I explain to Fitz they're really just coed fraternities that also function as fancy dining halls. Lewis parks nearby, and we follow him to Prospect Avenue.

We wait in front of the Cap and Gown Club house. It's more of mansion, with three stories of dark brick and elegant detailing. I discern a French château influence in the stonework and structure. In the yard, tall trees stretch their limbs toward the gray sky of the afternoon, their bare branches trimmed with frost.

Two girls walk onto the front steps, one Indian and the other redheaded. Prisha and her friend, I'm guessing. When Lewis sees Prisha, he literally runs to her. He sweeps her into an embrace while she laughs, the sound echoing in the quiet.

"Come on," I say to Fitz. "Let's give them their privacy."

He takes my hand, and we head toward campus. "Do you have a tour prepared for this school?" Fitz asks, steadying me when I slip on the icy sidewalk.

"I thought we could just walk together." We pass through an archway in a building with an actual turret. I focus on the warmth of Fitz's hand in mine. Today isn't about the school, it's about us. The campus is only the backdrop.

It's a beautiful backdrop, though. We explore for the better part of the day. I take in the snow-covered spires of the chapel, the stained glass, the intricately sculpted stone. The campus is a fascinating combination of old and new. We pass by Gothic dorms and brittle, modernist buildings of metal and glass. I need a full thirty minutes to examine every facet of the Gehry-designed science library. Fitz willingly obliges.

We grab coffee in the student center, kiss under the campus's enormous Blair Arch, and wander through empty quads of silent trees decked in snow. I insist Fitz take a photo of himself in front of the eating club of his namesake, F. Scott Fitzgerald. When it's too cold to be outside, we sit down for dinner in an Italian restaurant off campus.

It's bittersweet. Our first real date.

When we finish dinner, we head in the direction of my car. Earlier, we decided we'd spend the night in Princeton and drive to Boston in the morning. Prisha's friend, who is a saint, has graciously invited the four of us to sleep in her room. She'll spend the night in her girlfriend's dorm, while Lewis and Prisha will sleep in her bed. Fitz and I will share the futon. By now, I've run through the money my parents gave me for this trip, and I'd rather sleep in the eating club for free than book one of the two nearby hotels, both of which look fairly expensive. But I'm not eager to give up our privacy yet, and neither, I imagine, is Fitz. We walk slowly and silently to pick up our suitcases from the car.

Reaching the street where we parked, I pull out my keys. "So . . ." Fitz begins, "should we take the bags over now?"

We both know it's what we're doing here. We both know it's not what we want to be doing.

"In a minute," I say.

I lean back onto the car door and pull him to me. The kiss is breathless, consuming. I fumble for the handle and open the door, our mouths never parting. We tumble together into the back seat. I'm stretched out across the seats, Fitz on top of me, drinking me in with every kiss. There's no mistaking where this is headed. I hold him close to me, loving how he fists his hand in my hair, how his lips are a contradiction of soft and demanding, patient and wanting. I lower my hand to his belt buckle, waiting for him to gently push me aside. He doesn't.

"You're sure?" His voice is hushed. "Just because it's our last night—"

"I'm sure," I exhale. I've never been surer. His lips are an avalanche, burying me in him. I don't fight the feeling over-taking me.

While he wrestles his shirt off in the tight confines of the car, I pull mine over my head. The alley where we're parked is dark and deserted, and our car is nestled between a high wall and a hedge, protected from view.

Fitz reaches into his backpack. I feel my eyebrows spring up when he pulls out a box of condoms.

"You didn't strike me as the type to come prepared," I say. We're sitting side by side on the seats now.

Fitz removes the plastic square from the box, looking amused. "I'm aware that was a dig at my manhood," he replies. I laugh a little, having not intended the slight. "But I'm going to allow it," he continues, "and say Lewis insisted I buy them today at the gas station."

"Ah, that explains it."

Fitz nips my ear playfully. Even the brief brush of contact fires anticipation through me. "Are we here to make jokes at my expense? I thought you had other plans."

"Just you wait," I whisper.

We kiss, and then we come together, for real this time. It's not easy, climbing into his lap, kicking off our shoes, shimmying out of our jeans without hitting our heads on the roof. Fitz laughs when I lose my balance, nearly elbowing him. It's kind of awkward, and kind of hurried, and completely perfect.

I don't even remember the cold outside, burning with the heat of our bodies pressed together. Fitz traces his fingers up my thigh, and I run my hands through his hair, past his chest, farther down. His lips nearly never leave mine, like we're breathing through each other. Sweat beads on his brow. His heart is pounding, passion and anticipation and probably nerves fusing in one rhythm. He interlaces our fingers, and then the world becomes huge and bright and beautiful.

The whole time, I'm here and only here. We're an hourglass on its side, the sand suspended, hanging in temporary eternity.

After, I rest my head on his chest, our breaths quieting while he strokes my arm. He presses a kiss to my forehead, and for once my mind is wonderfully blank. I'm not thinking of tomorrow or the next day or the next. I'm utterly in the moment.

The moment, which I'm learning to cherish. I remember wanting only a week ago to reach up for the stars, the yawning ceiling of the world. For a few more months, the precious path from moment to moment will be enough. For a few months, the stars will wait.

FITZ

～

WE PULL ON our coats afterward and deliver our bags to Prisha's friend Madeleine's room. I try to play it cool, like it's no big deal I just had sex with Juniper in her car. But it's a really big deal, and I'm not cool about it. It's possible the permanency of the smile I'm wearing will require medical attention. I know Juniper notices, though she doesn't mention it—she only keeps throwing me smiles in return.

There's a hammock strung up between two trees outside, and we bring down a blanket we find in the dorm. The night air is cold, not freezing, and while we still need multiple layers, I consider the temperature a tiny gift from the universe. Wrapped in the blanket and in each other's arms, we rock in the hammock, staring up into the sky the way we did at Brown.

"I won't forget a moment of this," Juniper says.

I press my lips to her temple. "High praise from you," I reply, repeating our exchange from the rooftop. I know she'll remember perfectly.

She laughs, and *fuck* will I miss her laugh. "You *said*, 'High praise from the girl who remembers everything.'" Raising her head, she looks me in the eye. "And I meant I'll cherish every memory."

It takes the breath from my lungs. I realize right then— none of it helped. The decision not to go home tonight, the "getting goodbyes out of our system," the knowledge from the start that this couldn't last. None of it lightens the inescapable pain of us ending in the morning. I reach for the one sliver of hope I can see.

"Maybe this won't be goodbye forever," I say. Juniper bites her lip nervously. "I just mean," I rush to clarify, "if it's meant to be, maybe we'll find each other again."

I'm relieved when Juniper smiles. "Yeah," she says. "Maybe one day I'll walk into a pastry shop to buy cannoli and you'll be in line in front of me."

"Or I'll run into you at a party where I don't know anyone," I reply. Juniper turns from me, wiping her cheek.

"Serendipity," we say together.

"Fate," I add quietly. It doesn't feel like it could be anything else. There's a providence to it, a perfection I can't explain.

We fall silent, just enjoying the rhythm of our heartbeats, the comfort of being close. Finally, Juniper speaks. "What's the word for this? For this exact moment?"

I run through every word I know, discarding adjectives and gerunds, nouns and antiquated usages. I kiss her when I have my answer.

"It can't be described," I say. "Not with words."

As I look up at the sky, with Juniper's head on my chest, the truth settles onto me. I'll be looking into this field of stars from the front porch of my home tomorrow. Except it won't be the home I left a week and a half ago, and it won't be the home I'll know years from now. I hear the word *hiraeth* in my head, and it's in Juniper's voice.

Holding her close, I think of homes unreachable and people, lives, memories that continue anyway.

ACKNOWLEDGMENTS

THIS IS A book about family, and writing Juniper's and Fitz's journeys wouldn't have been possible without our own parents and grandparents. It owes to Emily's grandfather Don, who embodies the importance of family (and who asks every time we visit when our books will be turned into movies). The Ramírez family was meant to be a tribute to Emily's grandmother, Catherine, and the traditions she's passed down from the Contreras family to the Robles family, through the Selleks and to ours. For us, it's not tamales, but the best enchiladas and guacamole there is. So much of Juniper was born hearing your stories while watching you turn taco shells in hot oil without burning your hands.

We were fortunate enough to take college trips like Juniper's and Fitz's, and that's entirely due to the support of our parents. It's a privilege we don't take for granted, and one that not only inspired this book but also helped us make our own decisions about our futures. Thanks for sitting through endless nearly identical information sessions and walking into some of the grossest freshmen dorms with us.

Our agent, Katie. We'll never forget how you read this

book overnight. You were the first one to tell us this story was special, and you've been our champion in every way we could dream of. Like you did with Megan and Cameron, thank you for hearing these characters' voices and helping them find their way to the page.

Dana Leydig, thank you for every thoughtful question and direction you brought to developing this book. Authors always dread getting their editorial letter, but yours was nothing but inspiring, and we're very grateful for how constructive, insightful, and (dare we say) fun the process was. You're the Moira to our Stevie in this production of *Cabaret*.

We're indebted to those who've helped us portray the nuances of Fitz's and Juniper's stories with authenticity. Thank you in particular to Michael Hayden for talking to us about his experience growing up in the United States and seeking out his birth family after being adopted from another country. Your story could fill multiple books, and we're grateful you let it inform a piece of ours. Thank you to Dora Guzmán, our authenticity reader. While Juniper's family is drawn from ours, one experience is not representative of every experience, and your comments helped fill Juniper with a life of her own.

To Tessa Meischeid, thank you for being the best publicist we could ask for, and for having the coolest book-cover-themed nails. To Felicity Vallence, thank you for inciting cover-color wars and branding us #Wibbroka. So much of what makes Penguin Teen special is because of you. Thank you to the intrepid marketing Penguins, James Akinaka, Kara Brammer, Caitlin Whalen, Friya Bankwalla, and Alex Garber.

If we were on a road trip down the coast, we'd want you in our car. To Kristie Radwilowicz, for (three times now!) exceeding our imaginations with gorgeous and iconic cover design. To our copyeditors, Abigail Powers, Krista Ahlberg, Janet Pascal, Kaitlin Severini, and Marinda Valenti, thank you for your diligence and impeccable thoroughness (and for one unforgettable discussion of the nuances of pumping gas in New Jersey).

Part of the writing process for us is the coffees, the text chains, the head-clearing hikes in between the pages. For these things, we're very grateful to our friends in the writing community: Alexa Donne, Alyssa Colman, Aminah Mae Safi, Amy Spalding, Bree Barton, Bridget Morrissey, Britta Lundin, Dana Davis, Demetra Brodsky, Derek Milman, Diya Mishra, Farrah Penn, Gretchen Schreiber, Kayla Olson, Maura Milan, Robyn Schneider, Sarah Enni, and Simone DeBlasio. To our friends not in the writing community, some of you love YA and some of you don't, and all of you have read our books and listened to us talk about publishing. It means the world.

Finally, to the readers who we've met in person or online, who've told a friend to pick one of our books up, who've roasted us on Twitter (never change) or campaigned for cover colors, and who've given us handmade fan art, you're the reason we get to keep writing books and the reason it's worth it.

TURN THE PAGE TO READ

AN EXCERPT FROM

"This delightfully feminist rom-com has characters that feel like friends and will surely appeal to fans of Sarah Dessen."

—BuzzFeed

One

"BITCH."

I hear the word under Autumn Carey's breath behind me.
I guess I earned it by daring to walk ahead of her to reach the
dining hall door. I cut her off while she was examining her
reflection in her phone's camera, trying to decide if her new
bangs were a bad choice. Which they were. Part of me wants
to whirl around and tell Autumn I don't have the *entirety of
lunch* to walk behind her, but I don't.

Instead, I tilt my head just enough to tell Autumn I heard
her, but I don't care enough to respond. I have things to do.
Autumn's not remarkable enough in any way to hold my attention, and I've been called that name often enough, under
enough breaths, for it not to hurt. Not from a girl like her. It's
hardly an uncommon thought here. *Cameron Bright's a bitch.*

I throw open the door and walk outside. The sun sparkles
on the fountain in the heart of the courtyard, encircled by
low hedges and lunch tables. It's about a billion degrees out
because it's September, when Los Angeles gets apocalypti-
cally hot. I head for the stairway to the second-story patio,
under the red-tiled roofs and cream-colored arches of the
school's mission architecture.

I notice heads turn in my direction. The girls watch me with half worship and half resentment, the boys with intrigue. In their defense, I do realize I'm . . . well, hot. I'm a natural blonde, and I have the body that comes with running six miles a day.

A sophomore girl stares from the railing with the undisguised interest of someone who doesn't realize she's been noticed. I give her a *what?* glance, and she drops her eyes, her cheeks reddening.

I'm popular. I don't entirely know why. I'm hardly our school's only hot girl, and it's not like I'm rich. I'm not. My dad is, but he's lived in Philadelphia since the year I was born, which is not a coincidence. He sends a check for my tuition and my mom's rent, and nothing else. And I'm not popular because my parents have won Oscars or played for sold-out stadiums or were groupies for Steven Tyler. My mom could be considered an actress, but strictly of the washed-up, C-list variety. She had roles in a couple of commercials and stage plays when I was in elementary school. From there, it's been a downward trajectory to watching daytime soaps on the couch and job searching on the internet.

I'm uninteresting among my classmates, honestly. Beaumont Prep—the top-ranked, priciest private school on the West Coast—is full of the children of the rich and famous. Actresses, entrepreneurs, athletes, musicians.

Then there's me. I live forty minutes away in Koreatown. I drive a Toyota I'm pretty certain predates the Clinton presidency. I don't set trends or post photos of myself on Instagram that get thousands of likes around the world.

Yet I'm popular. Undeniably and unquestionably.

I find our usual table overlooking the courtyard. Everyone knows the second-story patio is ours, the best view to see and be seen. No one's here yet, which gives me the opportunity to pull my notebook from my bag and write down a quick list, organizing my thoughts.

To Do 9/8
1. Pick up peer-reviewed Wharton essay

2. Conditioning run

3. Econ homework

I know there's a fourth item. I'm itching to remember it, and it's not coming. I use lists to unwind because I get edgy when things feel disorganized and out of my control. The way I feel right now, trying to remember the final thing I have to do today—

"You could come over tonight . . ." croons an obnoxious male voice, unmistakably Jeff Mitchel's. Two bags drop to the ground at the table behind me. I roll my eyes as a female voice replies.

"You're not going to Rebecca's party?" The girl's tone is bashful and obviously flirtatious. I wince. Jeff Mitchel is the worst. Rich, spoiled, and just attractive enough to make him insufferably entitled. He gets straight Ds, smokes pot instead of going to class, and enjoys impressing girls by "treating" them to five-hundred-dollar dinners at Daddy's restaurant.

"Not if you're coming over," Jeff replies. I hear fabric rustling, telling me there's been physical contact. Of what form, I don't want to know. But I have a list to finish, which won't happen with *this* playing out behind me.

Gritting my teeth, I round on the two of them.

I find Jeff in his popped-collar glory, one hand on the white-jeaned knee of Bethany Bishop. Bethany, who's had her heart broken by nearly every one of Beaumont's dumbasses of record, a string of careless rich guys and philandering athletes. I have neither the time nor the inclination to watch this one cross the starting line.

"Really?" I drag my eyes to Bethany. "You're flirting with *him* now?"

Bethany flushes, glaring indignantly. "No one asked your opinion."

"You just got dumped." I ignore her. "The whole school knew. You ugly-cried by your locker for *weeks*. I'm not interested in having to walk past that again on my way to Ethics every day, and Jeff's a worse guy than your ex—"

"Hey," Jeff cuts in.

I fire him a glare. "Don't get me started on *you*." I turn back to Bethany. "Honestly, you're decently attractive. I mean, your wardrobe needs updating, and you have a really annoying laugh. But all things considered, you're a six-point-five for Beaumont. Jeff"—I fling my hand in his direction—"is a two. You could be doing way better," I tell her encouragingly.

Bethany grabs her bag. "Screw you, Cameron." She walks off in a huff, not realizing the huge favor I've done her.

Nobody ever does. When they're not calling me *bitch*,

people have told me I'm overly honest. I know. I know I am. When you grow up with a dad like mine, whose unwaveringly direct commentary came with every one of the rare visits and phone calls we've had throughout my childhood, it's just an instinct. He's never wrong, either, even when his words hurt. Which they do—I know he's a jerk. But he's a successful jerk, with Fortune 500 profiles and penthouses on two continents. With every critique he's given me, I could wither under his words and feel inferior or I could rise to them and become a better version of myself. I've always appreciated his honesty for that.

Bethany clearly sees things differently.

"What the hell?" Jeff asks, irritated. "Bethany was one hundred percent going to put out. You owe me."

"Please. *You* owe *me* the ten minutes of my life I'll never get back."

He eyes me, his expression changing. His raised eyebrow makes me gag. "I could give you ten minutes," he says in a voice he must imagine is seductive.

"I'd rather die."

"Damn, Cameron," he says. "You need to loosen up. Do the world a favor and get yourself laid. If you keep up this ice-queen routine, eventually there won't be a guy left who'd do the job."

"As long as you're first on that list." I'm ready for this conversation to be over.

"You don't mean that. Come on, you're coming to Skāra tonight, right? I'll be there. We could—"

But I don't hear whatever it is Jeff Mitchel wishes we could do tonight, because his offer, while thoroughly disgusting, reminds me of the missing item on my list. I return to my notebook and start writing.

4. Find out if soccer team is going to Skära

I may be a renowned "ice queen" on campus, but I won't be for much longer. Not if a certain member of the soccer team comes to the North Hollywood nightclub where one of the cheerleaders is having a huge party tonight.

"Are you even listening to me?" Jeff whines, demanding my attention.

"Of course not." I look up in time to see my two best friends approaching. Elle Li levels Jeff a look of such pure disgust she doesn't even have to utter a word. Jeff picks up his backpack and *finally* gets out of my sight. I swear, she has a gift.

"Permission to rant?" I hear characteristic exasperation in Elle's voice. She drops down across from me, Jeff entirely forgotten. I close my notebook as she and Morgan place their lunches on the table.

Morgan has her brilliantly blonde hair in an elaborate braid. She's wearing a Dolce & Gabbana dress, but Morgan LeClaire could wear sweatpants and she'd look like a movie star. Because she pretty much is one. Her mom's a record executive, and Morgan's hung out with the Donald Glovers and Demi Lovatos of the world her whole life. She decided she wanted to act when she was ten, and a year ago her agent began booking her roles in local indies. On the bench next to Elle, she looks bored, and I get the feeling she heard the first half of Elle's rant on the walk over from the dining hall.

Elle flits a perfectly manicured hand through her short, shiny black hair. She's five foot two, and yet everyone—teachers included—agree she's the most imposing person on campus.

Which is why I'm not about to interrupt her. "Permission granted," I say, waving a hand grandly.

"MissMelanie got the Sephora sponsorship," Elle fumes, her British accent coming out. She grew up in Hong Kong until she was ten and learned English at expensive private schools. "I made multiple videos featuring their lip liner. I even did a haul video where I spent seven hundred dollars of my own money on makeup I don't need. I wrote kiss-ass-y emails to their head of digital promotions—for nothing. For them to go with an idiot like MissMelanie, who mixes up 'your' and 'you're' in her comments."

Ellen Li, or Elli to her 15 million YouTube subscribers, is one of the highest-viewed makeup artists for her online weekly tutorials. Every week she creates and models looks for everything from New Year's Eve parties to funerals. She's been on *Forbes*'s Highest-Paid YouTube Stars list twice.

Despite my complete and utter lack of interest in makeup or internet stardom, Elle and I are remarkably alike. She's the only other person I know who understands how desperate and careless 99 percent of this school is. Elle's unflinchingly honest, and she'll do anything to achieve her goals. It's why we're inseparable.

And it's why I know she can handle a little attitude in return. I cut her a dry look. "You know you're acting incredibly entitled, right?"

Elle hardly even glances in my direction. "Obviously," she says, hiding a smile. "I'm *entitled* to the Sephora sponsorship because of my hard work, just like I'm *entitled* to have you listen to me unload without complaining because I've come to every one of your interminable cross-country races."

To be fair, this is true. Elle and Morgan have come to pretty much every race I can remember. They're often the only people in the bleachers for me. They first came when I was a freshman, when I'd invited my dad because he happened to be in town for the week to woo investors for an upcoming stock offering. I'd gotten my hopes up he'd come and see me win. When I crossed the finish line, he wasn't there—but Elle and Morgan were. They surprised me by coming, and it was the only thing that kept me from being crushed.

"You two are terrible," Morgan says, shaking her head. "I don't know why I'm even friends with either of you."

Elle and I don't have to exchange a look. We round on Morgan in unison. "You're an honor student, you're nice, you have cool, rich parents," I start.

"You're an actress, and you're gorgeous," Elle continues.

"You're too perfect," I say.

"No one *but* us could handle being friends with you," Elle finishes flatly.

Morgan rolls her eyes, blushing. "You guys really are the worst."

I shrug. "But you love us."

"Debatable," she delivers with a wink. She pulls out her phone, probably to text her boyfriend, Brad.

I catch the time on her screen. *Shit*. There's only ten minutes left in lunch. I have to drop off the essay I peer-reviewed and pick up mine from the College and Career Center. I shove my notebook into my bag and stand. "Morgan," I say, remembering the final item on my list. "Would you ask Brad if he knows if the soccer team's coming to Skāra tonight?"

Two pairs of eyes fix on me immediately. It's a reaction I knew well enough to expect. "What do you care about the soccer team?" Elle inquires. "You're not considering ending your two-year streak of lonely Friday nights with a hookup, are you?"

"What's wrong with a little window shopping?" I reply lightly. I throw my bag over my shoulder and leave, eager not to be interrogated.

I head in the direction of the College and Career Center. Passing the courtyard fountain, I pointedly ignore Autumn Carey and her friends glaring in my direction. I could not care less. If every glare I earned, or didn't earn but received nonetheless, bothered me, I'd drown in the judgment.

I quicken my steps to cross campus in time to pick up my essay. The College and Career Center pairs up seniors to read and review each other's college essays. It's mandatory, unfortunately, given the utter disinterest I have in my classmates' opinions on my college prospects. I was paired with Paige Rosenfeld, who's outstandingly weird, but luckily I don't have to talk to her. Her essay was about feeling like she couldn't help a classmate who was being bullied, and I gave her only a couple comments. Learning about Paige's personal life isn't exactly item number one on my priority list.

I have *my* essay to worry about. It needs to be perfect. I

worked for the entire summer on the draft I submitted to the CCC. Writing, rewriting, reviewing. I even had Morgan's boyfriend, Brad, who's on track to follow in his dad's footsteps to Harvard, edit it with permission to be harsh, or as harsh as Brad's capable of.

Because I need it ready, polished, and perfect by November 1. The deadline for the Early Decision application for the University of Pennsylvania's Wharton School.

It's my dad's alma mater. Even though we've never lived together, even though our relationship is admittedly dysfunctional, I've long wanted to go where he went. If I got in, he'd know I could. If I got in, we'd have Penn to share.

I walk into the College and Career Center with minutes left in lunch. It's empty, and I cross the carpeted, overly clean room to the student mailboxes. I drop Paige's essay off, then head to my box. The envelope with Paige's comments on my essay sits on top. Hurriedly, I slide the pages loose and start scanning the red ink in the margins.

Which . . . there's plenty of. I feel my heart drop, then race. I didn't plan on particularly caring what Paige Rosenfeld had to say about my essay, but faced with this treatment, it's hard to ignore.

I flip to the final page, where I find Paige has written a closing note. I force myself to focus on each sentence, even when I want to ignore every word.

This just reads as really, really inauthentic. Anyone could write this with a couple Google searches on UPenn. There's no "you" in here. Whatever reason you want to go there, tell them. Try to find a little passion—and then start over.

I frown. Who is *Paige* to tell me what's "authentic"? She doesn't know me. It's not like her essay was brilliant either. If I'd cared, I could have written her a note criticizing her trite choice of topic and overdramatic descriptions. Beaumont hardly has a bullying problem.

It's embarrassing, reading feedback like this on writing I was proud of. The worst thing is, though, I know she's right. I was so wrapped up in being professional that I didn't get to anything personal.

But I refuse to be discouraged. I'm not like Bethany. If I could be broken by harsh words, I would have given up a long time ago. I *will* rewrite this essay, and I *will* get in to UPenn.

Inside my bag, my phone buzzes. I pull it out on reflex and find a text from Morgan.

The soccer team will be there. Looking forward to whatever you're planning . . .

With half a grin, I flip my essay closed. I drop it into my bag, my thoughts turning to tonight.

Two

I'M LATE TO SKĀRA BECAUSE FRIDAY-NIGHT TRAFFIC on Highland is horrendous, and I had to hunt for half an hour for parking because I didn't want to pay seventeen dollars for the garage. The club is on the top floor of a huge mall on Hollywood Boulevard, between tall apartment complexes and art deco movie theaters. I have to dodge tourists clogging the curb chatting in languages I don't recognize and taking photos of the Hollywood Walk of Fame.

I finally reach the door, and the bouncer waves me in. The club is typically twenty-one and up, but tonight Rebecca Dorsey's dad rented the place out for her birthday. They won't serve us drinks, obviously, but people find creative ways to raise their blood alcohol content.

Under the erratic lighting, I spot him immediately.

He's leaning on the velvet couch near the edge of the dance floor, laughing with the rest of the soccer team. He's the picture of perfect carelessness. The picture of perfect hotness, too. He's tall, built like the varsity athlete he is, and his smile stands out in his corner of the club. I watch him reach up with one arm to rub the back of his neck, pulling up the hem of his Beaumont soccer polo, exposing the strip of dark skin above his belt. It's a nice strip, a really inviting strip.

This is my moment. I just have to walk up to him, join the conversation, and then lead him to a place where it's just the two of us.

But I can't.

The music pounds uncomfortably in my ears. I can't even walk past the kitschy sculpture by the door.

I've wanted this for a year. I've planned for it. Why can't I do this? It's possible I've forgotten how to flirt. I've been rejecting guys for two years while developing this crush in secret. What if I've forgotten how this particular game is played?

I watch him roll his eyes at whatever idiotic thing Patrick Todd's saying, and I know what's coming next. His eyebrows twitch the way they do every time he's preparing one of his effortless comebacks. He's wonderfully no-bullshit.

It's the first thing I ever loved about Andrew Richmond. Even when he was new to Beaumont, I noticed his quick and imperturbable humor. Our friendship deepened because we both felt out of place among our wealthy, glamorous class-mates. Andrew had the added difficulty of being black in our predominately white school. For one reason or other, we both entered Beaumont feeling like outsiders.

I've talked to him countless times, but never in this con-text. Not even crappy pickup lines are coming to mind. I need help.

Feeling my heart race with frustration, I sweep the dance floor for my friends. People I know and people I don't fill the crowded, darkened room. Morgan, dressed like a hipster on a Beverly Hills budget in a strappy gold dress with a beaded headband, perches on one of the L-shaped white couches near the balcony. She's eyeing Brad with that eagerness I've learned to recognize—and avoid. I know where their night's headed, and I won't be interrupting *that*.

But in front of the bar, Elle's running a finger down the arm of Jason Reid. Ugh. I have no problem interrupting Elle's completely indefensible hookup plans. Before she can pull Jason into a dark corner, I cross the room and grab her by the elbow.

"Cameron!" she protests.

I ignore her and usher us both into the ladies' restroom. I close the door, and Elle walks past me. I give the restroom a once-over. It's filthy, and the dimmed lights don't hide the spilled drinks and littered tissues on the floor. In one stall a girl in a sequined dress holds her friend's hair while she dry-heaves over the toilet.

"I hope there's a very good reason you pulled me away from Jason," Elle says, raising an expectant eyebrow.

"Other than the obvious?" I reply, my goal momentarily forgotten. I've explained to Elle a dozen times why I disapprove of Jason. He's an annoying, airheaded actor who adores nothing more than his own reflection. He has a girlfriend, who I'm guessing isn't here—and who I have to hang out with every day during cross-country after school. "You know I don't condone this."

"If I wanted your opinion I would have asked for it," she replies. "Why'd you pull me in here?"

My nerves catch fire. Andrew's out there only feet away. I

pace the disgusting restroom floor, running a hand through my hair in frustration. "Do you have a shade of lipstick that's, like, seductive?"

Understanding dawns in Elle's eyes. "You *are* interested in one of the soccer players. Tell me who."

"Andrew."

"Andrew *Richmond*?" Elle starts to smile.

"Do you have any lipstick or not?" I ask loudly, crossing my arms.

Elle's watching me with skepticism and a hint of humor. "For your information, I don't just carry around a complete color palette wherever I go. If you're going to borrow my makeup, you're going to need to text me beforehand what you're wearing and how much sun you've gotten that day. I don't just *have* lipstick for you."

"Fine." I level my gaze with hers. "I'll go borrow Morgan's. I have plans for the night, and if you won't—"

Elle sighs. "Come here," she orders. "You'd look awful in what Morgan's wearing."

With a swell of satisfaction, I lean on the counter, facing away from the mirror, and watch Elle pull out no fewer than four shades of lipsticks from her purse. She proceeds to mix them on her hand and then dab the color on my lips with one finger. Elle's a professional and a perfectionist. I knew she'd have something.

"For years you have me do the dirty work of discouraging every guy interested in you," she says, holding my chin while she paints my lips. "Now you're chasing Andrew Richmond. Would you care to explain?"

"No, I would not," I reply shortly. I could explain if I wanted to. For months I've had a list of reasons to break my no-dating rule for Andrew. *He makes me laugh. He's objectively gorgeous. We're both runners. He's committed. He's proven he has goals and works hard. I don't want to die a virgin.*

"It's because he's new blood, isn't it?" she goes on, ignoring me. "He's new to the popular crowd. He just made varsity soccer, he's the only guy here who hasn't dated every blonde within reach—he's exciting. And you haven't had enough time with him yet to know he's as lame as every other guy."

"I've known Andrew for years," I fire back. "I'd know if he was lame. Like I know with Jason." I cut her a pointed look, which she brushes off. "Andrew's . . . different."